HOLY GHOST

Truly, I owe this book to Julia Douglas.
She embodies the words of the Spanish writer
Baltasar Gracian: "True friendship multiplies the good in life
and divides its evils. Strive to have friends,
for life without friends is like life on desert island ...
to find one real friend in a lifetime is good fortune;
to keep them is a blessing."

~Kelly Conway

HOLY GHOST

A NOVEL BY

K.D. Conway

K.D. Conway

Website: kellyconwaybooks.com
Email: contact@kdconwaybooks.com

The cover image "Witches Walk" is from
www.travelinspirations.yahoo.com
"The Second Coming," by William Butler Yeats
Versions of the poem briefly stated, "For the want of a nail the kingdon was lost," have been quoted by numerous writers from William Shakespeare to Benjamin Franklin to James Baldwin.

ISBN: 9798692555519
Imprint: Independently published

Table of Contents

Introduction

The Spanish Civil War tore Spain apart from July 1936 to April 1939. The war was a tragedy and the backdrop for countless unspeakable horrors. Atrocities were carried out by all sides, and the war took a massive toll on Spain. Its population in 1936 was about twenty-five million people, and by the war's end in 1939, three hundred thousand soldiers were dead, two hundred thousand civilians were executed by mob violence, five hundred thousand people were in exile, with another five hundred thousand being detained after the war.

This war captured the world's attention. Fighters from all over the globe descended on Spain to defend freedom or faith. Most of the fighters came to support the newly formed Spanish Republic, notably the famous Lincoln Brigades from the United States, but some men and women also came to support Franco's forces. Hemingway and George Orwell both went to Spain to support the Republicans, and from their experiences they wrote compelling books. Paul Robson gave a concert in Teruel for the Republicans when the city was captured from the Nationalists. From the ashes of the bombing of Guernica, Picasso created his masterwork in which, using his paint brush, he condemned the Fascists and the vicious war they perpetrated. The status of the siege of Toledo was the worldwide daily headline for weeks. The war was a *cause célèbre*.

The Spanish Civil War has been called a practice ground for WWII, and here in America, we use the metaphor of our Civil War for a quick comparative shorthand. It was neither: it was not a practice run for WWII, and it was very dissimilar to the American Civil War. This civil war had Spanish causes, crosscurrents, and characteristics. It was a uniquely Spanish catastrophe.

Holy Ghost is a novel. The book tells the story of three young people caught up in this tumultuous time. It is not intended to be a detailed history or a political polemic. The story begins in the autumn of 1923, when Spain is an unstable, brittle place that has been reeling from over three hundred years of failures, humiliations, defeats, and dysfunction.

Going back as far as the 8th century, Spain was witness to a distinctive history. Around the year 720, Pelayo, the king of Asturias, a kingdom in Northern Spain that was the only part of Spain that had not been conquered by the Islamic invasion from North Africa, began the counterattack against the Moors. The Reconquest of Spain, lasting almost eight hundred years, slowly pushed the Moors back towards to Africa. This Reconquest catalyzed the development of Spain's unique brand of militant Catholicism.

In 1492 the Reconquest was completed; in that same year Ferdinand and Isabella financed Columbus's mission to "discover" the new world. For nearly one hundred years after Columbus' maiden voyage, Spain dominated the world; it expanded its foothold in the New World, and in return gold and plunder poured back into the country. It was a golden age for Spain. Salamanca was one of the world's great universities; the arts and literature of Spain flourished; the country produced giants such as Velazquez, El Greco, Cervantes, Saint Teresa, and Saint Ignatius Loyola.

At the country's zenith, Charles V, peering from his throne as Holy Roman Emperor, could see that Spain controlled most of the New World, plus the Low Countries, much of Italy, Austria, and some of France, Germany, Czechoslovakia, and Hungary. Before it was said of England, it was first said of Spain, that the sun never set on its empire.

But at some point, the rot began to set in—maybe beginning in 1588 when the Armada was defeated, and the British took control of the seas. Slowly, over time, Spain fell into decline. It lost most of its possessions, and from 1807 to 1814 it was the battleground for Napoleon's Peninsular Wars. Three hundred to four hundred thousand of the then ten million Spaniards died in these wars. The country was ravaged.

Following this disaster, Spain struggled throughout the 19th

century to establish a functioning liberal democracy and to catch up with other European countries in terms of basic human freedoms and economic development. In 1873, the First Republic was declared, collapsing eighteen months later in 1874. Then in 1898 more ignominy fell upon Spain: the Americans routed the Spanish in the Philippines and Cuba. There was little left of its once vast empire.

As we meet our characters in 1923, Spain is like an aristocratic family that has lost its great wealth, but whose pride and vanity are still fully intact. Spain was a backwater where millions lived in abject poverty, and Catalonia and the Basque Country, its most prosperous and advanced regions, were restless for autonomy or outright independence. Spain was ruled by the ineffective King Alfonso XIII; but in reality, it was held by the grip of the army, large landowners, and a conservative Catholic Church.

Separatism plays an important role in Holy Ghost. Spain is a country of many regions, where literally a different primary language is spoken in every corner of the country. In one corner is the Basque Country where Basque is the primary language; in the northwest is Galicia where Galego, a language close to Portuguese, is spoken; in the southwest, in Andalusia, a rapidly spoken version of Castilian Spanish is the mother language; and in the northeast is Catalonia, where Catalan is native.

These differences in language, and related culture and history, combined with varying levels of economic development, have created significant friction in Spain. When our book begins— as it largely remains today—the Basque Country and Catalonia enjoyed greater industrialization, wealth, and standards of living, creating strong tensions, a desire for autonomy, and with the most radical voices calling for independence.

The Catholic Church also features prominently in the story. The church was a powerful and complex force in Spain which came under unprecedented attack during the civil war period. Leading up to the outbreak of the civil war, the church, which was seen as an enforcer and beneficiary of the old order, was the target of multiple horrific attacks.

Shortly after the establishment of the Second Republic in April 1931, between May 10 and May 13, 1931, over one hundred convents and other religious buildings were set alight in riots that started in Madrid and then spread throughout the country. Objects of great cultural and artistic value were destroyed; some convent cemeteries were vandalized, and dozens of people were killed or injured. Perhaps most scandalous of all, the new Republican government did nothing to prevent the vandalism, violence, and destruction of property, with Minister of War Manuel Azaña saying, "All the convents of Spain are not worth the life of a single Republican, and if the Guardia Civil is deployed, I resign."

At the outbreak of the civil war, anti-clerical violence exploded in Republican-held territory. These attacks were most acute in the first few months of the war, when religious were literally hunted. Over the course of the war, it is estimated that between forty thousand and three hundred thousand people were murdered for their faith. These numbers included 13 bishops, 4,184 priests, and 283 nuns. The killings varied by diocese, with one location reporting almost 90% of their clergy was murdered.

The attacks on the clergy were frequently atrociously gruesome: a parish priest put through a parody of Christ's crucifixion; the Bishop of Jaen and his sister murdered in front of two thousand celebrating spectators; a priest thrown into a corral with fighting bulls where he was gored into unconsciousness, and afterwards one of his ears was cut off to imitate the feat of a matador after a successful bullfight; a priest was castrated with his sexual organs stuffed in his mouth; there were numerous accounts of the people being forced to swallow rosary beads, thrown down mine shafts, or being forced to dig their own graves before being buried alive.

Holy Ghost is set against this complex background in Spain: the end of the monarchy; the emergence of democracy in the Second Republic; the creaking fault lines of separatism, and the mixture of reverence and hatred for the Catholic Church. From 1923 to July 1936 Spain descended into chaos at an accelerating rate. This *milieu* sparked the three-year civil war. The country was torn apart.

Note on the Historical Fiction in *Holy Ghost*

*H*oly Ghost is a work of historical fiction. It is not intended to be a detailed history or political polemic; it does, however, use the key historical events and people as background for its story.

The following key events which take place in the book are meant to be drawn accurately, and without bias:

- The coup in 1923 by Primo de Rivera
- The exile of Miguel de Unamuno in 1924
- The death of Gaudí in 1926
- The abdication of King Alfonso XIII in April 1931
- The establishment of the Second Republic in April 1931
- The burning of the convents in May 1931
- The massacre at Casas Viejas in 1933
- The right-wing election victory in 1934
- The revolution in Asturias in 1934
- The left-wing election victory in February 1936
- The peasant uprisings in Andalucía and Extremadura in 1936
- The murders in Madrid in July 1936
- The coup in July 1936
- The sacking of the Montana barracks in Madrid in July 1936
- The battle in Badajoz in August 1936
- The battle for San Sebastian in September 1936
- The siege of the Alcazar in Toledo in September 1936
- The killing of Basque priests by Nationalist forces in September 1936
- The confrontation in Salamanca between Unamuno and General Astray in October 1936
- The death of Unamuno in December 1936
- The battle for and exodus from Malaga in February 1937

- The bombing of Guernica in April 1937
- The Anarchist vs Communist Battle in Barcelona in May 1937
- The Bishops' letter in support of The Nationalists in September 1937
- The battle for Teruel from December 1937 to February 1938
- The Fascist bombings of Barcelona in March 1938
- The battle of the Ebro in October 1938
- The fall of Barcelona in January 1939
- The fall of Madrid/end of the war in April 1939

The three main characters in the book, Xavier Bidertea, Montserrat Costa, and Jaime de la Calzada are fictional, as are their families and immediate friends. The rest of the characters are real. These historical characters include:

- Deniel y Pla, Catalan: Bishop of Avila and Bishop of Salamanca (1876-1968)
- Miguel de Unamuno, Basque: writer, philosopher, university professor (1864-1936)
- Miguel Primo de Rivera, Spanish: aristocrat, soldier, dictator (1870-1930)
- Ernest Hemingway, American: writer (1899-1961)
- Antoni Gaudí, Catalan: architect (1852-1926) •Francisco Franco, Spanish: soldier, Nationalist, dictator (1892-1975)
- King Alfonso XIII, Spanish: monarch (1886-1941)
- José Sanjurjo y Sacanell, Spanish: soldier, head of the army (1872-1936)
- Francisco Frutos y Valiente, Spanish: Bishop of Salamanca (1883-1933)
- Manuel Azaña, Spanish: lawyer, writer, politician, Republican (1880-1940)
- José Antonio Primo de Rivera, Spanish: lawyer, founder of Falangist Party (1903-1936)
- José Castillo, Spanish: police officer (1901-1936)
- José Calvo Sotero, Spanish: aristocrat, politician (1893-1936)
- Manuel Goded Llopis, Spanish: Nationalist general (1882-1936)
- Lluís Companys, Catalan: lawyer, politician, Republican (1882-1940)

- Juan Yague, Spanish: Nationalist colonel (1891-1952)
- Gonzalo Queipo de Llano, Spanish: Nationalist general (1875-1951)
- José Moscardó Ituarte, Spanish: Nationalist colonel (1878-1956)
- Francisco Largo Caballero, Spanish: politician, Republican (1869-1946)
- Jose Millan-Astray, Spanish: Nationalist general (1879-1954)
- Ceferino Giménez Malla, Spanish Gypsy: civilian, Roman Catholic saint (1861-1936)
- Bartolomé Blanco Márquez, Spanish: civilian, Roman Catholic saint (1914-1936)
- Jaime Hilario Barbal, Catalan: priest, brother, Roman Catholic saint (1898-1937)
- Josemaría Escrivá, Spanish: priest, founder of Opus Dei, Roman Catholic saint (1902-1975)
- Domingo Rey D'Harcourt, Basque: Nationalist colonel (1885-1939)
- Anselmo Polanco, Catalan: Bishop of Teruel, Roman Catholic saint (1881-1939)
- Ramón Serrano Suñer, Spanish: soldier, politician, brother-in-law of Franco (1901-2003)

This period, 1923-1939, in Spain is fascinating, and disturbingly, there are many parallels to our time.

I hope you will enjoy *Holy Ghost.*

K.D. Conway

HOLY GHOST

Cesar could not understand what had happened in the mountains. He could not grasp the idea that anyone could set mountains on fire. At Colell he reveled in the sight of them, and would never forget how they looked at Christmas, all covered in snow. As for the trees ... there were times when he thought they had souls. During the nights he had spent in prayer, every now and then he had gone to the window, and if the moon was shining, or if a light in the patio was burning, had watched the poplar leaves trembling as though greeting him, or at times weeping slow tears. No one was capable of setting fire to them deliberately! Not to mention the cypresses, which seemed to him the trees that had the most reason to believe in God.

—Jose Maria Gironella
The Cypresses Believe in God

Book One

Youth in Bloom

Book 1
Chapter 1
San Sebastian, Spain
July 10, 1923

Xavi Bidertea stood out as he walked along the long promenade. He was tall, lean, and handsome; he had the distinctive features of a Basque: thick dark hair, strongly delineated facial features, and soft olive complexion. Nearing seven thirty p.m., Xavi and his parents walked along *La Concha* beach; it was the nameless time between the late afternoon and the fall of night. In full mid-summer, on a warm cloudless day, the sun remained high in the deep blue sky, its light glistening and dancing on the tranquil, sheltered, crescent-shaped bay. Between the promenade and the bay, children laughed loudly and played on the long, sandy beach beside blue and white bathing tents.

Passing through the Belle Époque Old Town, they crossed the bridge over the River Urumea which split the town. Over the bridge was the Barrio Gros situated in front of the city's other beach, Zurriola. This broad beach, unlike *La Concha*, was not sheltered, and large waves off the Cantabrian Sea rolled in, crashing near the shore. The town and its beaches were seated below green mountains: to the north France and to the east Pamplona and Navarre. The city was jewel-like, being blessed by its setting near the sea and below the mountains.

This place—this beautiful city, below the green mountains, with its beaches, bay, and the sea beyond—created an irresistible pull on Xavi. As he walked along, he felt a tinge of sadness, mixed in with excitement about his impending departure for university in Salamanca. Deep down he felt the hold this place had upon him. In his heart, he believed his sparkling city would always bring him back. It was home.

As the Biderteas ambled along, they spoke French among

themselves and either Spanish or Basque to the numerous friends and acquaintances they passed. They were making their way to a traditional Basque restaurant, Arzak, where the going-away dinner for Xavi and the others was just beginning.

Xavi, along with Father Extebarri, were leading ten teenage boys from the local Jesuit high school along the Camino Frances across northern Spain. The hike, with its arduous climbs, long dusty walks, and numerous pilgrimage sites, created a kind of brotherhood, and had become something of a rite of passage for a select group of local boys. The group had taken over the restaurant for the celebration, and the boys were in boisterous high spirits about their upcoming thirty-five-day hike from just over the border in France to Santiago de Compostela in faraway, mysterious northwestern Spain.

Xavi's mother Maria was a highly educated woman. She was a well-known doctor who had lived in San Sebastian for twenty years; but even so, her competence in the local language remained shaky, and when large numbers of Basques gathered, it seemed to her that rather than speaking, they created an unpleasant mix of unintelligible sounds.

The boisterous group of young people speaking loudly in their native language created a cacophony that startled Maria; she clutched Xavi's arm and said in her native Catalan, "Stay close to me."

"Of course, Mother, of course," Xavi said, reassuring her.

After exuberant greetings all around, the group sat down for dinner. The dinner was impressive in its simplicity and abundant in its display of local products. A parade of delicious seafood: soft, white kokotxas, rosy red tuna belly, tender squid, and grilled turbot. Accompanying the seafood were beautiful, ripe, bright red tomatoes, and plump white asparagus from Navarre.

As the simple feast wound down, Father Extebarri, the group's leader, tapped his glass and rose to address the boys and their families. Father Extebarri, in his mid-thirties, was round and cherubic looking; he seemed to always have a cheerful smile on his face. His overall countenance and demeanor were warm and welcoming. He emanated a simple, gentle, kind holiness.

"What a meal we just had! A big thanks to our hosts!" Father Extebarri paused as the group yelled out their enthusiastic endorsement for the wonderful meal.

After a few moments, the applause died down and Father Extebarri resumed his talk, "Thank you all so much for joining us. Tonight we get on a bus and head over the Pyrenees to France to the small village of Saint-Jean-Pied-de-Port. We will sleep in the church of my good friend Father Arregetui—a good Basque I should add, and tomorrow we will rise early to begin our journey from France, across into northern Spain, and all the way to Santiago de Compostela."

Father Extebarri continued, "Your sons will be in the good hands of Xavi Bidertea and me. Many of you know Xavi." Xavi politely smiled as Father Extebarri pointed him out. "He is an exceptional young man, and we are making our fourth walk along the Camino together. He is an accomplished outdoorsman who has been hiking these mountains and sailing this sea with his father since he was a small boy. He is also our resident linguistic expert as we navigate France and various regions of Spain ... fluent in Basque, of course, French, Spanish, and if we ever need it, Catalan. Together we will safeguard your children to Santiago and back home again."

"Finally, we ask one thing from you as we make this pilgrimage. We ask your prayers. We ask your prayers for a safe journey. We ask your prayers as we confront the hardships of the trail. We ask your prayers for the deepening of our faith and fellowship as we make this pilgrimage."

Father Extebarri then requested the group to rise. "Through the intercession of St. James we ask our Lord for his guidance and protection. Let us say the *'Our Father'* together."

Then, in unison, the group prayed those ancient words: *Our Father who art in heaven ... but deliver us from evil. Amen.*

After the solemn prayer, the dinner broke up. As the boys headed to their buses Xavi's mother pulled him aside. "Xavi, I will miss you very much while you are gone."

"But, Mother, this is the fourth year I have done this journey," Xavi mildly protested.

"I know, but when you return, you'll be off to university in Salamanca, and that makes this trip the more difficult for me."

Then Maria clutched her son tightly, placed her mouth next to his ear, and whispered, "Promise me that you will come back soon and safely. Promise me."

"Yes mother, I promise," Xavi softly replied.

Book 1
Chapter 2
Roncesvalles, Spain
July 12, 1923

At seven a.m. Monsignor Olazábal came into the dormitory of the ancient monastery at Roncesvalles. The sun poured in through the windows, and the group of boys remained motionlessly asleep.

He leaned down and poked Father Extebarri in his sleeping bag and whispered, "You had quite a day yesterday, didn't you, Father? Come and have a coffee and tell me the whole story."

Father Extebarri slowly roused himself and made his way with Monsignor Olazábal to the Monsignor's residence near the church. There, over a strong cup of coffee and piece of crusty bread, he recounted what had happened the day before: "Yesterday after mass in Saint-Jean-Pied-de-Port, Father Arregetui happily sent us off. We filled our canteens with water, packed our packs with food and were on our way. It was warm and humid, but we made good time to the first rest stop at Orisson."

"Did you have any sign of the bad weather coming?" Monsignor Olazábal asked.

"No, no, and the boys were in awe when they arrived to Orisson. You know how it is there ..."

"Glorious ..."

"It is, and like a balcony of the Pyrenees with peaks all around, punctuated by deep valleys and peaceful, green pastures. The boys felt intense satisfaction that they had completed the first steep ascent of our journey."

"Then what happened?" asked the monsignor.

"Well, Xavi, he felt something different. The warm and humid air concerned him ... he knew what it meant."

"The air was heavy yesterday."

"He's seen many warm, humid mornings turn quickly to tumultuous afternoon storms, and so he pulled me aside and said we needed to get these boys over the mountains quickly."

"Even at a brisk pace you still had five hours of hiking ahead of you from there," the monsignor commented between bites of toast.

"We did, at least five hours; and to his word Xavi kept us moving quickly, even as the skies began to darken. At around two we passed back into Spain from France, and from there, as you know, we had one last ascent to reach Col de Lepoeder."

"But by two the weather had already turned, and you had no place to shelter yourself up there!"

"No, none at all, and we agreed we needed to push on to the Col and then down to the monastery as quickly as possible. So we continued on, and in the forty-five minutes it took to reach the summit, the weather really began to crash down upon us."

"It was dark by midafternoon yesterday."

"Not quite like night, but close to it. The rain, which had been mostly a drizzle, now began to pour down. Loud claps of thunder and bolts of lightning were all about. The wind picked up, and it whistled around us on the summit. But the worst of all was the fog; it so was disorienting, it was hard to discern up from down."

"Dear Lord, you could not have been in a worse place to catch that weather."

"We had no choice but to continue on. We couldn't stay there, exposed to the storm."

"So …?"

"Xavi huddled the boys together on the perch of the Col. They were silent. They had become afraid. He laid it out to them: we needed to get down to Roncesvalles; we must be extremely careful getting down this mountain; and most importantly, no one could get separated from the group. He then began to lead us down, taking special care of the smallest boy in the group, little Inaki."

"Xavi and the boys arrived here at about six p.m., but you weren't with them?"

"No…"

"What happened?"

"Somehow I got separated."

"Oh no…"

"Near the Col, the trail splits…."

"I know this place well. It's a dangerous spot"

"In any case, in the poor visibility I must have made some sort of misstep—"

"Into the steep, rocky chute down?"

"Yes."

"It's treacherous there."

"It is, and after several minutes I realized I was separated. The stones were icy slick, the rain was pelting down, the wind was howling, and from time to time the lighting lit the sky. I was lost. It was terrifying."

"I can only imagine. After Xavi and the boys arrived, we dried them off and got them settled … it must have been around seven p.m., and it was then that he said you were lost between the Col and the monastery. He told me he was going back up the mountain to find you."

"I don't know what I would have done—"

"I told him to be careful, that people get turned around, lost, in these mountains, or worse they slip or fall, but he was calm, and emphatic; he was not leaving you up there alone."

"I don't know what would have happened if he hadn't come for me."

"Were you able to find some shelter?"

"I crouched under a tree to get some cover from the storm, but even so I was drenched and exhausted. It was about ten o'clock when I saw a small light and heard him calling for me. I felt relief and joy—"

"He was a light in dark places—"

"He was, and together we slowly made our away down through the pouring rain, over the slippery stones. At about midnight we passed by the small stream which leads to the monastery, and then we were here."

"Praise God! What an ordeal."

"Yes, praise God."

"Father, you know Xavi did something exceptional?"

"Yes, I know."

"Climbing back up that mountain in that terrible storm…."

"He has an unusual combination of skill, courage, and physical stamina. He is a special young man."

The sudden exposure to the harsh realities and acute dangers of the natural world had been a shock to the boys. They slept deeply, and at around eight a.m. Father Extebarri gently nudged the group to get moving.

After breakfast, and before setting out, the monsignor gave the group a tour of the monastery. He recounted the story of Count Roland, Charlemagne's nephew, who in the 9th century, along with his army, were slaughtered in the trees between the Col and monastery as they were in retreat to France, with Basques and Moors in hot pursuit. The boys loved stories of ancient knights and battles and were wide eyed about what they heard.

The monsignor continued on, "I have one more story for you. Between Roncesvalles and the next village, Burguete, just two kilometers away, you will pass through woods, an enchanting canopy of ancient trees. The woods exit onto the large Cross of Santa Maria de la Blanca. It is a beautiful walk, mesmerizing in a way, and this place tells us so much about our Basque heritage and about the interplay between good and evil in our world."

The boys sat in full attention while the monsignor paused, waiting for his story to unfold.

He continued, "each of us here shares one essential trait: we are Basque."

The boys each nodded their agreement. "For those of us who live in this tiny corner of the world our Basqueness defines us. We are an ancient people. No one knows for sure when we got here and from where we came. And our language … our language, it is as old as time itself; some say it came from the Garden of Eden, others from the devil himself. It is not like any other language in Europe.

"The Garden of Eden!" Inaki blurted out.

"Yes, from the Garden of Eden because our country is a kind of Eden, too. We like to say we were here before the Romans arrived, and we were here after they left."

He paused as the boys laughed at the old joke which held a powerful truth.

"Our traditions and culture are ancient, some predating the arrival of Christianity, and some of these ancient traditions involved worship of dark, pagan symbols. And even though we are fiercely loyal and devout Catholics, the most Catholic of all the Iberians, pockets of these ancient beliefs remained in place, unchanged for hundreds of years.

One of these practices was a form of witchcraft. Over time, as Catholicism ascended, this witchcraft became more and more isolated; it was pushed farther into the remote corners of our country. As they became more ostracized, these witches sought out isolated caves and woods to perform their foul acts and rituals. Here in the wood between Burguete and Roncesvalles was one of those places."

"What type of things did they do?" Inaki asked.

"They worshipped strange creatures; they did unspeakable things. These acts go against everything we know to be true. They go against everything we know is right."

"But what about the cross that we will see?" Inaki pressed.

"In the 17th century, after these foul practices were finally stamped out, and to show that Catholicism had conquered these woods, that it had won, that good had triumphed, the cross you will see this morning was placed there."

The boys, all ten of them, had their eyes fixed on the monsignor. They seemed once both fascinated and terrified.

"Remember boys that good and evil have always coexisted, and even so today this battle is being played out here in our country."

Xavi watched the group, and he could sense them stirring, unsure of the meaning of the Monsignor's words. He imagined them wondering whether it was a story, a warning, or some sort of call to action. For him, he understood it as all three. He was certain good and evil coexisted, and he believed one must choose between them. For Xavi, the choice was personal, and manifested in actions. He had already chosen his side.

"Okay, well, that is enough ghost stories and the like; you must be off, as you have more ground to cover today on your way towards Pamplona. Away you go," the monsignor said, smiling and sending them on their way.

Father Extebarri pulled the monsignor aside, "I cannot thank you enough for how you took in the boys last night. Thank you … truly."

"Oh please, Father! You know here in our monastery we have been taking in pilgrims of all types for almost eight hundred years. You follow a long line of weary travelers coming over that mountain. Oh, and by the way you just missed American author Ernest Hemingway who came through here last week."

"Really? Here in Roncesvalles?" Father Extebarri said, eyebrows lifted in inquiry.

"Yes, he stayed in Burguete as a base for fishing trips up in the mountains before he and his group headed on to Pamplona for San Fermin."

"Maybe we will run into him in Pamplona."

"Perhaps, and you won't be able to miss him. He has a big personality; he was quite enamored with our local wines and spirits. I have heard that he and his group emptied almost all the bottles in the village," the monsignor said with a laugh.

At that the group departed and set out in the direction of Pamplona.

<hr />

Book 1
Chapter 3
San Sebastian, Spain
August 18, 1923

Just before noon Maria Bidertea assembled with the other parents of the young pilgrims to wait for the train from Logrono to arrive. They were excited and anxious to collect their boys after their journey to Santiago.

"*Hola señora* Bidertea," Inaki's mother said. She was searching for Maria Bidertea, as she emerged from the crowd of parents with her husband in tow.

"*Hola,*" Maria Bidertea replied.

"We are a little confused about Inaki's return."

"I am as well?" Maria responded.

"We went to the school to find out about the boys' return. The school secretary said she had received separate telegrams from different churches in Santiago and Ponferrada about Inaki and Xavi's train," Inaki's mother added.

"Hmmm, the school sent a messenger to our house, and I heard the same, but I assumed they must be returning on the train with Father Extebarri."

"Yes. That's probably right. I hope so anyway."

Together the parents waited near the platform.

One by one the boys came off the train—all except Xavi and Inaki.

Not seeing their son, Inaki's parents called out to one of the other boys, Martin Lardizábal, "Martin, where is Inaki? Is he with you?"

"Well, no, just after O Cebreiro he fell and was hurt—Xavi stayed with him."

"What?" Inaki's mother asked.

"Yeah, we're not sure where they are right now."

"Not sure … ?"

"But I wouldn't worry about either of them. They are both as tough as they come," Martin said in an upbeat, street-smart sort of way, and then he wandered off to meet his parents.

After all of the boys had exited the train, finally, Father Extebarri disembarked. Maria and Inaki's parents pushed forward to confront him. He looked fatigued, worried, and worn down; he was less upbeat in his retelling of what had happened to Inaki and Xavi than was Martin.

"I'm certain they are both fine. I trust Xavi."

"Father, what happened? Where are they?" Maria Bidertea insisted.

"We were almost thirty days into our journey, on the last legs before reaching Santiago. We had just passed into Galicia at O Cebreiro; the boys were full of exuberance and enthusiasm when it happened."

"When what happened?" Maria Bidertea demanded.

Father Extebarri drew a deep breath and continued, "We were coming down the mountain from O Cebreiro. I was at the lead when I heard the trail crash down behind me. I circled back; I was sickened by what I saw. I looked down below and there was Inaki at the bottom of a ten-foot fall-off of the path. He was motionless and bloodied."

Inaki's mother was overcome with dread. She crumbled into her husband's shoulder. "Is he dead? Is he dead Father?" She blurted out.

"No, no, he is not dead."

"Tell us! Tell us then what happened! Where is he?!" Inaki's mother cried out.

"I can't lie, when he fell it was terrible."

Inaki's mother gasped; instinctively, her husband put his arm around her.

"I had no idea of how we would get to him; then Xavi stepped forward. He saw that he could cinch himself down to him using the rope in his pack."

The parents remained silent.

"Then he tied the rope to a tree, and slowly he made his way down the drop off. He crouched to him, and finally Inaki began to move."

"Oh my God!" Inaki's mother cried out.

"His head was still bleeding, but fortunately it was just a superficial wound."

Inaki's mother crossed herself and raised her head towards the sky.

"The real problem was his ankle; it was clearly severely sprained or broken."

"And so how did he get back up?" Maria asked.

"Xavi put him on his back, and using the rope, he was able to slowly cinch himself back up to the path."

"Oh *señora* Bidertea, thank you for Xavi!" Inaki's mother said, showing a little relief.

"But where are they now?" Maria Bidertea demanded, ignoring the compliment of her son.

"Well that's the thing ... I am not really sure."

"What!" both mothers exclaimed in unison.

"After a short rest, we began the slow hike down the hill. Xavi carried Inaki on his back. Thank goodness he is the smallest of the boys. Martin and I carried the packs. After four, or maybe five hours of slow going we came to a farm. We were fortunate to meet a Galician farmer and his wife; they who immediately recognized our problem. They took Inaki and Xavi in."

"Yes, and then what?" demanded Inaki's mother.

"Xavi and I talked it over, and we both came to the same conclusion—that we should split up. I should continue on and Xavi would tend to your son. So I am not sure exactly where they are. On their journey back here I am guessing."

"Father, how could you?" Inaki's mother blurted out.

Inaki's father, who had been quiet to this point jumped in, "What the Father says is right. They had no choice but to split up. I know Xavi will see our boy back. I trust him." His words had a calming effect.

"Believe me, I am just as anxious to see them as you are," Father Extebarri added.

At just past seven p.m. the train from Bilboa arrived in San Sebastian. Upon arriving Xavi helped Inaki down off the train steps onto the platform. First, he ferried the backpacks and Inaki's crutches from the train car. Then he climbed back up the steps, placed the boy's arm over his shoulder, and connected together, they navigated the three stairs from the train to the platform.

They made their way slowly back to the old town. They passed the Zurriola beach where the waves rolled in as they had done six weeks before when they had left on their adventure. They passed over the bridge from the new part of town to the beautiful, old Belle Époque quarter. The going was slow. Inaki was not yet competent with his crutches, and every few feet an old friend or acquaintance would stop them to ask, "What happened?"

They gave a short version of the story and politely moved on towards the boy's house in the port.

Inaki, the oldest of five children, came from a simple, happy home. His father was a fisherman and his mother a housekeeper. When they reached the door of their flat, they could hear the screams and laughter of his brother and three sisters inside. Xavi knocked, and shortly came Inaki's mother who pulled the door open. Wearing the worry from the news of earlier in the day, and in her kitchen apron, she was transformed when she saw her little boy. At first, stunned to see him on crutches, her face quickly broke into the happiness of a mother reunited with her son. She hugged him and cried tears of joy.

"Aitor, come! Come quickly. He's back!" she called out to her husband.

The father came from a back room. Being a fisherman, he had seen many calamities at sea, and even death on occasion, but on seeing his little boy back at home, safe, his rugged stoicism melted away; he enthusiastically joined as the family hugged Inaki.

After a few minutes, the family's focus turned towards Xavi. "How can we ever thank you enough for saving our son?" his mother asked.

Xavi humbly deflected the question and said that he must get home himself, as he too was overdue.

"Of course, of course," Aitor said. "But please wait one moment. I have something I want you to have."

In a few moments Aitor came back. "Father Extebarri explained how he fell and how you rescued him and carried him off the mountain. Inaki will fill in the other details later, and for now they are not important anyway. What matters to us is that he is back and safe because of you."

"You are too kind. It was what needed to be done, and I was the only one in the group who could do it, so I did it."

Aitor continued, "In any case I want to show our gratitude to you."

"That's not necessary."

"It is just a small and simple item, but it has great meaning to me. Please take this medal, this medal of San Sebastian. My grandmother gave it to me, and I have always worn it on the sea. Many times, in storms and difficult circumstances, I have clutched it for strength and faith. It has never failed me, and I hope it will do the same for you wherever you go and whatever trials you face."

Xavi was deeply touched by the simple gesture. He felt uncomfortable taking the medal, but he could sense he would offend the man if he did not take it. He put the medal around his neck. "Thank you. I will treasure this medal as you have. I will wear it always."

Xavi said his goodbyes and gave the boy one last hug. As he left them, joyous laughter chased after him, creating the lasting memory of his long journey back. His friendship with Inaki had been cemented.

It was just a five-minute walk from the simple flats in the port to the fashionable district of the city by the cathedral. The doorman welcomed Xavi as if he were a soldier returning from battle in a faraway land. He rode the elevator to the fifth floor, there he opened the door to his family's spacious apartment; he called out to his parents saying, "I'm home," as if he just gone around the corner for milk.

His mother leapt from the dinner table and grabbed her son.

"Where have you been? Oh, I'm so happy to see you!" she exclaimed, her initial reaction summarizing her conflicting emotions.

"Xavi come sit with us; come have some dinner," she added.

He took his seat at the table and slowly began to recount what had happened over the last three weeks, picking the story up after he and Inaki had separated from the others.

"The couple who took us in were Galician farmers, kind, country people. They gave the boy a bed and I stayed in the stable with their cows. After several days Inaki had recovered enough to make the journey to Ponferrada, but as these were simple farmers, the journey was slow and arduous by horse and cart.

Once we arrived to Ponferrada we got him to a hospital, where the doctors set his ankle and made him a cast. Inaki, being Inaki, became an instant favorite of the nuns." Recalling his impish personality brought a smile to Xavi as he recounted this part of the story.

"But that was nearly two weeks ago, why didn't you come home then?" his mother asked.

"The doctor told me the break was bad. It seems he may always have a limp, and he needed some days of rest before we set out back to San Sebastian. I did not want Inaki to be alone; it was up to me to bring him back safely," Xavi replied.

"Once the doctors cleared him to travel our route on the trains was slow: Ponferrada to Astorga; Astorga to Leon; Leon to Burgos; Burgos to Bilboa; and then here," concluding his recap of the recent events.

"I am so proud of you." His father added the last word. After dinner, his father hugged his son and headed to bed, while Xavi and his mother lingered in the kitchen.

"Xavi, of course I know you did the right thing—you always do. It's just, as I told you before you left, I will miss you terribly when you go to Salamanca for university, which now is just a few days away."

While Xavi was a quiet force of nature, his mother was an extroverted one. Highly intelligent and willful, she let her feelings and desires be known. "I have arranged to take off a week off from my practice to come to Salamanca with you. I will help move you in. And besides, I have heard it is a beautiful city; I have always wished to visit it."

As was often the case, his mother's forceful behavior caught Xavi flatfooted and with little room to maneuver. Seeing the deed was done, and that in any case she would be a helpful companion in Salamanca, he hugged his mother and retreated to his bedroom, and to a well-deserved rest.

Book 1
Chapter 4
Palma de Mallorca, Spain
August 23, 1923

The Costas were one of the great families whose fortunes and history were intertwined between Catalonia and Mallorca. In the year 1229, the family's ancestors arrived with King Jaime I of Aragon to reconquest the island from the Moors. The venture was a success and the knights who assisted Jaime instantly became the island's aristocracy.

Montserrat and Magdalena Costa left their family's summer *palacio* near the ancient center of the city, Plaza Cort, at around nine thirty a.m. They walked through the old town, passing by many beautiful ancient structures, majestic civil buildings, and other *palacios*. They also made their way in front of the city's glittering jewel: its magnificent gothic cathedral, a massive structure supported large buttresses built right next to the sea. Shortly, they reached the port where the family's large sailing schooner awaited.

"Montse, I'm so sad this is our last sail…I love our days here!"

"Another summer in paradise passed by so quickly."

"But I'm so excited for the big party Saturday night!" Magdalena exclaimed in a girlish tone as they neared the sailboat.

"One thing at a time, Elena. Let's make our way to Sant Elm first."

Montserrat Costa was just two days from her eighteenth birthday, and only a few days from leaving for university at Salamanca. She and her fourteen-year-old sister had spent every one of their summers on this beautiful island. They passed their days in the island's warm summer sun, in and around the crystal-clear, blue Mediterranean waters, hiking in the nearby hills and mountains, and visiting tiny villages; life here seemed to go on as it always had.

"*Bon dia, señorita* Costa," Captain Salom warmly greeted the girls in the local Mallorquin language, a close cousin to their native Catalan, as they boarded the boat.

"Oh please can't you just call me Montse, like all my friends do?"

Miguel Salom, a forty-year-old Mallorquin, had worked for the Costa family since he was Magdalena's age. "Yes, of course you are my friend, but I am in the employment of your father, and my respect for him supersedes our friendship ... so where to today, *señorita* Costa?"

Montse knew she would not win the point, so she moved on to the more immediate question of the route of the day. "It's our last sail of the summer, and Elena and I think we would like to sail to Sant Elm. We can moor the boat there, swim, have lunch ... maybe some fresh seafood, or some *paella*, and then return to Palma."

"The winds will be perfect to sail to Sant Elm, warm, but not hot, and with a brisk southerly breeze."

The captain maneuvered the boat into the Bay of Palma, where the sails caught the summer wind. The buttresses of the massive gothic cathedral receded in the distance, and slowly they rounded Cap de Cala Figuera and he changed their heading to west, southwest towards Sant Elm. Over their years of sailing together Captain Salom had taught Montse the basics of handling the boat to the point that he was now comfortable turning it over to her for short stretches in calm waters.

"*Señorita* Costa, come ... take the wheel."

Montse was grinning and enthusiastic as she took over the boat; the captain, sitting nearby, kept a close watch. She confidently barked out commands to the other hands, who in turn looked to the captain to nod his final ratification of her orders.

Captain Salom watched Montse guide the boat, and he thought of what a remarkable young woman she was, and what a future she had. Outgoing, bright, and worldly, she was confident, but was kind to people of all stations and never condescending. Her family had been able to offer her a rich banquet of life's choices, and she had consumed them all ravenously.

As he oversaw Montse guiding the boat, he could not but also notice her physical transformation; she was no longer soft and a little pudgy like her younger sister. Montse turned heads. She had become a striking young woman: her long raven hair was thick and fell to the middle of her back; she had dark, piercing eyes; soft pink lips; and a light brown complexion, all layered upon a thin, but firm and athletic build.

As the small natural bay of Sant Elm came into sight Captain Salom took back control of the boat, mooring it just offshore from the little fishing village. Sant Elm was at the beginning of the Tramuntana Mountains, the mountain range that made a spine along the whole of the north of island. The mountains and the pine trees that grew on them came right down to the sea. It was a stunning place which stimulated the senses: warm, clear, shimmering blue water; endlessly sunny skies which were backdropped by craggy mountains; and the air was scented with the mixture of pines, citrus, and the salty sea. It was an alluring spot.

The captain looked at his watch; it was just about one p.m.; he suggested that they row the girls ashore for lunch in the little port.

"No, no, we prefer to swim in. Bring a couple of towels, and our sundresses and sandals; we will dry off and change there," Montse requested.

Going ashore by rowboat Captain Salom outpaced the girls and was waiting for them when they finished their swim to the shore and walked up to the soft, white, sandy beach. After drying and changing in one of the bathing tents, the girls went to the small beachside restaurant of *señora* Vincens. *Señora* Vincens' husband was one of the village fishermen, and each day in the summer season he would bring her some of what he caught, and she would prepare it simply, over a grill with olive oil and fresh vegetables.

The proprietress was well aware of the Costas' status, but Montse would not allow her to be deferential. Spending summers in Mallorca, far away from Barcelona and its mansions, exclusive schools, country clubs, stables, and the elite set of international people who occupied them, had exposed Montse to the rugged life of simple people. She had deep respect for the nobility in their routines and the happiness they seemed to take from them.

She also saw that many of these local people had a deep Catholic devotion. She regarded this faith and adherence to its old rituals as quaint but outdated. She viewed these beliefs more like superstitions, which she deemed to not be really harmful to the extent they did not create barriers to the march of modernity that no longer needed religion as a foundational underpinning.

As lunch was finished, the proprietress addressed Montse to say her goodbyes, "*señorita* Costa, the crew tells me you are to return to Barcelona tomorrow."

"We are."

"I want to tell you how much my husband and I have enjoyed having you and your sister visit again this summer."

"Oh, *señora*, Elena and I love it here. Coming here, eating your food…what a joy it is."

"*Señorita* Costa, you are too kind."

"No, really, thank you truly for all the hospitality you give us," Montse replied.

Señora Vincens added one last thing to their goodbyes, "I know you are sailing back to Barcelona tomorrow, and I will pray to Sant Elm, the patron of our little village, and the protector of sailors, that you make a safe journey."

"Thank you, *señora*."

The girls returned to the boat and began the sail back to Palma. The woman's last words stuck with Montse. She rolled them over in her mind; they were kind and well meaning, and yet so out of place in the modern world—almost like a garish painting in a handsome room. After several hours of sailing the Cathedral of Palma came back into sight, and Montse began to think of her birthday party in Barcelona and what would await her in Salamanca.

Book 1
Chapter 5
Barcelona, Spain
August 25, 1923

It was late in the afternoon on the day of Montse's birthday party, and the Costa household was buzzing with activity when Luisa Costa heard the clock chime six p.m. Luisa Costa was a beautiful and elegant woman. She, like her husband, was from a great and old Catalan family. She was intelligent and highly educated, having studied in Switzerland and Paris. Her days were full. Wife, and mother of three children, she was also a patroness of the arts and music in Barcelona, and she oversaw the management of the family's' homes here, as well as in Palma, and Paris.

Luisa and her husband Joan had been in the same orbit of high Catalan culture since being children. Finally after Joan returned from university in England, they began a courtship that led to their marriage.

The depth of their love affair was nothing like its appearance of being an arranged marriage between two grand families. Joan cut a tall and graceful figure; he was unfailingly polite and strikingly handsome; he was admired by his male peers and flirted with by women of all ages. But Joan had only eyes for Luisa from the first moment he met her. At age sixteen, when seeing her at a party, he had been struck by the *coup de foudre*, and from that moment on, even though it would be almost seven years until their formal courtship started, there was only room in his heart for Luisa.

The Costa family was prominent in the Catalan merchant class. Their interests were broad and included shipping, textile production, and book and newspaper publishing. In the years since World War I had ended, the economy roared along, and their interests and enterprises always seemed to be in the right place at the right time. The scope of their wealth enabled them to never give money a thought. They concerned themselves with their family, growing their dynasty, their many sincere and deep friendships, the arts, progressive ideas, and Catalan identity.

The chime of the clock triggered Luisa. "Where is Montse? She needs to get ready for the party!" she asked with alarm to Elena.

Just then the front door opened and Montse bounded into the foyer of the grand house and bolted up the stairs to dress.

"You, your father, and I are greeting guests beginning at eight thirty, so you must be ready," Luisa said as her daughter whizzed past her.

For Montse, such elaborate preparations were an unusual event. She stopped heads with her natural beauty; she wore no make-up and typically kept her hair in a simple ponytail; she shunned the fancy attire her peers wore, favoring simple outfits or clothes suited to her sporting activities: riding, tennis, hiking, sailing, and swimming. So, several hours later, at just before eight thirty, when, looking like a princess, Montse calmly walked down the large, circular staircase that connected the two floors of her family's grand home to her mother and father waiting in the foyer below, they were stunned by her transformation—she was radiant. Montse, at the age of eighteen, was a beautiful young woman.

Her outfit was the latest fashion from Paris: A pale pink dress that had two narrow straps over her shoulders and that hung to her mid-calf. The dress exposed her athletically toned, bronzed arms and upper back, and, more prominently, her recently developed and alluring *décolletage*. Montse's dark hair was worn up, as was the fashion, and she had one of the maids do her make-up.

Together with her parents, she walked through the French doors that connected the house to its garden. There, set among towering pines and cypresses, fountains, and flower beds, were a dozen tables, each seating twelve people. The sun had just set, and the light of the Chinese lanterns gave the garden a soft glow.

Montse and her parents greeted the guests as they arrived. The guests included close family, long time family friends, esteemed business relations, members of Barcelona's artistic class, some of Montse's friends, and a couple of friends each for Elena and for Montse's older brother Jordi.

Also at the party was Enrique Pla y Deniel, the Bishop of Avila,

Spain. His status as a bishop had no bearing on his invitation or presence at the party. The bishop was there because, being from grand Catalan family himself, he had been a childhood friend of Luisa's. He was also Montse's godfather.

The party was a cosmopolitan affair. It was easy to imagine similar gatherings at the same time in Paris or in the grand estates outside of New York. The guests mingled for several hours sipping champagne and nibbling on *hors d'oeuvres*. They spoke among themselves in Catalan, French, and even some English, but hardly a word of Spanish wafted into the night air.

At about ten p.m., the guests sat down to dinner and the toasts to Montse began: first from her sister and brother; then from her godfather, Bishop Pla y Deniel, and finally from her parents. The toasts were delivered in the styles particular to each individual, but they all shared common themes: her unique intelligence, her kindness, her generosity; that she was becoming a very modern woman; and, most of all, of the unbounded potential of the life unfolding ahead of her.

After dinner, at about one a.m., the music started, and Montse took turns dancing with her father and other family members, and even Bishop Pla y Deniel, before accepting the request of her brother's friend Tomás Ferrer. Like Jordi, Tomás was twenty-one; he was the son of a prominent leftist Catalan writer and was studying law at the university in Barcelona. Montse could not help but notice him. He was strikingly handsome, with thick, dark hair, and a countenance exuding keen intelligence. After they danced, she kissed him on the cheek and whispered, "I hope Jordi is bringing you to our post party luncheon tomorrow."

"I wouldn't miss it," he answered back.

At about three a.m. the music died down, and the guests dispersed into the warm night. Montse, glowing, made her way to bed.

Book 1
Chapter 6
Barcelona, Spain
August 26, 1923

At around two thirty in the afternoon, the lunch guests began to arrive at the Costa home. They would be thirteen in total: Joan and Luisa; Montse; Elena; Jordi and his handsome friend, Tomás (a place next to Montse having been made for him on her specific request); one of Luisa's sisters, Marta, and her husband, who had come from Andalucía for the party; Joan's brother and sister together with their spouses; and Bishop Pla y Deniel. They were all Catalans with the exception of Marta's husband, who was an Andalusian Marquise.

The group gathered in the main sitting room. The room was a testimony to Luisa Costa's elegant and sophisticated tastes and her patronage of emerging artists who were Catalan or had a Catalan connection. Notably, the room housed several paintings dating from Picasso's stay in Barcelona in the early 1900s, various works by the emerging artist from Barcelona, like Joan Miro, and more traditional works by the impressionist from Valencia—the Catalans believing Valencia to be a rightful part of greater Catalonia—Joaquin Sorolla. The combination of the beautiful room, the afternoon light pouring through the French doors, and the sublime collection of art was mesmerizing.

The guests sought out the intimate connections that could not have been made at last night's party. Bishop Pla y Deniel sat with Montse and explained to her how close Avila was to Salamanca, and that he would be happy to welcome her to his city. He added for good measure that he would personally give her a tour of the sites and legacy of the great Spanish saint, St. Teresa of Avila. Montse, having read the works of St. Teresa, readily acknowledged her enthusiasm for the invitation.

After Bishop Pla y Deniel excused himself, Montse's Aunt Marta came to sit with her. The aunt was the favorite of her parents' siblings. She possessed all of her mother's positive attributes without her imperiousness. But like her mother, she could be very direct, "Montse dear, tell me why university in Salamanca? First you are a Catalan, and beyond that, you could go anywhere … Paris, England, or even to the United States."

"Aunt Marta, yes, I am Catalan first and foremost, but I also love Spanish literature and art. Cervantes—is there a greater book than Don Quixote?" she asked rhetorically. She then continued, "I love the great Spanish artists as well: El Greco, Velazquez, Goya. There is no better place for me to study this literary and artistic heritage than Salamanca."

"That's all true."

"And I will be closer to you!"

"It's settled then! You must come visit us for *Semana Santa* next spring. If you promise to visit, I will give your mother my full endorsement of your choice," Marta replied, only half kidding about influencing her mother.

"Seville, that mysterious golden city, the birthplace of Velazquez; I have always wanted to visit it!" Montse added.

Nearing four p.m. the guests headed to the dining room and were seated at the large, formal dining room table. Before the meal began Bishop Pla Y Deniel said a short grace, to which the group of mostly nominal Catholics politely, but unenthusiastically followed along.

The meal started with a traditional gazpacho soup served with a chilled white wine. The cool zest of the crushed tomatoes combined with the wine was perfect for a hot, Barcelona late-summer day. As the soup bowls were being cleared the discussion meandered to politics, the usual suspects being accused of their usual misdeeds: a bloated Spanish bureaucracy, an incompetent and oversized military, and an anachronistic monarchy.

Feeling themselves on friendly grounds, most of the group took a turn batting this *piñata*. None of the Catalans, save the Marta and Bishop Pla Y Deniel, had ever lived in non-Catalonian Spain, and they easily played along with the usual recycled rumor and hyperbole about their Iberian cousins.

Finally, Marta's husband, the Marquise, pushed back, "Spain has an unmatched legacy of accomplishment; we discovered the New World, and we are still a mighty power."

Loud guffaws were heard about the table. In deference to the Marquise, the discussion had been in Spanish, but with the heat rising it was at this point that Jordi's friend Tomás rose up—he emanated charisma—and switched to Catalan, "Here, you are not in Spain, you are in Catalonia!"

Bishop Pla Y Deniel, an erudite man whose study and life experience enabled him to see both sides of this long-standing, unresolved debate, interjected himself, speaking in Spanish, "This is Montserrat's birthday and going away luncheon; we are best served to leave politics for another place and time."

The group seemed to re-collect its sanity and manners and nodded in agreement—all of them except for Tomás. He sought out Montse, leaned over, placed is mouth to her ear, and whispered, "I want to see you when you return from school, and I will find you so that we can be together away from this place."

Tomás, stood up and moved away from the table. He was wild-eyed; looking like a dashing revolutionary; and again he shattered the politeness and elegance of the luncheon. Switching from Spanish to Catalan he said, "I represent the next generation of Catalans. We will not be so patient and polite with these idiot Spaniards. *Viva Catalonia, viva Indepedenzia!*" He left the dining room and rushed from the house. Montse's eyes followed him out.

"What did he say?" asked the Marquise.

"You do not want to know," Marta dejectedly replied.

Book 1
Chapter 7
Haro, Spain
September 12, 1923

Don Pedro de la Calzada lived in a modest but comfortable house on his small vineyard just outside the village of Haro, in the La Rioja region of Spain. Don Pedro was a widower with two sons: Juan, twenty-five years old, an officer in the Spanish Army serving in Spanish Morocco; and Jaime, eighteen, who was about to start university in Salamanca.

Tomorrow was one of the most important days of the year for Don Pedro; he needed to complete the harvest of the grapes from his vineyard. He required all the hands he could muster for the harvest, and both of his sons were home to help. In addition, the local parish priest, Father Fernandez, the school headmaster, as well as about fifty hired hands joined to bring in the grapes.

Don Pedro retained his family's noble title, if not its wealth, which had been dissipated over the generations. Don Pedro did not long for the lost riches, as he believed his real nobility lay not in his title but in his integrity, his self-assured pride, and his conscientiousness. He seemed not to care two *pesetas* about his material diminishment; what mattered to him was that his sons would be true Spaniards, and that they would carry his values forward and protect Spain from all manner of heresy.

Don Pedro's deeply conservative outlook was summarized in the three words of the Carlist flag on display in the house's small entry. The words emblazoned on the red and yellow horizontally striped flag were, "*Dios, Patria, Rey.*"

Like his father before him, he had served in the Spanish Army. Don Pedro was in Santiago de Cuba when, after very fierce fighting, the Spanish positions were overrun by Teddy Roosevelt and his Roughriders. The defeats in Cuba, and subsequently in the

Philippines, were crushing for Spain's collective psyche. These disasters shattered Spain's self-image of being a world power.

As Spain retreated from the world scene, Don Pedro also retreated. He retreated to tend to his vineyard—to tend his sons. Though he was now living a quiet rural life, he stayed connected to the politics and happenings of Spain by reading right-wing newspapers, frequent discussions with Father Fernandez, and from the periodic visits of his son Juan. Don Pedro was very troubled by what he read and heard about his beloved *patria*.

Don Pedro and his sons sat down to dinner at just before nine p.m. The housekeeper had prepared a simple meal of *tortilla patata, croquetas, jamon,* and *chorizo,* all to be washed down with a bottle of strong red wine from his cellar.

Just after their first bites Don Pedro wasted no time quizzing his son. "Juan, how is the situation in Morocco?"

"Father, we remain on our heels. We have not recovered from the debacle of 1921. We have fallen back, and now we are in a stalemate."

"Hmmm ...," his father growled.

"If the politicians in Madrid would get out of our way, we could finish the Moorish riffraff off in no time at all," Juan said in succinct summary.

"We seem to be again approaching some sort of tipping point. The politicians' continued incompetence and corruption is unsustainable. There are powerful forces in this country that will not stand by and watch this malaise and decline," Don Pedro added with an ominous and knowing tone.

Don Pedro then came back to Juan and asked, "Who is your commander now?"

"Lieutenant Colonel Franco."

"How do you find him?"

"Father, I tell you I will follow this man anywhere. He has an unusual combination of personal bravery, cunning, and tactical genius. He has been in Morocco for ten years, and it is said he should have been killed by the wounds he received from a Berber machine gun in 1916. The native Moroccans fear and respect him; they call him *Baraka* ... a man of good luck."

"Juan, you are the future, the protector of Spain. The history and values of Spain are in our blood. Always remember from where we came."

Juan and Jaime knew this was the cue to listen attentively to one of their father's lectures on the greatness of Spain—about which they both held the same views.

"We stopped the Moors from overrunning Europe, and after seven centuries we pushed them back to Africa. At the same time we discovered the New World. Writers like Cervantes and artists like Velazquez have illuminated the world's minds, and saints like Dominic, Teresa, and Ignatius Loyola have elevated the world's souls. Never, ever forget our heritage and the greatness of the Spanish spirit."

Juan lifted his wine glass. "To Spain!"

Don Pedro and Jaime responded with raised glasses. "To Spain!"

It was easy for Jaime to raise his glass; he too had absorbed his family's conservative political views. These views had been reinforced during his four years of Jesuit high school at Our Lady of Remembrance College in Madrid. During his time away he had grown up both physically and intellectually. He was now almost a man; he was a classically tall, dark, and handsome Spaniard. He excelled in school, particularly in Spanish literature and history. His was in accord with his father's worldview and his brother's sense of duty.

The family finished their meal with a simple flan, and Don Pedro reminded the boys to be at the vineyard at six thirty tomorrow morning.

Book 1
Chapter 8
Haro, Spain
September 13, 1923

At just before six fifteen on the second morning and final day of the harvest Don Pedro and Jaime made their way to the maintenance shed, which had been converted into a dormitory of sorts for the hired harvesters.

"We made good progress yesterday. We should be able to complete the harvest today. Thank God, because these grapes provide us everything for our living," Don Pedro advised his son.

Jaime nodded his understanding as his father continued, "We are fortunate our land is so fertile; we could sell twice what we can make."

It was in Don Pedro's nature to deliver little sermons imbued with wisdom and life lessons at every turn. He believed his mission was to teach his sons not only how to grow grapes but also how to grow their character: to know what was important versus trivial; what to fight for; what was right, and what was wrong.

Jaime was not a rebellious young man; in fact, he was serious, almost prematurely responsible, and he accepted his father's sermonettes as fact. He had without questioning or resistance taken his father's world view on as his own. He too believed in God, Country, and King. He too believed in a united and great Spain. Having lived in Madrid for four years, he had seen the corruption of the stifling bureaucracy and the greed of the small-minded politicians. He also had no time for the separatist currents that flowed just a few towns over in the Basque Country, and more pointedly, the arrogant, condescending attitudes of the rebellious Catalans. *What have they ever done that is noble and grand? All they want to do is make money; they are like the Jews Isabella expelled: penurious, pushy, and self-centered. They should be proud to be Spaniards, to be part of great history and culture, rather than always going on about their unique identity.*

The family was all of a like mind. Spain was sleep walking into a crisis, a disaster. The country needed a revival. A revival of its spirit, a revival of its soul, and a revival of its purpose. Spain had been a great nation, perhaps the greatest of nations, and it was time it healed itself and reclaimed this mantle. Jaime was convinced his next step in life, university in Salamanca, would help prepare him part to be a part of this revival.

When Don Pedro and Jaime reached the shed, the workers were sitting at long tables eating a hearty breakfast. Providing a place to sleep and meals to eat was part of the vineyard owner's obligation to the workers, and as many of the harvesters had been coming to Don Pedro's vineyard for a number of years, they mingled more like friends than a boss with his hired hands.

At around seven a.m., everyone made the short walk to the vineyards and assumed their positions in the production line of sorts that took the grapes from the vines to Don Pedro's truck. Most of the workers cut the grapes from the vines—that was the hardest job. A smaller number of men went up and down the small alleys between the vines and collected the cut grapes into large baskets. These baskets were then delivered to the back of the truck, from where they were taken to large open wooden containers.

At just after one p.m. and the work of clearing the vines of their grapes was done and the workers stopped for lunch and their afternoon *siesta*. Fed and rested, the workers had one last task to do: stomp the grapes and begin the process of turning the plump red fruit into high quality bottles of delicious red wine. After the hard, nearly back breaking work of the last few days, this was a joyous task. The workers watched and cheered as several of them began dancing barefooted in the grapes.

The job of stomping the grapes was complete by about seven thirty in the evening, and after the fresh burgundy colored juice was placed into large wooden barrels, the workers cleaned up for the celebratory dinner.

Don Pedro had always treated the harvesters with sincere hospitality, and the feast he had prepared for them reflected this deep respect and appreciation for their work. To start, a large selection of cheese and sausages were passed on trays that seemed to never be empty. For dinner, as was his tradition, he served tender, succulent roast suckling pig, and of course wine from his cellar flowed in abundance.

After dinner Don Pedro became the paymaster and handed out envelopes rewarding each of the harvesters for their effort; his payments were always on the generous side of fair. The combination of abundant wine and good pay kicked the party into overdrive. Guitars and other instruments emerged, and the group was consumed by laughter, dancing, and singing.

Along the way it seemed all the important things in life were toasted: family and friends; the grapes and the wine; God, the Pope, the Church, and King and Country.

It was just about two a.m., before drunkenness and exhaustion nearly extinguished the party, Don Pedro made one last toast. "Here is to my son, Juan's brother, your friend, Jaime. Jaime is to shortly leave for university in Salamanca—may he achieve great scholarship and make true and lifelong friends there. *Viva* Jaime!"

"*Viva* Jaime! *Viva* Jaime! *Viva* Jaime!" the harvesters shouted. Jaime was enveloped in joyous embraces and showered with wine.

Book Two

Coming of Age

Book 2
Chapter 1
Salamanca, Spain
September 15, 1923

After traveling all the day before by train from San Sebastian, Xavi and his mother had spent the night in a small hotel near the university. They set out at around ten a.m., making their way to the housing office of the university to get Xavi's housing assignment. It took but a short time for Xavi and his mother to be captured by the charm of the city.

Salamanca, situated in the arid plains of western Spain, sitting on several hills by the Tormes River, had seen the long march of history. Passing by its Roman Bridge gave immediate testimony to how much the picturesque city had witnessed. Hannibal had laid siege to it, and the old Roman Road, the *Via de la Plata*, intersected it. The Moors had come and gone, and after they left, a royal university was founded in 1218.

Salamanca was one of the original four great universities in Europe, along with Oxford, Paris, and Bologna. It was the center for learning and theology in Spain. It was uniquely beautiful; it seduced its visitors with the magical elixir that was created when the sun and blue Iberian sky poured down on the pale sandstone of the buildings. The city radiated a golden, beguiling glow.

Xavi and his mother had never seen a place with such rich array of varied, and beautiful buildings. Around every corner and small square was another style of architecture, another notation of style that marked the progress of Spanish artistic and religious expression. Beyond the Roman Bridge, small sturdy Romanesque churches made way for the inspirational sweep of gothic buttresses; Renaissance palaces were transformed into the uniquely Spanish creation with their highly decorative, plateresque facades; and in the center of the city lay the majestic, baroque *Plaza Mayor*.

Salamanca's *Plaza Mayor* was said to be the most beautiful plaza in Spain. The three storied square, anchored by the city hall, was shaped as an irregular rectangle. Numerous round arches created a covered arcade that bordered the main plaza. Eighty-eight columns supported these arches, and above every one of them was a medallion commemorating a great figure in Spanish history. All around the plaza were restaurants and cafés. It was alive with students and local people. The city teemed with vitality.

Xavi and his mother, entranced by the city, lost their way, and hailed a local. "Where is the housing office of the university?"

"It's quite near, just up the street in the main square of the university. You will know you are there when you come to a large statue of Fray Luis de Leon … you can't miss him," the man kindly replied.

They came to the square over which the large statue loomed.

"Who is he, Mother?"

"Some old professor I recall."

They did not linger, and they made their way into the housing office.

"Xavier Bidertea, let's see. Ah yes, here it is. Xavier Bidertea, you will be in an apartment on the twenty-two Calle Liberos. You will like this apartment; it's comfortable, and it's very conveniently situated just around the corner from here."

"Can you tell me who my roommate is?"

"He is already checked in and he seems to be a quiet and polite young man from La Rioja. His name is Jaime de la Calzada."

"Thank you."

"You will enjoy your time here."

As Xavi and his mother veered from the square up the Calle Liberos, towards number twenty-two; the city was buzzing with activity. The street was full of students arriving and moving into their accommodations, and out of the corner of his eye, to his right, across the street, he did a double take of a beautiful dark-haired young woman. His mother kept him moving, and in short order they arrived at his new lodgings. Before entering the building, Xavi looked back for one more glance at the striking young woman. They walked up two flights of stairs coming to Xavi's new apartment, where they met two young men already moving in.

"*Hola*, I'm Xavi," Xavi said, extending his hand to the younger appearing of the two young men.

"*Hola*, Xavi, I'm Jaime. Welcome," Jaime warmly reciprocated Xavi's greeting.

The boys then proceeded to make introductions all around and exchange brief life summaries. Having located the apartment, Xavi returned to his hotel to begin the process of transporting his suitcases and belongings. After several of hours of back and forth, and brief conferences about what would go where, Maria Bidertea suggested they all should take a break and head over to the *Plaza Mayor* for lunch.

Maria Bidertea felt the warm glow of motherly pride as she saw that her son and his new roommate immediately got on so well, talking about mutual interests and places they both knew. Haro, being not far from San Sebastian, they had many experiences to compare with each other; she sensed they would become friends. Maria graciously played the host when the bill came, and after paying she suggested they tour the square.

They strolled slowly along the inside perimeter of the plaza, stopping from time to time to note and study the historical figures captured on the eighty-eight medallions displayed on the columns of the plaza: Cervantes ... Saint Teresa ... Charles V ... and many other great Spaniards, as well as the occasional foreigner, like Wellington, who were recognized on Salamanca's historical honor roll. This was the Pantheon of Spanish greatness.

Across the plaza was Monserrat Costa, and she picked Xavi out of the groups of young people mingling with their parents. From afar she could sense he had calm presence about him. She guessed him to be a Basque with his olive complexion, dark hair and eyes, and pronounced nose. She instantly felt a form of attraction that was new to her. It immediately felt deeper than the chemical attraction she felt with Tomás.

Maria and the boys ambled their way toward the medallion of Cervantes where Montse was conversing with another young woman. As they stopped to study the great man's medallion, Maria heard the familiar tones of her native Catalan. While his mother noted the young woman's language, Xavi recognized it was the same beautiful girl he had earlier seen in the street. Maria, on hearing her native tongue, introduced herself and the young lady eagerly replied in Catalan, "*Bon dia,* I am Montserrat Costa, and I am just starting university here. My friends call me Montse."

"*Bon dia,* I am *señora* Bidertea and this my son, Xavi. Though I am married to a Basque, I am Catalan, born and raised in Barcelona."

"Ah, me too!"

Maria continued on with Montse, comparing notes on life in her native Barcelona. Xavi, realizing her mother's Catalan discourse was excluding Jaime and his brother, interrupted and transitioned the conversation to the more inclusive language of Spanish.

Before they said their goodbyes Xavi, Jaime, and Montse realized they would see each other Monday morning, as they were in the same orientation session with the University's proctor, Miguel de Unamuno.

"*Hasta el lunes,* Montse."

"*Igual,* Xavi," Montse said with an engaging smile.

On the way back to the apartment Maria whispered to Xavi, "I think she is maybe somehow related to the famous Costa family in Barcelona."

Xavi did not give any thought to his mother's whisper, rather Montse's beauty and easy way of being were what stuck in his mind.

Walking nearby Jaime steamed; he found it so infuriating when Catalans used their language to exclude Spaniards. *Damn Catalans!* he thought.

Book 2
Chapter 2
Salamanca, Spain
September 17, 1923

Xavi and Jaime woke up for the first day of university with a mixture of nervousness and anticipation, combined with sad resignation over the loss of their summer days and their easy, simple pleasures. But more than anything, they were also excited to meet the great man: Miguel de Unamuno.

Miguel de Unamuno was a giant. He was famous throughout Spain for his intellect and the force of his character. Unamuno, a Basque born in Bilbao, fifty-nine years old, was the proctor of the University. He established his intellectual prowess at an early age, and by age twenty he had mastered eleven languages so that he could read foreign authors in their own tongues. He was an essayist, novelist, poet, and philosopher. At Salamanca he taught Greek, classics, and a course on his hero, Cervantes.

He was also a soulful man. He had married his childhood sweetheart, with whom he had ten children. He said of matters of the heart: *It is sad not to love, but it is sadder to not be able to love.*

Unamuno's relationship with religion was enigmatic. For his whole life he had struggled with faith, religion, and doubt, saying: faith that does not doubt is a dead faith. He specialized in paradoxes.

More recently, in 1922, he had taken the controversial position of supporting the right of Protestants to worship in deeply Catholic Spain. Unamuno was a highly principled iconoclast.

Xavi and Jaime made their way past the Fray Luis de Leon statue to a lecture hall that held about fifty freshmen waiting for the Professor. On their way in they saw Montse, looking as attractive as she had the day before, and Xavi enthusiastically waved to her to join them.

Professor Unamuno entered the room. He had a gray presence: His hair and beard were gray, and he was wearing a gray suit. The students waited for him to begin speaking. After taking a few moments to survey the new students, he started simply, "And so it begins—your journey here at Salamanca."

He spoke firmly, formally, and with conviction. Every word was in its place and seemed to carry significant weight; he made no superfluous commentary.

He continued, "You are now in the procession of the great river that eternally flows and connects our past to our future. Just a few steps from here we are reminded of the great ones who come before us. Go to the *Plaza Mayor.* Study the medallions. Learn their stories. These famous men and women speak to us, always. Listen to them.

"Coming into this hall you passed by the statue of Fray Luis de Leon. He defines the square. He speaks to us too. He studied here. He taught here. He excelled in Greek, Hebrew, and Latin. He was a man of letters, and he edited books for Saint Teresa.

"He also translated biblical texts to Spanish to make them more accessible. Certain parts of the Spanish Church, then as now, were rooted in an outdated and anti-Christian view of the world, and for this he was put before the Inquisition. They imprisoned him for four years, but they did not break him. When he returned here in 1576, giving powerful testimony to his fortitude, he famously started his first lecture on his return by speaking these simple five words, '*as we were saying yesterday.*' The great river continues. You are now in its flow."

He paused, transitioning, "Before Fray Luis, Columbus was here to confer with the geographers of the university. He came to review his plans and discuss the viability of his proposed journey; and after he discovered the New World, it was the philosophers and theologians from here who debated the rights of the Native Americans. Here the Dominicans, whose beautiful church many of you walked by this morning, stretched our conception of the universal rights of man.

"In these buildings, scholars thought about natural law, and their erudition was so prominent that their works became world renowned as The School of Salamanca. These scholars tackled thorny problems of theology, as well as the practical problems of the day, in the fields of law and economics. Their frameworks still inspire us today.

"And I cannot speak of your predecessors here without high-lighting Cervantes. Cervantes, who suffered so much, was here as well. Cervantes, who is perhaps the world's greatest failure. Cervantes, who absorbed so much pain and so much failure to create Don Quixote and Sancho Panza."

Once again, he paused, and Xavi sensed he was winding up for something important to him. "And this leads us to today, or more precisely to what has happened in our country four days ago. Four days ago a flamboyant playboy, the Marquise of Estrella, Captain General Miguel de Rivera, supported by King Alfonso XIII, led a coup. The general is a fool and an amateur.

"We have seen this story countless times before. The people demand democracy and the elites, initially, condescendingly tolerate it, only to ultimately squash it. Besides being morally wrong, these people are incompetent and out of touch.

"Here at Salamanca we promote learning, scholarship, excellence, and progress. In Madrid, a cozy club of aristocrats safeguard their narrow, selfish interests. I have not spent my life in pursuit of knowledge and truth in order to remain silent. I will speak out, I will write, and I will use the full force of my knowledge and life experience to denounce this coup.

"Welcome to Salamanca. Welcome to the flow of Spanish history. Jump in, take your place in it."

Professor Unamuno finished his talk; he took no questions, and without haste left the lecture hall. The young students in the hall were quiet; they sat stunned by the force of what they had just heard.

After sitting motionless for a few moments, Montse suggested they go get a coffee and digest what Unamuno had said. Xavi, Jaime, and Montse made the short walk to the *Café Novelty* in the *Plaza Mayor*. After the coffees were delivered, Montse jumped in, "Professor Unamuno, he is as impressive as he is reputed to be, and unfortunately he is so right about our country's politics."

Jaime, still sore from their encounter yesterday, was quickly inflamed. "Get off your Catalan high horse!" he snapped. "All you

Catalans do is strike and prattle on about autonomy. General Primo de Rivera is a patriot who believes in Spain and the restoration of our greatness."

Xavi watched and listened. He had little interest in politics and was not inclined to one side or another. Rather, he was called by his intuition that both Jaime and Montse were to become important friends to him. "Now, now, Jaime, be a gentleman with our kind Catalan *señorita*; and please, Montse be respectful to my proud Spanish roommate."

For the moment Xavi's words salved the tension, and the conversation moved on to the schedule of classes, books to be bought, exploring the new city, and how much they looked forward to taking their coffees at *Café Novelty*.

Book 2
Chapter 3
Salamanca, Spain
November 12, 1923

Montse collected the mail and immediately noted an envelope of heavy linen stationary carrying elegant calligraphed letters and an ornate red wax seal from the town of Avila. She opened the letter from her godfather…

> *Dear Montserrat,*
>
> *I was delighted to have received your letter and to hear of your happy arrival to Salamanca. It would be a great pleasure to host you and your friend here in Avila. Please contact my secretary and arrange the date and details.*
>
> *I look forward to seeing you very soon.*
>
> *Warmly,*
>
> *Most Reverend Enrique Pla y Deniel*
>
> *Bishop of Avila*

She immediately thought of a weekend alone with Xavi exploring the old walled city, its churches and *palacios*, following the steps of Saint Teresa; she went to seek him out to tell him the exciting news. He was studying at the *Café Novelty*. "Xavi, guess what?"

He was charmed by Montse. Beyond her beauty, her enthusiasm, her seemingly boundless energy, her positive air uplifted everyone she met. Xavi found her captivating, entrancing. "Montse you constantly surprise me; please tell me what it is."

"I just received a letter from a friend of mine who is a priest in Avila, and he would like to host us for a tour of the city," she explained coyly. "Would you come with me?"

"That's wonderful. Yes, of course I will come," he then thought for a moment and added, "but you know I could not go without bringing Jaime along as well," he said firmly.

Montse was stuck out on a limb. She dearly wanted time alone with Xavi, just him, but she was also certain his condition was a serious one. "Okay, okay, let's all go. I will make the arrangements."

———

Book 2
Chapter 4
Avila, Spain
November 25, 1923

Montse, Xavi, and Jaime had arrived in Avila by train early in the previous evening. Over dinner they had laid out the outline for their Sunday: connect at eight a.m. for breakfast; head to the cathedral; meet her priest friend after the nine-a.m. mass; tour the city; have a late lunch with the priest; take the eight-p.m. train back to Salamanca. It promised to be a full and interesting day in the old, walled city.

Avila sat, lonely, high on a tabletop of a treeless Castilian plain. The ancient, stumpy walls, standing about thirty to forty feet above the brown plain below, punctuated by eighty-eight guard towers and nine gates, completely encircled the city; the walls created a defensive perimeter of almost a mile and half. They gave silent testimony to the city's turbulent history. During the war to reconquest Spain from the Moors, the city saw the constant back and forth of pitched battles, leading it to become virtually uninhabited. Later, in the 16th century, after the Christian conquest, the town flourished once more. Churches and palaces sprouted up, and most importantly, the greatest of Spanish saints, Saint Teresa of Avila, emerged to become one of the most prominent of all Catholic mystics.

Over the last several centuries the town had again fallen off the map; nearly forgotten, almost sad really, seemingly stuck in a different time and place: the 16th century world dominated by Saint Teresa. Yet in Avila, the spirit of the great saint was palpable everywhere you walked. Ambling through the narrow, cobble-stoned streets, the presence of the deceased Carmelite was still felt as if she remained alive.

At breakfast Montse finally revealed the secret of her relationship with the so-called priest they would be meeting. "I need to tell you something … the priest we are meeting is an important man of the church."

Xavi and Jaime followed along with Montse, and their quizzical expressions showed their desire to hear more.

"Yes, the priest, well he is actually the Bishop of Avila…."

"What, how?" Jaime exclaimed.

"He is a childhood friend of my mother from Barcelona, and he, Bishop Enrique Pla y Deniel, is also my godfather," she added sheepishly.

The boys were dumbfounded. She was mostly silent about her family and background, and while the little ins and outs of her daily life occasionally gave indication that Montse came from a world of wealth and privilege, she spoke little of her life in Barcelona; they did not have a clear picture of how elevated her life there was.

As she disclosed her relationship with the bishop, Xavi recalled his mother's words: *I think she is somehow related to the famous Costa family in Barcelona.*

For now, her background and her life in Barcelona mattered not, and in fact, having the bishop lead the tour of significant places of the city would open doors that would have otherwise remained shuttered to them.

After breakfast, the three of them walked the short distance through the narrow streets to the cathedral. Xavi led them to a pew near the front of the church. Bishop Pla y Deniel presided over the Mass, and in his homily he spoke about St. John of the Cross, a contemporary of Saint Teresa who also lived in Avila, and who was considered, next to Saint Teresa, to be the second greatest Spanish mystic.

"St. John of the Cross was born near here in 1542 to a *converso* family. He was a contemporary of, and confessor to, our great Saint Teresa. As a Catholic *converso*, and like our Church, he combined the Old and New Testaments to follow the path of mysticism in his journey to know God. He died at just forty-nine, and in his short life he accomplished much amid significant turmoil in his world. …"

After the homily Xavi and Jaime took communion, but Montse

stayed in the pew and did not take the Eucharist.

When the mass concluded, a cathedral priest took them to the sacristy to meet the bishop. He warmly greeted his goddaughter *"Bon dia*, Montserrat."

They exchanged several sentences in Catalan before she made the introductions of Xavi and Jaime in Spanish. Without delay they set out to see Avila.

They started out by touring the cathedral, various palaces, and the ancient Romanesque Basilica of San Vincente.

The basilica sat just outside the walls of the city where there was nothing to stop the wind that was piercing as it cut across the high, Castilian plain. Admiring its ancient portico from outside, there was no shelter from the cold. Under the crisp blue skies they lingered, captivated by the church's squat Romanesque simplicity, which was somehow so much more appealing than the ornate Gothic cathedral.

"The basilica was built in late 12th century, as the Romanesque Period was about to be superseded by the Gothic," the bishop commented.

"Your Excellency …?" Jaime asked with a tentative tone.

"Yes, Jaime."

"I'm sorr, but what is a basilica?"

"A good question, as with so many things, we pass by them without really understanding them. A basilica is a designation given to a church that has special significance, whereas a cathedral, like where you heard mass this morning, is the seat, the church, of the bishop. The Cathedral of Avila is my church, Jaime."

"Ah, okay, but what is so significant about San Vincente?"

"First, as you can see, it is so pleasing to the eye in its shape and symmetry; and the stone, like many of the buildings in Salamanca, is the soft color of sandstone, which seems to radiate in the Castilian sunshine."

"It does. It glows somehow, and its dimensions invite you …" he said shivering in the cold wind.

"It seems the Romanesque is attached to the world, to the ground really, while the Gothic attempts to soar to Heaven. The stones give us a theology lesson, don't they?"

"I'm sorry, I'm not following exactly, Your Excellency." Jaime said a bit puzzled.

"Living here on earth or soaring towards heaven …"

"Or perhaps both, as Saint Teresa did," Xavi interjected.

"Indeed, as Saint Teresa did…. We will see that a bit later, but first let's go inside the basilica."

They walked in the church, and under its barrel vaults which held up almost windowless, thick walls, the bishop continued. "Jaime, to your question, it is a basilica because it holds the relics of two martyrs from the time of Diocletian. Our faith, and the turmoil surrounding it, are very old. One must never forget that. Faith and turmoil always go hand in hand."

They left the basilica and passed back through the thick walls to reenter the city; they turned their focus to Saint Teresa. The bishop led them to her home, the Convent of San José, where they were met in whisper by the Mother Superior. In the cloistered convent, silence was a constant presence; the impact of the silence was immediate; it was refreshing, restorative like a cool breeze on a warm day. Thanks to the intercession of the bishop, the Mother Superior led them into the convent's inner reaches that few outsiders had ever seen.

As they walked the silent halls the Mother Superior whispered the outlines of the saint's remarkable life. Montse, Xavi and Jaime leaned into her softly spoken words with acute interest.

"Saint Teresa, how can I say this, she is a saint, near to God, and in a human sense, a towering figure of … for, all mankind."

The Mother Superior led the small group a few more steps and stopped. "On two occasions she gave up a life of comfort for this … she was from a wealthy *converso* family, but she was called to God, and at age twenty she entered a Carmelite Convent, but not this one, one that was lax in its practices."

They walked in silence a few more steps and entered a small room with a narrow bed with woolen bedcover and simple cross above it.

"This was her room. This was her life. She left the comfort of her previous order to focus on this simple, you might say harsh, life of contemplation. We still live under the rule Saint Teresa established in the late 1500s. We are a mendicant order …we have no real possessions … *discalced* … shoeless."

Moving a step or two further into the room she continued, "This was her desk. This is where she wrote. She was an inspired genius and a brilliant revolutionary. Teresa had a clear vision; she was persuasive; she was a natural leader, and she was able to stretch minimal resources to prove the power of her vision to a world of disbelieving critics and skeptics to create this new order of Carmelites."

The Mother Superior made a strong impression on Xavi. She exuded a strong intelligence, and an aura of beauty emanated from beneath her brown Carmelite robes; her white undergarment accentuated her soft, kind face. Her spirituality and simplicity, her certainty and serenity, were deeply attractive in an unusual way, he thought. Her connection to God was powerfully present to him.

The Mother Superior continued on in her soft whisper, "We are an order that is cloistered. We dedicate ourselves to contemplation and asceticism, and our daily life is ordered around prayer, manual labor, abstinence, fasting, charity, and fraternity.

Saint Teresa stressed that discipline and obedience were the keys to moving closer to God. Her vision immediately found an unoccupied place in the world, and many convents rapidly sprouted up to follow her ideals. It still brings us immense peace to this day."

The Mother Superior concluded the tour by providing an overview of Saint Teresa's mysticism and writing. "Saint Teresa traveled and documented a spiritual journey that few had ever made. She went from solitude to prayer, to an ever-deepening connection to God that created a sense of actual physical connection for her."

The Mother Superior then paused and opened a book she was carrying. She began to read from it in her whisper:

I saw in his hand a long spear of gold, and at that point there seemed to be a little fire. He appeared to me to be thrusting at times into my heart, and to pierce my very entrails; when he drew it out, he seemed to draw them out also, and to leave me all on fire with a great love of God. The pain was so great, that it made me moan; and yet so surpassing was the sweetness of this excessive pain, that I could not wish to be rid of it ...

"This is the love of God we seek ...," she said as her whisper trailed off to silence.

The Mother Superior walked the group out. Montse, Xavi, and Jaime were each deeply moved. The silence of the convent had had more impact on them than did all of the pitched voices of protest they often heard on the streets of Salamanca—mystical silence trumping clanging discord.

As they were leaving, Montse took the lead. "Mother Superior, this has been deeply moving, I, we, truly thank you. Is there anything we can do to show our gratitude?"

"Well perhaps you would like to buy some of the cookies we bake? As you can see, we live a life of material poverty. Anything you can offer is of great help and will be greatly appreciated."

"Of course, of course."

Stopping on the way out, they took three small bags of sugar-covered cookies, and Montse took several large *peseta* notes from her purse in exchange.

"Oh, *señorita* Costa, that is too generous," the Mother Superior mildly objected.

"No, no, it will mean much more to you and your sisters than could ever mean to me."

"Thank you … what a truly Christian thought."

From the monastery, the bishop took them back to his home, the Episcopal Palace of Avila. There he led them to his private dining room for lunch. They drank a rough Castilian red wine, and over dark, rich *Rabo de Toro* stew, *Manchego* cheese, and a simple *flan* they talked robustly for three and a half hours.

The bishop spoke of growing up with Montse's mother, and Montse was delighted to hear sweet, previously unknown stories from her mother's childhood. They also quickly observed that he was a very educated man who spoke Catalan, Spanish, French, Italian, and Latin. He emanated wisdom, good judgement, and the cautious approach of a good politician.

Xavi and Jaime described their families and backgrounds, and with Montse they spoke of a settling into a pleasant life in Salamanca, and how they were forming a strong three-way friendship, even if they did not always see eye to eye on everything.

The bishop picked up on this point, "Oh, Montse, I see. It is good to have friends with diverse viewpoints … as long as they are not heretical."

"No, Your Excellency, Xavi is very circumspect, a good Basque Catholic, and an excellent listener who asks the right probing questions that always seem to get to the heart of the matter. Really, the conflict that often bubbles up is between Jaime and me. He is a very traditional Spaniard, and I, well, you know, I am a Catalan through and through. And, with the current political situation, we frequently seem to be stimulated to intense disagreement."

The bishop did not take the bait to pick a side. "Yes, Montse, you have always been the high-spirited gir, ever since your baptism; you cried when the water was put over your beautiful little head." They all had a laugh at the bishop's anecdote.

"And your name, coming from our mystical mountain near Barcelona, well that is as Catalan as can be," he said with a laugh, "but you know there are so many other things to discuss than politics, today being such a vivid reminder of that. We were in the footsteps of greatness. I suggest tonight you contemplate Saint Teresa rather than the latest fight between Unamuno and Primo de Rivera, or the issue of the day between your Catalans and Jaime's Spaniards."

As the lunch was ending the bishop made a toast. His tone was no longer of a careful politician, but rather conveyed the affection of a godfather. He told them how much he had enjoyed his day, how refreshing and energizing it had been to be with special young people. "You are each different, from different regions of this amazing country of ours, and I am heartened by each of you and by the talents you bring us. Whatever your view of the events of the day in Spain, you remind me our future is bright."

"*Salud,*" was heard all around the table.

"Thank you for this wonderful day. I must be off to prepare for tomorrow. My driver will take you back to your hotel to pick up your luggage and then to the train station. Thank you again and may God be with you."

On the train back to Salamanca they were energized.

"What a day!" Montse said after they had settled into their seats on the train.

"Thank you, Montse, for all of it," Jaime said.

"I never realized what a revolutionary Saint Teresa was," she added.

"Revolutionary?" Jaime said, objecting to the very nature of the word. "She is the patroness of Spain. You can't be more traditional than that, Montse!"

So it was, Xavi thought, *that even Saint Teresa became the fodder for politics between a Catalan and a Spaniard.* For him, the great saint was different. She was a giant. She was an inspiration. Saint Teresa was a combination of the Romanesque, attached to the earth, and the Gothic, soaring to heaven.

In a quiet moment while Jaime was in the dining car, Xavi looked intently at Montse, their eyes connected, locking their souls together for a moment, and he said, "You are an enigma to me, Montse."

"Whatever can you mean?"

"You marvel at our great Saint Teresa, and you are exceedingly kind and reverent with the Mother Superior, your godfather is a bishop, but you do not take communion?"

Montse interrupted him before he could finish his question. "Not tonight, Xavi. In time, but it's not for tonight."

Book 2
Chapter 5
Salamanca, Spain
February 24, 1924

The sky was maya blue on a bitingly cold, winter afternoon. Even inside the *Café Novelty* the frigid, winter air seeped in. Xavi sat a table with a coffee, bundled up and immersed in his studies. Outside, across the square, he caught sight of the great professor coming towards the cafe. Unamuno, along with several other professors, was scurrying along to get out of the cold.

The group surrounding the professor appeared somber, downtrodden, and the professor himself wore a stoical countenance. At the bar Xavi could hear Unamuno say, "One last drink before I go." Xavi was confused.

Just after the professor took a sip of his wine, he noticed Xavi, and made his way toward him. "Hello, Xavi, I am glad to see you before I must go."

"Go? Go where? Go when?" Xavi replied.

"Yes, go. For five months I have been speaking and writing about the illegitimacy of this new regime and the coup that propelled it. I believe in speaking the truth and letting the chips fall where they may—and now the chips are falling."

Xavi's face turned pale with worry.

"There is no point in going into the details of my dispute, and I do not have the time in any case, but the long and short of it is I am being sent into exile to the Canary Islands. I am being shunned away and silenced once again—as I was in 1914," the professor said, without betraying any of the sadness he must have been feeling.

Xavi knew the feud with Primo de Riviera was escalating, but he had no idea it had come to this. Everyone knew the new dictator was prickly and was cracking down on dissent, but somehow, he thought of the professor as too revered, as too famous—too great for exile. He had imagined he might be reproached, but nothing beyond that.

In shock, he asked simply, "What will you do?"

"I will go, and I will take solace in one of my heroes, Fray Luis de Leon, and I will anticipate my return to this place to which I given much of my life and which I love with all my heart and soul. I will be back. ..."

Unamuno continued, "In any case I am pleased to see you before I leave. You have an exceptional mind and character. You are unusually open to the world, and you are able to hold conflicting ideas without closing yourself off. With this trait, or because of it, you have developed a special type of kindness, a charity of spirit. I had hoped to watch this grow over your time here; alas, this will not be possible now. My leaving wish for you is to implore you to stay this course, even though events and life's circumstances will make this path feel shaky beneath your feet at times. Xavi, I know you are a young man of deep faith. I once had this type of faith ... I had even imagined becoming a priest ... and I wish you well on this journey. There is no higher purpose than following the calling of your beliefs. I have much to do before I take my leave. I must go now."

The only reaction that came to Xavi was to rise and silently embrace the great man, as if he were his father.

After Professor Unamuno left the *Café*, Xavi took his things and went to find Montse, to tell her of what had happened.

Word of Unamuno's fate spread quickly through the city, and later that evening Montse and Xavi went to the professor's house. They were amongst the several hundred students and professors gathered to protest, to protect, and to give their support to Unamuno. When the guards came to collect the professor for exile, a great commotion ensued, and a riot nearly erupted, but in the end the might and the threat of the soldiers' guns prevailed. The great man was taken away.

After the disturbance died down, the crowd seeped away. Montse and Xavi returned to the *Café Novelty* to take a coffee. There, they shared silence and heartbreak.

Book 2
Chapter 6
Salamanca, Spain
May 24, 1924

Spring came early to Salamanca. Montse, Xavi, and Jaime sat together outside on the terrace of the *Café Novelty*. Enveloped by
warm air and the sweet smells of the blooming trees and flowers,
they were beginning to wind down their school year.

The threesome had settled into a comfortable friendship of
which Xavi was the fulcrum. Montse and Jaime were learning to
stay away from the subjects of Spanish politics and Catalan autonomy, and with that impediment removed, they found attributes in
each other that they genuinely liked and admired, characteristics
that would have remained hidden away if they had remained fixated on the issues that divided them.

The impending end of their first year at university left them all
unsettled, with mixed emotions. They were no longer freshmen;
they had learned the city, the routines of being students, and they
each had excelled in their studies. They were pleased to be returning to their families and to rest and recharge. But also there was
something else—they shared a common thought: they would miss
the exhilaration and freedom of being in university, but beyond
that, they knew they would miss the friendship that they had developed. They each knew that there was nothing at their home
bases that could replace what had been built at Salamanca.

Sensing the mixed feelings that hung over their table, Montse,
always being the most outgoing of the three, broke the silence:
"Why don't we plan to meet up this summer? We can go to a place
that is special, a place that is unique to one of us ... do a show and
tell of sorts."

Xavi seconded the suggestion. "I like that idea, and I think I
know the perfect itinerary."

"What are you thinking? Tell us." Jaime asked.

"You two can come to my home San Sebastian for a few days, and then we can go the *Fiesta San Fermin*—experience Pamplona, the region of Navarre, and the Basque people and culture."

"The bulls ...?" Xavi added.

"Yes, the bulls. We can arrive to Pamplona for start of the *fiesta* on July 6th. Xavi, how about you and I run with them?"

"Count me in," Xavi highlighted his agreement with the idea. "We can watch the procession, sing the local songs, dance the Basque dances, and drink with the locals. I have been to Pamplona for *San Fermin*, but never as a runner ... it could be a great holiday for all of us."

Montse enthusiastically added, "It sounds wonderful." The sweet ring of her endorsement for the summer rendezvous immediately lifted the tinge of melancholy that had been hanging over the three friends.

"I will get us three more glasses of wine!" Jaime added.

As Jaime left the table Montse's and Xavi's eyes connected in a deep and romantic way.

Book 2
Chapter 7
Pamplona, Spain
July 7, 1924

A t just before eight a.m. Montse extended herself over the balcony of her room in the *Hotel La Gran Perla* and peered up and down the *Calle de la Estefeta*. The street below was very narrow, perhaps no more than twenty feet wide, and was bordered by four and five story apartment buildings on both sides creating the impression of a narrow urban canyon. She was perfectly positioned to oversee the chaos which was to momentarily unfold on the street below. The runners, and the bulls that would be chasing them, would both rush by as they careened toward the bull ring just several hundred yards away.

The raucous, joyful, and chaotic scenes of the festival could not have been more different than the tranquil days they had spent the previous week. Before arriving in Pamplona Montse, Xavi, and Jaime were together for a week in San Sebastian, most days taking Xavi's father's small sailboat out to explore the charming little fishing villages nearby, to the east and west of the town. At night, together with Xavi's parents, they would go out to the restaurants and bars of the various quarters of the city. During this time Maria Bidertea and Montse developed a tight bond. Often, they would separate from the group, like a mother and daughter, and could be heard going back and forth in Catalan, punctuated by giggles and laughter.

The previous morning Montse, Xavi, and Jaime had made the short train trip from San Sebastian to Pamplona. They arrived in time to find a place in the *Plaza Ayuntamiento* just minutes before *Txupinazo* was launched at noon, exploding high above the plaza, signaling the start of the weeklong festival. After the rocket was fired, they sang, danced, drank, and laughed with the local Navarrese until well after midnight; they collapsed into their respective beds from exhaustion, happiness, and a little bit of drunkenness. As the night was ending, they agreed they would all meet for coffee after the running of the bulls at the *Café Iruna* next door to the *Gran Perla*.

At precisely 8:00 a.m. another rocket was fired off, this one signaling the release of the bulls. The bulls' pen was only six or seven hundred yards away, and in several minutes the collective chaos of the bulls and the runners were under her balcony. *Oh the sound of it all!* The shouts, the banging of hoofs on cobblestones, were apparent to her before the first of the runners emerged. The runners, all in white with red neckerchiefs, were spread out along the street. Some of the pack was ahead of the bulls with heads craned backward to see how large was the space of safety between them and the charging, sharp, white horns; others were behind the pack; some, who had fallen, were still playing the dead in hopes that they would not be trampled upon, and still others sought refuge in the nooks and crannies of the buildings along the street. The mayhem passed by at great speed, making it impossible for her to pick out her friends. In a few moments, the crowd was gone and out of view as they made their way toward the bullring.

Montse nervously finished dressing and headed to the *Café Iruna* to drink her first morning coffee; there she waited in worried anticipation for her friends. She would never forgive herself if because of her chirpy suggestion in Salamanca that one or both of them were hurt, or even more unthinkable, killed by a bull or by the crush of the crowd.

Shortly after nine a.m. Xavi and Jaime came into the bar: united, ecstatic, and victorious. The three of them entered into a tight, collective embrace of relief and joy. They then recounted their short adventure—the whole run being less than a kilometer long—how after the crowd asked for the blessing from *San Fermin* that the rocket went off and madness reigned. The bulls passing them just before they entered the bullring, they both agreed that they were surprisingly fast and frighteningly large.

The crowd at the bar was united by the common experience of the run and the corresponding rush of adrenalin. Friends were easily made. The pattern of yesterday's activities began to be repeated with, *"Mas vino y mas cerveza,"* being frequently shouted from all corners of the bar.

After lunch, at about three p.m., Jaime gave in to his exhaustion and headed next door to the hotel for a *siesta*. Jaime was not alone in needing some sleep, and suddenly Montse and Xavi found themselves nearly alone in the bar. With Jaime gone they instinctively switched from Spanish to Catalan. They spoke of what a great year they had in Salamanca and of how their friendship had made it so. They recounted the silly things that happened, their slight drunkenness making these recollections seem more funny or significant than they had actually been at the time. They edged nearer to one another.

Montse drew close to Xavi. At that moment, all that was present to her was his handsome face, his dark eyes, and his moist lips. The longing she had felt from the first moment she had met him was growing towards irresistibility.

It all happened in an instant. The barriers collapsed, and she leaned in, drew him to her, and kissed him—kissed him passionately. He returned her passion, attaching tightly to her soft pink lips. She interrupted the kiss to whisper in his ear, "Xavi, I love you, and I have since I first met you in the *Plaza Mayor* in Salamanca." Time stood still.

After first pulling closer to Montse, Xavi reacted as if he had been shocked; he pulled away, his mood changed.

"I can't, Montse. I can't." He suddenly got up, rushed away from the table, and hurriedly left the bar.

Montse was stunned and confused. She felt hollowed out, devastated. She had held this secret passion to herself for almost a year. Nearly every day she was with Xavi, and each of these days she had kept a lid on her feelings, even as they continued to grow. She was now in her beautiful bloom, and many boys pursued her, handsome young Spaniards, many with perfect provenances.

Mostly she ignored their advances, but on occasion she would give in and agree to a coffee, a study session, or rarely, to share a meal. The pattern of these encounters became predictable: as these young men, entranced by her, became intent to push forward, she would invariably lose any of the scant enthusiasm she may have had.

It was no use. These boys had no way of knowing that they had no chance to access her heart. They were being held to an invisible measure that Xavi had set. She had broken the harnesses that had kept this passion in check, and now it was out, and this secret could not be recaptured. Montse was hurt and embarrassed. She felt a sense of panic.

A few feet away a table was occupied by a group of Americans—a party of hangers-on; they seemed to be in the wake of the writer Hemingway, who also had run with the bulls. *Americans' drunkenness was different,* she thought with a tinge of condescension, *so quickly veering to becoming overly loud, rude, and abusive.*

For several hours one of the Americans had been leering at her, and as his drunkenness increased his subtlety waned; when Xavi left the bar, Montse suddenly found herself alone with the man. The drunken American, sensing this was his moment, moved in. He hovered menacingly over her. She attempted to tell him to go away, but the alcohol and the language barriers impeded her pleas. He became increasingly grabby and aggressive. She was still reeling from the disastrous kiss, and now this …

Just then, Jaime returned from his *siesta* to the bar. He immediately sensed Montse was in an uncomfortable, or maybe even dangerous situation; he rushed in. He forcefully grabbed the American by the collar and pushed him back. He made it clear, the way strong men do, to move away and clear out. The American made a move toward Jaime, but Jaime aggressively leaned into this counter threat. No translations were needed.

The American recognizing his disadvantage barked to a friend, "Let's get out of this dump. Let's go find Hemingway."

Montse, still stunned, was gratified by Jaime's unflinching show of strength. He was not all bluster, play *machismo* and bravado the way she viewed many Spaniards were. He had been there for her when she needed it. But she could not dwell on this now. With the threatening situation defused she went back into her emotional freefall.

"Jaime, I want to go," she exclaimed.

"Yes, I will take you back to the *Gran Perla*," responding to how he understood her request.

"No, Jaime, I'm so upset I need to leave the city. I need to get to Barcelona. Take me to the station so I can get the next train home.

You can organize my things and have them sent to me. Please Jaime, understand how upset I am," she pleaded.

Jaimé thinking that the American had been even more unpleasant in the moments before he had arrived, immediately acquiesced, "Of course, Montse, anything, of course."

Book 2
Chapter 8
Barcelona, Spain
July 20, 1924

Montse's mother had noticed that her daughter had not been herself since returning from Pamplona. She did not bound in and out of the house; she did not fill the house with joyful air. She mostly stayed in her room, taking her meals in private; her normal exuberance had been dampened and the Costa household was less bright because of it.

Luisa Costa found it of no use probing Montse as she was unwilling to speak of what might be wrong or what had transpired on her trip. So, when Luisa Costa received in the daily mail a letter from San Sebastian, she imagined it was somehow connected to her daughter's malaise, and she hoped that it would provide some medication for whatever wound her young heart may have suffered.

"Dear, you have a letter here from your friend in San Sebastian," she called out.

Montse hastily came into her mother's study, took the letter, and simply said, "Thank you, Mother." Then she scurried upstairs to the safety and privacy of her room.

She recognized Xavi's handwriting; she sat down on her bed she took a deep breath and opened the letter.

July 12, 1924

Dear Montse,

I hope this letter will find you well in Barcelona.

Jaime told me what happened to you in the Café Iruna. I am so sorry about this, but I am grateful he was there to step in and protect you. He mentioned that this skirmish deeply upset you and that is why you needed to leave for home without saying goodbye. Perhaps what he said is true, but I cannot help but think that your leaving may have had more to do with what happened between us just before I left the Café.

I do not want to hide or bury what happened between us there that day. I feel no shame, embarrassment, or regret about that moment, and I hope you do not, will not, either. Montse, the truth is that I have very deep feelings for you, and they were also born from the first moment we met. My first reaction to your kiss showed the depth of these feelings.

Yet for me romantic love is a complicated matter...

You are my truest friend in this world, so I share this with you, something that no one else, including my parents, knows. For a number of years I have felt a call to God. The voice of this calling, and the path to which it calls me is not something I can or want to ignore, or resist. After I complete my degree at Salamanca I intend to enroll in a seminary and become a priest. This is the path I am called to follow, the love I need to pursue. God's voice is calling me to take this path. The strength of its call grows stronger in me every day.

You are a remarkable and beautiful woman...the most striking and magnetic woman I have ever known. I wish I could let my feelings run to you the way they desire to, but I cannot. I cannot allow myself to fully fall for you because, given what I have told you, this would be a lie before God, and in the end, it would only bring down anguish on both of us. I hope you will understand this.

Regarding Jaime, we stayed together for two more days before we went our separate ways. During that time what happened between you and me never came up. I assume he is not aware of what transpired between us, and I will never tell him.

Besides God, no one is as important to me as are you. I pray that when we arrive back to university in September you, Jaime, and I can return together to the serene, sunny days that radiate in glorious Salamanca.

Montse, please remember this: I did not reject you, rather I choose God.

With Great Fondness,

Xavi

The letter brought on a new torrent of hurt, anger, and deep, deep disappointment. She laid the letter down on the bed, curled up on her side and began to sob and convulse with tears.

Book 2
Chapter 9
San Sebastian, Spain
August 4, 1924

"Xavi, there's a letter here from Montse," Maria Bidertea called out with a playful tone to her son.

"I so liked her when she was here. I hope we will see here often … she seems to be the perfect companion for you," she added with an air of happy knowingness.

"Thank you, Mother. I am going to walk down to the beach." Xavi took the letter and then made the five-minute walk to one of the benches in front of *La Concha* beach.

He sat himself down on a bench, and opened the letter; it was monogrammed, and written on heavy, fine stationery.

Montserrat Costa

July 24, 1924

Dear Xavi,

I received your letter several days ago, but between traveling to Mallorca and stabilizing my emotions I have been delayed in responding to you.

After reading what you wrote I cried all afternoon and evening; I did not even take a break to have dinner with my family. When I got up the next morning, I decided to hate you, thinking hate would be the shortest and easiest path to forgetting about you and forgetting the feelings I have for you.

I tried to hate you. I tried to summon vitriol for you, but it was no use. I do not hate you. I love you, still.

Not being able to hate you, I thought hating God would be the next best remedy. This was of no use either. My connection to Him is too superficial for that. Xavi, my relationship with God and Catholicism has been largely ceremonial, or maybe decorative is a better word. The ceremonies of my Catholicism have been beautiful, opulent affairs, like the unveiling of a sumptuous new painting in a gallery of a fine home. But these rituals have had no lasting impact on me. Like that painting, which seemed so special on the day of its unveiling, but whose impact fades away almost completely to the point where one can walk by it for days without even noticing its existence.

Xavi, in all of this, I did realize something else: I admire your relationship with God and His goodness. I felt a presence, maybe His presence, so strongly when we were in Avila. It was a strange sensation, the absences of desires, or frustrations ... I felt so content there for a few moments. It felt like impenetrable happiness. I imagine it is what you feel often. I envy you for this.

I am not able to betray my feelings for you, but I am also not willing to lose you from my life either. I plan to return to Salamanca with these feelings intact, and under control. Let us build on our friendship, and the joy your company gives to me.

Love,

Montse

PS... I will spend much of the next month sailing here in Mallorca and I will be reminded of the blissful days with you and Jaime journeying to the little villages near your home. I look forward to seeing you very soon.

Xavi placed the letter in his lap. There in front of him on the beach he watched the children playing near the blue and white bathing tents and the sea beyond. Looking out towards the horizon was a sailboat, and he could not help but think of Montse —perhaps she too was sailing far away on a different sea. She had written a candid, powerful letter; there was no artificial or sentimental backtracking. For a few moments all he could think of was the beautiful and spirited young woman, Montserrat Costa, Montse. Somehow, he knew their lives would remain connected.

Book 2
Chapter 10
Seville, Spain
April 1, 1925

The train between Salamanca and Seville passed through seemingly endless vistas of olive and almond groves sprouting up from the rusty, red soil. Over the noisy background of the clitter clatter of the train passing on the tracks, Montse, Xavi, and Jaime talked freely and laughed often. They were on the homestretch of their second year at the university in Salamanca, and the moment was filled with excited anticipation; they were heading to Seville to spend the long Easter weekend with Montse's aunt.

Montse had stayed true to the letter she had written to Xavi. Her romantic love for Xavi was unabated but, as promised, she kept it contained deep inside of her heart, and, as a result, their friendship had grown even deeper. The aftermath of their brief romantic interlude had served to make them focus more on each other's character and inner being. Having set aside the romantic attraction, they each realized that the glue which made the deep friendship was strong, and seemingly unbreakable.

"Montse, you have told us precious little about your aunt or the weekend itinerary. We are almost there; don't you think it's time that you fill in the details?" Jaime asked.

"Okay, okay. First of all I adore my Aunt Marta. She has always been my favorite aunt. She married a wealthy Andalusian—a marquise, I think."

"You think?" Jaime asked quizzically.

"Yes, he is a marquise," she clarified uncomfortably.

"First a bishop now a marquise, you have quite a backstory don't you," Jamie said, pursuing the opening.

"Oh please, that has nothing to do with me. I'm a university student at Salamanca just like anyone else," she said simultaneously pushing back and closing that discussion down.

"In any case my aunt and uncle have a home, a *palacio*, in Seville and a large *hacienda* in the country. They plan to take us to the *Semana Santa* processions in Seville on Good Friday, and then out to their *hacienda* for mass and Easter lunch, before we get the late train back to Salamanca on Sunday evening."

"Thank you for opening some amazing doors to us." Xavi added.

"I wanted to come too you know! Even though the Andalusians seem from another country, or even another world, as compared to us Catalans, I have always wanted to see the spectacle of the *Semana Santa* processions. When my aunt invited me, I jumped at the chance ... and of course it makes it so much better that she was happy to extend her invitation to you two as well. It should be a memorable weekend."

As Montse's voice trailed off as they heard the conductor call out, "Next stop is *Sevilla Estacion Santa Justa.*"

Book 2
Chapter 11
Seville, Spain
April 3, 1925

Seville was a wonder. It was a glorious, mysterious city bathed in soft colors and glowing light.

The three friends spent all day exploring the city's barrios and backstreets, and they quickly concluded it was not like any place they knew.

After Columbus discovered the New World, Seville was the port of entry for ships returning from their journeys. Gold and plunder gushed into Seville making it the world's richest, most important city in the 16th century. Everywhere, around almost every street corner, there seemed to be another charming, tree-shaded plaza. Churches and *palacios* abounded. But what was most striking to them was the sensuality and mysteriousness of the city: the beautiful women shrouded in their *mantillas*, the smell of orange blossoms, the honey-colored buildings shading the narrow streets. It was intoxicating.

At just before midnight, in the minutes that separated Holy Thursday from Good Friday, Montse, her aunt and uncle, Xavi, and Jaime took their seats near the cathedral. They, along with tens of thousands of others from Seville, of all classes, were there to watch the most holy of the *Semana Santa* processions. Throngs of people packed the procession route that wound its way to the end point at the cathedral. The crowd was silent and somber as they waited for the first and oldest *Hermandad* to arrive.

Semana Santa was an ancient and sacred ritual in Seville. For a year leading up to Holy Week, nearly every one of the dozens and dozens of the city's churches had a brotherhood which organized the procession of *pasos* depicting the passion of Jesus Christ and the suffering of his mother Mary. The gilded, ornate floats were carried by four *costaleros* who bore the weight of the massive structures on their shoulders. The floats were led by clergy and acolytes, sometimes accompanied by a band, and always surrounded by *Nazarenos*.

The *Nazarenos* were spectacularly unusual. They were penitents in procession, dressed in uniform robes and wearing matching conical hats—*capirotes*—which covered their faces and had only small slits for their eyes. Historically, the *capirote* had been worn by criminals to mark them with shame; they had morphed to become a mask to create anonymity for the sinners seeking silent, anonymous forgiveness.

The first procession, *El Silencio* Brotherhood, which dated back to 1340, finally arrived. The *costaleros* shouldered their float which depicted Jesus carrying his cross, followed by another float of the suffering Mary. Surrounding both floats were *Nazarenos* robed in black robes and *capirotes*. The silence was sacred. It was humbling.

After the procession of the *El Silencio* came that of *Jesus del Gran Poder*. The quiet of the night was broken by the band playing their trumpets and pounding their drums. The rhythms of the music were hypnotic. The *Nazerenos* of this Brotherhood wore glistening black robes and *capirotes*.

The next procession to come was the most famous. *La Hermandad de la Macarena*. This brotherhood was known for the immense strength of the *costaleros* who endured the fourteen-hour long procession from its home church to the cathedral and back. More importantly, the men carried a sacred statue of Mary, *La Macarena*. *La Macarena* sat on a float of white flowers and dozens of white candles, and She was surrounded by hundreds of the brotherhood's *Nazarenos*. Mary was painfully sorrowful. Her tears visibly pouring down her pallid face. The crowds came to see Her, to revere Her, and to seek Her intercession.

Along the way, and just before *La Macarena* reached the cathedral, a famous *flamenco* singer, Manuel Torre, began an extended *Saeta*. The *Saeta*—coming from the Latin word *Sagitta*, meaning arrow—was a highly emotional, spontaneous song sung in *flamenco* style. The *Saeta* channeled the Virgin's pain and suffering; it truly seemed to be an arrow that pierced all who heard it. Many in the crowd began to weep.

The overall effect of seeing the processions for the first time was overwhelming. Xavi and Jaime mostly saw it as it was intended: a highly pious, if somewhat flamboyant Catholic display—something uniquely Andalusian.

For Montse however, it seemed bizarre and repulsive. It struck her as incongruously out of touch with the modern world.

As the sun began to rise the group made their way back to the *palacio,* each separated in their own thoughts and impressions of what they had experienced.

—◦—

Book 2
Chapter 12
Casas Viejas, Spain
April 5, 1925

It was about nine thirty on Easter morning when Montse, her aunt and ancle, Xavi, and Jaime split up between two cars. It took about twenty minutes to travel from the gracious, whitewashed *hacienda* to the humble village with its small parish church. On the way to the Church of *Nuestra Señora del Socorro*, Our Lady of Help, as the others conversed, Montse could not avoid noticing the abject poverty that ringed the outskirts of the village.

As the group walked into the church, the contrast between the life of abundance of her aunt and uncle and the peasants' nothingness troubled her. This was not the urban, working poor she had occasionally rubbed against in Barcelona, or the simple life of the humble villagers she knew in Mallorca. This was a grinding, inhumane kind of poverty which she had never seen before. The peasants here appeared gaunt and hungry; their eyes were lifeless and glassy with sadness and fatigue. Some appeared closer to death than to life.

Inside the small church, the vivid separation between rich landowners and the poor who worked their estates was physically manifested in the arrangement of the church. The privileged occupied the majority of the pews leaving the few peasants who did attend, mostly without seats, standing, or pushed outside.

These images stayed with Montse all through mass. They blocked out the words the priest pronounced: "He has risen … died for our sins … a message and meaning for eternity, for us all."

After mass, as they headed to the cars Montse said to her uncle, "I would like to take a tour of the village. Can your driver stay behind and take me back to the house for our Easter lunch?"

Her aunt Marta intercepted the question. "Of course, but really dear there is nothing to see in this village. It's rather a dreary place."

"Perhaps, Aunt Marta, but I am here, and I want to see it. I will be back before lunch," she replied clearly and said in such a way that she would not be dissuaded by her aunt's comment.

She saw it all. The poverty, the total lack of possessions, or even, in some cases, the lack of even the most basic house. The worst of all of it was the children. Their faces, sunken by hunger, lifeless, already fatigued from the poor luck of their draw in life. She felt sick. She was disgusted.

She returned just before the lunch that was served at two p.m. After the forty days of sacrificing during the Lenten season, the sumptuous lunch and variety of sweets were warmly welcomed. Throughout lunch Montse's aunt and uncle learned about Xavi and Jaime; and reversing the flow of conversation, they expressed their deep gratitude for being included, for being able to see the *Semana Santa* processions.

All the while Montse stayed uncharacteristically silent. Finally as the back and forth with Xavi and Jaime slowed down, her aunt took note. "My dear, you have hardly said a word. Are you well?"

Montse responded in a sad and serious tone, "Well no, my dear, dear, Aunt Marta, I am not well. I feel sick by what I have seen the last several days. The excesses of the *Semana Santa* contrasted with the horrific poverty in Casas Viejas. Floats decorated in gold, and here, a lunch of abundance, while just a few minutes away I saw with my own eyes that many of these poor people will not have a meal of any type on Easter."

She paused, and others around the table were in stunned silence, their faces and movements in their chairs displaying their discomfort of where the discussion was headed.

"I cannot help but conclude that Spain is wrapped in a strange and strangling false piety. It is as if you Spaniards are perpetually wearing some sort of mask, a *capirote* of sorts, in order to avoid seeing what is right in front you. Perhaps you should spend less money on your extravagant processions and *fiestas* and put your hand out to your brothers and sisters in the next village. Just a few minutes away from here people are literally starving!"

Montse landed a direct hit on everyone at the table. She immediately could see from their silent, ashen faces the wound she had inflicted on her favorite aunt and the young man she dearly loved.

Her aunt Marta, a gracious and socially skilled woman, veered the conversation away from those troubled waters, asked if anyone wanted an after-lunch liquor, and about the time of their train back to Salamanca.

Montse fell silent. She was deeply conflicted by the strength of her convictions and the awareness that she had hurt people she dearly loved. On the train back to Salamanca not a word was spoken.

—•—

Book 2
Chapter 13
Salamanca, Spain
April 12, 1925

The incident at Easter lunch lingered with Montse. Normally she traveled through her days completely certain of what was right and wrong. She was unused to holding conflicting ideas in her mind; and more than anything, she was distressed by the emerging feeling that she had been wrong in her etiquette, though not in the content of what she had been said. She had come around to the uncomfortable idea that she must atone for what had been said at lunch; it was clear to her, apologies were required.

> *Montserrat Costa*
> *April 12, 1925*
> *Dearest Aunt Marta,*
> *I am writing you this letter in deep apology for how I behaved at Easter lunch. I know that my comments were deeply hurtful to you and Uncle Carlos.*
> *The events and scenes I experienced on Good Friday in Seville and in Casas Viejas on Easter deeply disturbed me. The contrast between the opulence, and now I choose my words carefully, in some moments, decadence, in Seville, and the abject poverty, and hollowed out emptiness I witnessed in Casas Viejas, is still something I am struggling to understand. I am struggling less about the origin, nature, political and social causes of these contradictions, than what I, Montserrat Costa, young woman of great privilege and means, should do about it.*
> *My dearest Aunt Marta, please do not read these words as in way a justification for my hurtful outburst on Easter. There is no excuse for how I behaved, and these two things should operate on different emotional planes. I am deeply disappointed in myself,*

as I know that I hurt you and Uncle Carlos. For this I am truly, terribly sorry. This hurt is particularly painful for me to endure knowing how much I adore and love you and given how generous you were to me and my two dear friends from Salamanca. Please forgive me.

With My Deepest Affection,
Montse

She sealed and stamped the letter and then set out to look for Xavi. On a warm Saturday midday her first guess was that she would be able to find him studying outside the *Café Novelty*. Writing the letter to her aunt had bolstered her sense of mission; when she found him sitting outside the *café*, she was serious and forceful, "I need to talk to you."

She replayed the outline of the apology that she had used with her Aunt and waited for Xavi's response.

"Of course, I accept your apology, though I do not think you owe me one. I understood what you were feeling, and I could see over lunch how deeply upset you were. I pray that God may guide you to find a way to use your time, talents, and resources to help the forgotten and abused people of our country. Let some good come from this."

His simple and supportive summing up gave Montse an immense sense of relief. He came to her and gave her a deep, strong hug. She had not felt his touch since that day in Pamplona; it was restorative. His wisdom and kindness further endeared him to her.

"Xavi, where is Jaime? I need to make my amends with him as well," she concluded.

"I believe he is at our apartment. Thank you Montse, good luck with Jaime. God's speed with your vocation."

Montse knocked on the door and Jaime replied, "Come in, it's open."

"Hello, Jaime, I need to speak with you about what happened at Easter lunch."

Before she could get much farther, he sternly cut her off. "Yes, you do. You were terribly rude to your aunt and uncle, and secondarily to Xavi and me."

After being showered with grace by Xavi, she was shaken by Jaime's harsh tone. She regrouped, and again laid out her apology. Slowly Jaime's distress began to subside and his chides became milder and more tolerable.

Finally her friend pivoted to a way forward. "You know, Montse, I've been thinking that your view of Spanish rural life has been unfairly colored by what you saw in Andalucía. I would like you to see another side of it. Why don't you and Xavi come to La Rioja for the wine harvest just before we return to school next September? I have already spoken to Xavi; he is excited for it. What do you say?"

She was relieved. "Okay, Jaime … on one condition."

"What's that?"

"That Xavi and I do not get any special treatment. That we sleep where the other harvesters sleep and eat what they eat. I need to see what it's really like."

"Okay, okay, but you must also promise to come for a few days before the actual harvest and keep my father and me company. I want you to see La Rioja," Jaime countered.

"I accept."

Montse was relieved the apologies were behind her. She thought of how she could best help the forgotten people of Spain and of the wine harvest with her two special friends.

Book 2
Chapter 14
Haro, Spain
September 18, 1925

Prior to the wine harvest, Montse and Xavi spent five days in the de la Calzada house. During those cloudless, warm, and sunny days, while Jaime and his father prepared for the harvest, Xavi showed Montse the nearby towns and little villages, some in La Rioja, others in neighboring Navarre, and many of them on the Camino Frances, the principal route of the Camino Santiago. At night they would all gather for dinner and discuss the travels of the day and the impending harvest.

On one of those days Xavi took Montse to the tiny village of Puente La Reina. There, they walked over its ancient bridge, built for pilgrims almost a thousand years earlier. This bridge was an essential point on the Camino. Several routes met there, and it was the only way across the River Arga. The bridge was a special place for Xavi, and he desired to share it with her. Together they walked to the middle of it, where they stopped.

"Montse, stop here."

"Okay. ..."

"Close your eyes; imagine the millions of pilgrims that have passed over this exact spot on their route to Santiago de Compostela."

"I can see them...."

"What do you see?"

"They are with their packs, staffs with water gourds, hats turned up with a scallop shell—"

"Yes, that's it. That's the traditional image of a pilgrim."

"There are a countless number of them."

"Do you recognize any of them?"

"No. They aren't faceless, but they seem like the everyman."

"Most are, but some are famous too. Imagine St. Francis Assisi, Lorenzo de Medici, US President John Adams, who passed this way after he shipwrecked in Finisterre on his way to Paris. Each time I have walked the Camino I have stopped here to remind myself of the flow of history."

Her eyes remained closed when she added, "A steady stream of them throughout the ages."

"We are all pilgrims."

"Xavi, it is an amazing thought to be part of this stream of humanity isn't it?"

"It is. It is part of this pilgrimage to Santiago. The continuity of our faith, of our desire for faith."

"But I'm not exactly sure what you mean by being a pilgrim?"

"The essence of being of a pilgrim is—"

She interrupted. "Never mind about that, it is enough to be here in this special place with you."

———

Consistent with the agreement she had made with Jaime, once the harvest started, she and Xavi moved into the shed with the other harvesters. At dawn of the second day of the harvest Montse heard the rustling of some of her fellow fifty harvesters. On her small cot, covered by a simple brown wool blanket, she rolled from her side to her back and slowly opened her eyes. Her first thought was how tired and sore she was from previous day's work in the vineyard. In the spirit of her request, they were put on the lowest rung of the harvesting team: they were cutters, bent over all day clipping the grapes by hand from the vines.

As the workers sat for breakfast, Don Pedro de la Calzada laid out the outline for the day: complete the picking by midday; crush the grapes in the afternoon; and, most importantly, drink, eat, sing, dance—and get paid in the evening.

The day went as Don Pedro had said it would, and by late afternoon Montse found herself being called into one of the containers to crush the newly harvested bright purple grapes with her feet. She relished the dance on the grapes. Her easy way, lack of airs, and natural beauty immediately made her a favorite of the other harvesters. She danced on the grapes, her hair tossing about in the light breeze, and her white dress becoming purple from the juice. It was magic. They cheered her on. Xavi, Jaime, and Don Pedro, knowing her story, were amazed by how easily she fit in; each in his own way smitten by her.

Following dinner, and after the pay envelopes were handed out, including ones to Montse and Xavi, who took them just like the others, the music, singing, and dancing commenced. Montse looked around and saw how Don Pedro, the local priest, the village teacher all mingled and mixed together with the workers; it was such a different Spain from the one she had seen in Andalucía.

She was slightly drunk; she danced with everyone and no one in particular, finally spinning her way towards Xavi and Jaime. Putting an arm around each one of them, pulling them into a tight huddle, smiling and giggling, she thanked them for showing her another, different side of Spanish life, "I have been to Xavi's home, and this week here at this wonderful *fiesta* at the de la Calzada home; next summer you will come to Barcelona to let me show you the treasures of Catalonia."

Even if they had wanted to oppose her request, which they did not, there was no denying Montse.

Book 2
Chapter 15
Barcelona, Spain
June 8, 1926

The breakfast room of the Costa Estate opened onto the garden, and late spring light poured in on Xavi and Jaime.

"Montse will want to show us Gaudí. This is the city of Gaudí," Jaime volunteered.

"Yes, I imagine she will," Xavi replied.

"The *Sagrada Familia*, the Park *Güell,* and probably then to the Gothic Quarter."

Xavi nodded his agreement while eating *Pa Amb Oli,* toast with tomato.

The day before, Xavi and Jaime had met in Pamplona, and from there they had taken the train together to this sprawling, Catalan port city. Montse met them late in the evening at the main Barcelona Train Station, she was with the family's driver who took them to the family estate in a *Hispano Suiza.* The boys felt almost like royalty in the elegant sedan.

"Good morning. Are you ready to begin explore Catalan culture?" Montse said, as she bounded into the room.

"Okay, Montse, and where do we start? Maybe in the 15th century when Isabella made Catalonia a part of Spain?" Jaime joked.

"Very funny, Jaime. No, not with Isabella, Jaime, but with Gaudí! Of course with Gaudí—he is the indispensable Catalan."

Continuing on she added, "He built and renovated many grand homes in Barcelona, and my parents got to know him well. One of his former assistants will lead us around today—Josep Sala. We call him Pep."

A few minutes later Pep, who looked to be in his early 30's, arrived in his modest car and he and Montse warmly greeted each other in Catalan. After introductions to Xavi and Jaime, Pep told them that they would start their tour by going to a sacred place.

"First, we go to the place that is the origin of Montse's name—a mountain about an hour away from Barcelona we Catalans call Montserrat."

"Sometimes I wondered if she doesn't come from another planet," Jaime said, teasing.

"Very funny, Jaime. I see you are in a good mood this morning," she replied with a laugh.

"It's otherworldly, that's for sure. You'll see," Pep added. "But it's really where we start our tour of Gaudí."

On the way to Montserrat, Pep drove and began to fill in the details. "Gaudí was born in the early 1850s, to very modest means. From early on he was fascinated by design. He enrolled in school with the intention to become an architect, but he was a poor student. Amazing as it seems now, his teachers thought him extremely unintelligent because he was seemingly unable to follow the outlines and plans typically used by architects."

"Okay, but why go to a mountain to learn about an architect?" Jaime asked.

"We go to Montserrat because it is an ancient and sacred place for us Catalans and the source of Gaudí's inspiration."

"How so?" Xavi asked.

"It is located amongst low mountains that rise up not far from Barcelona. They look like they are composed like rock fingers—serrated mountains."

"Montserrat! I get it," Jaime said.

"Yes, exactly. In this special place, the Benedictine Monks have had a monastery since about the year one thousand."

"Nature and Catholicism …," Xavi observed.

"Yes, they are at the core of understanding him," Pep replied. "And afterward we will go to the project that has preoccupied him for years, the *Sagrada Familia*. Here you will see in practice how he blends nature and spirituality. It is a uniquely Gaudí vision of the world."

As they made their way towards the monastery, the serrated mountains grew up in front of them. Pep welcomed them to the sacred spot. "Here we are. Once we park the car, we'll take the funicular up to the monastery. When we get there please go on your own. Explore the church; touch its Black Madonna; smell the air, the way the pine scent mixes with the salt air of the Mediterranean; look at the shapes of the mountains and the trees; try to sense and feel what he must have felt as a young man. Discover his inspirations. Go and find Gaudí."

After several hours, the group reconvened and headed back to Barcelona. Over lunch the ambiguity of the first stop bubbled up in Jaime, and he asked Pep a pointed question. "Okay, Montserrat —it is a very beautiful and Catholic place, but what does it have to with buildings and architecture?"

"Gaudí is deeply Catholic. A mystic—"

"Like Saint Teresa," Jaime responded.

"In a way. Montserrat shaped and inspired Gaudí. The combination of the beauty of nature and the monastery moved him. He came to believe that architects could not design anything new; he believes God had already created all the important shapes in nature—and they are not stylized."

"Not stylized?" Xavi asked.

"Yes, like the serrated rocks and tall pines at Montserrat, they are irregular, not uniform in shape."

"Interesting…," Xavi commented.

"Now to the *Sagrada Familia* you will begin to see how this all ties together."

In the car, on the way to the *Sagrada Familia*, Pep explained that the architect had designed many things: homes for wealthy Catalans; municipal buildings; Episcopal palaces; beautiful parks, like the Park *Güell*, but that for the last ten years he has dedicated himself solely to building this church.

When in the late afternoon they pulled up in front of the church, the boys' senses of order, symmetry, and traditional church design were pummeled. Their heads were spinning. The *Sagrada Familia* was incongruous. Four giant towers, looking like drip sandcastles, had been bolted onto the very traditional chapel. It appeared more like pile of rubble than the beginnings of a grand church.

"What is it?" Jamie blurted.

"The church is intended to honor the Holy Family, our families, and in particular to welcome poor, simple people. This church is for the forgotten people of Barcelona."

"It doesn't make any sense," Jaime objected.

"Gaudí took over the project after the base of the very traditional church was completed, and he intends to build something that embodies nature and God's creation. He says only God creates, and that he merely copies."

Pep shepherded the group towards the building. "Let's go inside to the workshop and see if we can find him."

The guide, who had worked the church's workshop, knew the site well. Looking around he saw several workers, but there was no sign of Gaudí. He then led Montse, Xavi, and Jaime to his workplace. There they saw many miniatures of the three porticos that were planned, "he envisions his designs in three dimensions, so he rarely uses drawings, building large scale models instead."

Pep described the models and the effect Gaudí was working to create.

"I see ... I see," Xavi said.

"Now can you understand why we started at Montserrat?"

"I can," Xavi replied.

"The towers will resemble the serrated mountains of Montserrat; the pillars of the nave will be shaped like the trees."

"It's fascinating," Xavi added.

"When it's done—a long time from now—the light will pour in from the windows above. ..."

Xavi, thinking of the special place between Roncesvalles and Burguete, commented, "Like the feeling of being in a canopied forest."

"That's it," Pep replied.

"I cannot say I like it much, but it is amazing," Jaime said. "More practically though, at the rate they are working, it will never get finished."

"True, the project is chronically low on funds, and Gaudí has devoted himself completely to it. He often goes door to door asking for money; he probably is out on the streets searching for funds as we speak. His dedication has become an obsession. He goes days without changing his clothes, and he sleeps here in the workshop."

"Why?" Jaime asked.

"He is a man of very, very deep faith, and he knows the church will not be done is his lifetime. He is fond of saying *'God is not in a hurry'*," Pep added.

Montse sensed the energy of the tour began to wane, and as she had seen all of these sights many times before, she volunteered, "Okay, okay, this was a great tour, but now it's time to go get a drink!"

"Pep, thank you for a surprising day. You have been a wonderful guide," Xavi said.

"Yes, you were great, thank you," Jaime added.

Pep left after he dropped them at a café near *Las Ramblas*. Leaving the car Montse added, "I told Tomás we would meet around six at *El Quartre Gats*."

"Who is Tomás?" Jaime asked.

"A good friend, and when I am home, I see him often."

Before Tomás arrived the first glasses of wine were delivered. Jaime toasted Montse and her generous hospitality and then led a second toast to Catalonia. "Here is to Montse and her glorious Catalonia; may it always be a proud part of Spain."

Montse sipped and laughed a bit, "That is a better toast for me, but I would not make it when Tomás arrives; he takes his Catalaness very seriously. He might hear those as fighting words—literally, I mean."

A few minutes later Tomás arrived. He had an electricity about him; Jaime and Xavi watched closely as he and Montse greeted one another very warmly, embracing as something more than friends. Xavi could see a magnetic chemistry between them, and it made him uncomfortable. For the first time he was confronted with the consequences of his choice.

Book 2
Chapter 16
Barcelona, Spain
June 10, 1926

It was late in the afternoon when Montse, Xavi, and Jaime arrived back at the Costa home. Montse was exuberant. The last three days with her friends—Xavi especially—had enabled her to see Barcelona over again as if it were all new. For a few moments, which made her heart sore, she allowed herself to hold hope about a life with Xavi. The last time she had felt this much joy, and the freedom which rose from it, were the moments in the bar in Pamplona just before their kiss.

Bounding into the drawing room with her friends she found her mother and father and several of their close friends. Her joyfulness crashed hard into the somber mood that hung in the air. "What's wrong—why does everyone seem so glum?"

"Gaudí is dead," her mother responded.

"What? How? We were just in his workshop two days ago." she was stunned and shocked.

"This is what we know: Gaudí, lost in his thoughts, as he was wont to be, was hit by a tram three days ago. Because he was dressed so poorly, he was thought to be a beggar. He was taken to the indigents' hospital. He was found two days later and died shortly thereafter.

"The funeral is in two days. We will all be going. Montse, if your friends will be coming with you, they will need proper clothing," her mother said matter-of-factly.

Though her mother had said little, Montse was outraged by her pretension and condescension. But the more powerful feeling that came over her, for the first time, was how unexpected turns could crash into, and break apart, life's moments of joy.

Book 2
Chapter 17
Barcelona, Spain
June 12, 1926

At noon, the horse-drawn cortege carrying Gaudí's body started out from *Las Ramblas*. Behind the funeral carriage were a few policemen, high church officials, municipal authorities, and members of the great families of Barcelona including the Costas. Three miles away, at the *Sagrada Familia*, Xavi and Jaime made themselves a part of the sea of Catalans that that had rapidly emerged to honor the great man.

It seemed to both of them that all of Barcelona must be out to say their final goodbye to Gaudí. The crowds on each side of the streets of the three-mile-long funeral procession looked to be at least ten-deep.

Gaudí's funeral unified Barcelona: rich and poor, left and right. Xavi, understanding the language, and Jamie, sensing the emotional milieu, both quickly grasped what had drawn so many people: deep faith, Catholicism, the desire to say a final thank you to the man who had built so many of the city's most famous buildings and parks, and perhaps the largest contingent of the crowd, who saw the funeral as a symbol of Catalan exceptionalism, and as a way to silently scream out for Catalan identity and autonomy.

The carriage finally arrived at the church. There, laid to rest in the crypt, Gaudí become a permanent occupant of the building about which he had become obsessed, and, probably, about which he was thinking the moment when the tram struck him down.

After the funeral mass, Xavi and Jaime returned to the Costa home. It was the middle of the afternoon. There the Costas and a small group of their family and friends gathered. The group, including Tomás, continued their mourning.

Tomás sensing Jaime to be a true "Spaniard," verbally poked

104

and prodded him to highlight the superiority of Catalan culture. "You see today how united we are? How we celebrate our culture, our greatness?" Tomás said boastfully.

Jaime remained respectfully silent; he pulled Xavi aside to the corner of the large drawing room. "Even though I cannot understand their words, I feel their emotions. This feeling of distinctiveness, of superiority, of Catalaness, runs very deep in these people. Reading about it is one thing but being in it creates an entirely different perception. They are different, and this yearning they obviously have runs very deep and boils quite hot."

"You finally see it firsthand."

"Yes, and it is on a collision course with the rest of the country and our sense of Spanish destiny."

Xavi did not comment. There was nothing to add. Speaking their language, and also being a Basque, he understood this sense of distinctness, this longing to be separate. But owing to his own deep faith, he thought more of Gaudí and of the mysteries of God's plan, than of the politics of the day—which he thought would always rise and recede like the tides of the sea.

Book 2
Chapter 18
Madrid, Spain
March 12, 1927

The train from Salamanca arrived at the Atocha train station in Madrid. Montse, Xavi, and Jaime left the station and made the short walk to the Prado Museum.

The friends were three of the fifteen students from Dr. Gonzalez's senior Art History course. They were in Madrid to pursue the assignment they had been given: visit the country's main museum; find a painting that spoke to them; then write a paper about why it did.

Inside the museum Jaime laid out course of action. "We should split up to explore the museum and each find our own painting."

"Jaime, you are the expert on Madrid, where should we meet afterwards?" Montse asked.

"Well, it's just after noon now, so let us plan to meet at bar *La Delores* at … say, four-thirty. It's just across the street in the writer's quarter, behind the Palace Hotel."

And so they set off to explore the museum. They each slowly toured the vast collection: several dozen paintings by Velázquez, including *Las Meninas,* which dominated a whole room; and nearby the walls of several rooms that were emblazoned by the vivid colors and elongated shapes of El Greco; the life of Goya was on display through his paintings, from his pleasant scenes of rural life, to his luscious paintings of the Duchess of Alba, to the massacre of the 1808 resistors, to the dark, terrifying paintings from his life's end. They also passed by the bizarre, horrifying images by Bosch, which were too frightening over which to linger. They inspected all of these paintings, and yet as wonderful and evocative as they were, none of them spoke to them.

At about a quarter till five Xavi walked into *La Delores,* and a few minutes later in came Jaime. Together they waited for Montse, who finally arrived at five-thirty. They drank *cañas* and nibbled on strong *Manchego* cheese. They each wore the satisfied face of a job completed.

On their second round of *cañas* Jaime finally volunteered his selection. "Okay, I'll go. For me, it's *Charles V on Horseback*, by Titian."

"Of course you would select that one," Montse said in a mildly teasing tone, "But, really, Jaime what about it?"

"It's a large portrait, grand in scale and composition."

"It commands its gallery," Xavi added.

"It does, as it shows Charles V, Holy Roman Emperor, all powerful, striding victoriously after his triumph over the Protestant armies. That is how I like to think about my country: strong and triumphant."

"Jaime, always the old-fashioned Spaniard, aren't you?"

"After four years, Montse, you should know my innate patriotism is never far from the surface," Jaime said, giving as good as he got.

"I guess I'm a slow learner." She laughed as she took a sip of the small glass of beer in front of her. "Okay, I will go next."

She paused for a second, collecting her thoughts and emotions. "My painting is one of the lesser-known great paintings in the Prado. It is also a large painting. It is by the 19th century Spanish artist Antonio Perez Gisbert."

"I'm not sure I know it," Xavi interjected.

"No perhaps not, but you surely know the subject."

"What is it?"

"The execution of General Torrijos and his companions on the beach at Malaga."

"Of course, those tragically famous events," Xavi replied.

"It is a beautiful painting. It is a moving painting. It shows the moment in 1831, when, after their rebellion against Ferdinand VII failed, General Torrijos and his supporters face execution on a beach near Malaga."

"I have seen the painting, but never knew the details," Jaime interjected.

"Gisbert captures the painful, poignant moment of the end. In the foreground a few of the general's men lie dead, already executed. In the center of the painting, to where your eyes are drawn, you see General Torrijos and about a dozen others waiting for their final leave. There are several Franciscan priests who comfort them."

"The general is noble, unafraid of his fate," Jaime interjected.

"Yes, Jaime, exactly. He awaits his end, far from the triumph he imagined, and near his eternal judgement."

"But Montse, you have never shown any inclination to religion."

"It's not that. I chose it because of the painting's power, the nobility of General Torrijos, but more as a reminder that the Spanish people have long sought a freer, more just, democratic, and progressive society."

"It's time for more *cañas*, not politics, Montse," Jaime replied to his friend. *"Tres cañas, por favor,"* he called to the bartender.

As the beers were poured, their foaming heads frothing over the edges of the glasses, Jaime recalled in his mind the violent disagreements in the first year of their friendship, and how it all seemed to change after he had stepped in to help her in the *Café Iruna* in Pamplona. *Perhaps people are not easy to change, but rather events awaken them to see things that would have otherwise remained obscured,* he thought.

"I guess it's my turn," said Xavi.

"Yes, let's hear it, which painting did you choose?" Montse asked.

"I chose *The Descent from the Cross,* by Roger Van der Wyden."

"I could have guessed that one," Montse said while Jaime nodded in agreement.

"This painting so powerfully describes the emotion - the pain of this moment. We see Mary Magdalene, Joseph of Arimathea, Nicodemus, The Virgin Mary, John the Baptist, and several others overwrought and overcome with emotion—each of them, showing a slightly different shade of despair, all with tears streaming down their faces."

"It is great painting no doubt, an emotional painting." Montse said.

"Without the Resurrection there is no..." Xavi paused momentarily, he seemed to be searching deep within himself to find the exact words to connect to his feelings, "there can be no reconciliation, no consolation without this moment of agony and pain. It's the ultimate mystery, the ultimate triumph."

"The pain is so vivid," Montse said softly.

"In several ways. The limp body of Jesus being taken from the cross, hands and feet bleeding from the nail wounds," Xavi added.

"It's almost gruesome," Montse added.

"And the effect it has on everyone else in the painting. His mother collapsed, ashen; John the Baptist attending to the fallen Virgin Mary; the others mourning, the grief on their faces, each expressed with a different emotional tone."

Montse wanted to reach over and touch Xavi, caress his hand, she loved him so, but she didn't.

"The Crucifixion of Jesus is the indispensable moment of our human existence."

That was it. She was silent in her knowledge of Xavi's vocation, and Jaime was silent because there was nothing he could add to how his friend had summed up his faith.

They finished their *cañas* and nibbled their cheeses. The three friends were unified in their silence. Their lives had come together in Salamanca, but as their art selections highlighted, they were distinctly different in outlook, personality, and temperament.

Nominally they were all Spaniards, but their connections to each other were stronger than they were to their country. They were near the starting line of their adult lives, and the inclinations they had brought to Salamanca, had, over four years, sharpened and hardened into distinct, fully developed worldviews. They were bound on separate paths.

Book 2
Chapter 19
Salamanca, Spain
June 4, 1927

Xavi, grinning, in his graduation robes, holding his diploma, sought out his parents and Father Extebarri in the crowd after the graduation ceremony.

Xavi's mother embraced him, and after she released him, so did his father, and finally the priest in turn. It was all hugs, smiles, and tears of joy.

Finally, Xavi's mother broke the silence "We are so, so proud of you!"

"Yes, Xavi it's wonderful what you have done here." His father added.

"Thank you."

"Will you finally tell us what is next?" Xavi's father said, glowing in anxious anticipation.

"Well, that is what I have been meaning to tell you …"

"What, Xavi, what?" his mother chided happily.

"I have decided to stay here in Salamanca."

"Law school perhaps?" his father coyly suggested.

"No, not law school, something else."

"You are going to study to be a professor like Unamuno?" his father added.

"No, not like that either. It is something that has called me for some years now, and the call has grown stronger and stronger."

He paused, and his parents stared at him, eyes wide open, expressing confusion and anticipation, and Xavi, understanding that as the next step in his life journey was only half revealed, he must continue.

"I have decided on a different path … I've… I am going to become a priest. I start in the seminary here in a couple of weeks."

Instantly his parents' faces went from puzzled to stunned. Father Extebarri, sensing the awkward moment, moved himself a few steps away from the family.

Xavi could see his parents needed time to digest the news, so he moved to change the subject, "We need to get over to the *Café Novelty*; we have a table for lunch with Montse and Jaime and their families."

He was relieved for the break.

The *Café Novelty* had been a special place and second home to Montse, Xavi, and Jaime for the last four years. The café, perfectly situated on the graceful *Plaza Mayor* served many functions: café, student lounge, luxurious restaurant, billiards parlor, and even a dance hall. Inside was a microcosm of Spain: to the right, merchants, manufacturers, and right-wing politicians routinely gathered to discuss matters of the day and harangue about the decline of traditional Spanish life. Separated by the invisible barriers that divide people, on the other of side of the café, artists, poets, and professors assembled to discuss books, art, poetry, and to bemoan the state of Spanish politics.

When the Biderteas and Father Extebarri arrived, the others were already seated. Montse was joined by her parents, her brother Jordi, sister Elena, her aunt and uncle from Seville, and by her godfather, Bishop Pla y Deniel; Jaime was there with his father and brother Juan, who was in his officer's dress uniform.

The group mixed politely but uneasily in Spanish. The distinctions in class, language, and outlook that plagued Spain were on display at the graduation luncheon. Even at such a joyous event these differences were not easily masked over. The conversation finally began to flow more freely when the new graduates reminisced about their time in Salamanca and their next steps in life.

Montse spoke of how her four years in Salamanca had put the privilege of her life into perspective and how she wished to use her position and skills as a writer to spotlight the injustices in Spanish society.

"I am going to be a reporter at my father's newspaper in Barcelona, *El Progressiu*. My first assignment will be to write on the plight of the peasants in Casas Viejas."

Her parents nodded in knowing approval, while Don Pedro de

la Calzada seemed puzzled. Maria Bidertea, who saw Montse as almost perfect, only could feel the sadness for what might have been for her son.

Jaime next volunteered about his journey. "I have spent hours with the medallions on the plaza. I can hear them whispering to me, 'come, help restore our glory'."

"I always knew you heard voices, Jaime," Montse teased.

"Montse, this is my future I'm talking about," Jaime snapped back.

"I'm sorry, Jaime, I just thought we needed to lighten things up a bit."

"In any case, I feel the call to help restore the glory of Spain. I will be going to Zaragoza to enroll in Officer Training at the National Military Academy General Franco just opened."

Don Pedro and Juan appeared to rise in their chairs, elevated by pride, while the Costas wore expressions of mild, politely-expressed condescension, and the Biderteas seemed lost somewhere else.

"What about you, Xavi?" Joan Costa asked.

"Today is a time to look back, to make an accounting."

All at the table nodded agreement.

"My journeys on the Camino Frances with Father Extebarri, continuing on to Finisterre, the end of the world ..."

It seemed that these journeys, the idea of pilgrimage, lifted the table; they all began to listen intently.

"The end of world?" Joan Costa asked.

"Yes, the place where pilgrims would continue onto after reaching Santiago. Finisterre—literally, the end of the world, the farthest point people knew of."

"Why there?" Joan Costa probed.

"It's a beautiful, small peninsula, covered in pines, high above the roaring Atlantic Ocean in Galicia. But really, it's the spirit you feel, an overwhelming inner peace. There in the shadow of a large cross it is tradition to burn a piece of clothing, the shedding of your past. Watching the flames flicker as night falls makes you realize you are changed ..."

"Changed by what?" Joan continued on.

"Pilgrimage. Life is a pilgrimage."

The table was silent, rolling over Xavi's words in their minds.

"And also, I need to thank the bishop."

"Me, Xavi?" Bishop Pla y Deniel asked.

"Yes. For the day we spent in Avila, the day with Saint Teresa. She is also an inspiration to me."

"What are you saying, Xavi?" Don Pedro de la Calzada asked.

"I will tell you, Don Pedro, but one other thing."

"What is that?" he responded.

"Professor Unamuno ..."

"Unamuno?"

"Yes, Don Pedro. More than all of his books of philosophy, his words of encouragement have inspired me, filled me with a sense of vocation."

The table was silent. They were waiting for the shoe to fall.

"I am starting in the seminary here."

Montse dropped her head with an air of sadness; Jaime smiled as if to say, "Of course." Xavi's parents, still digesting the news, were expressionless; the bishop and Father Extebarri showed the satisfaction that they were getting a new club member that they knew and liked; and Montse's family looked completely lost.

The momentum of the luncheon faded. The table became a stage for awkward silences. Even at such a celebration the brittle fault lines of Spanish life groaned and creaked.

The three young people, so fundamentally different in so many ways, had come together, putting these differences aside, to see the good in one other. They had grown inseparable as a result. When they added their families and their backgrounds to the mix, these bonds seemed to be weighed down and overwhelmed. The initial joy of the get-together could not bear this weight; it slowly lost its energy and ended enveloped with an air of sadness.

Later that evening Xavi heard a knock on his door. It was his mother.

"Can we take a walk?" she asked.

"Of course, Mother."

The lamps were lit in the *Plaza Mayor*; the soft light created a glow on the medallions as Xavi and his mother ambled past them. There, his mother continued the conversation they had started earlier that day.

K.D. Conway

"Your decision to join the priesthood, well, it caught me by great surprise, and it has been tossing and turning in me since you told your father and me about it earlier today. I was upset all through lunch."

"I could see it."

Maria Bidertea continued, "Once this turmoil began to subside, I was able to ask myself why this so upset me? Xavi, the simple answer is that it did not fit in alignment with my 'plan' for you: a life in San Sebastian; an esteemed career; wife and happy marriage, maybe with Montse; and beautiful children, my grandchildren, to finish off the picture. A life continuing in my orbit.

"As your father pointed out to me—why is he always so rational?—you have always seemed to be guided by some type of special of calling. I am often reminded of it when I see Inaki's mother or father, or when we see Father Extebarri—he told us what you did on the mountain above Roncesvalles. I can see you have always been called to some higher purpose than the comfortable life like your father and I have. I know this, Xavi. You should take this path."

"Oh. Mother, thank you. This means so much to me." He paused for a moment and then continued, "May I share a recurring thought that has driven me?"

"Yes, please ... I want to know."

Xavi continued, "I often think of the story in Matthew's Gospel of the three servants who had been given different amounts of coins by their master, and then what they did with these gifts. I do not know how many coins God has given me, but I know I am compelled to make the most of them—and, in the end, that is what really matters."

"God has given you many coins. You will become an exceptional priest."

Illuminated by the soft light from the lamps, surrounded by the greatest figures of Spain's history, mother and son tightly embraced.

Book Three

The Center Cannot Hold

Book 3
Chapter 1
Salamanca, Spain
April 1, 1928

Salamanca was aglow on Palm Sunday. Warm spring sunshine bathed the city and well-dressed families strolled around the *Plaza Mayor*, carrying the palms they had just received at mass. Xavi, a palm cross in hand, left mass at the cathedral and made his way to the *Café Novelty*.

One of the small joys of living in Salamanca was that being a university city, there were newspapers from all over Spain: local papers, papers from Madrid in Spanish, papers from Barcelona in Catalan, and even one or two papers in Basque. Xavi took a few *pesetas* from his pocket and bought a copy of *El Progressiu*. He placed his coffee and a slice of slightly runny *tortilla patata* down on one of the small, round outside bar tables, and there he perused the paper: the headline immediately jumped out at him...

Disgrace in Andalucía
Montserrat Costa
Casas Viejas, Andalucía

Today, on Palm Sunday, the good and noble families of Seville will attend Catholic services. They will dress in their finest new suits of clothes; the ladies will look beautiful and the men handsome. They will tour the churches of the city to inspect the be-flowered *Semana Santa* floats that will wind their way through the streets to the cathedral during Holy Week; they will make their prayers to the various statues of the Virgin on display; and some of them will even contemplate heaven and eternity. Afterwards they have fine lunches and eat special cakes. Seville will glow. All will be happy.

But less than an hour away in Casas Viejas, there will be none of these serene scenes. In rural Andalucía people live in destitute poverty and deplorable conditions. They live in makeshift houses, and most of them will go hungry tonight. Seeing the emaciated, sad children is the worst of it. With hunger banging away in their stomachs they will not be thinking of processions, or heaven, or of eternity. They will only be thinking of how to survive until tomorrow while living in this unnecessary, grinding poverty.

He read on as Montse mixed statistics and personal stories to create the one-two punch of hard facts and heart-breaking tales. As the story continued on, he could feel her righteous indignation building to its final crescendo.

This unbearable poverty that exists nearby to the pious grandeur of Seville are like two chemicals which should not be placed beside one another; they are an innately unstable mixture. These circumstances are a disgrace. Spain, wake up, before these elements combust in a violent explosion!

Well, she really did it, he thought.

Her well-crafted words had fired a hot, burning arrow into the heart of traditional Spain on the eve of the country's holiest week. Montse wrote it in Catalan, for the Catalans, to shame Spain. As a Basque who spoke Catalan and who lived in Spain, he knew for certain that there was nothing a Spaniard detested more than to be reproached by a Catalan. He knew this article would cause outrage across Spain.

He thought of his beautiful friend who wrote with such fortitude and candor. But beyond thinking of Montse, he also felt, for the first time, the building of the instability in Spain. He was training to be in the business of saving souls, and he wondered how long it would be before this building tension, which his friend had highlighted, would affect his chosen profession.

Book 3
Chapter 2
Barcelona, Spain
November 23, 1929

After Joan Costa returned from his trip to the United States, he had hardly spent a moment at home with his wife and family.

Day and night for a week he spent in meeting after meeting, surveying the trajectory of the business interests that made up his family's empire. The news skewed from uncertain, to worrisome, to outright disastrous. The waves from the economic bomb that had exploded in New York when its stock market crashed were beginning to come ashore in Spain. The picture of what was, and what was to come, came clear to him. He knew he needed to bring his family together to sound the call for caution.

The family dinner proceeded as normal. Luisa spoke of the upcoming opera season; Jordi, who ran a family textile business and saw but a piece of the puzzle, spoke of his hunting trips in the hills of the Catalan Pyrenees; Montse, now a burgeoning journalistic celebrity, discussed what injustice she would tackle next for *El Progressiu*; and Elena, studying at the University of Barcelona, described the convergence of the ideals of feminism and Catalan autonomy.

All the while Joan appeared to listen, he was consumed by worry; he did not really hear any of it. Finally he took over and commanded the dining room. "I am just back from New York, and the news there is dark," he started out ominously.

The faces of his family seemed perplexed as if hearing a foreign language. "When I first arrived on October 15th the mood of the city was jubilant. It was like a party to which everyone had been invited—from taxi drivers to captains of industry. The fine hotels and restaurants were full, and the good wine flowed. The city radiated energy and optimism.

"Then came October 29th and the New York Stock Exchange crashed. I was in New York on this awful day. It was devastating; it was a total panic. Many people believed the markets would rise forever and had borrowed vast sums of money against this bet. They were immediately wiped out. Many people took their own lives. The change in the mood in the city was palpable."

Montse was puzzled. "Yes, this sounds terrible, but the Americans are so prone to excess—what does this all have to do with us?"

Joan thought for a moment and recalled an old verse he had learned in school in England. "Let me try to explain it to you with this poem I learned years ago. First in English and then in Catalan he recited the lines:

For want of a nail the shoe was lost.
For want of a shoe the horse was lost.
For want of a horse the rider was lost.
For want of a rider the message was lost.
For want of a message the battle was lost.
For want of a battle the kingdom was lost."

"Oh, Joan, please do not speak in riddles! Tell us what it is." Luisa Costa insisted.

"We live in Barcelona, the capital of Catalonia, which, for better or worse, is part of Spain. Everything is connected."

"Joan, please stop being so cryptic—what is it you want to tell us?" His wife chided him.

"This crash, which started in New York, will hit Spain hard. We live in a country at the mercy of others; we rely on borrowed and foreign capital. When this tide flows out, as it surely will, we will face a day of reckoning, and we already see the first signs of it, with orders cancelled and projects put off."

"He's right, for some reason we can't see, our textile orders have slowed down," Jordi interjected.

"Oh, Father, aren't you being too pessimistic?" Montse pushed back.

"Perhaps. I hope so, but I fear not."

"But it can't possibly affect us—affect the way we live!" Elena protested with the tone of youthful naïveté.

"It is true we live on a high hill, but it's not our finances about which I am worried."

"What then, Joan, what then?" Luisa said showing increasing frustration.

"Primo Rivera's dictatorship is already not very popular, and if the economy collapses, his last pillars of support will certainly come down with it. Once he goes, who knows what will happen—the king may very well be next to fall, and though we may despise Alfonso XIII as a fool ..."

He paused again and decided to share his worst fear, his premonition, "Everything might come apart."

"Come apart?" Montse asked.

"Spain is full of hatred. It is like a covered pot of boiling water, whose cover will not be able to hold the water if it begins to boil over. This is a time to be careful."

Montse sat wondering what this all meant—her father's words and, more so, his somber, serious tone. Her article on Casas Viejas was acclaimed, propelling her career to full bloom, and she was not lonely anymore as she was warming to Tomás. She was the daughter of a great Catalan family, and all of life's doors seemed open to her. From where she sat, she could not see any dark clouds forming on the distant horizon.

—◦—

Book 3
Chapter 3
Salamanca, Spain
September 5, 1930

Salamanca was abuzz. Primo Rivera's dictatorship had collapsed in failure, and it was said in all corners of the city that the great man, Unamuno, would be back at his beloved university any day.

Given the talk of his return, Xavi was not completely surprised when the professor walked into *Café Novelty*. As he entered, all the patrons, left and right, rose in applause to salute his return.

It was not easy for the professor to make his way across the café. As the applause died down, many old friends, acquaintances, and well-wishers stopped the professor. They hugged him, shook his hand, and provided deeply warm greetings. He was the exalted hero.

Eventually the adulation died down; the patrons returned to their tables, and the professor made his way towards Xavi.

"Dr. Unamuno, what a joy to see you back!"

Unamuno reentered the city like his hero Fray Luis de Leon. "Xavi, it is so good to see you again and to smell the air of Salamanca. This city, this university, is a part of me, even though it has been six years, it feels like I never left. I'm happy to be back; I am an Iberian at heart, and this is home for me."

"Not a day passed here that we did not speak of you; please, can you tell me where you've been since last, we met?"

"Of course, of course. After I last saw you here, I was exiled to the Canary Islands, but quickly I was able to escape to Paris. Once there I wanted to get as close as possible to Spain, and to be with my Basque people in France, so I located myself just over the border from San Sebastian in Hendaye. There I continued to speak out against the Primo Rivera government until he resigned, and once he left, I was able to return home."

"But enough of that, enough about my troubles, Xavi, tell me about you, tell me about your friends, tell me about how youth is blossoming," Unamuno said.

"Well, Professor, do you recall my friends Montse and Jaime?"

"Yes, I think so … she was the beautiful woman from Barcelona, and Jaime, he was the hot-headed Spaniard."

"Yes, that is Montse and Jaime."

"And where are they now?"

"They are both in Barcelona. Montse writes for *El Progressiu*, and Jaime is now an army officer stationed there."

"On opposite sides of the same coin so to speak then—and you, why do remain in Salamanca?"

"The calling you saw in me remains strong. I expect I will complete my studies and be ordained next May."

"Ah yes, yes, I am very pleased for you."

Unamuno paused, and Xavi sensed he had more to add. "Given your chosen profession, I have something important to tell you. A warning of sorts. …"

"A warning? Please, Professor, tell me."

"Since I have returned to Spain, I have spent much time with the people who desire to fill the vacuum that Primo Rivera left. With your head deep in your books of theology I doubt you think much about our situation here in Spain?"

"No, not much."

"It is careening downward at a truly frightening pace. The economy is in rapid decline and the king's position is tenuous. The forces that have been suppressed—liberals, socialists, trade unionists, anarchists, Catalan and Basque separatists—sense an opening, and each, with their own world views and agendas, have come together in common cause to create a new Spain—a Republic they say."

"What does that mean, Professor?"

"Well, they don't agree on much—except that the King must go. After that, their visions diverge radically, and in some cases disturbingly, in frightening directions."

"What does this have to do with me?"

"I know these agitators well; they believe they can flatter me for an endorsement of their point of view. Some of them are driven by a noble, progressive vision for Spain, but many of these groups are motivated by hatred and settling scores."

"Settling scores? With whom, about what?"

"Listen to me."

Xavi leaned into the professor, as if waiting for a forthcoming secret.

"The principal score they wish to settle is with your church. They say they hate the church because it is backward and an impediment to change. Some of this may be true, but it also must be said their hatred is driven by something deeper and more sinister."

"I don't understand? Sinister?"

"Most of these people are godless. And with godlessness comes extreme hubris—the idea that there is nothing superior in this universe to their own egos. They hate the church, and by this I mean the true church, not the one of shallow symbols, because the true church unflinchingly holds a different view of man's place in the world: that there is a set of principles, right and wrong, that exists separate from their hubris. They hate this mirror held up to their shortcomings, to their small-mindedness. Xavi, please listen to me."

"Yes, I'm listening, Professor."

"Be cautious. These people have degrees, but they lack wisdom. Many of them cloak themselves as democrats, but really they are just well-educated thugs."

"Professor, I am so happy to see you again, and I am grateful for your counsel; but as these people believe they have a job to do, so too do I have a mission, a destiny, which you know I believe is driven by the Holy Spirit. Of course I hope my path does not collide with this type of violence and hatred, but I also will not go out of my way avoid it."

"You have grown, but you have not changed."

"Men and women of faith, who live in the world, often collide with men and women who hate them because of their faith. Professor I know you were once a man of deep faith, too, so I know you know these ancient words: *God's will be done, on earth as it is in heaven.*"

"Yes, so it is true. May God's will be done, but still, please be careful, Xavi."

Book 3
Chapter 4
Haro, Spain
April 13, 1931

There were several newspapers laid on Don Pedro's dining room table. Each of them blared a common theme: "Spain Rocked", "The Left Ascendant." These headlines left no room for doubt: the left wing, anti-monarchist parties had dominated the national elections.

An earthquake had hit and shaken Spain's foundational pillars. And, depending on whose news analysis you read, Spain was either poised for a renaissance built on liberal values and universal freedoms or was staring into an abyss of unimaginable horror.

Don Pedro knew which future he saw.

He despaired for his beloved country, and more than anything he was deeply worried about his sons, both of whom were officers in Spain's conservative army. How would they fare in the coming period of acrimony and chaos?

Don Pedro's sons had arrived for his birthday, but this was no party; it was a family conclave. After clearing the newspapers, over a simple dinner of red wine from their vineyard, a hard *Idiazabal* sheep's cheese from the nearby Pyrenees, and rusty red local *chorizos,* they discussed changes washing over Spain.

"Juan, how did this happen? What is the news from Madrid?" Don Pedro asked his son.

"Father, more than anything it's the economy—people want a change—they are fed up."

"But don't they realize what they have chosen will make our situation even more difficult?"

Juan waited respectfully for his father to finish. "The worst of it is not yet in the papers."

"What?"

"It's the king. Alphonso XIII is weak. And with these election results, his position has become untenable. As I hear it, the king summoned the head of the army, General Sanjurjo, to ask him if he still maintained the support of the army; when Sanjurjo would not confirm the army's support, he knew the game was up. It is rumored that he has decided to abdicate and to flee Spain."

Both Don Pedro and Jaime audibly gasped.

After a few moments, Don Pedro moved on. "When? How long does he have?"

"Days, not weeks," Juan replied solemnly.

The table went silent. Don Pedro considered the news; it triggered a primal instinct; he needed to protect his sons.

"Look at both of you: officers in the Spanish Army, serving your country. I am so proud, but I fear we are approaching a time when everyone will need to choose—a time with no middle ground. If it comes to this, and God help us if it does, this will be a perilous time. You will each need to follow your conscience, but there will be no safe harbor. As officers in the army you will be on the front line, and you will likely find chaos all around you. Both of you, be careful. Jaime, you in particular need to watch yourself when you return to Barcelona. The Catalans are very volatile."

Jaime thought of all he had heard. He was not surprised to hear that the king had lost the support of the army, as he had heard these murmurings amongst the officers in Barcelona; but yet he could not imagine the total crumbling of the foundations of Spanish society that his father foreshadowed. Spain's pillars—the army, the church—*they will always remain in place*, he thought.

Book 3
Chapter 5
Barcelona, Spain
April 18, 1931

When Jaime returned to Barcelona there was dancing in the streets and the feeling of revolution in the air. A strange mix of music, exuberance, and vulgarity was everywhere.

There were no Spanish flags to be seen; only Catalan banners and flags for the new Republic of Spain flew in the city.

In truth, Jaime could feel the joy; many Catalans danced their traditional circle dance, the *Sardana* and waved the flag of the new republic. At the same time, he also saw something more menacing: young people, men mostly, often drunk—full of hatred. Though he spoke little Catalan, the messages were clear.

"Fuck the King!"

"Fuck Spain!"

"Fuck the bosses!"

And, also, so strange, and truly frightening he heard shouts of, "Fuck the church. Fuck God!"

His commanding officer wanted no provocations of the Catalans. He ordered the enlisted men to the barracks and officers to go onto the streets only in their street clothes. For the first time in Barcelona, Jaime thought of himself as an occupier.

He walked along in his street clothes as he made his way to meet up with Montse at her favorite restaurant, *El Quatre Gats.* Their moods were at polar opposites: Montse was exuberant; Jaime was worried and anxious.

Montse greeted Jaime with joyful exuberance. "Oh, what a few days it has been here! Spain is no longer a monarchy! We have a democracy, a republic! We are witnessing history. The elections. The abdication of the king. The creation of the Second Republic! I wish you could have seen the city on the day when the king abdicated.

Not since the funeral of Gaudí have I seen so many people in the streets of Barcelona, but not in sadness and mourning, rather in joy and anticipation. It was glorious, jubilant. The people came from everywhere. People of all classes and backgrounds. They danced the *Sardana*; they sang traditional Catalan songs; they shouted out *'Viva Catalonia;'* and they waved Republican flags!"

"Sounds like quite a party," Jaime said with a sarcastic tone.

"Oh, Jaime, it was pure joy. There is an anticipation for a new, democratic, modern Spain. We are witnessing the birth of a new nation. You and I can be among the leaders of a new Spain!"

Jaime was in shock at what he heard. "Montse, I am sorry, but this is not how I see it."

"No, Jaime, that cannot be!"

"I experienced something completely different last night when I returned to Barcelona in my officer's uniform. When I left the train, I heard curses. A man passed by me and called out *'Porc Espanyol'* When I got into a taxi the driver ignored my instructions and told me to speak Catalan. He would not respond to me in Spanish, and I had to get out and get another taxi."

"You know people's emotions are running high, and some of them have lost their heads for the moment. You shouldn't worry about these little annoyances."

"Little annoyances! Officers here in Barcelona are told that it is not safe to go out in our uniforms ... to not provoke your people."

"Really, Jaime! We are on the cusp of something very momentous for our country. We should celebrate ... maybe some champagne."

Jaime resisted Montse's exuberance. "I'm sorry, but I don't feel like celebrating."

"Oh, Jaime, I'm sure you are making too much of your taxi and your uniform. Let's celebrate. Days like these don't come along often. Stay and have dinner with me and Tomás."

He was silent for a few moments considering Montse's invitation. He hated Tomás, but he adored his beautiful friend, and the honor of their friendship carried the day. "Yes, okay, I will stay."

After a few minutes Tomás arrived. Jaime was forced to admit to himself that he was a presence. *What was it about him?* he thought, *his good looks, his air of certainty, his aggressive march through the room?* People turned their heads as he walked by. He had a strong charisma.

He greeted Montse with romantic affection, which she returned. There was an intense, electric chemistry between them. Turning to Jaime, Tomás immediately began pushing the Spaniard. "Welcome to Catalonia."

Jaime held his tongue and mostly listened observantly as Tomás went on about the new world that was dawning. He spoke of lofty ideas, theories, principles, and the onset of a revolution.

Jaime watched Montse listen. She seemed bound to Tomás by a physical connection, not by agreement with his ideas. *Is she even listening to the nonsense?* he wondered.

Finally Jaime interrupted, "Tomás, I don't understand this talk of a revolution? We have a republic?"

"Yes, my Spanish friend," said in such a way that made it clear that they would never be friends, "It is called a republic now, but this is just a veil for the revolution to come."

It was all coming so quickly Jaime did not know where to begin. "What revolution? What do you mean?"

"Everything from the old order must be washed away: the monarchy, the aristocracy, the army, and above all, the church. No bosses. No property. No God!"

Jaime's blood, which had been simmering from the first moment of Tomás' arrival, quickly rose toward a boil. "I will not even speak of what you imply for our country, but only of the implication for Montse and for me. There is no room for Montse's family, and her way of life; no place for me as an army officer; and no place for our beloved friend, Xavi, who is to be ordained in a few weeks."

"First, I love Montse, of course, but we have no need for this excessively opulent bourgeois way of life. What we have will be provided for all equally, by the people."

"What nonsense!"

"Listen to me, *Espanol!* As for you and your army, that is different. We will trim it the way a sheep is sheared for its wool. You may continue to serve of course, but in an army that serves the revolution and the people. Your army will no longer be a destination of privilege, for the privileged. And as for Xavi, and his church, it will be destroyed, buildings torn down, and its priests and nuns reeducated to serve the people, not this god they have made up."

It was too much. Jaime did not know when exactly the line was crossed, but somewhere in his diatribe Jaime broke. "Tomás you are mad!" he shouted.

He felt an intense urge to get up and to physically confront Tomás. Yet, he realized his place, in Catalonia, amongst Catalans, in the first days of the Second Republic; he was alone and hopelessly outgunned in a hostile land. "Tomás this is not the place for this, and I hope it never does come to that, because if it does, we will be on opposite sides of this fight."

"Oh calm down, *Espanol,* we are all friends here," he said with fiendish tone. "Order more drinks while I use the bathroom."

After Tomás stepped away from the table Jaime turned to Montse, "Did you hear him? He is crazy, he is dangerous!"

"Oh, Jaime, don't pay too much attention to what he says, I never do. He is an idealist, but in the end they all compromise and become reasonable. He just wants a more just Spain."

"I'm sorry, I don't see it that way. He is a zealot. He is dangerous, very dangerous. Please give him my best, but I must go before it turns ugly in this restaurant. I will see you next month at Xavi's ordination in Salamanca. Goodbye."

Jaime could not stand another moment in Tomás' presence, and he was unnerved by the flow of events. He was also unnerved by his friend. How could she be so cavalier in the face of such a dangerous situation? How could she be so joyful when the country was clearly falling apart? How could she not see the evil hatred flowing from Tomás?

It's all madness, he thought.

Book 3
Chapter 6
Salamanca, Spain
April 25, 1931

If the foundations of Spanish society were starting to quiver in Catalonia, in the large industrial cities around the country, and among the very poor in Andalusia and Extremadura, inside Salamanca's ancient cathedral the Catholic Church's ways and traditions went on, unchanged and unmoved, as they had done for hundreds of years.

While the choir sang like angels descending from heaven, the ordination mass began with a procession that went on for several minutes. First, dozens of priests and seminarians, including Father Extebarri and Inaki, who limped in, permanently hobbled from his fall as a young boy, and now himself a seminarian in Bilboa; then came Xavi with the nine others who were being ordained. Finally completing the procession were Bishop Pla y Deniel, and at the very end the Bishop of Salamanca, Francisco Frutos y Valiente.

The cathedral was full of guests and well-wishers. A contingent of the crowd was there specifically for Xavi, including his parents, Montse, Jaime, Jaime's father, his brother Juan, and Professor Unamuno.

The mass proceeded as any mass until the after the readings were read. At this point the candidates for ordination were presented, and their qualifications were witnessed. The bishop then confirmed their intention. "We choose these, our brothers, to the order of the priesthood."

To his words the congregants responded, "Thanks be to God," and applause rang out thunderously in the huge old church.

As the applause subsided, Bishop Frutos y Valiente took the pulpit and gave his homily.

"We are so proud of these young men who we welcome to the

131

priesthood. As we confer this special place in our church on them, each of you should remember that through your own baptism each of you gathered here today is called to share in Christ's mission as priest, prophet, and king.

"Kings having not only authority, but also the duty to care for their people in need. This is an important duality, and as we have seen in our country, a vacuum is created when a king exercises his authority but does not exercise his responsibility to care for the lowest, poorest, and least fortunate amongst his subjects.

"Prophets, the messengers sent from God to speak the truth— even when it is unpopular. Today as Spain descends into moral relativism and chaos, we must each act as prophets to speak out for what we know to be universally true.

"And finally as priests. We can all act as priests by our daily actions. By saying grace, by making the smallest sacrifice for someone else, you participate in the priestly mission of Christ—the priesthood of all believers.

"But it is these ten young men who are our focus today. Let us contemplate their lineage to the first apostles of Jesus. It is an unbroken line from the original twelve to these ten men today. Let us contemplate their call to not just love one person, but rather for their commitment to universal love of all people.

"These ten young men are exceptional. They are the perfect warriors to fight against the errors encroaching on modern Spain."

After the bishop finished his homily the ordination rights continued. The candidates were asked various questions confirming their commitment to the priesthood, their loyalty to their bishop, and to preach and live the gospel. They each answered, "I do" to these examinations.

The questions continued. Finally coming to the confirmation of their commitment to a celibate life.

Upon hearing Xavi say, "I do," Montse's heart sank. The door officially swung shut. She felt deep sadness and loss.

Their commitments made and witnessed, the candidates, in an act of extreme humility laid themselves prostrate on the ancient, hard-stone floor while the litany of saints was sung, slowly, hauntingly by the choir.

Kyrie, eleison

Christe, eleison
Sancta Maria, ora pro nobis
Sancti Michael, Gabriel, et Rafael, orate pro nobis

Jaime found the chanted orations haunting, moving …
Omnes sancti Angeli, orate pro nobis
Sancte Ioannes Baptista, ora pro nobis
Sancte Ioseph, ora pro nobus
Sancti Petre at Paule, orate por nobis

As chants rang through the Cathedral he began to weep.
Sancti Ioannes et Iocabe, orate por nobis
Sancte Matthee, ora por nobis
Omnes sancti Apostoli, orate por nobis
Sancte Marce, ora por nobis

Through his tears he looked to his left to the great professor, Unamuno, was softly weeping as well.
Sancte Augustine, ora pro nobis
Sancte Benedictine, ora pro nobis
Sancta Teresa, ora pro nobis

Finally he peered to his right and there was Montse.
Kyrie eleison
Christe eleison
Kyrie eleison

The effect of Xavi and the others lying prostate on the cathedral floor while the chants rang through the cathedral was overwhelming. Montse's head was tilted forward, her face in her hands, tears seeping through her fingers.

Finally, after the chanting ended, the bishop laid hands on the ten young men and they were ordained. This final act conferred upon them tremendous new power. They could baptize; they could anoint the sick; they could hear confession and forgive people's sins; and most importantly, as Jesus had first done at the last supper, they could turn the bread and wine into the body and blood of Christ.

As the mass ended the new priests processed out. They were beaming. The spirit that filled them at that moment lifted everyone in the church. The crowd was jubilant, and radiant with joy.

After the mass, the bishop hosted a small reception at his palace for the new priests and a select few guests. Professor Unamuno reaffirmed how proud he was of Xavi. Bishop Pla y Deniel took special note of Xavi's capabilities, and told him that if he ever needed anything in Salamanca, he knew who he would call.

Also there were his parents, their sense of loss having been transformed into enormous, unimaginable, unspeakable pride for their son's vocation.

Others took turns congratulating and hugging him. In the rush of the crowd he confirmed to Jaime that he would see him in Madrid in a couple of weeks.

Finally Xavi found Montse. Her joy was layered on a thicker foundation of impenetrable sadness.

"What is wrong, my dear?"

Montse thought for a moment and realized she should not let this time pass without including him in her private world.

"Can we find a quiet corner to speak?"

"Of course, of course. In the back of the garden, among the flowers, there is a bench. Let's go there," Xavi responded.

Sitting next to Xavi in the shade of the bishop's garden, the flowers of spring were blooming all around them; even among the glorious new bloom, Montse's sadness shone through. "Xavi, as you know I have been seeing, in a romantic way, my brother's friend Tomás, and my coming here created a lot of tension between us."

"Why, Montse?"

"Tomás hates the church, and by extension, he hates you. He hates the reality of you, and he hates the idea of you as an abstract concept. The idea of priests and sacraments is anathema to him. We argued ferociously about this. Somewhere in this argument it crossed over from being a philosophical debate to a personal invective. When he realized that I had had feelings for you—that I still have feelings for you—he became volcanic with anger. He began to make all kinds of crazy threats."

"Oh, Montse, I'm so sorry—don't worry about me."

"No, Xavi, don't say anything."

He leaned toward her to listen more closely.

"This fight did the opposite of what he had intended. He brought the feelings I had for you back to the surface; and today, when you took your vows—your vow of celibacy, I felt a great loss. I have had every advantage in this life, and yet the one thing I have truly wanted, maybe needed, is lost to me, forever."

She began again to weep. Xavi wrapped his arms around her and consoled her on the small bench in the back of the beautiful garden, with only the flowers as witnesses.

Finally Montse got up to leave. "Here, please take this." She handed a letter to Xavi. "I don't know when next I will see you, and I want you to have this note ... I will never forget this day."

Xavi remained on the bench as Montse walked away, through the garden, then out of his sight, and out of the reception. She was gone.

—◆—

Book 3
Chapter 7
Madrid, Spain
May 12, 1931

Xavi took a break from the conference for newly ordained priests he was attending in Madrid to meet Jaime, Jaime's brother Juan, and three of Juan's fellow officers at *Bar Delores*. At around five-thirty p.m. Xavi arrived, and there were greetings of "Father Xavi!" all around, though in truth, he was still having trouble getting used to his new moniker.

One of the officers pushed forward to the bar and asked if he would like a beer.

"No, no thank you. A coffee will do. I am saying mass at seven at the Convent of the *Discalced Carmelites*. After mass maybe."

Xavi then sought to persuade the men to come to mass with him at the convent. "It is a beautiful church, and the cloistered nuns have a rich tradition. Come, you'll see."

"Father, with due respect, a church is a church," one of Juan's friends responded.

"No, no. This is a special place. This order of nuns is said to have raised the money to ransom Cervantes' freedom. Without them there would not be Don Quixote, or the wise squire, Sancho Panza."

Partly intrigued, but more out of a sense of obligation, the men accompanied him on the short walk to the church of the convent, and except for five or six others spaced out among the pews of the small church, it was empty. The nuns were not in the main church. They were to the side of the altar, behind a grill, in their cloister. As the mass began, their beautiful voices, rising in song, floated from behind the bars separating the church from the convent.

"It seems as if they are angels," Jaime whispered to his brother.

"I'm glad Xavi made us come," Juan whispered back.

Jaime returned to contemplation and thought of how entrancing it all was: the small, beautiful baroque church, the singing of the sisters, hidden behind the grill that separated the church from the cloister, the watching of his friend say mass. He felt complete tranquility.

He was a million miles away from the bubbling chaos in Barcelona. *If only time could stand still; if only the whole of Spain could feel the peace of this moment,* he thought.

The mass headed, as all masses do, inevitably towards the consecration. At the ultimate moment, when Xavi closed his eyes and lifted the host to the sky, there was a very loud commotion—men shouting and pounding furiously on the door of the church entrance. The noise interrupted Xavi. He turned around and lowered the chalice to the altar and gazed to the back of the church. At the same time Jaime, Juan and the other officers also turned their gazes towards the source of the disturbance.

Suddenly a mob of about twenty men burst through the doors, arriving with them were the smells of smoke and gasoline. The leader of the throng called out, "Get the fuck out of this church before we burn it down!"

Xavi's instincts kicked in. He placed the host back in the chalice, took his vestments off and sprinted toward the back of the church; his friends followed him. At the prospect of a confrontation with a group of strong young men—as opposed to cloistered nuns—about half of the rabble ran away.

"You will not pass into this church. You will not lay a finger on these holy women. Leave now," Xavi shouted at the mob.

"He is not alone. We are officers in the Spanish Army, and we stand with the father," Jaime said in unquestioning support.

"And before you go, we'll take your torches and rags. You will do no harm tonight!" he added sternly.

At this point one of the men snarled and swore at Jaime and spat on Xavi. Juan, acting the older brother, moved forward and threw one ferocious punch that sent the man to the ground. "Now give us your torches and rags and get out!" Juan said fiercely

The combination of Xavi's force of will and Juan's physical force quickly won the battle. The torches and rags were collected; the mob dispersed.

Standing in front of the church, as his adrenalin began to sub-side, Jaime could see smoke coming from behind the area of the Prado.

Maybe another convent? he wondered.

"We need to get to that smoke. We need to see what it is and what can be done. Let's go!" Juan added with urgency.

"You go, I want to stay here with the sisters. I want to make sure they are okay. Let's meet back up at *Bar Delores* later," Xavi added.

He stayed with the sisters for several hours and finally the Mother Superior broke the sacred silence of the convent. "Father Xavi, you may go now," she said simply.

"Sister, are you sure?"

"Yes, Father. We thank you sincerely, but there is no more to do here. We trust in the Lord for our protection," she added.

Xavi felt the spell of her silent faith. He desired to stay under it, to stay with these women, but he knew he must honor the Mother Superior's request.

"Goodbye, Sister."

"Goodbye, Father. Thank you. God bless you."

Moved, exhausted, he left the convent to meet his friends a few blocks away back at the Bar Delores. Now he needed a beer. At just before midnight Jaime, Juan, and the other officers arrived. Their faces were covered with soot.

Jaime was in a righteous rage. "We got to the other convent. It was burning. The police and firefighters were there, but they were doing nothing! We took their hoses and put out the fire. The nuns there were terrified, but safe. I have never seen anything like this. Who would attack nuns? What kind of animals would do this? And even worse, what kind of cowards would stand by and watch? I am disgusted by what I have seen tonight. Is this what we get from democracy? Is this what we get from our so called Second Republic?"

They left bar at just after one a.m. As they stepped onto the street from the bar, they could see many fires were still alight and smoke pluming all around the city.

—·—

Book 3
Chapter 8
Barcelona, Spain
July 1, 1931

News of the interview with the Minister of War in *El Progressiu* was buzzing all around the barracks. It was said that Montserrat Costa, on the strength of her reporting about Casas Viejas, her distinctly progressive point of view, and, of course, her family's connections, had secured an interview with Manuel Azaña.

Getting Azaña, the newly appointed Republican Minister of War, the second most powerful man in Spain, to sit for an interview for a Catalan newspaper was a journalistic coup. The interview was conducted in Spanish and appeared in *El Progressiu* in both Spanish and in a Catalan translation. All of Spain took notice. Montse was no longer just a journalist. She was now a leading actor in the play.

Hearing of the interview, Jaime left the barracks and found a kiosk where he bought the newspaper. He found a café, ordered a coffee, sat down, and began reading.

El Progressiu: Thank you for taking the time to talk with us, we know how busy you are as we establish our new Republic.

Azaña: Thank you for having me, for giving me the chance to address the Catalan and Spanish people. And thank you for your articles on the poverty in Casas Viejas. Your work was important in highlighting the injustices in our society, the injustices our government will address. You, too, are important in building our new Republic.

El Progressiu: That is kind of you to say. I am doing what I can to help build a new country too. We all want a more just society. As a start, *señor* Azaña, please give us a little background on your life.

Azaña: I was fortunate to have been born to an afflu-
ent family that could offer me great privilege. Unfortunately, this happiness, this peace of my childhood, was
pierced at a young age when both of my parents died.

El Progressiu: Oh, *señor* Azaña, that is such a sad note.

Azaña: Yes, yes, it is. And I think from this sadness grew
a compassion for people, a sensitivity to the suffering of
others. I know we can have a more just country. In spite of
this unhappy circumstance of my childhood, and because
of my family's position, I was able to attend university. I
received my law degree at Zaragoza in 1897 and my doc-
torate at the University of Complutense in Madrid in 1900.

El Progressiu: What did you do after university?

Azaña: Initially I practiced law, but my passion was
really politics. Along the way I worked in your field as a
journalist in France in WWI. After the war I returned to
Spain to focus on the situation in our country.

El Progressiu: You were a vocal critic of the monarchy,
correct?

Azaña: Yes, of course. In the 1920's I spoke out about
Primo Rivera, and by association, the king. In 1930 I was
signatory of the Pact of San Sebastian calling for the ab-
olition of the monarchy and the establishment of a republic in Spain.

El Progressiu: How did you get to that point of view?

Azaña: In comparison to France, and other advanced
European nations, Spain is woefully backward. Spain
needs to be transformed. We need to become a progressive society like our European neighbors. Now we have
a true democracy, a republic. Now we can transform our
country. The monarchy was an anachronism.

El Progressiu: Was it only the monarchy to which you
objected?

Azaña: No, no, of course not. Many of our institutions
are repressively conservative. The army, but more than
any other, the church is holding Spain in chains.

El Progressiu: Let's begin with your views of the army,
as the Minister of War they are particularly important.

Azaña: It's simple, the army is bloated and outdated. We face no threats here in Spain, and we are no longer an Imperial power. The army must be downsized, and the officer corps trimmed. The army must serve the people, and not the reverse, as has been too true throughout our history.

Jaime's temper was boiling. How could Montse do this? How could she facilitate this heresy? After another sip of coffee, he read on...

El Progressiu: You mentioned the church in Spain, can you elaborate?

Azaña: There can be no doubt that the church is an impediment to creating a modern, progressive society. Its stranglehold on education, charities, hospitals, and the like must be broken. These institutions must be secularized. In addition, I believe there is no place in a modern Spain for their mediaeval processions and festivals. These strange, truly bizarre spectacles, like the *Semana Santa*— medieval in their outlook—men in capes and masks; they must be outlawed.

El Progressiu: Regarding the church, I want to turn to what recently occurred in Madrid and in several other cities. A number of churches and convents were attacked and burned. Many people, even those in favor of The Republic, were shocked by this violence, and even more so by the Government's response to these incidents. What would you tell these people?

Azaña: Let me be very clear: all the churches in Spain are not worth one Republican life ...

The interview continued on, but Jaime could read no further. He threw the paper down on the bar table in disgust. He thought, *You bastard! You coward! You pompous intellectual! I was there. I saw innocent nuns attacked. I saw them tremble as the police did not come to help them. I held a hose that put out fires! I—we, will never forgive you for this, and we will never forget your callousness!*

141

Book 3
Chapter 9
Barcelona, Spain
January 17, 1933

Tomás waited impatiently for Montse at the *El Quatre Gats*. *She's been gone for three weeks, and now she makes me wait!*
Montse had left Barcelona to cover the unfolding tragedy of Casas Viejas in Andalucía. Waiting for his girlfriend to arrive, Tomás re-read her account from *El Progressiu* printed three days earlier.

Massacre at Casas Viejas
Nation Outraged
Montserrat Costa

Too much tragedy for one little village.
First the grinding poverty; now the horrific massacre.
During the early days of January, anarchists marched into Casas Viejas. These revolutionaries against all institutions, both ancient and modern, raised their fists in revolutionary furor. They chanted their theology: No God and no masters! Though they were loud in their voices, and extreme in their views, they were peaceful.
The progressive government of Premier Azaña, fearing these protests would metastasize into an attack on the hard-won democracy of the Spanish Second Republic, sent in the military. Most villagers, sensing the building tension, like a tea pot beginning to whistle, and fearing the worst, fled.
All that was left in the sad little town was a standoff between the anarchists and the military, that found sev-

eral dozen peasants holed up in the house of Francisco Cruz Gutierrez.

On January 12 tragedy befell Casas Viejas. No one knows the exact chain of events that led to the massacre, or why the army lost its nerve and patience, or who gave what orders. What we do know is that troops under the command of Captain Rojas somehow set the house alight.

Some minutes later a young woman, Maria Silva Cruz, emerged from the smoldering, small mud house with a baby in her arms. She and her baby survived. Twenty-four others did not. After the fire died down to embers, the charred bodies were found. *Señora* Cruz and her baby shouted out in lamentation; their cries swirled with the smoke to make a ghoulish mix.

How could this happen? How could a peaceful protest end in a massacre? Where can our democracy go from here? What can be said of the noble intentions of minister Azaña?

There are too many unanswerable questions...

As Tomás continued reading the article, Montse arrived. She greeted him with a travel-weary hug.

"Hello Tomás," her smile unable to mask her fatigue.

"Where have you been? You submitted this article three days ago!"

"Yes, I took a detour on my return."

"A detour, detour where?"

"Oh Tomás it was terrible! I was so sickened by what I saw that I went to see my friend Father Xavi in Salamanca."

"What? How can he help? Or maybe he gives you other comforts the way it is known that these priests do?"

"How dare you! Stop!" Montse snapped back.

Tomás, seeing he had pushed his hatred of Xavi, and all that he stood for, as far as it could be pushed, pivoted to launch a different attack. "Do you still admire the 'great' Azaña?"

"Yes, I admire Azaña, but he is in a perilous position."

"Can't you see there is no difference between left and right governments? They are both corrupt! They are both power hungry!

Both sides will kill innocent people when it serves their purpose. We need to tear the whole system down; we need to erase history, start our society over, from scratch."

"Oh Tomás, sometimes! What is wrong with you? Twenty-four innocent people are dead. I saw it. I was there as the stand-off crossed into murder. The horror, the insanity, has exhausted me."

"Montse, I am trying to protect you."

"From what."

"The hypocrisy of all organized parties, left and right."

"Tomás, please, spare me the political theory. This is a time for mourning."

Book 3
Chapter 10
Palma de Mallorca, Spain
February 23, 1933

Jaime was finding his way in new surroundings. While Barcelona was bubbling with tension, Mallorca was bucolic. He sat down to write his father, to allay any worries he might be carrying.

Dear Father,

I have now been in Mallorca for a couple of weeks, and I am starting to settle in.

It could not be more different from Barcelona. It is a quiet, mostly rural island. The scenery here is varied and almost universally spectacular. Palma sits on an expansive and sparkling bay, but in other places there are many secluded coves. At all of these beaches the sea is a translucent blue. Surprisingly, there is an imposing mountain range, the Tramuntana, which splits the northwest side of the island from a flatter, agricultural plain. Everywhere there are trees: pines, almond, citrus, and olive. The olive trees, some thousand years old, twist and turn in gnarly, ununiform shapes. The sights and scents of the island give one a sense of being in a garden paradise.

The people here—the Mallorquins—are simple, kind, though somewhat guarded with outsiders. They speak a form of Catalan, but they do not seem to have any of the Catalans' independent spirit or condescending arrogance. I do not feel any of the tension that was a constant presence in Barcelona.

Professionally, I am pleased to be under the command of General Franco. He earned the respect of his men in Morocco, and, from what I knew of him at the Military Academy, I liked him very much.

For now, General Franco's career has lost its shine. His Military Academy is shut down, and he is on the wrong side of War

Minister Azaña.

So, father, here I sit in Mallorca. I am under the command of a man I like and respect, but I am in a bit of a backwater (a beautiful one though at that). For the moment, I am far away from the troubles that brew on the peninsula.

Very Fondly,

Jaime

Book 3
Chapter 11
Barcelona, Spain
November 3, 1933

Montse met her mother and father in the small dining room of the family estate. It was now a rare treat to be home and to share a meal with her parents. Though she lived just a few minutes away, their lives were slowly drifting apart. Her journalism put her on the front line of the brewing turmoil, and when not in front of her typewriter, she spent more and more time with Tomás. "Good evening, Mother; good evening, Father."

"It's so good to see you; we never see you anymore," Luisa Costa replied.

As they settled in, the maid served a simple, hearty fall meal of *Arroz Brut* with rabbit. "It's always good to be back home. I was hoping for this some *Arroz Brut*."

"Good, and how is Tomás? Is he still involved with those radicals?" her mother sniped.

"Oh, Mother, really! He is just doing what he can to build a new Spain, a new Catalonia."

"You look very tired, fatigued really."

"Well, I am. Wherever there is chaos in this country, I seem to find myself in the middle of it."

"But why you, darling?"

"Because it's vital. Events are moving so fast now: the massacre of Casas Viejas, the anarchists and their rallies, the Falangist's and their rallies."

"It sounds dreadfully draining."

"It is. It's physically and emotionally taxing, and sometimes it even feels dangerous."

"Oh, my dear, must you put yourself in harm's way like this? There are so many beautiful things to see and do here in Barcelona."

Montse let her mother's comment pass by her, and she continued, "Plus I am worried."

"Worried? About what?" her father inquired.

"Deep fissures are opening everywhere."

"So I feared."

"Tempers are flaring, and hate is spilling out. If a person thinks you disagree with them, they either shun you or shout at you."

"Is it like this all over Spain and not just here in Barcelona?" her father probed.

"Yes, everywhere. People are at each other's throats. Something is going to break, and I don't know what that will look like if it does, but it frightens me … I'm scared."

"Oh, Montse, you are too young for all this," Luisa said sympathetically.

Her father jumped into the conversation wanting to get the latest news and feel from the ground. "You are just back from the campaign in Madrid, how does it feel to you?"

"The parties of the right are ascendant. Our government is failing."

"Failing?"

"Between the anti-clerical reforms and the impact of the burning of the convents, conservative and moderate Catholics are angry and mobilized. Providing woman the vote may backfire, as so many women are tethered to Catholicism, either superficially or devoutly."

"Oh these people! Will they have to be dragged into the 20th century kicking and screaming?" her mother exclaimed.

"Perhaps … but it is not just the right that is the problem. The government has also lost the support of the far left. The far left—people like Tomás—are likely to boycott the elections."

"Why? That is crazy." her father asked.

"They, Tomás for example, see both sides as equally corrupt and fatally flawed. They want to start over, rebuild society from the bottom up. Every time I try to reason with Tomás, he brings up the massacre at Casas Viejas. There is no rebuttal to that horror."

"Oh this idea of utopia is so ridiculous! Why not just modernize our country and become more like France?" her mother responded.

"I know, I know. It is a terrible situation. The idea of building a democratic, progressive Spain, and creating an autonomous Catalonia, is slipping away. I really cannot tell you where this is all heading."

Her parents went quiet, and between bites of the rice, her father broke the silence. "Were you at the Falange rally in Madrid this week?"

"I was. I need to finish the article on it."

"What do you make of Primo de Rivera's son, José Antonio?"

"He is something different."

"What do you mean?" her father asked, his eyebrows raised.

"He is not at all like the foolish playboy his father was. There is something unusual, quixotic, about him. First off, he is a good-looking young man. He is also a very well-educated and articulate. He speaks both English and French fluently."

"Being handsome and speaking languages is not enough to lead a country, Montse!" her mother interjected.

"True, but he also has something else too, something very unusual. He has the sense of right and wrong of a nobleman. They say he was expelled from the army because he punched a general who had insulted his father."

"Hmmm," Joan murmured.

"He also seems to have a poet's heart. He talks about big ideas that are not easily classified as right or left. He is of course staunchly Catholic, but he does not talk like the aristocrat he is. He uses terms like responsibility, community, and fatherland. He uses sweeping, grand, and compelling imagery."

"I see ..." Joan Costa added.

"On the other hand, frighteningly, he does not appear to shy away from the idea of using force to achieve his vision. He is a compelling and charismatic figure, and many young people, young men mostly, are flocking to him, flocking to the Falangist Party."

"This is fascism!" Joan exclaimed his objection.

"Maybe ..."

"Why maybe, Montse?" he asked.

"It is too easy to lump him in with others like Hitler or Mussolini. In my opinion, this is a mistranslation of his ideals and philosophy. He represents something different."

"What do you mean?" her father probed.

"Honestly, in many ways his vision for Spain is closer to Tomás' than it is to his father's."

"Really, how so?"

"He is a bit of utopian also but built on Catholic ideals. My worry is ..." she said as her voice trailed off.

"What, what is your worry, dear?" her mother implored.

"My worry is that these idealists, on both sides, will soon be quick to violence. Neither group seems prone to compromise."

"All utopians are extremists wrapped in soaring rhetoric," Joan concluded.

"Spain is tearing itself apart. Can we finish eating, I am hungry," Montse said, signaling an end point to the subject.

—•—

Book 3
Chapter 12
Avila, Spain
November 20, 1933

In his palace, in the heart of conservative, Catholic Spain, Bishop Pla y Deniel sat at a desk in his private office. In Avila he was as far from the building turmoil as one could be in Spain. Yet even from this high ground he could sense the waters of trouble were rising quickly.

Spread out across his desk were papers from around the country. They all had the same story: the right-wing parties had swept the elections. Perusing the papers, he started with *El Progressiu*.

Right Wing Parties Make Strong Comeback
Reforms at Risk; Left Threatens Retribution
Montserrat Costa

Yesterday's sweeping results for the right-wing coalition confirmed what most observers had perceived in the run up to yesterday's election: that is, the right-wing parties were energized, and the center left parties were fragmented and discouraged.

Right wing voters, led by Catholics, landowners, the military, and the urban bourgeoisie, used the ballot box to make a counter revolt against the reforms instituted by the leftist government. These voters, who saw their way of life under attack and their long-standing privileges being threatened, launched a counter revolt yesterday. Their ballots spoke in a loud and clear voice: the government's reforms were ill conceived, poorly executed, too hastily implemented, or mostly unnecessary. This point of view will now dominate the new parliament.

While the right is ascendant and speaking with a unified voice, the left is fragmented and discouraged that its reforms are moving too slowly. The current left-wing government, sailing into the head wind of an economic collapse in Spain and fighting deeply entrenched, powerful, conservative interests, as well as suffering the aftermath of the horrible massacre at Casas Viejas, is now in retreat.

The far left, notably in Catalonia, rural Andalucía, and industrial Asturias largely sat out the elections. The trade unions and intellectuals of the anarchy movement seem to perceive little difference between Spain's political parties, and they can be heard beating the drum for revolution and total overhaul of the country. It appears they are not reading a Spanish script, but rather from the notebooks of the French or Russian revolutions that justifies extremism, threats, and politically motivated violence.

From here, in the near term, a new government will be formed, and reforms will grind to a halt. The conservative institutions in our country will happily go back to doing what they have always done. The country awaits on edge for the left to mount its counterattack.

The bishop put down the paper.

He could not help but be proud of Montse. She wrote clearly and forcefully. She was now an articulate young woman. His goddaughter had become an important and powerful voice in Spain.

The bishop had another thought too: he was worried. He, like everyone else in Spain, was moving beyond abstract concerns about politics and now was trying to assess what this brewing turmoil would mean for him personally. The bishop in Salamanca had recently died, and there was talk that he might be chosen to fill that post. Going to Salamanca, with its university and famed seminaries, would be a more prominent posting, but would its churches be more or less likely to be burned down; would he more or less likely to be hunted there?

—◦—

Book 3
Chapter 13
Palma de Mallorca, Spain
June 2, 1934

Jaime took a break from packing his things. He was on the move. He was following General Franco again, this time to Africa. Before he departed Mallorca, he wrote his father one last time.

Dear Father,

I am writing to you as I gather my things to head to another assignment: I have been instructed that I am moving to The Army of Africa in Spanish Morocco.

It seems my fortunes and postings are now tethered to those of General Franco, and with the arrival of the new government his star is again ascending. He has been assigned to lead our Army of Africa. I am happy for the general, but I cannot help to feel from first-hand experience how politicized our military has become. Rather than merit and valor establishing the basis for an officer's value, it is frequently who you know and how you curry favor. This is no way to run an army! It is a recipe for treachery and false loyalties amongst the officers.

I am sad to leave Mallorca. The mild weather, the beautiful beaches, craggy, pine-covered mountains, the white-blooming almond trees along with the kind simplicity of the people here has been a wonderful tonic for me. One reads of the chaos and violence beginning to engulf the Spanish Peninsula, but I feel a million miles away from any of that ... here we live in a paradise, a bubble of sorts.

I am proud to be serving in the Army of Africa. It is our country's best fighting force ... Spanish Morocco may be farther away from the mainland, but it will put me closer to any turmoil that may break out there. If there is any real trouble in our motherland, we will be called to deal with it. Let us pray that now that the right wing controls the government, order and sanity will be restored.

I am told that Tetuan in Spanish Morocco is a lovely place and that the officers there live like kings. No matter how beautiful Mallorca is, or Morocco may be, nowhere can be as alluring as home. I miss watching the fruit ripen on the vines, and the certainty of the rhythms of life there. Sitting here, overlooking the deep blue Mediterranean Sea, I can close my eyes and imagine the vineyard being a carpet of soft green rolling up and down the hills of our land.

I miss you ... I miss all the life you gave me and Juan.
Jaime

———

Book 3
Chapter 14
Salamanca, Spain
November 7, 1934

Jaime left the train station at Salamanca and headed directly to see Xavi in his office at his parish church, St. Martin of Tours.

"Is Father Bidertea in?" he asked the secretary.

Before she could answer, Xavi, on hearing his friend, came out and gave him an embrace. "What a happy surprise! What brings you to Salamanca?"

"I came to see you," he answered with intense seriousness.

"Okay, let's go to the *Café Novelty* and get a coffee."

"No not there, somewhere out of the way, somewhere quiet," Jaime replied.

The words caught Xavi by surprise. He picked up on his old friend's serious tone and mood.

"Yes … I see. Let's go to the cloisters at *San Estaban* church. We won't be disturbed there."

It was a short walk to the ancient cloisters of the Dominican church. Xavi knew they would find secluded, peaceful refuge in the sheltered garden. On the walk over, Xavi could sense there was a disturbance brewing deep within his friend. He seemed agitated and looked to be suffering from a serious lack of sleep.

"Tell me—" Xavi started, and before he could finish his sentence, the traumas haunting Jaime began to pour out.

"I am coming from Asturias. I have seen horrible things."

"Yes, I have read about how difficult it was," Xavi said in a way he hoped would reassure his friend.

"No, not difficult, horrific."

"I'm here for you, Jaime."

"I saw things, well pick your description, that were hideous … grisly … ghoulish … nightmarish. I saw a complete breakdown

155

of our world and the rules that we learned are supposed to govern it. What I saw—it is not something you can read about in a newspaper."

Xavi was not expecting to hear any of this and struggled for a moment on how to best help his friend find relief. "Tell me what happened."

Jaime lost himself in thought for a few moments, as he seemed to be carefully cataloguing the events from the beginning. Then he started in from the first few insignificant details that over a few weeks grew into his nightmare, "Well, you know the political situation in our country is unstable, breaking down, right?"

"I know the government seems to be ineffective, alternating between left-wing and right-wing parties. I also know the economy is very bad. I see so many desperate working people in my parish."

"All of that is true. People are getting fed up. You used the right word—desperate."

"Yes, good people who have lost their jobs, their livelihoods. There is nothing worse than hopelessness; it is how the Devil breaks down our souls."

"I am not a theologian. I am a soldier. What I see is that these conditions lead to violence."

"What happened in Asturias seems horrible."

"It was. It really started after the last elections; the anarchists and radical trade unions started to agitate."

"I know, Jaime, but as I said, I really do not pay much attention to politics."

"As always, it started in Barcelona."

The word Barcelona took Xavi away for just a moment, thinking of Montse: *Was she okay? Was she in the middle of all it somehow? Was she safe?"*

Jaime continued on, "The radicals declared a general strike and a Catalan Republic, but it only lasted ten hours there and then collapsed. But in Asturias this fury exploded. You know of course of Turon?"

"Yes ...," Xavi said sadly.

"There, the fanatics stirred up the miners and killed thirty-seven de la Salle Brothers. Their crime? They continued to teach as they always had. From there the violence escalated into a full revolution, and always churches—not banks, not government buildings—were the first targets."

"I know, I know it is a terrible thing for people to die because of their faith."

"But, Xavi, the insurrection continued to grow. They overwhelmed the local police and marched on Oviedo. After they burned the cathedral there, finally the government said enough was enough. General Franco was called in to put this revolt down. That is how I got there."

"I see."

"I have known the general since military school, and I have served him as an officer for several years. I like and respect him. He is a decent and fair man, but I tell you, when he is called to action, he comes with cold calculation and ruthless efficiency. He is not a compromiser. He comes to win."

Xavi remained silent, watching his friend closely as he recounted his story.

"And with the Army of Africa, he brought the Moorish troops as well."

"Moors in Asturias?"

"Yes, calling Moors to Asturias. Ironic isn't it. The only place in Spain that they never conquered. But it was telling as well."

"Telling …?"

"General Franco is a devout Catholic and Spaniard through and through, but he considers communists and anarchists lower than Moors."

"I am not sure God would see it that way."

"In any case, the fighting was fierce, many were killed on both sides, but after a few days we overwhelmed the miners."

"Jaime is it this battle that so disturbed you?"

"No, Xavi, no. The battle was intense, and death was all around me, but no. I am a soldier."

"What then?"

"It was the atrocities afterward ..."

Sensing they had arrived at the headwater of his distress, Xavi gently prodded his friend, "Talk to me, Jaime, talk to me."

Jaime paused, and then slowly resumed, "The killing, no … murdering … of surrendered men. The raping of their women as they looked on, no one protecting them—all of this done with a kind of gusto. And I hate to use this word for what I saw, but it is the right word—joy."

Xavi was shocked. For a few moments he said nothing. There was nothing more to dissect, nothing more to pull from Jaime's soul. He saw it for what it was: a form of confession, without the actual ritual, or penance of the sacrament. Jaime had come to unload this burden and seek comfort.

His friend sobbed, and Xavi consoled him with a silent embrace. Finally, after many moments the sobbing abated, and they unlocked. Xavi then let Jaime sit silently for a time and finally asked, "Do you want to make a formal confession, my friend?"

Jaime paused and floated off in thought. "No, Father—not at this time. I just needed to tell someone. I needed to unburden myself of all of this."

"Anytime, anytime, I am here for you as your friend, and if you ever need it, as a priest."

Book 3
Chapter 15
Salamanca, Spain
January 22, 1935

Xavi returned to Salamanca from San Sebastian. He had gone home to see his parents just after the celebration of the Three Kings, the day of Epiphany, on January 6th, and had stayed through *La Tomborrada* celebration on January 19th.

The parish secretary met him as he arrived. "Father Bidertea, Bishop Pla y Deniel wants to see you."

"Me? Did he say why?"

"The assistant said it was important. They want you to go to his office in the palace as soon as possible."

As Xavi walked towards the residence, he had no idea why the bishop would want to see him. He had met him a handful of times over the years, mostly because of his friendship with Montse. Adding to his curiosity was the fact that Bishop Pla y Deniel was to be consecrated as the new Bishop of Salamanca in a few days; he imagined he must be extremely busy.

Upon arriving at the residence, he was met by an assistant. "Hello, Father Bidertea. His Excellency does want to see you. He is in a meeting at the moment. Please wait while I tell him you are here."

Several minutes later the assistant came back, "Follow me, the bishop will see you now."

The bishop met Xavi at the door of his private office. "Sit down, Father Bidertea. Tell me how you have been."

"Well, Your Excellency, I am just returning from San Sebastian. I extended my holiday a bit and was able to experience *La Tamborrada*."

"Ah yes, I have heard of your *La Tamborrada*. The whole city comes out to drum, don't they?"

"Yes. Children, their parents, and their grandparents. All together they come to drum and to celebrate."

"Remind me again, why you do this drumming?'

"It started as a protest to Napoleon's occupation. Because no dissent was allowed, women pounded on their wash basins as a sign of their discontent. Now it has become the biggest festival in our city."

"You Basques are an interesting bunch."

"Yes, yes we are."

The bishop thought for a moment. "It is also then a good place to take the temperature of *your people*?"

"Yes, Your Excellency, it is," Xavi answered without volunteering any of his observations.

"Well, Father Bidertea, tell me what you heard, what you saw, what you felt."

Xavi thought of how to answer the man who was to be his new bishop. He proceeded honestly, factually and without varnish. "Your Excellency, the situation, it is very unsettled."

"How so?"

"Your Excellency, being a Catalan, you know how the impulse of separatism stirs the emotions of the people. To me it feels like a period of great anticipation. It seems to me that the Basque people are waiting for an opening …"

Xavi paused for a long moment searching for the right word, "… an escape path."

"Hmmm … yes, I know this impulse and the fervor it stirs."

"Your Excellency, you being from Barcelona, I imagine you would have seen these feelings there as well."

"Indeed. We are in unsettled period, and perhaps, approaching a dangerous time. This is, in a way, why I asked you here today."

"I'm sorry, Your Excellency, I don't understand."

"Father, I am new to Salamanca, and as you yourself point out, this a turbulent time."

"Excuse me, Your Excellency, I don't see how I fit into that?"

"I need an assistant who not only knows the city, but who is also skilled and resourceful in other ways. Montserrat has told me much about you: your knowledge of languages; your ability to sail; your familiarity with the mountains; and, most importantly, your courage and constancy."

"I think Montse may be exaggerating my capabilities, Your Excellency. I am just a simple parish priest."

"Father, she is extremely fond of you—so fond I would say it is best for you and your vows that the two of you are separated by hundreds of miles."

The bishop peered directly at Xavi, as if to reinforce his point, and then continued. "I am not here to remind you of your vows or speak of my beloved goddaughter. Allow me to get the point. I wish for you to be my private secretary here in Salamanca."

Xavi was stunned. "Excuse me, Your Excellency. Your Personal Secretary?"

"Yes, exactly. I have long watched you from afar, and besides Montse's commentary, I have my own view of how valuable you can be to me, to the church."

Still a bit shocked, and not knowing whether to be flattered or to protest, the best he could do was to weakly offer up his current duties as an obstacle. "Your Excellency, what an honor, but what about my parish, St. Martin of Tours?"

Switching to a satisfied smile, the bishop responded, "Do not worry, Father, I know your bishop."

———

Book 3
Chapter 16
Salamanca, Spain
February 18, 1936

The run up to the elections had been exhausting. Incidents of serious violence, by both sides, were widespread. The shouting and hysteria had worn the country out. Bishop Pla y Deniel, like everyone, was glad they were over, and he hoped for the best—while, secretly, like most people who were religious, or believed in traditional values, or owned as a much as a cow, feared for the worst.

"Father Bidertea, do you have the newspapers? We need to study the results."

"Yes, Your Excellency, I have papers from all over the country. Would you like to start with Montserrat's article?" Xavi replied to the bishop.

"Yes, yes, let's start with her article."

Spain Moves Back to the Left
Popular Front Wins Convincing Victory
Montserrat Costa

Yesterday the Popular Front, a coalition of progressives, socialists, trade unionists, and separatists, won a narrow victory over the current center-right government in numbers of votes, but achieved a large victory in terms of seats in the parliament.

In the run up to the elections the Popular Front pounded opposing candidates on the issues of falling wages, the flagging economy, and the brutal handling of the Asturian revolution. The left campaigned on the promise that it would re-accelerate the reforms that the current government had reversed. It is now expected these reforms will focus on redistributing agrarian property and trimming the power of the church and the army.

Leaders of the Popular Front expressed the hope that this election would permanently mark the end of right-wing governments, enabling Spain to accelerate the development of a modern, progressive nation.

Shouts of election fraud were widespread among right-wing politicians. In addition, as always, there is the specter of the army injecting itself into politics and composition of the government. However in spite of the shadows cast by the army, it appears Spain will transition itself to a return of the progressive government that will implement much needed reforms.

While the country remains tense and deeply divided, the left now has the whip hand ...

The article continued on, but the bishop needed no more words to comprehend the situation.

"My dear Montserrat is so young and naïve. She cannot see the storm that is coming. Yes, it is true the elections have gone back and forth for the last five years, but it is also true the army will not sit back, watch chaos unfold, and see its privileges trimmed. At some point the radical left will push the army too far, and then there will be a violent counterattack. The military will not wait on the ballot box."

Xavi also saw the gravity of the situation. "Your Excellency, what should we do?"

"I want you to begin an inventory of our most important relics and works of art. We must have a plan to move these pieces to safe places before the storm hits."

"Yes, Your Excellency. I will start on this today."

"Father, I hate saying this: I am concerned deeply for our country, for our church. The tinder for an all-out civil war is brittle and dry. Any day a spark could ignite a conflagration."

Xavi remembered the evening in Madrid. He had seen the fires before. He wasted no time dispatching the bishop's request.

Book 3
Chapter 17
Barcelona, Spain
May 20, 1936

Montse found her mother in the sitting room with a letter lying on a table in front of her. She looked pale and seemed a million miles away.

"Mother what is it? I came as soon as I could after your phone call. You look like you have seen the devil himself."

"I feel as if I have ... read your aunt's letter."

Dearest Luisa,

Circumstances are grave here in Andalucía.

After the elections, empowered by the leftist rhetoric of 'free land' for everyone, the peasants have begun to take the agrarian reforms into their own hands. Without law, or any civilized pretense, day by day in Extremadura and here in Andalucía they have raided farms and estates taking them for themselves. Sometimes these confiscations were peaceful, often they were not. In either case the local authorities looked the other way and did nothing to protect private property, or indeed the safety of the landowners. It is an unbearably painful outrage that I know all too well from firsthand experience.

Several weeks ago, fearing for my safety, Carlos sent me away from our hacienda back to Seville. I begged him to let me stay, but he would not hear of it. Four days after I left for Seville, a mob attacked our property. Our foreman, who has been with us for twenty-five years, was killed and Carlos was beaten senselessly. We were able to rescue him to a hospital here in Seville. There he lies in a coma.

Luisa, my husband lies inches from death and our estate has been taken. I am enraged. I am angry with the politicians, and the police ... and I must tell you, even though it pains me deeply to say so,

I am also angry with Montserrat. Why was it necessary for her to write those articles on Casas Viejas? Her words did nothing but incite people who had worked peacefully on our estates for generations.

Montse felt nauseated. She could read no farther.

"Oh, Mother, this is all so terrible."

"I feel sick for my sister."

"Yes, but I am not responsible for what has happened. I did my job and I reported what I saw."

"I know, I know that."

"The conditions there were terrible, they were feudal," she responded with a combination of remorsefulness and defensiveness.

"Dear, dear, Montse, of course you are not responsible for your Uncle Carlos being in a coma, or for their estate being taken. But what I wonder is have we passed the point of no return."

"What does that mean?"

"Are we approaching some sort of apocalypse? A time which splits families apart—sets father against son, brother against brother, sister against sister, aunt against niece."

"Oh God, I hope not. I can't believe it's come to that."

"I am worried … and please don't take this wrong, but I must ask: How is your relationship with Tomás?"

"What do you mean?" Montse responded, as if her mother had hit a tender nerve.

"What I mean is, he is the man in your life, and he often gets very agitated. Everything seems to be about politics, and he has moved farther and farther to the left."

"He just wants a better Spain, a free Catalonia," Montse responded.

"Maybe, but I have to ask because no matter how privileged we are, no matter how famous you have become, no one can be fully protected from what seems to be brewing."

"Mother, Tomás is very loving; he is completely dedicated to me."

"Then why haven't you gotten married?" Luisa asked pointedly.

Montse was deeply surprised by the question, but she was conscious of not adding to her mother's distress, "He doesn't believe in marriage. He believes it is an outdated, bourgeois institution."

"What a load of nonsense! Your father and I are modern and

progressive people; we are true Catalans. I can't imagine not being married to him."

"Tomás may have some extreme political views, but he loves me, he really does."

"I can see that. I can see he loves you, but … and this may be uncomfortable for you … do you love him?"

"Oh, Mother, don't ask." Montse sighed. "I wish I could have what you and father have, but I do not. I love Tomás of course, but I am, I have been in love with someone else for a long time—someone I cannot have, someone who fills my heart and touches my soul."

"Xavi …," Luisa murmured.

Montse continued, "What I am going to do? Love someone who can't love me? Life goes on. Believe me there are many, many women who would give anything to have Tomás."

"There is so much that hurts right now. Montserrat, I have suspected what you say has been the truth since your days in Salamanca. I wish so many things were different right now."

"I know. I am building my life as best as I can. I try not to allow myself to think of any other possibilities."

"This is a time for caution, and part of caution is being careful whom you trust."

"What are you saying?"

"Remember you are part of a great family, and now you are also a well-known journalist. Be aware there may come a time when we are hunted because of our wealth, our provenance, our prominence, and your reputation. Be careful with Tomás."

Book 3
Chapter 18
Salamanca, Spain
July 15, 1936

Xavi hurried into the bishop's office with a copy of *El Progressiu*. "Your Excellency, I am so sorry to interrupt you, but it is urgent that you read Montserrat's article."

"Yes, of course, Father. Sit with me while I read it."

Madrid, Nation Torn Asunder
Montserrat Costa

Normally in Madrid on a bright, sunny July day, lovers stroll together hand in hand in the Retiro Park; sightseers walk in wonder past the *Cibeles* statue and its flowing fountain, and art enthusiasts are transfixed in the Prado by some of humanity's greatest achievements.

Today in Madrid no one pursued these simple pleasures. The city split itself into two rival camps. These sides, one not really knowing the other, faced off against one another in vicious hatred. This morning there were competing funerals. Each funeral draped in sadness. Each service mourned a fallen father, a fallen son.

After the last goodbyes were said, the funerals became competing gangs looking to settle scores with the other using fists and guns.

How did it come to be? How did the situation in Madrid unravel so precipitously?

There is so much hatred in Spain, flowing so fiercely, that it is hard to remember where it all started. Regarding the present sad events, we know that earlier this week on

July 12, Police Lieutenant José Castillo was murdered by four Falangist gunmen. They took their signals from their leader José Antonio Primo de Rivera. Lieutenant Castillo had committed no crime and done no wrong. He was murdered for being an anti-fascist, for being a socialist.

The next day, in the *Cortes*, *La Passonaria*, Delores Ibarruri, stood up and called out the right-wing leader José Calvo Sotelo, saying "this man must be silenced." Later that evening the police came to his door and arrested him, though he had committed no crime and had Parliamentary immunity. On leaving he said to his wife, "I will call later, if these fine gentlemen do not blow my brains out first."

And blow his brains out they did. His body was dumped that evening in the city cemetery.

So today we witnessed two funerals for two Spaniards who held different beliefs, who, by all accounts both loved their country, but who were killed by angry mobs who would not allow them to hold divergent beliefs. In two cemeteries mourners mourned, families wept, and dirges played. Sadness rained down as sadness does on funerals.

The only difference? One funeral ended with the leftist clenched fist salute, the other with the fascist raised palm.

In sacrilege to these deaths and their mourning families, rival mobs from the competing funerals were not able to contain their rage. No one knows who threw the first fist, but at the end of the day four more Spaniards were dead, and in a few days four more coffins will be laid into the ground.

The bishop laid the paper down. He tried to hold back his tears.

Finally, he looked up and said simply, "This is the spark. We are descending into total chaos. Pray God for the safety of all who we love and all who we shepherd … please go gather our relics and precious pieces of art and move them as we planned."

—·—

Book Four

Horror and Tragedy

Book 4
Chapter 1
Salamanca, Spain
July 19, 1936

The summer night was hot. Xavi was sleepless. He tossed and turned. He peered at the clock on his bedside table, it read 2:35 His bedroom window was open; warm air and silence poured into the room. He listened intently for sounds: gunshots, or shouts, but he heard none.

There was no doubt in his mind that an explosion was coming. He was not alone; everyone in Spain sensed the period of escalating, retaliatory lawlessness and anarchy had run its course. Everyone knew, that, like in a play, the scene needed to change.

Over the last several days Bishop Pla y Deniel was constantly on the telephone. The conversations were hushed and private. Occasionally Xavi would catch a word or two: "The army" … "General Franco" … "Spanish Morocco." He wasn't able to piece together the equation, but he imagined it involved calculations about the launching of a coup to restore order.

Xavi hadn't slept much since reading about the dueling murders in Madrid. As his fatigue grew his mind became less focused. He prayed partial prayers … "Hail Mary full of grace …", but he couldn't finish it. He thought of those he cared about. He thought about the people of Spain, the people in the Basque country, the parishioners of his former parish.

He rolled over in his bed again and kicked off his sheets. It was impossible to ward off the warm air. He was perspiring and knowing that sleep would not come any time soon, he chose to focus his attention on those he really loved, those he deeply hoped were in God's hands tonight. He prayed for their safekeeping: his parents in San Sebastian; Jaime in the Army of Africa; and Montse in Barcelona, the place which would likely be the

epicenter for the coming blast....
He continued restlessly awake.

————

Book 4
Chapter 2
Barcelona, Spain
July 19, 1936

Montse and Tomás lay motionless next to one another in her bed. For the last three nights they slept fully clothed, at the ready. The bedroom clock showed 3:58 a.m.

Like everyone else in the city, they both were on edge, waiting for the tension to be broken, for an explosion to come. The rumors were swirling everywhere that the army was fed up with the chaos and lawlessness. There was word of trouble in Spanish Morocco, and that a coup would be launched at any moment. They knew whatever mischief the army might start, they were ready, and they would repel it: Tomás with bullets and Montse with words.

Boom!!!

A horrific explosion pierced the stillness.

"Tomás! Tomás what was that!?"

"That was it! That must be the start of it!" he exclaimed. "Let's go!"

They bounded into the night air. "I am going to *Placa de Catalunya*," Tomás added urgently.

"I'm going with you." They rushed out of the apartment onto the street.

As her eyes adjusted to the darkness, Montse became aware of people, ordinary citizens like her and Tomás, in the thousands and thousands, coming from everywhere, filling the streets. Many of them had rifles, some carried grenades, and others just had rocks.

In the darkness she could feel their collective intention. They were unified in the purpose of defending Barcelona from the coup, from the army, from the forces that repressed modernity.

The coup had begun. Many rumors were swirling, but the consistent theme Montse heard was that the army had had enough, and that they were finally sparked to action by the murder of Calvo

Sotello. The word was that several thousand soldiers had left their barracks in the dark and were marching in the streets of Barcelona, to capture the city and to take the government. Spanish democracy, the Republic, the future of Spain, was at risk.

For the first few hours of the morning, she could get no accurate pulse of the tide of events—it was chaos. On one side there were tens of thousands of ordinary citizens and a few Civil Guards, Assault Guards, and local militias; and on the other side several thousand troops of the Spanish Army that had turned on its government and its people.

As the sun rose, she could see what she had previously smelled: The city was enveloped in smoke. The air was filled with the sounds of bullets firing and bombs exploding. There was no pattern. The army had shattered what peace remained in the city, and a new form of chaos reigned. At any moment Montse could not tell who held the advantage. Misinformation abounded, and bodies began to pile up, unattended, on the streets.

By late morning it seemed the soldiers leading the coup had broken through. Word came that a column of rebel troops had taken the telephone exchange and occupied several important hotels. There was despair amongst the defenders and many whispers: "Has it been lost? Are we doomed …?"

Then, as the sun rose high in the midday summer sky, the news came that most of the army troops had been pushed back. They were returning to their barracks. The mood swung wildly. She observed there was nothing like the exuberance of men who saw themselves as soon to be dead and were somehow saved. Cheers rang out. It was time for retribution. The rebels must be crushed.

The heart of the counterattack was the telephone exchange. Montse made her way there. She could see the Spanish Army column, that just hours earlier which had captured this vital link to the outside world, was now surrounded and hopelessly outnumbered. Even as she hated idea of the coup, she was repulsed by the idea that it was only a matter of time before all of these men would be overwhelmed, captured, wounded, or killed.

And so, it was by nightfall that General Goded, leader of the coup in Barcelona, surrendered. A few shots could be still be sporadically heard, but it was over. The battle was short, violent, and deadly.

Montse attempted to get counts of the dead and wounded; this counting was hellish work. The hideous estimates varied wildly, but as best she could tell, there were many hundreds dead and several thousand wounded. It would take days to get a more accurate count.

She still thought in headlines; she considered how she would report it, how she would write it. The coup had been put down. Barcelona was saved. The citizens were triumphant and jubilant. The Republic survived!

—■—

Book 4
Chapter 3
Barcelona, Republican Spain
July 20, 1936

In the late afternoon Montse sat at her typewriter, exhausted from the turmoil, and up against a deadline for her story. She was pounding out the final words describing yesterday's events when Tomás returned to her apartment.

"Where have you been? I have been so worried about you."

"With my comrades," he declared with notable satisfaction.

"Comrades?" she responded quizzically.

"Yes, Montse."

"What does that mean, comrades?"

"Yesterday we put down a coup and started a revolution."

"I'm sorry Tomás, I'm not really following you?"

"After the traitors surrendered, there were still a few holdouts in Drassanes barracks. This morning we finished them off and captured the thousands of rifles that were there. After that, a group of us went to see Companys."

"You mean Lluís Companys, President of the Government of Catalonia?" Montse responded.

"Yes."

"Why did you need to see President Companys?"

"We went to make it clear to him who had defeated the coup. We went to make it clear to him who would be in charge of Barcelona going forward."

"In charge of Barcelona? What do you mean in charge of Barcelona?" she asked.

"We told him that we, the Central Committee of Antifascist Militias of Catalonia, would be in charge of the city going forward."

"Do you realize who you were talking to?"

175

"I did…."

"Companys has given his life trying to build a Catalan Republic—he spent most of the last two years in jail for his commitment to our cause. What did he say?"

"What could he say? In truth it was us, the anarchists, who saved the city, who saved Catalonia from the reactionary forces of Spain. We have the guns. We are now the power here in Barcelona."

Montse was stunned. Tomás' strong views had crossed the line to dangerous extremism. "I cannot talk about this right now. I need to get my article to *El Progressiu* before the publication deadline."

She typed her last few words, took her pages from her typewriter, and rushed out into the streets.

Everywhere she looked were the dead, alone or in piles. Catalans attended their own, but no one attended the Spanish soldiers. The once proud young men began to rot in the summer heat. She felt sick.

She hurried on. The city smelled of fire and tasted of ash. She passed by a burnt-out church; its precious, sacred objects were cast in a heap in front of it. A few blocks on, just before the offices off *El Progressiu*, she passed another church in ruins. This one ghastlier than the last: tombs of nuns cast open and skeletons strewn on the pavement.

She saw, smelt, and even, she thought, tasted death. It was apocalyptic. Montse doubled over and retched.

She stood up slowly, wobbly, recovering her balance slightly, she thought, *what is this madness that has descended on my city?*

Book 4
Chapter 4
Barcelona, Republican Spain
July 21, 1936

At around nine a.m. Montse got up and dressed. She had not slept one moment all night. She could not shake the images, the smells, and the tastes of the prior day. She was haunted by it all.

After she dressed, she found Tomás in the kitchen, having a coffee. Montse had already seen enough of this so called "revolution." It was time to confront him.

"Tomás the city is a nightmare."

"What can you mean—we were victorious?"

"Militias, mobs really, roam the streets with rifles; they travel as if they are packs of wild animals; churches are burned, and tombs are desecrated. What is this?"

"Montse, I told you, it's a revolution. A great revolution."

"Stop with that! We have a democratic republic!"

"Not anymore. We have a revolution. A revolution to overthrow and overturn all the old ways, including this bourgeois republic."

"And you approve of the burning of the churches and the desecrating of scared tombs? This is not revolutionary. It is barbaric. It is nihilistic."

"Like in Russia, the first thing that must be torn down is the church, their myths and fairytales, this nonsensical illusion of God."

"This is not Russia, Tomás! We are in Catalonia. We are in Spain!"

"Montse, if you wish to remain a liberal progressive, a Republican, you may do so, but know you will be on the wrong side of history and on the wrong of things—on the wrong side of me."

Montse was shocked. Shocked at what she had seen, and what her lover had said. At that moment, her mother's words of caution

177

came to her: *Be careful with Tomás.* She now saw it clearly; her mother had been right. Tomás was dangerous.

The combination of the images she had seen, her fatigue, and Tomás' radical words pushed her past the breaking point. She was in no mood to debate political theory or how they might bridge their differences. She screamed. "Get out! You animal, get out of my apartment!"

Tomás slowly sipped the last drops of his coffee. He leered directly at her and replied smugly as he got up to leave, "Be careful Montse."

"What do you mean be careful?"

"You, your kind, your family, you are no longer the power here." He slammed the door as he left.

Montse had no time to contemplate the confrontation and the loss of her lover. She had more pressing concerns. *I need to get to my family. I need to make sure they are safe. I need to make them leave Barcelona.*

She rushed out of the apartment and made her way to her family's home. The passing of time and the hot summer sun intensified the grisly sights and smells. But she blocked them out. She had a mission.

Upon arriving at her family's estate she found her father, mother, and sister in a confused, disabled state. "Where is Jordi?" she asked.

Her father looked up with worry and sadness and replied, "Our textile factory was taken over by the workers. He was taken captive."

"Where is he now?" Montse demanded.

"I, I am not sure ..." her father replied with a defeated tone.

She could see her father was in shock. This grand man, he was a hero to her—so elegant, intelligent, worldly—he had been brought low by only two days of the horror. He was not thinking clearly. He was spinning, and he could not manage this crisis. She took charge.

First, she rapidly retold the events of the last days: the coup, the counterattack against the plotters; the jubilance at that the surrender; the horror of the churches being burned; the hungry, menacing, marauding look of the militias on the street; and finally, her personal battle, her clash with Tomás.

After recounting it all, she summed up what must happen, "Mother, Father, you are not safe here."

"Maybe it will pass," her mother said.

"No! You must take Elena and leave the city. You must leave the country. You must leave now—while you can!"

"We have to stay. We must be here for Jordi," her mother murmured.

For the second time this day, she channeled a force from deep within her, this time not out of rage, but out of love. "No! Mother, you must go, you all must go. You must go now! Everything is crashing down, and you must go while there are still ways to get out—to escape. In a few days you will be trapped."

"Where to? ... Our driver is nowhere to be found ... Where would we go?" her father asked in a soft, confused, tone.

"Get some things, what you can pack easily. Drive to France; from there you can go to our apartment in Paris. You must go now!"

The second time she said, "You must go now!" seemed to rouse her father from his shock. "Yes, yes, Montse is right. We must go. But you must come with us."

She had anticipated this moment, and she replied sternly, "No Father, this is my time to stay. To write about what happens, to tend to Jordi. You, Mother, and Elena must go now."

"Montse is right." Joan Costa said, ending the discussion.

They went to pack a few things, and a few minutes later her father drove away with her mother and sister. *When will I see them again? Will I see them again?* she thought, as her internal dialogue veered in a new direction ... toward a prayer.

After their car was out of sight she felt alone. And in her loneliness, she wondered where Xavi was: if he had been hunted; if he was dead; if his body was lying in the street somewhere, rotting in the sun.

Book 4
Chapter 5
Tetuan, Spanish Morocco
July 20, 1936

Jaime took a break from packing his vital items. He, and his fellow soldiers of the Army of Africa were shortly to be transported to the Spanish peninsula. As he packed, he began to compose in his mind the elements of his final letter to his father before leaving.

What is important? That he was the safe, of course. That the coup here had been a walk-over. In Spanish Morocco, the army had been met with more nonchalance than resistance. There had been only a few casualties, including one soldier, who broke his arm climbing a remote flagpole replacing the Republican flag with the Spanish red and yellow horizontal bars.

He also needed to report that he would be leaving for Seville shortly. To Seville with Colonel Yague, where General de Llano had secured a beachhead for the army. This was the beachhead from which Spain would be quickly liberated from the evil forces that had put it in a vice grip of darkness and chaos. He thought about it, and concluded it wasn't necessary to mention that they would be ferried by German and Italian planes. The liberation of Spain was about Spaniards. It was about Spanish glory.

He also wanted to ask for news. The reports about the progress of the liberation of Spain were spotty. Everyone knew Barcelona and Catalonia, would be difficult, but what about the other cities? What about Madrid? What about his brother Juan? Juan, in Madrid, how was he? What were the reports?

<del>◦—◦</del>

Book 4
Chapter 6
Salamanca, Nationalist Spain
July 25, 1936

Xavi returned from having a coffee at the *Café Novelty*. All was calm in Salamanca. The coup had met little resistance in the old university city ... just a few, almost harmless, left-wing professors shouted slogans at the Army. It was more of a protest than real resistance. Salamanca, as almost all of the conservative heartland of Spain, quickly submitted to the Nationalists. There was little fuss, and people paid almost no attention to the changing of the flags in the *Plaza Mayor*. There were now two Spains.

Xavi saw Professor Unamuno as he walked back to the Bishop's Palace, and even the great professor supported the army's actions. "Separatism and wanton violence must be stamped out. So yes, in a limited sense, I support the Nationalists. But soon, very soon, democracy must be restored—we cannot go backwards."

When Xavi returned to the Episcopal Palace, he found the Bishop surrounded by, and in deep study, of maps of Spain.

Without looking up the Bishop acknowledged Xavi, "Thank God General de Llano took Seville."

"Excuse me, Your Excellency?"

"Yes, had he not done so, there would be no way to get Franco's army back to the mainland from Africa."

"I see ..."

"The coup did not come off as it was planned. Too many of the big cities did not fall. It is easy to be deceived by the calm in Salamanca. Here, even Unamuno supported it."

"Yes, I heard. I just saw him. People are strolling in the *Plaza Mayor* as if nothing happened."

"Thanks be to God. It is not the case in Madrid, Bilboa, your hometown of San Sebastian, in most of Andalucía, in Valencia, and, of course, in Barcelona."

"I hate to think of Montserrat being cut off, of not seeing her articles."

"I'm afraid she will go silent to us. Barcelona is on the other side of a dark curtain."

Xavi paused, thinking of what Montse might be enduring; though he rarely saw her these days, it pained him to think that she was out of reach. "What comes next, Your Excellency?"

"I'm not exactly sure. It is like a boxing match: after the boxers have each landed their best punches, both expecting a knockout, but looking stunned, wobbly, only to see their opponent is still standing. I believe both sides are coming to the realization that there will be no quick knockout, that they will be going fifteen rounds against each other. It's a civil war now."

"Your Excellency, you speak as if we have a boxer in this fight?"

"We do, we do, Father. If the Nationalists do not win, we, our church, will be exterminated. There is no other way."

—•—

Book 4
Chapter 7
Seville, Nationalist Spain
August 10, 1936

In the first days of the coup General de Llano successfully took Seville. It was a brutal assault. His troops were vicious. In particular, they showed no mercy to the workers in the Tirana district of the city. Hundreds were rounded up and killed after the town was secured. There was little distinction paid between workers and fighters, between true Republicans and Anarchists.

General de Llano was not a stickler for niceties. He was a ruthless extremist. He hated in equal measure Socialists, Communists, Anarchists and Separatists. To him, the so-called Republic was just a vat for the foul ingredients of humanity. As far as he was concerned, the faster they were killed off the sooner the old ways would be reestablished.

Job one was a success: establishing the beachhead in Seville. It was to here that Franco's troops were ferried from Africa by their sympathetic Germans and the Italians supporters.

Having arrived on a German plane to Seville in this convoy, Jaime waited for his call to action. He was ready to fight. The plan was to move north from Seville and quickly strike a deathblow to the Republic by taking Madrid. He had no doubt the march to Madrid would be swift, and that soon Republican red, yellow, and purple flag would be torn down and supplanted by the red and yellow colors of the true Spain.

He was told his unit, with Colonel Yague in charge, would be moving out shortly. He made one last check of his mail and found a letter from his father.

Dearest Jaime,
This is the worst, most difficult letter I have ever written.
There is no easy way to say this —your brother was murdered.

On July 20th he was at his post in the Montana barracks in Madrid when his unit was overwhelmed by thousands of Republican troops and gangs of anarchists.

The senior officers, seeing that they were insurmountably outmanned, and that the situation was hopeless, waived the white flag of surrender. The white flag did not stop the assault. These—animals—this red riffraff—came to kill. They came with knives, picks, and axes. They committed barbarous atrocities in the barracks. Juan is dead.

I am inconsolable. There was no mercy, no honor, no basic human decency, no last rights, no proper Catholic burial.

This is not all—there is no word of the whereabouts of Ana and little Pilar. Communications with Madrid have been cut, and travel in and out of the city is restricted. It is all too much, and I am sick at the thought of Juan's wife and daughter living like prisoners in this alien land.

Jaime, my dear son, I do not know how I will escape this grief. As you reconquest Spain, please remember Juan, and please know what Godless evil you confront as you head into this battle. Kill them all!

Jaime was grief-stricken.

Images of his brother raced through his mind: long days with him in the vineyard, vivid thoughts of the last time he had been with them at Pilar's baptism. In his mind's eye he could see his brother with Ana and Pilar, his friend Xavi pouring sacred water over the beautiful baby girl's precious little head. After the ceremony, the celebration, an afternoon of joy, and a respite from the chaos boiling up all around Spain. He could not believe this would be his last image of his brother.

He was nauseated. There was sickness everywhere in Spain in these days, and right there and then, in a rage, he made a commitment to himself to avenge Juan's death.

He committed himself to killing them all.

—◆—

Book 4
Chapter 8
Salamanca, Nationalist Spain
August 21, 1936

It had been a month since the coup was launched. Salamanca remained calm. Life continued on as it had before. There was no conflict as far as Xavi could see from the Bishop's Palace.

The war seemed far away, that is, until he opened Jaime's letter. With just a few words the war landed in his lap. Xavi was not prepared for his friend's words: *Juan ... he was killed.*

But Jaime's letter was more than an expression of grief; it was an exhortation for help. Jaime wrote of his anger and his feeling of helplessness. Juan was gone; he would be avenged, but it was Ana and Pilar who needed urgent assistance. They were lost in Madrid, as if overboard at sea.

Jaime made a direct plea to his friend: *My father and I do not know where else to turn, you must be able to help ... maybe your bishop will know someone in Madrid ...*

Xavi put the letter down and left his office. Head down, he strode across the street to the cathedral, to the tiny chapel of St. Martin. The chapel was his refuge. Small, tucked out the way, covered by stunning Romanesque frescoes, it was the place where he sought peace.

As he knelt to pray, he noticed that even in this out-of-the way chapel, dozens of candles had been lit. *So many silent prayers,* he thought. Looking at the tiny wax pillars flickering in the darkened chapel he thought, *the candles do not have a side.* They were not color coded and divided, one group against another. He knew the church had taken a side, but he was not so certain that God had done so as well. There were heroism and atrocity on both sides.

The act of prayer calmed Xavi. It was as if God reached down into his soul and lifted his despair and worry away. It always seemed to work this way for him; when he called Him, He came and took away his pain and worry.

Clarity came to Xavi. He immediately saw what he was called to do. He must go and find Ana and her daughter Pilar—Pilar, the little girl he had baptized just months before.

Recomposed, focused, he walked back across to the Bishop's Palace and was told the Bishop wished to see him. There, the Bishop continued to study his maps of Spain, calculating the progress, and speculating on the next shoe to drop.

"Yes, Your Excellency, how may I assist you?"

"Father, the conflict is a month old now, and it is time we take stock of it and to lay out what should be done. First let's listen to General de Llano's broadcast to see if there is any news today."

In the short period of the conflict Xavi had grown to loathe the Nationalist general. Every night the general took to the radio … the signal of his broadcast was strong enough to be heard throughout Spain. He trafficked in hysteria, hyperbole, and threats. His purpose was terror.

Piecing it all together, the reports, the rumors, the nightly radio broadcasts by General de Llano, when one filtered out the propaganda, told of more or less a stalemate between the Republicans and the Nationalists.

"Yes, Your Excellency. However, I must say I do not find the general the best representative for the Nationalist cause."

"I agree. I too dislike the man, but amongst his nightly rants are often valuable little nuggets on the direction and progress of the war."

Yes, it is a war now, Xavi thought. *It's not a coup, or a conflict. It's a war. A civil war.*

At 8:00 p.m. sharp they turned the radio on, and from the little box the general howled his outrages. As always, he ranted about the communists and the Catalans—twin cancers he called them. These so-called cancers being a justification for whatever vicious assault or atrocity seemed necessary to rid Spain of them. Xavi thought General de Llano was disgusting.

Switching off the radio the Bishop concluded, "Father, there was not much in his mad ranting tonight. But we need to face the facts."

"Your Excellency, you are much more informed than I am—

how do you see it?"

"Here is how I see it: Certain generals decided that they had seen enough chaos in our country, and they launched a coup to restore order. The coup failed, a stalemate ensued, and this stalemate has morphed into a civil war, a bloody civil war."

"So it seems."

The bishop continued his summary, "The Republicans are currently in a dominant position. They hold most of the country and virtually all of the important cities: Madrid, Barcelona, Valencia, and Bilboa."

"Your Excellency, are you suggesting the conflict, this civil war, will be won by the Republicans?"

"No, I do not think so. For all their advantages the Republican side is torn apart with internal strife: anarchists against communists, both of them against true Republicans, and Catalans and Basques running for their independence. In addition, we, I mean the Nationalists, have a small but dedicated group of professional soldiers who are led by efficient, you could say ruthless, men. Also do not be surprised if the Germans and Italians press the scales our way—they detest the Marxists who are leading this revolution. For now we have a stalemate. In the long run I am betting on General Franco. Pray to God this will be the case."

"Your Excellency, we are churchmen—what does this mean to us?"

"Father, in a civil war everyone must take a side."

"Take a side …?"

"There is no such thing as neutrality in a civil war. There is no safe harbor. We may find some of the Nationalists, like General de Llano, abhorrent, and some of the acts of our troops to be atrocious, but at the end of the day this is a simple decision."

"How so?"

"One side proclaims its allegiance to our faith and our church; and the other side is aggressively trying to destroy it. I am a bishop, and you are a priest. We are shepherds of men. Our flock is dispersed and under attack. It is clear: We must gather them. We must save them. It's that simple."

"But here in Salamanca life goes on much as it always has," Xavi said quizzically.

"It's true. In fact, since the war started, we see more people than ever streaming into our churches. But in the red zones, it is a holocaust. The reports are nightmarish: bishops, priests, nuns, brothers, devout lay people—slaughtered in the tens of thousands. Churches burned, tombs turned open and laid bare, skeletons desecrated. Relics and irreplaceable treasures have been destroyed. For every religious killed or captured there are many, many more hiding in fear from the hunt."

"The reports of horrible—"

"Father, enough of ringing our hands; it's time for action. Here is what we are to do: we are going to rescue as many of our brothers and sisters in Christ as can be saved."

Whatever can he mean? Xavi wondered.

His Bishop then looked the young man squarely in the eyes; he intensely focused on him and said, "Father, I want you to lead this mission for our church. You need to rescue as many of our brothers in Christ as you can."

He paused and then continued, "This mission is to save the church in Spain. It is of the highest priority, and it has great visibility all the way to the top of the Vatican."

"Yes," Xavi stammered, "I can see how important this is, but what is the mission—and why me?"

"It is no accident you are here with me. There are many mysteries, but no accidents, in God's world. I have had my eyes on you since we met in Avila in 1923. You are uniquely skilled for this: your knowledge of languages, your outdoorsmanship, your intelligence, your thoroughness. You are both cautious and bold. This mission is part espionage and part rescue. I am highly confident that if anyone can do it, it is you."

Xavi, assuming this was meant as a compliment said, "Thank you, Your Excellency."

"Father Bidertea, one last thing. This will be extremely dangerous. You will be required to move in and out of enemy, Republican, territory. If you were to be captured, you would be treated as a spy and a priest. Your death would be certain and painful. You are not bound by your vows to accept my request. Father, think about it."

Xavi heard the Bishop's warning, but really, he only thought of

Jaime's request to find Ana and Pilar. "Your Excellency, I accept, on one condition."

"Yes, Father, what is that?"

"I need to start this project in Madrid."

"I'm sure that can be accommodated as there is much to do there. Father, you must think this over. Let us meet in the morning to discuss it further."

Book 4
Chapter 9
Salamanca, Nationalist Spain
August 22, 1936

The Bishop was waiting for Xavi when he went to see him first thing in the morning. "Come in, Father, come in. How did you sleep? Have you changed your mind since we spoke last night?"

"No, no, Your Excellency. I know what I am called to do," Xavi said calmly and firmly.

"Excellent. Okay, let's get down to the practical details."

The bishop paused for a moment then continued, "You will work directly with me. No one else is to know about this. No one, not even your parents—expanding the circle is too dangerous."

"Yes, Your Excellency." Xavi nodded his understanding.

On his desk was a rump sack, an odd accoutrement for a bishop's fine desk. Before explaining the purpose of it, the bishop opened his safe and took out an accordion folder. From it, he pulled out a French Passport bearing the name Patrick Azerbergui.

"Father, this will be your identity. When on your mission, in France or in Republican territory, you will be Patrick Azerbergui. You are Patrick. You are a French citizen from Saint-Jean-de-Luz. We choose this identity as we assumed that you, being from San Sebastian, would know Saint-Jean-de-Luz well."

"Yes, Your Excellency, I have been there many times."

Xavi inspected the passport; it looked real and the personal details seemed to match his own. "How did you get this? It appears to be an authentic French Passport."

The bishop smiled. "It is, Father, it is. As I mentioned yesterday, this mission has friends in high places."

The bishop continued, "When you are on your mission, when you are Patrick, I recommend you speak in French or Catalan. Speaking too much Spanish or Basque could raise suspicions about your true identity and purpose—remember these are dangerous times. The second item I have for you is this rump sack."

"But, Your Excellency, I have several of these," Xavi said in mild protest.

"Yes, Father, I am sure you do, but I doubt any of them have the unique characteristic that this one has."

Xavi looked puzzled as he carefully examined the sack.

The bishop gently took it from him. "Father, there is a hidden compartment in the back. This compartment is where you will keep things that should not be discovered by either side. When in the Nationalist territory you must keep your French identify hidden, and when elsewhere, vice versa. Also it is a place to keep the money you will need, and, of course, any small religious articles you may have with you. The compartment is sewn shut and after you have torn it open you will need to use this needle and cord to reseal it."

The bishop then pulled out three packets of money. "Here is one hundred thousand *Pesetas*, two hundred thousand French *Francs*, and ten thousand US Dollars. They are in large denominations so as to not use too much space. Be prudent but spare no expense. Do what you deem is necessary."

Xavi remained silent, taking in all the bishop was telling him.

"As you have requested to go to Madrid, we have arranged for your first mission to be the saving of five nuns who are trapped there. First you are to go to Perpignan in France. There you will see Jacques Latour at this address on the Rue de la Laterne. He will give you further instructions."

"Is that all? The whole mission seems vague and uncertain, Your Excellency."

"I give you few instructions. I sit here safely in my palace—I cannot imagine what uncertainties, travails, and dangers you will face. God has brought you to this point. You will be in His hands. The details I leave to you."

"I will do my best—"

"Not your best, Father. Do what you need to do to save our brothers and sisters. We are placing enormous faith in you."

The bishop paused before changing topics. "You will of course leave your priest clothes here when you are on your missions. And

one last thing, Father, you should not wear that medal of San Sebastian you always wear. I assume that your being from the city of
this saint's name, that this medal somehow has a special meaning
to you. You must remove it, as it will not be safe to wear it in the
Republican zone."

"I know what you are asking me to do. I understand about the
dangers, and I understand about my medal," Xavi touched the
medal as his thoughts floated back to the mob that had attacked
the convent in Madrid, to the nuns he saved that night.

He knew his mission.

Book 4
Chapter 10
Perpignan, France
August 26, 1936

Spain was now a divided country. It took Xavi two days to cir-
cuitously journey from Salamanca to Perpignan. First, he took
the train to Pamplona, an unbroken route across traditional, conservative, and Nationalist Spain. Crossing the ancient provinces
of Castile, Leon, and Navarre he saw no sign of the war. As the
train passed great estates and small family farms, he saw workers
laboring in the fields, seemingly unbothered by events elsewhere
in Spain.

Once in Pamplona, he made his way across town from the train
station. The small streets he traversed were a bit of a maze, criss-
crossing, meandering, until suddenly he landed in the town's main
square, the *Plaza Castillo*.

He stopped in the old square. The *Gran Hotel La Perla* and *Café
Iruna* were right in front of him, and the *Calle de al Estafeta* was
just off the plaza to his right. There, in the plaza, as mothers walked
slowly, arm in arm with their daughters, and as children hopped
and ran and laughed, he closed his eyes, and for a few moments he
called up the past. He was in July 1924. The bulls galloped by; local
families sang and danced; Hemingway and his party boisterously
celebrated—and Montse reached across to kiss him.

Where had it all gone? The time? The innocence? The country
itself? And where had Montse gone? Where was she now? *Please
God hold her safe.*

Xavi opened his eyes, turned away from the plaza and proceeded to the bus station. Pamplona sat in a plain below the Pyrenees,
the mountains that created a curtain between Spain and France.
He was only about twenty miles from the border, and he hopped
on a bus heading there; he got off in Valcarlos and he walked the

final few miles to Saint-Jean-Pied-de-Port in France. He was no longer Xavi Bidertea, he was now Patrick Azerbergui.

At the border, the French guard inspected his passport and waived him through with a pleasant, casual *"Bonjour."* From Saint-Jean-Pied-de-Port he took a train up to Bordeaux; a second train took him down to Toulouse; and finally, a third one brought him to Perpignan.

He headed to his pension where he dropped off his duffle bag. Next, he stopped for a coffee at a small *café*. He had never been to Perpignan before, but was immediately struck that the place was teaming with Catalan speakers. Everywhere adult men speaking Catalan were doing menial work: bellboys, bar tenders, taxi drivers, waiters, and the like.

Suspecting his waiter was one of these many Catalans, he asked, "Are you from here?"

"No *monsieur,* I am from Girona, just over the border in Catalonia, in Spain," he responded in wobbly French.

"Oh, I see …"

"When the war started it was an explosion. In addition to the actual shrapnel flying, people also flew. Thousands of us were blown here, scrambling across the border, taking what we could carry or stuff into our cars."

"Why did you feel you needed to leave?" Xavi asked.

"After the coup failed, immediately Catalonia became a lawless land. Years of hatred and envy were unloosed towards almost anyone who was middle class or above, or who was thought to be conservative, or who was seen as in way religious."

"Really?"

"Worse than you can imagine. With no law and no God, scores were settled quickly and violently. I owned a small factory and my wife, my children, and I barely got out. We were among the lucky ones—at least we are alive, and our family is intact," he said with a tone of deepest sadness and loss.

"Oh, I am so sorry to hear of your plight, *monsieur.*"

"We were able to bring a little money, but this will soon run out. I wait tables and my wife cleans houses. I do not know what we will do."

His instinct was to console the man in a religious way, but he thought better of reassuring him that God will provide somehow. Unsure of how Patrick would respond, he was silent.

The waiter continued, "Everyone there in Catalonia pretends that they invented a new world—'comrade this and comrade that'—that now everyone is an equal. What a farce! The educated, the productive, the faithful, have been imprisoned, exiled, or killed. Girona is now run by people with little education and lots of hatred—and Russians are everywhere there."

"Russians? In Girona?"

"Yes, all of Catalonia is teeming with Russians. The Republic is lost."

Xavi was moved but had no idea how to help. He left a generous tip. He departed feeling awkward and off balance. It pained him to not say that he would hold the man in his prayers.

He noticed something else: people who seemed to be watching him while he walked to find Jacques Latour. There was a strange, sinister feeling in the air in Perpignan. There were many men in shadows, in doorways; he felt distrust and suspicion.

Xavi came to the address he had been given for Jacques Latour on the Rue de la Laterne. The building was a small warehouse. The sign said, *"Les Amis de la République de Espagnole."* He looked over both shoulders before entering and then called out *"Bonjour,* I'm looking for *Monsieur* Latour."

Out of the shadows emerged a middle-aged man with dark bushy hair and a thick moustache. He inquired in French "Who is asking?"

"I am Patrick Azerbergui," Xavi said, not knowing if his name would open the way, and not knowing what would come next if it didn't.

Hearing the name Latour's demeanor changed immediately. "Yes, come in, welcome. I have been expecting you."

"Where am I? What do you do here?"

"I run a small charity. When the war broke out, I started *Les Amis de la République de Espagnole.* There is much to do. I understand you have come to help."

"I think so …"

"I have a truckload of supplies for you to take to Madrid. Here is the address to where you are to take them. Understood?"

"I'm not sure exactly," Xavi said haltingly.

"And if you have time when you get there, if you could stop and say hello to some friends of mine. Five women, they need special attention. They are at *Calle Lope de Vega 16*, apartment 5C. Can you remember that? *Calle Lope de Vega 16*, apartment 5C."

"Yes, I will remember that." Xavi said. He remained uncertain that he had understood the signal he was given.

"Remember these five women need you, they need your special attention. *Calle Lope de Vega 16*."

The second time Latour mentioned the women, it clicked for Xavi that this was the mission, the women, the five nuns. "Yes, I will see the women."

Finally, the man, after looking around and seeing no one about, reached over and embraced Xavi. He whispered in his ear, "Be very, very careful, Father. This is dangerous work you do."

Book 4
Chapter 11
Madrid, Republican Spain
August 28, 1936

Xavi arrived in Madrid late in the afternoon. It was sweltering hot. The summer heat had Spain in a stranglehold.

Two days earlier he had left Jacque Latour's warehouse. After he left Perpignan, he drove two hours toward the looming Pyrenees. Just before reaching the border, he stopped at an *auberge* for lunch. The place, and its proprietress, *Madame Chenot*, radiated warmth and welcome. He made note of it for his return—should he return.

At the border, the Republican guards welcomed him in French and Catalan, *"Bienvenue, benvinguts."* They hailed him as hero, a supporter of the cause, of the Republic.

Xavi made his way to Madrid through Barcelona and Valencia. Everywhere he passed, in the cities and towns, the people seemed jubilant, energetic. A revolution was afoot.

He did not share these feelings. He was not Patrick. He was not an aide worker to the Republic. He was Xavier Bidertea, a Catholic priest, and the other things he saw sickened him. Every church ransacked, burned, and in many cases their tombs thrown onto the streets, laid bare, bones strewn, stewing in the hot sun.

When he arrived in Madrid the mood was different. The city was on the frontline, just twenty miles away from the advancing Nationalist Army. In Extremadura, Badajoz had recently fallen, and the Nationalist troops were surging towards the city from the south and the west. Today, for the first time, the city had been bombed by Nationalist airplanes. This was no time for celebration, no time to fill the *cafés* to drink, to sing, and debate political theory. Madrid was at war.

Xavi parked his truck and checked into his hotel near the *Plaza del Sol*. As he set off on foot, nearly everyone looked harried, terrified, nervous, and worried. A stranger stopped him on the *Paseo Castellana*, and before Xavi could even say hello, the man blurted out, "The bombings were awful. It was all so alien and confusing. First, we heard a faint buzzing in the distance, then it grew louder... *'what could that be?'* Finally, the planes came into sight. They flew low and next we saw the bombs drop. They hissed as they twisted and turned, falling to the ground. Many people did not know to run for cover. Dozens of innocent people were killed and many more wounded. We are civilians. The Nationalists are murderers!"

Again, he did not know how to respond. He could see the horror. As a priest he felt he should run to the killed and wounded to attend to them. As Patrick Azerbergui, he was an aid worker who had to continue his mission. He detached himself, head down, and responded without real emotion, *"Qui, c'est terrible, je suis tellement désolé."*

He had to find Juan's wife and daughter. He had to rescue the nuns on the *Calle Lope de Vega*.

There was rubble from the bombings everywhere. He picked his way around the piles and loose pieces of buildings and glass strewn on the street, and after about fifteen minutes he arrived at the address Jaime had given him for Juan's wife: *Calle Claudio Coello* 47. The apartment was in a fashionable district and had a concierge. He rang the bell, and a middle-aged woman answered.

"What do you want?" she snarled at him.

Xavi stammered, *"Madame de la Calzada et sa fille, ¿s'il vous plaît?"*

The concierge looked both threatened and threatening. "They are not here. You need to go!" she replied in Spanish.

Xavi attempted to construct a follow up, but before he could get it out, she added emphatically, "You need to go. You need to go now!"

Discouraged, Xavi said nothing more and left; he needed time to regroup. While walking away, he noted there was another, younger, woman in the lobby who must have overheard the short conversation. She followed him out onto to the street.

"I heard you ask for Ana and her baby Pilar," she commented in Spanish.

She had a kind face, and something in her way made him believe he could trust her. He switched to Spanish, "Yes, Juan's brother sent me to find them."

"Ana is dead."

"What? How?"

"I do not know how exactly—there are too many dead to get all the stories straight. It seems she went to find her husband at the barracks. The mob murdered her too."

Xavi was struck low. "Are you sure? Are you really sure?"

"Yes, I am sure. The reason I know is that she asked me to care for Pilar while she went to look for Juan. When she did not come back, I asked about her and heard she had been killed."

"Oh, *Dios mio...*"

The woman continued, "That is not all of it."

"What do you mean?"

"Three days later an officer and his wife came to my door. The woman said she was Juan's sister and that she would take the baby. I was suspicious, as I had never heard that he had a sister. I tried to resist, but the officer took the baby from my arms and they left. Pilar was hysterical ... I am a wreck. First Ana and Juan were killed, and now their daughter—taken, kidnapped."

Xavi was horrified. He could not believe what he was hearing.

The woman continued, "There is terror everywhere. Friends killed and wounded, churches burned and looted, and now today the airplanes dropping bombs—but taking a child! You should have seen little Pilar's face when she was taken—fearful, crying, holding her arms out to me as she was carried away. I must not say more. You cannot trust anyone. Spies and snitches are everywhere. Friends turn on friends. I need to go."

She scurried back into her building. She did not look back.

Xavi was devastated. He had failed. How would he break the news to Jaime and his father?

He was in freefall. The only path forward for a redemption was the nuns. He could not allow himself to fail twice in one trip. The nuns. I must get to the nuns. I must save them.

He prayed for Juan and Ana, and he prayed for little Pilar, wherever she might be.

Book 4
Chapter 12
Madrid, Republican Spain
August 30, 1936

To the west of the city, not more than twenty miles from the center of Madrid, opposing lines had been drawn.

The Republican line was manned by a mix of a small group from the regular army loyal to the Republic, citizens of Madrid, and a contingent of the International Brigades.

It was an enthusiastic, if disorganized, lot. The citizen soldiers from the city often behaved as if they were on a picnic. On many days they came to the front around noon, fired a few shots, sang some revolutionary songs, had lunch with red wine, then returned to the city to boast about their valor, all in time for their evening dinner.

The members of the International Brigades were a different matter. They were unified in passionate hatred of the Nationalists. To them, the Nationalists were a new branch of the bad tree of Fascism. Hitler, Mussolini, and Franco were all vile enemies of their view of the world: a utopian world of equality; a worker's state, where the evils of capitalism and the ridiculousness of religion, Catholicism mainly, would be eradicated once and for all. Fascism must not advance a mile further they thought; in Spain the battle lines had been drawn. *"No pasarán,"* they shall not pass, was their cry.

These men were true believers, zealots. They came from America, Canada, England, France, Germany, Australia—all over, really. They were an odd mix, falling into one of two groups. There were the intellectuals: professors, poets, artists, and other assorted eggheads. Beside them in arms were true tough guys: truckers, longshoremen, and other union laborers—the vanguard of the workers movement. Their grievances with capitalism were not theoretical. They bore actual scares from their fights with the bosses.

In addition to hating Franco, they agreed on one other principle: their model for the future looked more like the Soviet Union than the United States. They were more Marx than Madison. Few spoke Spanish. Language differences didn't matter much; the job was easy: point your rifle straight ahead, defend the line, and kill as many fascists as you could.

Xavi arrived at the Republican side of the front. It was not hard to find French speakers, and he was welcomed as a brother in arms as he unloaded coffee, tins of meat, cans of fruit, and water. He served the men, and some women too. Their spirits were high, having just put the coup down in Madrid. They knew what had to be done: push Franco and his troops back into whatever cave from which they had crawled out. In their minds, there was no possibility that Fascism would prevail. They were on a mission to not only save Spain, but also the world.

As he passed out food and water, Xavi mingled with the troops and civilians. They quickly took to him, joking and calling him *"Frenchie."* He could see they were long on enthusiasm but short on organization and military discipline. All the while, he watched both battle lines, he scouted for a place he could cross to the Nationalist side.

At the end of the second day of serving the Republicans, after the sun went down on a warm summer night, Xavi went up a small hill, a small mound really, that he had previously spotted. The place was covered in a stand of pine trees, and from there he could see the Nationalist encampment. It was not more than hundred yards away.

Attempting to make himself invisible to both sides, slowly, he began to crawl on his stomach toward the Nationalist line. After a few minutes he stopped; he laid flat on the ground, as silent as could be. He was just a few yards from the Nationalist encampment and heard only Spanish spoken. There, vulnerable and exposed, Xavi took a white handkerchief out of his pack and said in Spanish, "Please don't shoot!"

The sentries saw him. They jumped to attention and pointed their rifles at him. He craned his neck upward and pleaded,

"Please don't shoot," and added, "I am a priest."

"Come forward! Keep your hands where we can see them."

"Okay," he said putting his hands up as if he were a prisoner.

"Who are you? Why are you here?"

"I am a Spanish priest, Father Xavier Bidertea."

"Really? You are more likely to be a communist spy than a Spanish priest!"

"Take me to your commander, and I will explain everything."

"No tricks, or you will be dead before morning. Give us your backpack."

Xavi followed the sentries, walking past men resting in sleeping bags. Soon they entered a tent. The officer was awake, fully dressed in his uniform and studying maps.

"Captain, this man tried to breach our line just now. He says he is a priest."

"What? What would a priest be doing out here crawling through the dirt?" the captain asked to no one in particular. "Well, Father, what's your story?"

"It's true, I am a priest. I am here trying to find a route to get five nuns to safety." Xavi's words floated away into the night air.

"That's a crazy notion."

"He had this," the young sentry volunteered, handing the captain Xavi's pack.

The young captain searched the pack, "Spanish Priest? All I see here is the French passport for Patrick Azerbergui."

"Please let me have my pack."

"Okay but remember, three rifles are pointed at you."

"This pack has a hidden compartment—let me show you."

The captain nodded to the sentries.

Xavi took the pack and opened the secret compartment. He pulled out his Spanish passport and shared it with the young officer.

"I see … and you also carry a lot of money?"

"Yes, I am on my own out here, and I have been instructed to do what it takes to save these poor souls who are stuck in hiding."

"Who sent you here?"

Xavi thought for a moment of two things the bishop had said, "Do not tell anyone," and, "Do what you need to do." He had no choice. The second guideline superseded the first one. "The Bishop of Salamanca. I have been sent to rescue priests, nuns, and other religious people from the Republicans."

The captain's face took on the look of bewilderment. "It's too strange for fiction."

"It's true."

"Perhaps, so, well, if things are as you say, what do you propose?"

"Tomorrow night, after dark, at 11:00 p.m., I would like you to start firing on the enemy lines. With this as a diversion, I will get the nuns across the lines and to safety. Can you do that?"

"Don't fuck me, Father. We kill people for less."

Xavi captured the man's eyes with his own. He let the silence hang in the air for several seconds. "I'll be here, Captain. I'll be here."

Xavi's words, and more so his powerful gaze, flipped the captain from suspicion to belief. "Okay … tomorrow night, the fire fight will start with full force at 11:00 p.m.," the captain said.

Book 4
Chapter 13
Madrid, Republican Spain
August 31, 1936

The words of Jacques Latour stuck in his mind. *Calle Lope de Vega 16, apartment 5C, can you remember that?*
In the mid-morning Xavi drove towards the address. Trucks were buzzing all about full of armed men and women heading to the front or just menacing the city.

He pressed the buzzer for 5C. A woman answered, "Who is it?"

"Je suis Monsieur Azerbergui." He waited for a reply. How would he establish himself as a rescuer and not a hunter?

"Why are you here…?"

Now he paused. *What's the password?* he thought. "I work for *Les Amis de l*a *République de Espagnole*. I am here to see friends of Jacques Latour."

The door buzzed open. Xavi entered the elevator and wondered what would come next. Arriving on the fifth floor he rang the bell at 5C. From the other side the woman's voice called out, "Who is it?"

"*Monsieur* Azerbergui from *Les Amis de la République de Espagnole*," He then added in Spanish, "I am here to save the sisters."

The door was opened by a dark-haired Spanish woman. She had a face that showed it had once been attractive, but which had been marked by too much worry. "Come in. I was told you might be coming," she said tersely, holding a revolver at her side.

"Are the sisters here?"

"First, your papers."

Xavi pulled out his French passport and handed it to the woman.

"It seems right. Let me get them," she said, putting the gun in a desk drawer.

Then, as if coming from out of the shadows, they appeared from a back room. Five of them as he had been told. In their habits, they appeared to range from a young woman to a woman in late middle age. Their faces expressed trepidation, sadness, and some relief.

The oldest sister stepped forward. "I am Sister Clara. Who are you? How do you plan to get us out?"

"I am Father Xavier Bidertea, traveling under the identity of a French aid worker, Patrick Azerbergui. I'm here to get you out of Madrid, to the Nationalist zone, to safety."

"Yes, but how?"

Slowly he explained it all. He recounted what he had been doing for the last several days: the hole in the line he had found, the fire fight that would start at eleven, and that in a short several minutes after that how they would crawl to safety.

"Can you and your sisters make the crawl, it's about hundred yards?"

"Yes," she answered abruptly.

"Sister, did I offend you in some way?"

The Spanish woman jumped into the discussion. "You have no idea what they have been through."

"No."

"Well, you should know," the sister said in a slightly scolding manner.

"Tell me, please tell me."

"We lived in a small community in a poor section of Madrid. Our vocation is prayer and helping the needy among us. We help men find work, teach women how to sew, instruct the children on God. We don't have grand ambitions. We do God's work out of the limelight, in small ways. Our convent had been in that neighborhood for over a century ..." her voice faded off.

"What do you mean had been?"

Slowly Sister Clara resumed, "It was July twentieth, another hot summer day in Madrid when it happened."

"What, what happened, Sister?" Xavi asked.

"After we returned from our weekly shopping, our convent was in an inferno ...."

She paused, bowed her head, and crossed herself. "There was no going back. We were panicked, petrified, in a daze really. One of the sisters suggested *señora* Gonzalez. She long has been our friend; thank God she took us in."

The Spanish woman, *señora* Gonzalez, inserted herself. "Once I settled the sisters down, I went to the convent to look for myself. It was terrible. The five other sisters that were there are ..."

Both women looked away for a few moments, until the *señora* resumed the telling of it. "Gone."

"Gone?"

"It was overrun by a mob; every sacred object—nothing of real value—was taken or destroyed, and finally the convent was set alight, as if to erase that it had ever existed."

"Oh my God, I am so sorry. But what about the other sisters?" Xavi asked.

There was a long pause and more sorrowful silence fell over the room.

"The others, our sisters—do you know what that means, Father? To be a sister for life?"

"Not exactly ..."

"One gives up everything. I should not say 'gives up.' It's a trade one makes, and for most of us we get a lifetime of unimaginable, simple joy. Even as a priest, you could never fully understand. These sisters, the ones who are now gone, they are mother, sister, friend, companion. They, and the love of God, are all we have in this world. We grow to love each other in inexpressible ways."

Señora Gonzalez jumped in. "The other sisters, the ones who were not out shopping, they were raped and killed."

Xavi was not prepared for the sudden shift and bluntness of the conversation. He was sickened. "*Señora*, may I use your bathroom."

"It's off the hall to the right."

Xavi closed the door and fell to his knees. He hung his head over the toilet and wretched. He was reeling—reeling from Ana and Pilar, from the raped and dead nuns, the bombings of the civilians, from the hatred that had been disturbed and unleashed from a deep hell.

He got up and splashed cold water on his face. He could not dwell on those things. The horrors were almost too paralyzing. He was called to do a mission. While the stakes now were higher, he

knew he been called before: in the Pyrenees with Father Extebarri, in a crevice where Inaki fell, stopping the mob at a convent in
Madrid on the night of the fires ...

Xavi steadied himself and thought, *It's time to save these five.*

He returned to the living room. "Dear sisters, I am so terribly
sorry for what has happened to the others ... but it is all the more
reason why we need to get you out of here immediately. First thing
we need to do is to get you some civilian clothes to change into for
the escape. *Señora,* can you direct me somewhere nearby where
we can buy some simple things to wear?"

"Yes," she said in a tone that expressed she was now willing to
cooperate with him.

"*Señora,* the sisters will be safe here for an hour or two?"

"Yes, Father, yes," she said with calm assurance.

When Xavi and *señora* Gonzalez returned, the sisters changed
into their new clothes. Xavi thought how lovely several of them
were with their faces and hair revealed. He noted they all seemed
to share a common physical characteristic: that is, their faces, even
the older nuns, seemed to show little effect of aging or worry.

"Okay, are you ready to go?"

Sister Clara declared, "No."

"No? What else do you need?"

"You need to hear our confessions before we go. If we are to die
today—"

"This is not your last day."

"We need to be able to present ourselves to God with clean
souls."

In agreement, one by one, Xavi took them into the bedroom.
He sat in a chair and they knelt before him. There, they each made
a confession. Mostly it was a minor sin here and there, a slight, not
fully helping with the cooking or cleaning, nothing serious—except in two cases.

The youngest nun was consumed by sadness and was deeply
morose. After the introduction to her confession she went on, "Father my sister was raped and killed in the convent."

Xavi had mostly heard the first confessions of small children:
an extra sweet after dinner, a bed not made, an unkind word said

to a younger brother, and the like. He found himself in deep and uncomfortable waters, as a priest, and as a man.

"Yes, they were all your sisters," he said, hoping he had found the right words.

"No, Father, she was my actual sister."

Xavi was struck. He felt sick again. The water was getting deeper ... too deep perhaps; there was no bottom anywhere in sight. "Tell me, please tell me," he whispered.

"I am twenty-four, and she was just twenty-one. I selfishly told her to stay because I wanted to get out that day for the shopping. It is because of me that she is dead. It should have been me. She is dead because of my selfishness."

Xavi immediately reacted, "Oh, Sister—you are confusing a sense of guilt with the act of committing of a sin. Believe me when I tell you, today there is senseless death everywhere in Spain. You need to do no penance for this. You need to honor your sister through your life's work. This starts tonight with your escape out of Madrid. When you get to the other side tonight say one 'Hail Mary' for your sister. Can you do this? Will you do this?"

His words, projecting the image of the "other side," of some future other than captivity and despair lifted the young woman's spirits.

"Yes, I will do that. ..."

The last confession was from Sister Carmen. She appeared to be about forty years old. Her tone was thoughtful, dispassionate. "Father, I have to come to question God. To question why this massacre? Why this hell has been unleashed?"

"Oh, Sister, you have seen too many terrible things; it's natural to doubt. Doubt is a part of faith; without doubt there would be no reason for faith. God exists. He was made man through Our Lord Jesus Christ. We know this. The fact of the matter is that we cannot know God's plan and His reason for things. We cannot know why these horrors are happening. Remember He is God, and we are not. God, and Spain, needs your devotion now more than ever; reflect on this as you say your rosary tonight—after you have crossed over the lines. Your courage and faithfulness may be your part in His plan. You have a role to play in all of this. You will see."

The confessions lightened the mood of the women, and the

group was ready to go. "We go under the cover of being aid workers. I am French, and my name is Patrick Azerbergui. You are to use your real names without annotating 'sister' to it. You must not let on that you are sisters, and I am a priest. Please try not to speak, and if so, say nothing to give yourselves away."

"Yes, Father," Sister Clara agreed.

"One last thing. We will serve the Republican troops. I know this may be repugnant to some of you. If you cannot do it out of Christian charity, then do it as means to helping to secure your freedom, as a way to get back to your mission."

As they left the center of the city, they began to sing. He could feel their joy … their holiness.

Once they reached the front line, the day played out as Xavi had envisioned. He and the sisters served the troops without incident, until just before nightfall.

The young sister, the one whose sister was raped and killed, was serving soup to the troops. Innocently, sincerely, one of the men thanked her, and, forgetting where she was, she responded in Spanish, "God Bless you."

The soldier peered at her in a wondering way. Xavi took note and inserted himself in French, "It's just a custom, like sending cards at Christmas—it doesn't mean anything."

"What are you babbling about over there, *Frenchie?*" one of the leaders said playfully. The good faith he had engendered in the few days as Patrick Azerbergui diverted the situation, and as night fell, they boarded the truck and said their goodbyes.

Lights off, he moved the truck towards the mound. There he parked out of sight in the stand of trees. They waited for the sounds of war to begin. At just before eleven Xavi pulled the sisters together, "At the sound of the gunfire we will go. I will lead; stay close and do not get up until we reach the Nationalist line. Do you understand?"

"We are with you, Father. Where you go, we will follow," Sister Clara said reassuringly. Her words moved him.

As the Captain promised, at 11:00 p.m. sharp, intense gunfire rang out from the Nationalist side, and then in return from the

Republican side.

"Okay, sisters, let's go. Do as I said: crawl quickly towards the Nationalist gunfire. Follow me. In a few minutes you will be free."

Several minutes later, they arrived at the Nationalist line; the young officer pulled the sisters up, one by one, and welcomed them to freedom. "We have been waiting for you," the young captain said.

"We will never forget what you have done. Never," Sister Clara said, embracing Xavi tightly.

"God has given you a chance. Use it. Make a difference, and please pray for me. I am sorry I can't stay, but I need to make it back across to the Republican side. I must get back to my truck."

"Father, you come and go like a ghost," said the captain.

"A holy ghost," added Sister Clara.

As he crawled between the lines, the gunfire slowly subsided. Back on the mound, near the truck, he heard the sound of singing floating through the night air. He swore to himself that angels had descended in the night.

Book 4
Chapter 14
Perpignan, France
September 2, 1936

Xavi passed through Catalonia and crossed the border to France without a problem. *"Bienvenue,"* the French border guards called out to him as he returned to France.

On his way down the Pyrenees to Perpignan, he stopped at *Madame* Chenot's *auberge*. *Madame* Chenot was a wholesome French country woman; she radiated friendly warmth. "You are back so soon, *monsieur?*"

"Yes, I thought I caught the scent of your onion soup as I crossed the border," Xavi playfully replied.

"The border? You are going back and forth into Spain?"

"I am … I am an aid worker; I deliver supplies to the Republic."

"The war has been good for business. When it started, we were flooded with Catalans fleeing, but now that flow has slowed to a trickle, and the stream of people is going the other way."

"What do you mean?"

"Look around you."

Xavi scanned the rustic dining room.

"Every day we get dozens of men coming to cross the border to fight with the Republicans."

He could see it, but more so could hear it. Some languages, like English, he could make out, and others he could not.

"From what I saw, they will have plenty to do in Spain."

"So it seems. How was it there? How did you find it?"

"Terrible, sad. It's not anything I would want you to imagine."

"That's true from what I hear from the Catalans fleeing too."

Madame Chenot stood above him as he was seated at the small, wooden table. He noted a religious medal hanging about her neck, a St. Bernadette of Lourdes, he thought. Xavi ventured

211

a bit farther. "Your medal, it's from Lourdes, isn't it?"

"It is. I am Catholic. I am a believer. We are not far from Lourdes, and I have been many times, but please not now. This sad hour is not the time to speak of religion. What may I bring you?"

Xavi understood. There was hatred in the shadows everywhere, probably here too, amongst the foreigners rushing into Spain. "Your onion soup, of course! I have been thinking of it since Madrid."

After his lunch Xavi made his way to Jacques Latour's warehouse. As he arrived, he saw another truck leaving.

"How was your trip? A success?" Latour called out.

"I did not even make a proper introduction last time I was here. How do I call you?" Xavi asked.

"You can call me Jacques," Latour replied with a large smile across his face.

"Okay, Jacques, about the trip—I did what you asked me to do."

"You saw my friends?"

"Yes"

"They are safe?

"Yes. Last I heard of them they were singing in the night."

"Singing? Excellent! I am sure I will hear from them soon," Latour responded. "Did you run into any problems … at the border, perhaps?"

"No, no problems. Though I did see hundreds of armed men crossing into Catalonia."

"Yes, thousands of people from France, Germany, England, and even the US are coming in to help the Republicans. Their cause seems so noble and romantic."

"Noble and romantic? You support the Republic, don't you?" Xavi asked with a perplexed tone.

"Let's just leave it there," Jacques replied. "What did you see in Spain?"

"It's worse than you can imagine. I have seen demons I never thought I would see. They have escaped from Hell and are running wild in the streets."

"I was afraid that's what you would say."

The conversation paused and Xavi saw a copy of *El Progressiu* on Jacques desk. "A paper from Barcelona?"

"Yes, I need to keep track of what's happening on the ground there."

"Do you mind?" Xavi asked, pointing to the paper.

"Be my guest."

Xavi picked up the paper, and right there on the front page, there she was. Montse was alive; she was still the cover girl.

Stalemate in Toledo ... Which Way the Republic?
Montserrat Costa

Toledo, La Mancha, Republican Spain

After the Nationalist Coup was thwarted six weeks ago, The Republic found itself in control of almost all of Spain's major cities, most of its industrial production, and all of its gold. But the Nationalists are slowly crawling their way up the perch The Republic occupies.

From Seville the Nationalists set out on their reconquest. They have taken Badajoz and most of Extremadura, and now there is intense fighting just twenty miles from Madrid. The Nationalists have showed themselves to be a professional, disciplined fighting force, and with the help of their Fascist allies, the Germans, and the Italians, they relentlessly march onward.

So as the Nationalists continue their march on, the Republican troops are consumed by a prolonged stalemate in Toledo. Toledo? Why Toledo one must ask? The old capital of Spain is a backwater. It is known for housing amazing treasures of history and art. The home of El Greco has no strategic or military significance. Nonetheless, Republican troops are preoccupied, obsessed really, with taking the city's old *Alcazar*. And what is the *Alcazar* now? It is a military school for boys run by a Colonel Moscardó who is said to love soccer more than soldiering.

While the Nationalists march on in seeming unity behind General Franco, we in The Republic squabble over the purity of left-wing ideologies and engage in a stalemate over an insignificant military academy in an out-of-the-way small town.

It is fair to ask six weeks after the Coup—which is now a civil war—are we heading to disaster?

Wow, her typewriter still runs red hot, Xavi thought. But also, he wondered about her change in tone? It seemed to him that something had changed for Montse.

"Read anything interesting?" Jacques asked.

"The usual back and forth," he responded, not knowing Jacques well enough to share his true sentiments. "So I saw a truck leaving when I arrived. You have others helping you?"

"Well, yes, we have many helping with our efforts—helping us both here in France and in Spain."

"Is there a lot of work to be done?"

"Too much," Latour replied wistfully.

"Hmmm, so we will likely see each other again?"

"You want to continue to help us, even after what you experienced?"

"Yes."

"Then, I imagine we will," Latour answered with a smile.

"If I were to need a boat, or a safe route to hike over the Pyrenees from Catalonia to France, could you help with that?"

"Yes, I'm sure I could. Of course your need for those things would depend on where our friends might be and what they needed."

Xavi reached over to shake Latour's hand. "I am pleased I could help. The spirit of your friends, the looks of happiness on their faces after they crossed the line, brought some joy back to me. It was a feeling I was beginning to lose sight of. It was worth the journey."

"Excellent."

"And I will never forget their singing …"

"Yes, the singing … Patrick, I can you see you are a fearless man, and a man of great skill, so I am sure I will see you soon and often. Unfortunately, I have many, many friends in dire need."

Book 4
Chapter 15
Haro, Nationalist Spain
September 5, 1936

Monsieur, monsieur, wake up, wake up! We are at the Bordeaux station," said the porter.

Xavi groggily roused himself. The train car was empty. "I'm sorry, I must have dozed off."

"*Monsieur,* you have been asleep since we left Toulouse."

"Oh ... I was more tired than I thought. God bless you."

Noting the surprised look on the porter's face, Xavi added, "And thank you. I need to find my next train."

The train from Bordeaux to Saint-Jean-Pied-de-Port ran through the vineyards. The images of the vines, heavy with their purple-red fruit, centered Xavi on what he must do on his next stop. He needed to go see Don Pedro de la Calzada. He needed to tell him about Ana and Pilar.

Somehow, he felt dread was worse than fear—more oppressive, like dark clouds collapsing onto the mountains. There would be no easy way to deliver this news. First a son, and now a daughter-in-law and a baby granddaughter. So many, so soon, lost to the war.

After Bayonne, the train veered inland, away from the sea, following the River Nive. The countryside of the *Pays Basque* was bucolic. Verdantly green pastures, sheep grazing here and there, tiny villages populated by Basques living in their whitewashed houses trimmed with rusty red shutters. The train stopped at Espelette, and there, an old Basque man, with his beret cocked slightly on his head, waved hello to the passengers getting off. Espelette had always charmed Xavi; it was a small Basque village with its houses covered with red peppers drying in the sun. Even before the war, the village had seemed like it was from another, simpler time.

As he approached Saint-Jean-Pied-de-Port, the Pyrenees rose

up in the distance. In the river a man fished as the waters bubbled past him. He was just a few miles from Spain, but really, he was a world away from the troubles there.

He disembarked at the old pilgrimage town, and just before reaching the border station at Valcarlos, Xavi made his Spanish credentials ready. There, he crossed back over into Nationalist Spain.

"What's your business, Father? Why were you in France?" the guard asked brusquely at the border.

"I was in Saint-Jean-Pied-de-Port. I went to see a friend, Father Arregetui."

"Hmmm ... okay. Be careful, Father, these are dangerous times."

He re-entered his country without warmth or welcome. From Valcarlos he made his way across Nationalist-controlled territory back to Pamplona, then to Logrono, and finally to Don Pedro's house in Haro.

The housekeeper answered Xavi's knock; she paused a moment, seeming not to recognize him without his clerical clothing. "You are Jaime's friend, Father Xavi, aren't you?"

"Yes, yes I am. Is Don Pedro here?"

"Please come in and let me get him."

Several minutes later Don Pedro shuffled out from his bedroom. He no longer looked like the strong, proud, and contented, middle-aged man he had last seen at Pilar's baptism. He seemed old, gray, and tired. He looked defeated.

"Xavi, you must be here because you heard about what happened to Juan in Madrid."

"Yes, yes Jaime told me."

"You coming means a lot to me."

"Oh, Don Pedro I am so sorry for you. I know how much you loved your son."

"It has been terrible. At night I toss and turn, dreaming it wasn't true, that I had been confused somehow. Then I began to silently scream out, 'Why Juan? Why not me, instead?'"

Xavi studied Don Pedro closely. He could feel his anger close to the surface.

"Those filthy reds. I hope every one of them is hunted down and killed. There is no place in this country for them. God Bless

General Franco."

Xavi neither agreed nor argued with him; he had already begun to see that the war was much more complicated than Don Pedro described it. On top of the pain, the grief, and the anger that were living inside him, he had to deliver the news of Ana and Pilar. It was a horrible piling on.

He felt it again, the oppressive darkness, the ... dread. "I am here," he stuttered to continue, anticipating how horrible this additional blow would be on the already severely wounded man, "I have some other news for you. Difficult news ...," he said with voice trailing off.

"Has something happened to Jaime? Is he all right?" he asked, almost lashing out at Xavi.

"Yes, yes, he is fine ... as far I know. I just had a letter from him."

"Oh God, I couldn't bear if something had happened to him."

Xavi continued slowly, "It's about Ana and Pilar."

"What about them?"

"Jaime sent me a letter. He told me about Juan, and he asked me to help find Ana and little Pilar."

"Yes, I have been so worried about them too. Ana's parents are nearby in Logrono. She needs her family near her. She and Pilar should be here in La Rioja; they should return to us."

He had come to the end of dancing around the dark news. "I'm so sorry, I'm afraid that won't be possible."

"What do you mean? Do you have news of them? Did you find them?"

"Don Pedro, after Jaime's letter, using the church's sources, I made some inquiries ... and I learned—"

"What did you learn? Tell me, tell me, what did you find out? How is Ana? How is my beautiful little Pilar? Where are they?"

"Don Pedro ... Ana is ... she is dead."

"God no!"

"How?" he finally asked.

"It's not clear, but as far as I could learn, she went to be with Juan at the barracks and she was ... she was killed there too. I imagine she died with your son. She died with the husband she loved."

"Oh my God no."

Don Pedro fell silent again and Xavi moved in to console him. After several minutes Don Pedro gained enough strength to continue, "But what about Pilar? We must bring her here, or to Logrono."

The dread had exhausted Xavi, but he forced himself to continue, "Don Pedro … she was … she was taken."

"What do you mean, taken? Kidnapped?"

"No, from I have learned I would say she was taken."

"What does that mean?"

"It seems an army officer and his wife took Pilar just after Juan and Ana were killed. She has not been seen or heard from since. My guess is that in the lawless chaos she was taken by a childless couple as their own. One begins to hear stories of this happening all over Spain."

After more silence, Xavi, beginning to feel self-pity for having to deliver the news added, "Don Pedro, I am so sorry to have had to come here with this."

Don Pedro staggered to a nearby chair, and he collapsed into it. For many minutes he was lost to Xavi. He was out of touch, unreachable.

After this long absence Don Pedro slowly arose. "Xavi, I am so, so tired now. I am going to my room."

Xavi kept his vigil for Don Pedro in the living room. After several hours, the man Xavi knew to be the vineyard foreman came in and asked, "Where is Don Pedro?"

"He is resting. He should not be disturbed," Xavi answered.

"Father, I know how difficult this time is for him, but the harvest, it came early this year. It will start tomorrow. We need him."

Book 4
Chapter 16
Haro, Nationalist Spain
September 8, 1936

For two days Xavi filled in for Don Pedro as best he could. The grapes were plucked from their vines, they were gathered, turned into juice, and put into wooden vats to begin their fermentation. The harvest was done without joy. At the end of the work, there was no dinner, no music, no dancing. The workers took their envelopes filled with *pesetas* and disbursed quietly. Don Pedro's sadness was a virus that infected everyone at the vineyard in 1936.

Xavi was reluctant to disturb Don Pedro. For three days Jaime's father had not left his room; but now as Xavi had to catch a train back to Salamanca, he was compelled to knock on his bedroom door.

"Don Pedro, it's me. It's Xavi."

"Come in," Don Pedro weakly replied.

"Don Pedro, how are you?"

"Weak, maimed ..."

It was a devastating self-assessment, but Xavi could not linger to console him. "It's all ... everything is ... so heartbreaking, but I must go. I need to get back to Salamanca."

"I know."

"We were able to bring all the grapes in."

"I fear it will be a foul vintage. But thank you. I'm not sure what would have happened if you hadn't stayed."

Xavi could see Don Pedro's tears welling up. He did not want to see him break down. He went to him and embraced him. "Don Pedro do not get up. I am not far away and can be here for you anytime you feel the need. Please know that."

"Thank you, Xavi, thank you."

Book 4
Chapter 17
Salamanca, Nationalist Spain
September 10, 1936

Xavi sat at in his office in Salamanca. It was stacked with papers; they were visible reminders that he had two jobs to do for an unforgiving bishop.

At around one p.m. the receptionist came in. "Father, a Captain Jaime de la Calzada is outside. He says he needs to see you."

"Jaime! He is my dearest friend. Please send him right in."

When Jaime entered his office Xavi was shocked. The war had taken such a toll on him. He was disheveled; his uniform was muddied and bloodied. But worse than his physical appearance was all the life appeared drained from him—almost as he remembered his father looking upon hearing the news of Ana and Pilar. There was no warmth, no greeting, no relief at seeing an old friend.

"Father, I need to see you. I have little time. I must get back to my unit by nightfall."

"Jaime, anything. What I can do for you?"

"You must hear my confession."

"Your confession …" Xavi's replied, his words clothed in a combination of surprise and empathy.

"Yes, my confession."

"Of course. Jaime, would you like to go to across the street to the cathedral, to a confessional?"

"No, here. Right here."

"That's fine too."

"I have been carrying this sin for three weeks. I can't carry it another step."

Jaime knelt before Xavi. He started with the customary preamble. "Bless me, Father, for I have sinned. It has been several years, … many years since my last confession."

"Jaime, my friend, tell me what weighs so heavily on your soul?"

Jaime started, circling his sin, like a boxer in a ring with his opponent. "I saw many horrible acts of violence when I was in Asturias helping to put down the revolution there in 1934."

"You told me."

"I saw things that were outside the boundaries of just conflict. I was very disturbed by it, but I did not personally participate in these acts of terror. I did not order them, and I do not believe I could have prevented them."

The air in Xavi's office was full of heavy silence as Jaime paused. Jaime slowed his pace as he moved closer to it, as he came face to face with the heart of the matter. "Today is different. I was part of an atrocity ..."

Xavi first had to control his instinct to gasp with shock and horror; instead, he gently put his hand on his friend's shoulder. "Tell me Jaime. Tell me what happened. Take your time."

"It was in Badajoz."

"At the battle for the city?"

"Yes. The city was heavily fortified, and even after days of bombing, the fighting was ferocious. Our attack was spilt into two groups. One group attacked through *Puerta de la Trinidad*. Their losses were staggering—they lost seventy-six of their ninety men. The group I was in attacked on the south side of the city through *Puerto de Los Carros*. We encountered little resistance until we were inside the streets. There, everything intensified. It devolved into hand-to-hand, and bayonet-to-bayonet fighting. It was like an oven in the city. The temperature was well over one hundred degrees, and without a breath of wind."

Jaime looked up at Xavi, imagining the luxury of passing the war comfortably in Salamanca, "Father, being here in Salamanca, in the Bishop's Palace, can you imagine what it's like?"

For a moment, Xavi wanted to tell Jaime about his other job, where he had been, what he had seen, but he knew it would be a self-centered distraction. This was Jaime's time, not his. "No ... not exactly," he said humbly.

Jaime continued on, "At some point in battle there are no strategies, no tactics, only finding the greater strength and will to kill the man in front of you. I killed three or four men in close combat.

Ultimately, we prevailed. The city surrendered."

"Jaime, this is how it is; it's the horror of war."

"I am a soldier; I am trained for this. My sin came afterward ..."

Xavi remained silent. It was not for him to coax the story out.

"After the battle, dozens, maybe hundreds of men surrendered. Others fled, but they were identifiable by the gunstock marks on their shoulders; they were hunted down and captured. Together they were all rounded up; hands tied, exhausted, defeated, trembling in fear, they waited for their fate. It came quickly. Colonel Yague gave the order to take them to the bull ring."

Jaime paused and Xavi could see that his friend had floated away, probably back to the bull ring.

"Yague huddled the officers together and said simply, 'we are moving onward to capture Madrid. We cannot carry these men with us, and we cannot leave enemy resistors behind us. Kill them. Kill them all."

Even after what Xavi had seen and experienced in Madrid, the blunt brutality of Yague's order stunned him.

Xavi composed himself. "Jaime, tell me, tell me what happened next? There is no sin that is beyond redemption. Please, Jaime, you need to get it out for your confession to be complete, for you to receive God's forgiveness and mercy, you must tell me."

Finally, after another long pause Jaime continued, "The prisoners, with their hands tied in ropes, were brought into the ring. They were put against the walls of the stands of the ring. Then they were shot. Then they were murdered."

Xavi was staggered again by it. "Jaime ... I'm sorry, my friend ... for this question ... but I must ..."

"Yes, Father ..."

"Did you ... did you ..."

"No, I did not pull the trigger."

Xavi felt a very brief respite.

"But I might as well have."

Jaime paused again and then said in a low, mournful voice, "We ignored their screams; we ignored their pleas for mercy; and in some cases, we ignored their Christian prayers. Instead, we howled with delight. We taunted them—dirty, filthy reds—and then we shot them. We murdered them. I could have stopped it, but I didn't."

Xavi recovered and began to lead his friend. "Jaime … do you remember the moment?"

"Yes, like it was this morning."

"What were you feeling?"

"Xavi I was filled with so much hatred after Juan was killed. I thought only revenge would wash this hatred away. I engaged in the taunts, and it is as if I too pulled the trigger of those machine guns."

There it was.

Slowly at first, then like a gusher it had come out. Jaime collapsed, weeping, into his friend's lap. To Xavi, Jamie's words and tears seemed to have yanked the demon from his soul, the way a barnacle is pulled from a rock.

Xavi allowed Jamie's sobbing to prolong. It was like a medieval doctor bleeding a sick man.

Finally, as the intense emotions began to subside, Xavi began to heal his friend. "Oh, Jaime, we know no man is beyond redemption; no one is beyond His grace. God's mercy has found you."

Xavi paused for several moments. His mind rushed to find the right words, the right metaphors to relieve the pain of this friend. "Jaime, your sin is very grave."

He continued on, as Jaime looked up into his friend's comforting eyes. "Remember the words of Isaiah, 'though your sins are like scarlet, I will make them white as snow.'"

"What does that mean?"

"Sin and God's forgiveness is the human story. My friend, the Bible, our church, they are a catalogue of stories of great sinners, even murderers who repented, were forgiven, were redeemed. Many have become remarkable saints. My heroes."

The words "stories of great sinners, even murderers" seemed to find Jaime. Xavi continued on. "St. Paul, before his conversion, was a persecutor of Jesus' followers. On his way to Damascus to arrest more Christians for persecution, he was struck by a vision of Jesus. Upon seeing this, Paul asked, 'Who art thou, Lord?' And the Lord said, 'I am Jesus whom thou persecutes ...'"

Xavi had opened a door into his friend's soul, and his words were beginning to seep in. "Jaime, the power of this vision caused Paul to lose his sight for three days. Upon recovering, his eyes were opened, and he was converted. He went from the persecutor to a warrior for Christ."

"Yes, St. Paul ..." Jaime murmured.

"Or think of Longinus."

"The centurion who he himself pierced Christ with his spear?"

"That's right."

"Tell me ..."

"What could be worse? He speared Our Lord when He was on the cross?"

"I understand ..."

"Then a miracle occurred. After spearing Him, he became nearly blind, but his sight was restored by the blood and water which poured out from Jesus. He then cried out 'Indeed this was the Son of God.'"

Pausing again, he could see and sense his words were connecting. The life was reentering his friend.

"What happened to Longinus after?"

"After the crucifixion? He left the army. I leave the rest of his story for you to discover. But I will tell you one other thing about St. Longinus for you to contemplate."

"What's that?"

"His spear is in one of the four pillars of The Basilica of St. Peter's in Rome."

"It's hard to imagine what a journey this must have been."

"Jaime, make this your Epiphany; make this the moment; have your sight restored."

"I want to see again."

"You will my friend, you will," Xavi said, again placing his hand on Jaime's shoulder.

"Xavi, Father, what should I ...?"

"Become a warrior for Christ like St. Paul. Have your sight restored like Longinus."

Jaime lifted his head and softly said, "Yes, Xavi, yes."

"Jaime, do you have sincere sorrow for what you have done?"

"Oh yes, Father, I do. The killing did not alleviate any of the pain of Juan's loss. It was like a boomerang that came back on me. Once the machine guns stopped, there was a stream of blood, so much blood that the floor of the bull ring could not absorb it.

I saw the lives I had destroyed. I began to imagine their brothers, their fathers—immediately I knew I was no better than the mob than had killed Juan. No, I was worse because I should have known better. I was worse because I am a baptized and practicing Catholic and a professional solider."

"Everything can have a reason, Jaime, even this."

"I am also ashamed that my Catholicism, when put to a real test, was only a symbol. It was like a Carlist flag, on display, waving proudly, but which turned easily with the wind. Xavi, my regret is overwhelming."

"Jaime, here is your penance. I ask you to do four things."

"Okay."

"First, study the life of St. Paul and the story of Longinus. Regain your sight."

"I will, but that is only two things."

"Most importantly is how you live. Go forward, and once you have regained your sight, execute your duties as a warrior for Spain faithfully, intensely, and in accordance with principles of St. Augustine's just war."

"Yes, I know St. Augustine, we studied him at the military academy."

"Finally, and this is the most difficult thing I ask, when it becomes possible, you must go make amends to those families in Badajoz."

"Return to Badajoz?"

"Yes."

"You're right. I need to go to Badajoz. I must survive this war to get back there."

"You must try to alleviate their pain. Jaime, can you do these things? Do I have your word that you will do these things? Do I have your word you will return to Badajoz?"

"You have my word."

"Jaime, please say your act of contrition for me."

"O my God, I am heartily sorry for having offended Thee, and I detest all my sins, because I dread the loss of heaven and the pains of hell, but most of all because they offend Thee, my God, who art all good and deserving of all my love. I firmly resolve with the help of thy grace to confess my sins, to do penance, and to amend my life. Amen."

"Jaime, I will now confer your absolution." Making the sign of the cross Xavi completed the confession, "Thereupon, I absolve you from your sins in the name of the Father, and of the Son, and of the Holy Spirit. Amen."

"Thank you, Father, thank you."

Completing the confession, Jaime stood up. Xavi paused to switch subjects, "Jaime, sit down, please. There is one additional thing I need to tell you outside the bounds of the confessional."

"What? What is it Xavi?" Jaime sat on the front edge of the straight chair beside Xavi's desk.

"After I received your letter, I made some inquiries about Ana and Pilar."

"Yes, please tell me."

"Jaime the news is not good." As he said it, he could see Jaime wince as if he was applying a blow upon a spot that was already severely tender. "There is no easy way of saying this so I will say it directly. Ana is dead, and Pilar … Pilar, she was taken."

"What? Are you certain? What do you mean, taken?"

"Yes, Jaime I am one hundred percent certain."

"Where is Pilar?"

"Lost … lost to the war."

Jaime slumped back into the chair and went silent for many moments.

"This war … this war. I know what I must do."

"What?"

"Do as you said. Anger and revenge are not the way forward."

Xavi considered telling Jaime that he had seen his father in Haro, but thought it had all been enough already. "God bless you my friend. I will continue to pray for you every day. I will pray for your safety and that this war end quickly."

"Thank you, Xavi, thank you."

Jaime rose from his chair and embraced his friend, to return to the battle. Xavi was certain he heard Jaime sobbing as he left.

Later as the day became evening, he sat down with the bishop to listen to General De Llano's nightly broadcast. General De Llano was particularly boastful.

"The Nationalist forces are on the march all throughout glorious Spain. Powered by divine providence, and led by our great generals, our troops are overwhelming the filthy reds everywhere we engage them. They are no match for us. First Seville, then Badajoz, and now Irun.

"With the fall of Irun the Basque border with France is closed off. Shortly, if San Sebastian does not surrender, its resistors will experience the same fate as those in Badajoz did. There is a bull ring there as well …"

Xavi did not remember another word after De Llano said Badajoz for the second time. "Your Excellency, please excuse me, but I am not feeling well."

Xavi rushed across the street to the Chapel of St. Martin. His mind was spinning, and the prayers would not come. The chaos and horror had exhausted him. Rather than prayers, it was a poem from university that rattled around in his mind:

> Turning and turning in the widening gyre
> The falcon cannot hear the falconer;
> Things fall apart; the center cannot hold;
> Mere anarchy is loosed upon the world,
> The blood-dimmed tide is loosed, and everywhere
> The ceremony of innocence is drowned;
> The best lack all conviction, while the worst
> Are full of passionate intensity.
> Surely some revelation is at hand;
> Surely the Second Coming is at hand.

What is this Second Coming, he thought? Could things possibly become worse?

Book 4
Chapter 18
Salamanca, Nationalist Spain
September 10, 1936

Xavi was in his office, making his way through the day's work when his phone rang. With the first word he knew it was his mother. She did not say hello, she just blurted out, "Your father has been jailed by the Nationalists."

"What? What happened?"

"San Sebastian fell yesterday, and they came for him. He has done nothing wrong. Why would they come for him?"

"Because he is a Basque."

"Because he is Basque?"

"They, the Spanish, the Nationalists, they hate the Basques."

"They would capture him because he taught a few children the Basque language?"

"Yes."

"Your father is a threat to no one."

"I know, I know. They hate our history. They hate our self-confidence, our self-reliance, our customs, and more than anything else, our language."

"Oh, Xavi, I am so frightened. The Nationalists have been brutal. They dropped pamphlets with pictures of dead bodies in Badajoz which said that this is what would happen to the people of San Sebastian if the city did not surrender."

Badajoz. There it was again, like a bad dream returning. "Are you okay, Mother, are you safe?"

"Yes, but we need to get your father freed. You work for a powerful bishop; you must be able to do something."

"Mother, I will be there tomorrow. One way or another we will get Father out."

"Come quickly, Xavi."

228

"Stay put, Mother. I am coming."

"And, Xavi, there is one more thing you should know."

"What else?"

"Neither Father Extebarri nor Inaki have been heard from in several days. There are reports that the Nationalists have killed many priests. Why would Catholics kill priests?"

"Mother these murderers are not true Catholics. They kill them because they are Basque. They kill them because they are filled with hate."

"Be careful coming here."

"Don't worry about me. I will see you tomorrow. We will rescue Father." *My father. Another victim of the war to rescue,* he thought.

"I love you, Xavi."

"I love you, too, Mother."

After Xavi hung up, he marched into the bishop's private office. The bishop was on the phone, and Xavi signaled he needed to see him urgently.

"Father, what could be so urgent as to interrupt me?"

Xavi forgot the formalities of addressing the bishop and launched directly into his point, "San Sebastian has fallen, and my father has been arrested."

"Yes, I had heard the city was about to fall."

"It's about my father! He is a threat to no one. His sole crime is being a supporter of the Basque language and culture."

"I heard you. You needn't raise your voice. I am still your bishop."

"I'm sorry, Your Excellency. I need your help."

"But with the Basques it can be complicated."

"You are the most powerful bishop in Spain!"

"Well yes, but Father, I'm not sure. It could be difficult."

"Your Excellency, with all due respect, going to Barcelona, Valencia and Madrid as a priest during this civil war is difficult; getting five nuns across a hostile line is difficult. This, Your Excellency, is inconvenient."

The bishop was stunned by Xavi's directness.

"Your Excellency, we both know you are a powerful man, and that you are well connected to many highly placed officers on the Nationalist side, including General Franco himself. Make some calls; do what needs to be done to have my father freed.

"I am going there tomorrow, and I expect by the time I arrive that he will be released," Xavi said with his tone bordering on insolence.

"Yes, yes I see that. I will make some phone calls to see what can be done."

—•—

Book 4
Chapter 19
San Sebastian, Nationalist Spain
September 14, 1936

Xavi was packing to leave for the train station when he heard a knock on his door.

"Come in."

The door opened and the bishop entered Xavi's room. "Your Excellency, I did not imagine it would be you. There is a chair in the corner, please sit down."

"No, Father, I will only need a minute. I came to tell you that your father is being released this morning."

"Oh, Your Excellency, that is wonderful news. Thank you. Truly, thank you."

"Father, this was not easy. The main factor that weighed in his favor is the work you are doing. The Nationalists believe in a united Spain, and they take a very dim view of Basque Separatism. They intend to make the Basque country truly Spanish. In the future, public expressions of your language and culture will be forbidden."

"Your Excellency, this is so misguided. For the most part we Basques are very conservative, Catholic people."

"It's not the time to discuss politics, Father. You need to get to your parents."

"Yes. Again, thank you, Your Excellency, thank you."

"One more thing."

"Yes."

"I do not believe I would be able to do get him freed again. Please counsel your parents accordingly. If I were you, I would advise them to leave the country."

"But they have lived in San Sebastian for thirty years," Xavi protested.

"These are complex, dangerous times, Father. I recall they speak French?"

"They do."

"The Basques have long and complicated relationship with Spain. Some Spaniards, some Nationalists, are going to see this as a time to settle some scores. They would be safer in France."

Xavi was stunned. The most powerful bishop in Spain was suggesting the parents of his personal secretary leave the country because his father taught some children the Basque language. Xavi said nothing. His face was blank.

"Be careful, Father. Return to me as soon as you can. You, and your parents, are in my prayers."

Throughout the long train journey from Salamanca to San Sebastian, Xavi thought about the bishop's words. As much as it pained him to admit it, the bishop was probably right. Xavi knew he could not be there to protect them. His parents should leave Spain. As the train rolled along, he imagined the right words to persuade them that they must leave their home, that they needed to go to France.

Arriving to San Sebastian, Xavi left the train station and walked near the Zurriola Beach. The waves crashed into the shore as always. In the late afternoon he crossed over the bridge of the river Urumea to the Belle Epoque old town. There was an eerie, unhappy calm hanging over the city.

The few people that were on the streets were mostly soldiers. San Sebastian seemed vacated. Half of its population had fled, and the other half remained in their homes in a state of fearful submission. His beautiful, vibrant city wore a thick blanket of sadness from its occupation.

When he arrived home, his parents greeted him with a mixture of love and relief. His arrival seemed to puncture the sorrow that had enveloped their home.

"Oh, Xavi, we are so happy you are here," his mother said with smiles and tears.

"Son, I do not know what you did, or how you did it, but I am so relieved to be out of jail," his father added.

"Yes, yes, it's good to be here, it's good you are out. We have much to talk to about."

"Let's sit like the old days, with wine, and some ham and cheeses and talk," his mother said.

While his mother went to the kitchen for some cheese, *jamón ibérico,* olives, and almonds, his father poured three glasses of red wine from Rioja.

"I'm sorry, I wasn't here sooner. I was caught up in some projects and, besides, I didn't think Gipuzkoa would fall so fast," Xavi started out, between sips of the wine.

"Neither did we. But once Irun fell, they shut the border to France, and then things moved rapidly."

"Most of the news we get in Salamanca about the situation here is slow or comes from General De Llano over the radio."

"Oh he is a horrible man. General Franco would do well to shut him up!" Xavi's mother replied.

"Yes, mostly he traffics in hyperbole and bravado, though he still commands the attention of my bishop every night. Enough of him, Father, tell me, tell me how it happened. How did San Sebastian fall?"

"It began with the assault on Irun." Xavi's father replied.

"It's clear whoever holds Irun controls the border to France."

"It's true, and both sides threw all their weight into the fight."

"Were the *Requetés* fighting with the Nationalists?" Xavi asked.

"Yes, the *Requetés* were there. Fearless as always. In their red berets, their hatred of anarchists and communists being greater than their loyalty to their Basque homeland, they attacked from Navarre."

"Did they tip the scale?"

"Not entirely. Really, I'd say it was the Germans and Italians that carried the day. Their bombers attacked the city mercilessly."

"And the Nationalists burned the city?" Xavi asked.

"No, as if the horror of the battle were not enough, the anarchists who had been defending the town, set it ablaze on their retreat. Xavi, Irun is destroyed; there is nothing left there. Since then, the Nationalists have slowly but surely been taking the whole province. Our province, Gipuzkoa, was captured, mountain by mountain, and village by village. And yesterday, they marched into San Sebastian unresisted. After only a month, the people are already exhausted by this war."

"It is the same everywhere in Spain. But what about you? How were you arrested?"

"As soon as the Nationalists arrived, they began rounding up undesirables and Basque 'activists,' they said. That is, anyone who promoted our language and our culture in even the smallest way. I was on their list. I guess teaching a few children our language is now an act of terrorism. It's absurd."

"Father, the Nationalists intend to stamp-out our culture and language."

"This is insane. We are deeply conservative. We are a very Catholic people, but still we are fiercely proud of our heritage and way of life too."

"I know that, but I'm afraid anything that is not truly Spanish is unacceptable to the Nationalists."

"Yes, I have already seen this. They, those who march under the imprimatur of the Catholic Church, like the *Requetés*, with crosses on their sleeves, are said to be killing Catholic priests who minister—give last rites—to our troops who are fighting for the independence of our homeland, the Basque Country."

"Mother mentioned Inaki, and Father Extebarri."

"They have been missing for days. There are reports of a massacre of priests by the Nationalists near Mondragon."

The implication was clear. He thought about Inaki and Father Extebarri for a moment; the crises were mounting too fast to handle; he needed to triage them. The fate of this mother and father came first.

"Father, it was my bishop who got you released."

"How can we thank him? He is such a wealthy and powerful man, what kindness could we show him?" his mother said.

"Yes, Mother, I know you are so grateful, I know that—but please listen to me—showing your gratitude to my bishop is not the issue right now. We have other, more pressing problems."

"Like what? What do you mean Xavi?" his mother asked.

"Mother, they will come again for Father. Some night, no one can predict when, you will hear a bashing on the door, and it will be them. They will come and take him—and when they do, I will not be able to help."

"But you said your bishop—"

Xavi cut his mother off to make the point firmly, "He made it clear that he had only one free pass for Father, and that it has been used."

Xavi's words changed the room. His mother and father went silent. Xavi had seen so much shocked silence recently that he had learned its cadences: the punch to the gut, the onset of severe distress, the severing of the line between emotions and thoughts. He knew to give them some time to think. He knew it would take some moments for what he said to be processed and for logic to be reconnected with his mother's and father's spinning emotions.

"Xavi, what do you mean exactly?" his father finally asked.

"Father, I think you know what I mean. You, and better still, you and Mother must leave San Sebastian as soon as possible."

His mother, still in a state of shocked confusion, added, "Where would we go?"

"Maria, we could go to Bilboa; we have friends there," his father suggested.

"No, not Bilboa. Bilboa will likely fall soon too. Out of Spain. You need to get to France," Xavi interjected.

"France? The border is closed," his mother protested.

"I will get you to France. I will get you to just over the border to Saint-Jean-de-Luz."

"How?" his father asked.

"Leave that to me. I am going to go work on it now."

As Xavi exited the apartment he turned around and added, "Be ready. Make a small pack of clothes and things … only what you can carry on your back. I intend for us to leave soon."

Xavi left his parents' house and went to find Martin, one of the boys who had gone on the Camino with him and Father Extebarri. Martin, even as a small boy, had been street smart, a wise cracker. When Xavi got to the port, he found Martin working on his boat.

"Hello, *Padre*," Martin yelled out with a big smile.

"Good afternoon, Martin. Why are you in such good spirits on such a sad day?"

"Well, yes I am. Now that the Nationalists are here there are more mouths to feed and fewer fishermen to feed them. For now it seems the war is good for business!"

"Always seeing the bright side, aren't you?"

Martin laughed loudly. "And what brings you here? The last I heard you were nearly the Pope."

"Ha, I am still a foot soldier in God's army."

"This isn't a social call, is it, *Padre*?"

"Not exactly. Martin, you always were the person who seemed to see and hear a lot—"

"Yes, Father, I have my ways, and you know I will always do whatever I can to help you."

"Have you heard about the killing of Basque priests?"

"Yes, that is some very nasty business, and I am guessing you are not asking in general, are you?"

"No. I am looking for Father Extebarri and Inaki."

"I figured as much. I have good news about Father Extebarri."

"How so?"

"He is in hiding. He is staying in the flat of a friend on the *Calle San Juan*."

"And what about Inaki?"

"I don't have anything for you about Inaki. I fear he was caught up at Mondragon with the other priests there."

"Dead?"

"Probably, Father, probably."

Xavi turned away from Martin. He did not want his friend to see him fighting off tears.

He composed himself and turned back to Martin, "Can you help me with something? It is dangerous. It's for Father Extebarri"

"Let me guess, you want to rescue Father Extebarri? Like you did back at Roncesvalles?"

"Not exactly like that, but yes."

"Count me in."

"Can you get him a message?"

"Of course."

Xavi and Martin huddled and laid out their plan, and a few minutes later they shook hands and parted.

Returning home, Xavi's parents met him near the front door and his mother said, "We heard what you said, and we trust you, Xavi. We are packed. When do we leave?"

"Tomorrow night we go."

Book 4
Chapter 20
Saint-Jean-de-Luz, France
September 16, 1936

Xavi, his mother, and father left the Bidertea's apartment at about eight p.m. They walked a short distance to have dinner at a small fish restaurant run by some old friends near the port. Each of them was carrying a small rucksack .

Aitor and his wife Estibalitz had run the small restaurant for years. Aitor happily managed the front of the house while his wife stayed in back and prepared simple, delicious meals from whatever came in off the boats. When the Biderteas arrived the restaurant was nearly full of Nationalist troops, all speaking Spanish; no Basque was heard.

Aitor greeted the Biderteas warmly and whispered in Basque, *"Kaixo,"* then switching to Spanish he added, "It is so nice to see old friends in these dark days."

"Yes, yes, we need our old friends more than ever now," Maria Bidertea responded.

"Aitor, would you do us a favor? Would you put our packs in the back while we eat?" Xavi asked.

"Of course, it is not a problem."

The Biderteas sat down for dinner. From time-to-time other officers would arrive, and upon arrival they would greet each other with the Fascist salute.

Maria could not help herself. "This is not a Spanish sign, this is an affectation of German and Italian thugs," she whispered in disgust.

Just before ten o'clock Aitor came to their table and reminded them of the curfew. "I am sorry to rush you along, but now there is a curfew. Amongst all our problems, this is a small one, but a problem, nonetheless."

"Yes, we are ready to pay now, anyway."

"Tonight, I will not take your money."

"Thank you, Aitor, may I have a word with you?" Xavi asked.

"Of course."

Xavi nudged him to the corner, away from the tables and traffic, "We need to go in back to get our packs, and we may need to linger a bit. Is it okay?"

"Yes. Martin mentioned this earlier when he delivered his fish today. Anything, Xavi, really anything for you and your parents."

Just before ten-thirty p.m. the Biderteas embraced Aitor and Estibalitz and said "Thank you, thank you. We are not sure when, but we hope to see you soon."

"Good luck, and may God watch over you tonight. Go now," Aitor responded.

The Biderteas then passed out of a back door and made the short walk toward the port. It was a dark night with no moon and a thin cloud cover. The narrow streets of the *Parte Vieja* were completely quiet. Only the cats were about.

They walked toward the place where the old quarter passes into the port. They heard a disturbance from some distance away near *La Concha* beach. The noise aroused the guards from around port and nearby on the promenade of *La Concha*. The Nationalist soldiers came running from all directions and converged on the site of the trouble. At that same moment, a man stepped from the shadow of a recessed doorway.

"Hello, Xavi." Father Extebarri said as he emerged from the darkness.

"We do not have time for long greetings. We have to go now while the guards are distracted. We need to get to the boat. Hurry!" Xavi said.

They hurried their way into port, to the slips, and there they climbed into a small boat that Martin had made ready for them. The four them nearly filled the small, open fishing boat. Xavi started its outboard engine, and they began to pull away from the little port.

He ran the motor at a low speed, making little noise. The boat passed slowly from the sheltered slips of the port into the bay of *La Concha*. The four of them remained quiet, and Xavi kept the running lights off and the motor almost noiseless until they were far away, out into the Cantabrian Sea.

It was pitch dark, but Xavi knew the turn up the coast toward France by heart. As they moved farther out into the sea, the lights of San Sebastian became but small twinkles. Far from the city, they began to converse in low voices.

"Goodbye my beautiful San Sebastian," Maria said wistfully while the others looked back upon the city lights in silence.

"Father Extebarri, I am so glad you made it," Xavi said.

"It's a dark time; Xavi, but you always seem to be there for me."

"None of that, Father."

"No, really, there is something about you. You seem to show up for me in my darkest hours, like a guardian angel," his voice was bathed in gratitude and sadness.

"Xavi, what happened back there when we left?" his mother asked.

"Well, Mother, it went according to the plan."

"According to plan?"

Martin and some of his friends made a scuffle. We figured that the guards would be on edge and would scurry from all around to pounce on them. It worked perfectly."

"What will happen to Martin?" his mother asked.

"I am guessing he will be spending a few nights in jail. In his way, he is a quite a guy. We owe him."

"If we ever get back …," his father said wistfully.

"Father Extebarri, where have you been? What happened to you?" Maria asked the priest.

"I have been in the war … ."

"You've seen a lot then," Maria responded.

"Too much. For the last three weeks I have been with the Basque troops fighting the *Requetés* and other Nationalists. The Basque fighters are not anarchists, communists, or foreigners. They are our friends and neighbors, mostly devout Catholics, who prize our homeland, who dream of the idea of an independent Basque Nation."

"That's all lost now isn't it?" Maria added.

"It seems so," Father Extebarri replied, his voice trailing off.

"Father, there are rumors about terrible happenings in the fields," Xavi probed.

"It's too true, Xavi."

The boat went silent again. The little motor purred along.

"A few of us priests traveled with the troops, saying mass, hearing confessions, tending to the wounded, and when needed, giving last rites. None of us ever held a gun. Then a few days ago, just before San Sebastian fell, we were overrun near Mondragón. The priests were tending to the wounded when the Nationalist troops converged on us; they overran us. When they came, they rounded up the soldiers who were not wounded—there must have been fifty to seventy-five of them. They bound their hands and took them into a nearby forest. Then we heard the sound of machine guns and the screams of grown men. It was ghastly; I cannot get it out of my mind."

"And what about the priests?" Xavi pressed.

"After they returned from the forest the Nationalists placed their focus on the wounded lying in the grass. One by one, they bayoneted each of the wounded soldiers, making sure they were dead; then, they came for the priests who attended the soldiers."

"And Inaki, what about Inaki?" Xavi said, dreading what he was sure he would hear.

"Inaki, hobbled as he is, he never got over that fall on the Camino—"

"No, I guess he didn't," Xavi added.

"He could not get away."

Maria gasped at the thought of poor Inaki trying limp away from the thugs.

"They murdered him."

Silence, and its frequent companion, sadness, crashed over and enveloped the tiny boat. Xavi only heard two sounds: the water of the mild seas splashing against the hull and the low whirring of the engine. The running lights glowed weakly in the dark as the boat moved up the coast towards France. They were truly out at sea,

After several minutes of collective silence, Father Extebarri continued, "You know, they were particularly vicious with the priests. They called us *'red priests and Judases.'* I witnessed a number of priests being murdered; I knew they would be coming for me."

"How did you survive?" Maria asked in a whisper. Even in the dark Xavi could imagine the horror on his mother's face.

"I placed myself under several dead men and played dead myself. They did not see me, and they passed me. It was like the Angel of Death seeing there was nothing to feast upon, and then moving on to stalk another house."

The water continued to gently lap against the hull as they silently contemplated the terror. Father Extebarri continued, "I lay there until nightfall, and I remember two things vividly. I was covered with the blood of two dead men, and the ghostly stillness of dozens of bodies lying all about."

Maria gasped, but Father Extebarri continued. "I did not want to go on, and I thought of taking my own life, but the pull in me to survive was greater than my despair."

"Thank God, Father," Xavi added.

"But how did you get back to San Sebastian?" Maria asked.

"I began to walk towards the coast, step by step, and by morning I was on the hills overlooking the sea by Zarautz. There, where the river Orio meets the sea—"

"We know the place," Xavi's father added.

"I collapsed into the water. The blood flowed off me, and it was like a baptism. I felt renewed. I continued on, walking for another day to San Sebastian. I got there just as the city was about to fall."

"Oh, Father Extebarri, that is so horrible," said Maria.

"Yes, but I live …"

"You do …" Xavi added.

"And I am here with you."

None of them could add to that.

Xavi and his father had sailed this route dozens of times, and even at night, in the dark, they knew the villages they passed by. They puttered past Hondarribia, and then towards Hendaye, the first town in France.

"There is Hendaye. We are no longer in Spanish waters. Soon we will be to Saint-Jean-de-Luz."

"Xavi, what are we to do when we get there?" his mother asked.

"We are going to the Church of Saint Jean the Baptist."

"Yes, I know Father Ganbarra well. He will take us in," Father Extebarri volunteered, feeling he had some worth.

"And what about you, Xavi, where will you go?" asked his mother.

"Mother, I will come with you to see Father Ganbarra, and then in the morning I need to be off, back to Spain."

"Why so soon?"

"I need to go back to San Sebastian."

"Why? It seems that it could be dangerous," his mother said.

"I need to go see Inaki's parents. I need to tell them ..."

The silence and sadness crashed down again into the boat as the lights of Saint-Jean-de-Luz came into view. Xavi steered the boat back toward the coast and into the harbor.

In the middle of the night there was no activity in the port or on the dark streets that led to Father Ganbarra's Saint Jean the Baptist church.

Father Extebarri knocked firmly on the parish house door. Father Ganbarra answered, "Oh Father Extebarri, I've been expecting you. Word came from a fisherman that you were coming. Come in, bring your friends in too. It's so late. How did escape?"

"Father, there is too much to explain right now. I will tell you all about it in the morning."

"Come this way. We have beds made up for you."

Book 4
Chapter 21
Burguete, Nationalist Spain
September 16, 1936

Early in the morning, Xavi quietly opened the door of the room where his parents were sleeping. "Mother, Father, I need to start back to Spain," he whispered.

"Can't you at least stay for breakfast?" his mother pleaded.

"I am not sure what difficulties lie ahead. I need to go."

"When will we see you again?" his mother asked with her eyes welling up.

"I will be back soon—and maybe often; please do not ask how. Here are two envelopes: one for you and one for Father Extebarri. They contain some money to help you get started here. I must go now."

"Where did you get this money?"

"Mother, not now."

"Thank you, Xavi. Thank you for getting me out, for getting us out," his father added as he embraced his son.

Xavi then hugged his mother and slipped away.

"He comes and goes like some sort of phantom," Maria said to her husband as their eyes followed their son until he vanished into the narrow of streets of the small French Basque village.

Leaving the train at St.-Jean-Pied-de-Port, Xavi was unsure of the situation at the border. He decided to avoid the border crossing at Valcarlos and to hike over the Pyrenees back to Spain. He knew the paths well that wound around the official crossings and that would drop him safely back down to Roncesvalles. After a few hours of hiking, the occasional farm sign changed from French to Spanish, signaling he was back in Navarre, back in Spain.

Xavi continued on. He made his way to the Col de Lepoeder.

Below him was Roncesvalles. He stopped there and thought when he was last here. It was 1923, with Father Extebarri, with Martin and the other boys, and with Inaki too. Intense sadness came over him.

The war was less than two months old, and he had already lost so much: his parents and Father Extebarri in exile, the soul of his best friend to the hell of battle, Juan and Ana dead in Madrid, Pilar in the arms of impostor parents, and Inaki in the ground in an unmarked Basque field.

Life was compressing itself. Each week now was like living a year. So much so, that it was hard to remember the exact details of important things that had just happened. *What were the names of the nuns?* he thought, trying to recall the exact details of what had just happened two weeks earlier in Madrid.

And finally he wondered, where was Montse? Was she still in Toledo, or back in Barcelona? Was she still the star, progressive journalist, or now just another dispensable bourgeois puppet? He closed his eyes and said a prayer for her: He prayed for her safety wherever she might be, and he hoped she too had made it to safety in France.

He was physically exhausted and emotionally spent. He felt deep loneliness. He missed Montse. He missed her as a man misses a woman. He longed for her warmth, her intelligence, her humor, and the beauty she brought to everywhere she went. He recalled the kiss in Pamplona … her missed her touch.

The sadness could be overwhelming. It came in waves. He thought of what Professor Unamuno had once told him about life's sad moments, its heartbreaks: *They are unavoidable, like the loss of my young son to meningitis; but either these tragedies overwhelm you, or you channel them to create deeper empathy for people, the ability to love more deeply.*

Remembering the professor's words fortified Xavi. *I need to love more deeply,* he thought. *Action is caring. It is by doing God's work I can channel my sadness. There is so much to do. There are so many people who need love now.* He got up, stretched a bit, and headed down the mountain for Burguete.

At about seven in the evening he passed the monastery and entered the beautiful, canopied path, the Witches Wood, that connects Roncesvalles and Burguete. Arriving at the place where the woods intersect with the Cross of *Santa Maria de la Blanca*, he heard a voice. "Stop! Go no further!"

The late day sun cast a long shadow from the tall white cross. Xavi was in the shadow of that cross when he noted the teenager in a *Requeté* uniform; the young man was really no more than a fit, fresh-faced Navarrese boy.

"Who are you? Whose side are you on?" the teenager barked.

How ridiculous, Xavi thought, that wearing this uniform, with its distinctive red beret, conferred the right to command an ancient forest.

"I am Father Xavier Bidertea. I am the secretary to the Bishop of Salamanca."

"I doubt it. Show me some ID," he said in a sharp tone.

Xavi showed his Spanish passport and papers which verified that indeed he did he work for the Bishop of Salamanca. "Okay, but what are you doing here?'" the soldier asked suspiciously, condescendingly.

"I'm hiking, and I am trying to get to my hotel just up the road in Burguete."

"It seems very strange to be hiking here in this time of war, but I can see no reason to hold you. Be careful, Father, you could be killed by either side out here."

"You too. You are too young to be barking at strangers. Go home, be with your parents, your family. Avoid all of this chaos."

The young soldier appeared hurt and confused by what Xavi had said, but he let him pass on to Burguete. Xavi was close to his hotel, and he needed to rest and recharge himself. He had one more stop before he returned to Salamanca. He needed to go back to San Sebastian to see Inaki's parents.

Book 4
Chapter 22
San Sebastian, Nationalist Spain
September 17, 1936

Xavi took the bus from Burguete to Pamplona, and from Pamplona he took a train the final fifty miles to San Sebastian. Xavi left the train station for Inaki's parents' apartment in the port. He recalled making this walk thirteen years earlier with Inaki. Inaki had hopped along on his crutches, awkward, but joyful. On that day, years ago, Xavi helped him along home to the ecstatic reunion with his parents and his brother and sisters.

He passed Zurriola Beach where the waves rolled in and crashed upon the shore; they continued as always, unaffected by the chaos and horror of the war. He crossed the bridge towards the port. He felt such deep sadness. *Channel it to love,* he thought—it was a hard task on this day. The sadness tried to overwhelm him, and it pushed him to the edge of despair. He continued on as he knew the hopelessness would drown him if he didn't.

He also felt more than a small tinge of guilt that he might have inspired Inaki to the priesthood, and that it had led to his grotesque, grisly, senseless murder on a nameless grassy hill. Almost every day it seemed he faced events and circumstances that tested his faith. So far, his faith had bent but had not broken. The fire wall of his faith was the knowledge that his trials were nothing compared to the eternal moments Christ spent on the cross—the moments that changed all of history.

Just before arriving at Inaki's parents' apartment, he ran into Martin. Martin was wearing a number of bruises, and he looked much the worse for wear. Martin called out to Xavi, and Xavi went over to him at his boat.

"Martin, are you okay?"

"I'm fine."

"It looks like you took quite a beating."

"They let me have it good."

"I assume that was not from the fight, but from what happened afterwards."

"Yeah, the soldiers, thugs really, hauled us in and pinned me as the instigator. I've had worse in the bars of Bilboa." He laughed.

"Martin, thank you for everything. Thank you."

"Xavi, as I said, anything for you."

"Not everyone would have done what you did. Not everyone would have volunteered for a beating, Martin."

"I was just glad to see your parents and Father Extebarri get out of here. For now, these goons seemed to have outlawed joy and happiness. They are a stern and serious bunch."

"Our city is sad, isn't it?"

"For now, *Padre*, for now. I will be giving them a wide berth while they are here."

"It seems they are here to stay."

"You more than anyone should know nothing stays forever. Hey, even the Romans left eventually," Martin said with a smirk.

Martin's tone—his unique mixture of loyalty, courage, and humor—were an elixir. Xavi spirits were lifted.

"Anyway Xavi, I thought you would be long gone and heading back to Salamanca; what brings you back here?"

"Father Extebarri told me about Inaki. I will spare you the details, but it is as you suspected."

Martin fell silent. The smile fell from his face, and he crossed himself. "May he rest in peace, Xavi. He was one of the really good ones."

"I know, I know. I need to go and see Inaki's parents. I need to tell them what happened."

"That is some tough duty, *Padre*. Tough duty. We all loved Inaki, and he had become a damn fine priest too."

"Well, in any case …"

"There will be some scores to settle when the time is right."

Xavi wanted to argue Martin out this instinct for revenge, but at this moment he couldn't find the rational for it. "Martin, I am very grateful to you for what you did to help my parents and Father Extebarri, if you need—"

Martin cut him off. "No, *Padre,* you and Father Extebarri

taught me to see the love of God, which I see even now amongst the occupation of these thugs. The beating I took is only a small repayment of what you have given me."

"God bless you, Martin; you have no idea what a comfort your words are."

"And God bless you too, Father, wherever you go. And I sense you don't spend all your days behind a desk in a bishop's palace."

As Xavi left Martin and headed to the apartment. He marveled about the different ways that people came to God and how they saw Him. He admired Martin. It wasn't entirely obvious, but he could see that beneath his sarcastic exterior Martin was devout. When the time had come for it, he had stood tall. Not all the piety was in the bishop's palace or the cathedral. There was more of it in the real world with people like Martin and the sisters in Madrid. The smile on Martin's face, and the singing of the sisters in the dark, these small acts had God's fingerprints on them.

Xavi came to the apartment. He wanted to turn around and leave. He wished for a moment that time could be turned back, that this war had not happened, and that Inaki had not been on that hill. If, if, if. But "if" could not be, and time could not be turned back.

He knocked on the apartment door. Slowly the steps came and Inaki's mother, in her apron, answered. She was together with her husband and two of Inaki's sisters. They were on a vigil; they had the look of people who were waiting for horrible news to be confirmed. He imagined that they had heard the whispers of it here and there, and that in spite of repeating to themselves, *it could not be,* they secretly knew it probably was.

Xavi delivered the news. He stripped out some of the details but added his interpretation, because it was true, and it would attack their despair: "Inaki was a martyr. He was killed for his faith, and this was the noblest death there is."

He did not stay long. He could not stand to see the raw pain play out in front of him once again. He could not bear to witness more of it.

When he left, he could hear the wailing and screaming. It was so different from the laughter and joy that had followed him when he last left the apartment in 1923.

Book 4
Chapter 23
Salamanca, Nationalist Spain
October 8, 1936

Alone is his office at the Bishop's Palace in Salamanca, Xavi perused his mail and noted a letter, postmarked from Toledo. It was from Jaime. The envelope was thick with pages; it was a long letter. He opened it immediately.

Dear Xavi,

I have been wanting to write since I last saw you, but it has been difficult. When I returned to my unit, we immediately left for Toledo. The order came from General Franco himself that Toledo would not fall, that Toledo must be liberated.

I have a number of things to report about Toledo, but that is not why I write. This letter is first a progress report of sorts ... a report on my soul.

Xavi, I am eternally grateful to you. I am in your debt for the way you heard my confession, with such empathy, with a lack of judgement, and with such clear instructions on what I must do—how I must rebuild myself. You cannot imagine what an ordeal it was to come see you. You cannot imagine the depths of the trepidation I felt about confessing my sin to you. We have chaplains here with us, but I knew it was only you who could separate me from my dread.

I wish I could say otherwise, but it would not be true; the road back has been difficult going. The memory of Badajoz is still with me, always with me. It is there almost every night as I toss and turn. I try to hide from the grotesque images, from the screams I still hear in the bullring. They follow me. I have not been able to escape them—anyway maybe somehow that is good; maybe the pain of this horrible memory is part of the healing.

These nightmares bleed into my days, as the war continues on.

249

The boundary between justified action and wanton killing remains narrow and blurry.

Notwithstanding this hard road you put me on, I have taken your penance instructions deeply to heart. I have begun my study of St. Paul and St. Longinus. I am heartened that after their sins, God called them to great faith. St. Paul of course, but really it is more the story of St. Longinus that has touched me.

I am particularly attracted to Longinus because, like me, he was a solider ... and like me, he participated in a gruesome atrocity. Please forgive me for comparing Badajoz to the Crucifixion, but it's just that his story speaks to me so personally.

You, and I suspect it was your intent, left it for me to discover the rest of his story; that is, after the Crucifixion he left the army to become a monk, to preach the word of God. You also did not tell me of the miracles attributed to him; that he was arrested for his faith and had his teeth and tongue pulled out so that he would be silenced. But God is not to be silenced, is he? Even without teeth and tongue he continued on, miraculously preaching until his death by beheading.

St. Longinus, soldier, monk, and martyr. He is the Patron of the Wounded, and it is easy to see that wounds come in so many forms in a war....

Xavi, these stories, these miracles are mesmerizing. One either chooses to believe them or not. I have come to the choosing of believing them. This choice is in large part because of you. I have seen what the power of faith can do. This life of faith you have shown me is not a straight line; it seems to be more of a journey, a pilgrimage as you say, than a spontaneous cure. What is the best I can hope about the screams in the bullring? That these cries diminish? That I will get a night without them? I cannot imagine they will disappear completely, can I?

I pray to God that I may live honorably, in His service; that these visions will begin to recede. Maybe this is right? Maybe that is how God lets it play out: that balanced against the Glory of God one should see the depths of the fires of Hell?

In any case, I know I will not feel a more lasting peace until I am able to make amends, face to face, to the survivors in Badajoz. As soon as this war ends, I will make my way there. I promise it to you.

As I said, I also write with other news from here in Toledo. You probably only see the headlines of what happened here, but I tell you that beneath the headlines is an amazing human story. A story of faith, hope, and courage.

After the War started about seven hundred troops and an equal number of civilians from Toledo took refuge in the old Alcazar. The Alcazar was of no significance. A Military Academy for boys. A school run by a Colonel Moscardó, whose only passion is soccer.

The Republicans, hungry for a victory of any kind—even if it was taking an insignificant Military Academy—gave the capture of the Alcazar insanely disproportionate importance. They launched attack after attack on the old building, laying siege to it, without the ultimate success for which they so yearned.

Early in the siege, they captured the son of the commander. The details of the Colonel's son's last moments are heroic. They should be remembered. After they captured the boy, they threatened to kill him if Moscardó did not surrender, but still the Colonel said 'No.'

Moscardó, like Abraham, was willing to sacrifice his son for his convictions. As the threats on his son escalated, Moscardó asked to speak to him by telephone. They had a short conversation in which he told his son that his duty would not allow him to surrender; that he should commend his soul to God and die a patriot. The boy told his father he understood; that he was willing to die for God and country.

Xavi, unlike with Abraham, the Angel of the Lord did not intervene, or at least not then; shortly after the phone call the boy was executed.

As the execution of the Colonel's son did not cause his capitulation, the Republicans brought in miners from Asturias to blow up the Alcazar—with the troops and civilians in it! The miners wired the building with explosives, and Prime Minister Francisco Largo Caballero came from Madrid, and posing for the cameras, pressed the detonator, setting off a massive explosion.

I know I should not feel this hatred, but I do. The Republicans, their arrogance, their condescension, their foolishness, makes me feel such contempt for them. What military purpose, humanity, or nobility is there in blowing up a building full of women and children? What they succeeded with at the Montana barracks with the killing of Juan and Ana, and the others, they failed at in Toledo.

251

And maybe this is where in the story the Angel of the Lord did arrive ... when the explosion failed to bring the building down, when its heroes survived. There is something really foul and evil about this communism that has overrun Republican Spain.

Upon their liberation, the joy and relief of the people was amazing. Their two months under siege gave them a special bond, a brotherhood you see among men who fight together. They persisted, and became, by and large, more resolved, more faithful—and even eight babies were born during the siege. Their lives will forever be marked as babies of the Alcazar. It was a blessing to see their faces and to feel their deep gratitude.

This is not all from Toledo.

After the liberation, I was in a bar, and there, lying unnoticed, were numerous copies of old El Progressiu newspapers. On many of them I could see Montse's byline. I had one of my fellow soldiers who speaks Catalan translate for me. It seems Montse took an increasingly critical tone of the siege, and its tactics, and he said she was particularly pointed about the preening of Largo Caballero when he came to detonate the building.

So even Montse saw what we see, the attack on the Toledo highlighted everything that is wrong about the Republicans: they fixated on a target with no strategic value, their tactics were ill conceived and disorganized, and they primped and posed in front of the cameras, confusing war with propaganda.

All of the Catalan and Republican journalists are said to have fled just before we arrived, so I guess she must be back in Barcelona. I thought you would want to know.

Having seen what I witnessed in Toledo...the fortitude of Colonel Moscardó, the courage and persistence of the ordinary men and women in the Alcazar, the stupidity and banality of the Republicans, makes me confident we will prevail. God willing, however long it takes. I pray God will spare me so I can complete the penance you have given me.

Please keep me in your prayers.
Jaime

Book 4
Chapter 24
Salamanca, Nationalist Spain
October 12, 1936

The liberation of Toledo was a *tour de force* for General Franco. He consolidated his power and was named *El Caudillo,* the undisputed leader of the Nationalist forces.

Today, October twelfth, Columbus Day; the day to celebrate Spain. Oh glorious Spain! Indispensable Spain! The home of the Spaniards. It was their culture, Spanish culture, that had pushed Islam out of Europe and back to Africa; it was the courage and vision of the Spaniards that discovered the New World. What other country could be the home to Columbus, the Conquistadors, Cervantes, and Saint Teresa?

Glorious Spain—her treasures and triumphs had been preserved from the barbaric Republicans. Tonight was a celebration of Spain—that is to say, Nationalist Spain. Oh what self-congratulatory speeches would be heard at the university tonight!

"Your Excellency, are you ready to go over to the ceremony?"

"Yes, Father."

"Your Excellency, what can we expect tonight?"

"It's Columbus Day. It will be a celebration of the Nationalists, of Franco."

"Who will be on the dais with you?"

"Unamuno, General José Millan Astray, and Carmen Polo Martinez-Valdes, General Franco's wife."

"Who is General Millan Astray?"

"General Millan Astray, quite an interesting character. He is maimed. He lost his left hand and his right eye in Morocco."

"That's terrible!"

"Yes, but perhaps his greater wound was to his manhood from his wife."

"Excuse me, Your Excellency, I don't understand?"

"Yes, it's true. When he married his wife, she announced to him she intended to remain chaste."

"It seems his current vocation, running the press office for the Nationalists, would be like sailing on the sea of tranquility."

"You, being a sailor—that is well said, Father."

Xavi and the bishop made the short walk from the Bishop's Palace to the university. It was warm in the late afternoon, and the sun showered down on the soft sandstone buildings of the city, creating long shadows. The play of the light and stone in Salamanca was bewitching.

When Xavi and the bishop arrived, they were among the about one hundred fifty people gathered in one of the halls of the ancient university. As the guests arrived, civilians and soldiers alike, they raised their arms in the Falangist salute.

Falangism, Spanish Fascism, was spearheaded by the poet and intellectual, José Antonio Primo de Rivera. Primo de Rivera was indisputably impressive. Dashing, brilliant, he painted in grand strokes. He had attempted to create an inclusive canvas for Spain's future. But now, Primo de Rivera was off the stage, in a Republican jail, waiting for the death sentence he had been given to be conferred upon him.

And so it was that Franco took Primo de Rivera's mantle, but he was not his heir. Franco was in no way dashing. In comparison to José Antonio, he was a small, and small-minded man. These straight-armed salutes which paid homage to Franco troubled Xavi. He had seen them in San Sebastian; he imagined they had been present when Inaki was killed; and that they were in the background when his parents and Father Extebarri made their way on a dark sea to France. But no, that was not it—that was not what was so troubling about them, it was that they represented submission to a form of mob mentality. They were homage to a lack of intellectual rigor. They represented everything that the great man, Unamuno, opposed.

"Your Excellency, I will be here in the first row if you should need anything."

"Thank you, Father."

And there came the professor. "Good evening, Xavi," Unamuno

said as he passed on his way to the dais.

Unamuno welcomed the crowd and introduced a prominent intellectual, José María Pemán. Pemán, was valuable to Franco's forces. He was an intellectual of high regard who wholeheartedly supported the Nationalist cause. He kicked off the evening with a passionate and highly crafted speech outlining the imperatives of a Nationalist victory. Spain must be unified. Spain must rid itself of communism and separatism.

Pemán finished and turned the floor over to Professor Francisco Maldonado. Maldonado lacked subtlety. He used words the way a butcher wields a knife. He launched into an attack on Catalonia and the Basque Country, calling them "cancers on the body of the nation." He added he was confident that Fascism would heal Spain. "Fascism, the healer of Spain, will know how to exterminate them, cutting into the live flesh, like a determined surgeon free from false sentimentality."

The words shocked and repulsed Xavi. He watched the bishop, who squirmed in his seat.

The Falangist crowd was in a frenzy, an uproarious, wild frenzy. From somewhere in the auditorium, someone cried out, "*Viva la Muerte!*"

General Millán Astray heard the cry and responded with, "*España!*"

The crowd roared, "*Una!*"

Millan Astray repeated, "*España!*"

In turn the crowd replied, "*Grande!*"

A third time, Millán Astray shouted, "*España!*"

The crowd bellowed out, "*Libre!*"

"*España,* one, great and free!" Millan Astray concluded. The crowd was near hysteria.

Xavi watched Unamuno. Xavi could see the professor was in distress. His discomfort was palpable. Knowing him as he did, he was certain he was working out a response.

Then, the great man rose slowly and began to address the crowd. "Quiet, quiet!"

Xavi was in awe of Unamuno. The power of his intellect, and the power of his character silenced the crowd almost immediately. He had an unseen power few people possess; certainly, it was a force his bishop lacked.

"You are waiting for my words. You know me well, and you know I cannot remain silent for long. Sometimes, to remain silent is to lie, since silence can be interpreted as assent. I want to comment on the so-called speech of Professor Maldonado. I will ignore the personal offence to the Basques and Catalans. I myself, as you know am a Basque, born in Bilboa."

Then Unamuno paused and gestured to Bishop Pla y Deniel, "And the bishop here, whether you like it or not, whether he advertises it or not, is a Catalan, born in Barcelona."

The bishop remained silent, motionless, expressionless.

Unamuno continued. "But now I have heard this insensible and necrophilous oath, *'Viva la Muerte!'* and I, having spent my life writing paradoxes that have provoked the ire of those who do not understand what I have written, and being an expert in this matter, find this ridiculous paradox repellent.

"General Millán Astray is a cripple. There is no need for us to say this with whispered tones. He is a war cripple, as was Cervantes. But unfortunately, Spain today has too many cripples. And, if God does not help us, soon it will have very many more. It torments me to think that General Millán Astray could dictate the norms of the psychology of the masses. A cripple, who lacks the spiritual greatness of Cervantes, hopes to find relief by adding to the number of cripples around him."

Millán Astray's face went red with anger. He was outraged, and staring directly at Unamuno, he responded, "Death to intelligence! Long live death!" provoking more wild applause from the Falangists.

Pemán, in an effort to calm the crowd and protect Unamuno, exclaimed "No! Long live intelligence! Death to the bad intellectuals!" Pemán did not have the stature of Unamuno, and so the crowd continued in its riotous applause.

Unamuno resumed; he re-commanded the room. "This, the University of Salamanca, founded in 1218, is the temple of intelligence. You are profaning its sacred domain."

He returned Millán Astray's stare. The temperature in the hall was rising rapidly. "You, you Nationalists, will win because you have enough brute force. But you will not convince. In order to convince it is necessary to persuade, and to persuade you will need something that you lack: reason and right in the struggle. I see it is useless to ask you to think of Spain."

The professor gathered his papers and concluded simply. "I have spoken." He then began to move off the stage.

Unamuno's words drove the crowd from murmuring, to frenzy, to chaos. Xavi could sense the danger in the growing hysteria. He was worried that the crowd was turning into a mob, and that they were focused on Unamuno.

Xavi placed himself between the professor and those who were incited to move toward him. Seeing Xavi, the mob monetarily delayed their rush forward.

At the same the time Xavi could see that while General Milan Astra was angry, he also worried for the Professor. He did not want this situation to spin out control. The distance and delay that Xavi had created was an opening.

"Professor, get to the side door; take the *señora's* arm." Unamuno, with Xavi at his side, took the arm Carmen Polo offered as his protection; it was his passage from danger.

Oh the irony! As the mob shouted out at him in anger, seeking retribution for his words, it was Franco's wife who led the professor to the safety of a quiet side street. And there, providing a buffer from the crowd in pursuit of Unamuno and Franco's wife, Xavi followed faithfully.

Book 4
Chapter 25
Salamanca, Nationalist Spain
October 28, 1936

After the events of Columbus Day, the city was a blaze with rumors about what would happen to Unamuno. The great professor was suspended from his position at the university, but what would happen next? Would he be sent into exile again? It was said Franco was so furious that he had considered executing him.

The bishop called Xavi in to inform him that Unamuno had been given his fate. Xavi feared for the worst.

"Father, I know you have known the professor for a number of years, and that you admire him greatly."

"Other than the saints, I have few heroes."

"In his way, he can be quite entertaining."

"Your Excellency, he is more than entertaining. He is a great man."

"Perhaps, and I myself have enjoyed his company many an evening as well. I believe, deep down, all that doubt and skepticism masks a strong faith, or at least a strong desire for faith."

"Your Excellency, the professor lives where few men can: the gray space between faith and doubt."

"Please do not try to make angels dance on the head of a pin, Father. His type of deep intellectual churning, his lack of complete certainty, is anathema to the Nationalists. While Unamuno is defined by his embrace of gray, they only see black or white."

"Your Excellency, where you have sent me, my missions, they are in fields of gray."

"That may be, but Franco and his people, they are certain of the importance and virtue of their cause. Unamuno's speech knocked over a hornet's nest."

"I know. I saw the swarm of hornets chasing him out of the hall."

The bishop peered at his secretary and continued, "Franco was furious. I do believe he seriously considered having him executed."

"Thank God not, but really? For a few words—for a few words that rang true?"

The words "rang true" hung in the air. The bishop studied Xavi. He sometimes wondered whether he had Xavi's full loyalty. The bishop understood that commitment was so close to, but so different from, loyalty. "In any case, Franco calmed down, and he concluded that the fallout from an execution would be too much to manage."

"The fallout? How so? General Franco seems to operate without concern for sanction?"

Again Xavi's words paused the bishop. "Yes Unamuno, even though he is not understood by foreigners, he is revered by them. Executing him would have been a step too far." The bishop paused again, and then added, "at this point …"

"So what was decided?"

"He is permanently stripped of his duties at the university. He will be kept under house arrest."

Stripped, Xavi thought. *What a word. To be made naked. To be embarrassed, held up for ridicule.* "Your Excellency isn't that a death sentence in a way?" his impertinence nearing the line that would trigger the bishop's wrath.

"Yes, perhaps, but it is done," the bishop answered tersely.

It seemed to Xavi, Unamuno was another Spaniard, another Basque, lost to the war. Another innocent caught on the wrong side. Like the nuns, like Inaki, like his parents. He had another mission to perform, another rescue to do. "Your Excellency, I want to visit the professor."

"In what capacity, Father?"

"As a friend."

"If you plan to go as a friend, then I suggest dress as a friend, and not as a priest, not as my secretary."

The message was clear. "I will take off my collar when I go."

"It would be best for you. It would best for me."

"As you wish, Your Excellency," Xavi concluded as the air in the bishop's office had grown tense.

After he changed, Xavi made the short walk from the Bishop's Palace to Unamuno's house on *Calle Libreros*, the bookseller's street—the street he and Jaime had first lived on when they arrived in Salamanca.

There were two guards outside Unamuno's house. Even in his civilian clothes they recognized Xavi.

"I am here on a social visit."

The guards stepped aside, and it was the Unamuno himself who answered the door. "Come in Xavi, come in."

"Professor, we may speak in Basque if you prefer."

"Yes, it would be nice to speak in my old mother tongue again."

Unamuno took Xavi into his study where they were surrounded by towers of books and papers.

"Xavi, I am glad you came. Since Columbus Day no one comes to visit anymore. It is one of the many sanctions of the hideous power they wield."

Often, and this was one of those times, Unamuno spoke a simple sentence that was both question and answer. Xavi waited for Unamuno to continue.

"And I am guessing your bishop did not appreciate your coming."

"He did not stand in the way."

"Xavi, I need to thank you for what you did, how you stood up for me. Your humble nobility continues to surprise me."

"Oh, Professor, it had to be done, and not even General Millan Astray wanted the scene to cascade out of control."

Xavi paused to study the room. Unamuno had near him, for comfort perhaps, his two most famous books: *The Tragic Sense of Life* and *The Life of Don Quixote.*

And then there was Unamuno himself. The long face, the thin, prominent nose, his grey hair, and grey beard—in another time he could have been a noble in an El Greco portrait. It occurred to Xavi, that Unamuno himself was his own paradox: a Basque through and through who appeared as a classic Castilian.

"I hate to say this, but you look tired, Professor."

"Xavi, I feel very tired. I am so sad to be losing the university for a third time. This time is the last time, I fear. But it is my students I will miss most. This house arrest, it is not itself a bother."

"You wouldn't want to travel again?"

"No, not really. I have rarely left Spain anyway. It is my home. Is suits my spirit."

"Suits your spirit?"

"Yes, Spaniards understand me. The English and Americans can't really comprehend my writing."

"Hmmm, how so? Translation?"

"No, it's not an issue of translation. They do not believe in the importance of death, the importance of struggle, as we do. But we can discuss that another day. That's not for now."

"But what about France? You spent so much time there?" Xavi said, wanting to keep the conversation moving.

"Oh the French! They seem to be either irredeemably frivolous, or obnoxiously condescending. They prefer to float above the suffering and struggle."

"Struggle, we have so much of that now, don't we?

"We do. You know the irony of the incident on Columbus Day?"

"No, I'm not sure what you mean?"

"I supported the Nationalists from the get-go. I supported the coup at first. I am wary of this separatism which threatens to break our country and Iberian culture apart. In addition, it was clear public order needed to be restored. I had hoped the military would enforce order and maintain the glue of our society."

"But you have had a change of heart?"

"Yes. They, Franco, have gone too far. They are too ruthlessly, recklessly, wantonly aggressive. They have substituted terror for persuasion. Force for intellect."

Xavi knew it was true. He had seen it up close already.

Unamuno continued on, "But, Father, I know your silence is not disagreement with me. I know you have too much intelligence for that. You are living in the gray too; you have for some time, haven't you?"

Unamuno's final phrase caught Xavi off guard. "I'm not sure what you mean?"

"I think you do—deep inside you do."

"Excuse me, no."

"I have been at this university for over forty years. I have seen many exceptional young people pass through here."

"I'm sure you have."

"But few as exceptional, as beautiful, as Miss Costa ..." The Professor stopped to see how directly his shot had hit Xavi.

The silence that came over Xavi told all.

"And I saw how she looked at you, how she revered you, the tears she cried at your ordination …"

Xavi remained silent, feeling confused and lost, and wondering where the Professor was headed.

"But you chose, didn't you? And you have chosen again. You see the gray, but you move forward anyway. You see the limitations of your bishop. Xavi, he does not have your character or deeply felt intelligence. But your choice is easy. The Republicans have devolved into communists and anarchists, and there is no limit to their hatred of your church. They are bent on destroying your most sacred possession, something more valuable to you than even the love of Miss Costa."

Xavi needed an exit. "Professor it is so good to be with you. It is so good to converse with you in our Basque language. I must go now. I will be gone for a week and perhaps two."

"How very odd. A priest traveling from his very safe confines while the bonfires of an anti-clerical purge rage. Whatever you are doing must be quite important. I will look forward to our next visit. As I said, I have few visitors anymore."

"I will come to see you again. I will come again when I return."

"Be safe my friend, be safe."

Book 4
Chapter 26
Perpignan, France
December 15, 1936

Oh my God, Patrick! What happened? Are you okay? Come to the back; that needs attending."

Xavi followed Jacques to the small bathroom next to the office in the back of the warehouse. In the mirror Xavi could see it finally, the deep gash over his right eyebrow. There was dried blood all over his face. His shirt was a mess, and near the wound itself it was still a wet, bloody ooze.

"Don't move." Jacques said as he cleaned his face with a wet cloth.

"Ouch, that stings," Xavi exclaimed as Jacques applied peroxide to the wound.

"It needs to be disinfected before we put a bandage on it. I think you will be able to get by without stitches, but that will leave a scar."

Xavi was still shaking as Jacques applied the bandage. "Jacques can I sit for bit, maybe a drink."

"Of course Patrick, of course. In my office. How about some *marc*?"

In the small office stacks of files and paper covered the desk. Jacques poured two glasses of *marc*. The rough liquor was new to Xavi. It was warm, hot almost, as it passed over his lips and tongue.

"A few sips of this will settle you, Patrick. You should carry a bottle in your pack—just in case."

"Perhaps," Xavi said as the liquor began to push back on the tide of adrenaline that had overcome his body.

"You were gone so long? What happened, Patrick? This wound is fresh."

"Can I have a minute? Could you refill my glass?"

"Of course, of course," Jacques said, refilling Xavi's glass.

With the second glass of *marc*, Xavi regained a sense of calm, and he began to recount what had happened. "After I left you, I spent three days living in the mountains, charting the paths over the Pyrenees between France and the Spanish border. I was watching the passes—which ones were being watched and which ones weren't. Jacques, these mountains are treacherous."

"I know, I know. What you are doing is extremely dangerous. I understand that."

Xavi continued, "After that I made my way to Girona."

Jacques stopped him. "Girona, what is like there? It is so close, and I hear terrible stories from there."

"It's a frightening place. No place for a priest, or, really, anyone decent."

"What do you mean, Patrick?"

"It's totally different than Madrid. Madrid is a city at the front of a war, focused on its defense. Girona is a city swept up in revolution."

"Revolution?"

"Yes, revolution. It is a dark and brooding place. It is ruled by zealots."

"Zealots?"

"When you are there you feel hatred flowing in its streets. They think they have outlawed God and owners. Their new rules look nothing like the world we have known."

Xavi paused and took another sip of his drink, "You know, it's very strange. I was in San Sebastian just after the Nationalists arrived, and the people there were stuck inside gripped by fear. In Girona people fill the streets; they smile; they call each other comrade, but there is no real joy—they seem to be in a trance."

"A trance?"

"Compliant, soulless."

"Strange."

"They have tried to chase God away. All the churches have been destroyed or closed. Add to this mix the Soviets."

"What do you mean, Patrick, Soviets?"

"There are many Russians in Girona. It is so odd to hear their strange language and attempts at badly accented Spanish and Catalan. They are everywhere in Girona; you can't miss them, and they seem to be very powerful. Girona is a Godless, dangerous place."

Jacques pointed to Xavi's forehead, "But this didn't happen there did it? It's too fresh."

"No—it was later."

"So why were you gone so long, much longer than I expected."

"I got to Girona and dropped off my supplies. As I said, it is a dangerous place, so I moved carefully. I went to the address where you said the six seminarians were; but there were only two there. They had been six, but in fear they had split up into three groups of two."

"They split up?" Jacques said with alarm.

"Yes, and I decided that reuniting the six would be too risky, and that I would take them over the mountains two at a time."

"That made sense."

"The intital trip had the usual difficulties of cold weather, fog, and snow—nothing for which I wasn't prepared, and ultimately, I got the first two here to France."

"Then what happened?'

"The next two." Xavi paused, and then continued, "They are lost."

"Lost? What do you mean lost?"

"They are lost in every way you can imagine. When I got to them, they were fearful, trembling, and in despair. When I told them who I was, and what was my purpose, they told me they were not going to come with me."

"Not coming with you?"

"Yes, they said instead they were going to turn themselves in. I tried to explain to them how foolish and dangerous that would be. They told me they were willing to trade their safety in exchange for names and locations of their classmates. I tried to argue them out of this, but it was no use. And one other thing"

"What?"

"Somewhere during their ordeal they broke; they lost their faith. They said they were going to turn me in."

"*Mon Dieu!*" Jacques exclaimed. "What traitors!"

"Jacques, none of us knows how we will bear up when we have our Calvary moment, do we?"

"No, perhaps not ..."

The small office went silent until Xavi picked up the story again. "So I left them and moved on to the last two."

Pointing again to Xavi's head Jacques asked, "Is that when this happened?"

"Yes, in the Pyrenees. The last two were very unfit after months without any real exercise or even daily walking routines, but they were joyful, optimistic; it seemed the ordeal had strengthened rather than weakened their faith. In any case, we moved slowly up the mountains."

"I'm listening Patrick, I'm listening."

"I have been in the mountains since I was a little boy. I know how they sound. I know the sounds of the wind, the sounds of the earth settling, the sounds of sheep moving—and I know the sounds of footsteps also."

"Footsteps?" Jacques repeated ominously.

"I have learned to judge their distance, too."

Jacques leaned in to listen intently.

"As we moved slowly up the path, the sound of the steps—I judged that it was from two men—was closing the distance on us."

"Did you say anything to the seminarians?"

"Not until the last moments."

"What do you mean?"

"When I sensed they were near us, and that we had no choice but to fight, I told them. I told them they would be the bait."

"What! The bait?"

"Yes, as the sun was going down, I told them. I told them we needed to fight, and that I needed them to draw the men in."

"Oh my God ..." Jacques said with trepidation.

"I told them that they would sit around a fire, and I would hide in the trees nearby, in order to take the men by surprise. They showed no hesitation. They said simply, *we live together, or we die together.* I won't forget that."

"Okay, okay, but what happened next?"

"We lit the fire, and I hid myself. In a few minutes the men, and as I had thought, two of them, arrived."

"What did they say?"

"They spoke in Catalan. They told the seminarians that they did not come for them, that they could go free. They said they came, they were hunting, they used the words '*hunting*,' for '*the priest*.'"

Jacques said nothing; his faced showed the fear as if he too had been on the mountain.

"They didn't flinch. *Live together or die together,* I thought as I waited for my moment, my moment to wield my branch."

The words "my branch" enabled Jacques to exhale.

"I saw my opening; I jumped out and stuck them with ferocious blows of the branch."

"Like David against the Philistines."

"Except it was one of the men who had the stone."

"The stone?"

"One of the men was felled instantly; the other staggered, fell to his knees, and recovered. Before I could apply another blow, he grabbed a large rock and struck my forehead."

"Oh no."

"I was stunned. Blood gushed out. It was then the seminarians passed their second trial of faith."

"What? Tell me."

"They picked up what was near them—small sticks and pebbles—they threw them at the man. It was enough to distract him, enough for me to recover a bit, to see what I needed to do."

"What did you do?"

"I picked up my branch and struck him with all the force I had. He fell to the ground. He fell before my feet."

"Did you kill them?"

"No."

"Why not? They would have killed you?"

"It wasn't necessary. I tied them to a tree, and on first light we set off again, making it over the mountains to France."

"But they know you now! They saw you!"

"It is not for me to pass the judgement of life or death."

"Well in any case, thank God you made it. You know, there are so many different chemicals that have exploded at one time in your country. It is difficult to keep all the actors straight; however, it is easy to understand our mission—save our church."

"Our church? Jacques, you do seem to be something other than a logistics manager."

"Patrick, the less you know about me the better. But, thinking you may require some sustenance besides the *marc*, I want to tell you about Ceferino Giménez Malla."

"Who is he?"

"An ordinary man. No one you should normally know. But as you speak of trials of a faith, I want to tell you his story."

"Tell me then."

"Giménez Malla was a Spanish Romani, a Gypsy, and a Roman Catholic."

"Was?"

"Yes, was. He was born poor and often went hungry as a child. About the age of twenty, he married his wife Teresa according to a traditional Roma ceremony. They were happily married for forty years. They had no children."

"The Romas, they live outside looking in here in Spain," Xavi interjected.

"As in most places. He was known for his honesty, and he became a leader in his community. Though he had no education, people would seek him out for advice."

"He sounds like a good man."

"He was. An example of his charity, he took in a local landowner, a Catalan, who was suffering from tuberculosis. The man had passed out on the street, and heedless of the danger of contagion, Malla, strong like an ox, hoisted the man on his shoulders and carried him home. The grateful family rewarded him with a sum sufficient to start a business buying and selling surplus mules that the French army no longer needed after World War I."

"Where is your story going, Jacques?"

"Bear with me, Patrick."

"I'm listening."

"Even though he was illiterate, and an outsider, after his wife died, Giménez Malla began a career as a catechist. He taught both Romani and Spanish children the Catholic faith. He was a wonderful storyteller, had a gift for catechizing children by telling stories. He became a member of the Franciscan Third order and the Society of St. Vincent de Paul."

"I see. Attracted to love and to the poor."

"Yes, exactly. But that is not the end of it, or the point of it. In

July 1936, when the Civil War erupted—"

"It seems to be always about this wretched war," Xavi interrupted.

"It does for now. It was then that Giménez Malla tried to defend a Catholic priest from Republican militiamen. They both were arrested and imprisoned in a former Capuchin monastery that was converted into a wartime prison."

"What monstrosity! To turn a monastery into a prison."

"Amongst so many. There he only had one possession: his rosary. He was told that he would probably be released if he gave it up. He refused to renounce his faith."

Xavi listened intently for the story's next turn.

"A guard is said to have asked him if he had weapons, to which he answered, 'Yes, and here it is,' displaying his rosary. On August 9, Giménez Malla and some others were taken by truck to a cemetery and shot. He died holding the rosary in his hands, while shouting, *Long live Christ the King!* They killed an old man, a Gypsy, because he would not give up his rosary. This is whom we fight against. Remember that."

"Whom we fight?"

"I am with you, Patrick. Enough said. Do not ask more."

"Jacques, please don't worry about me." Xavi pointed to his head and continued, "This will heal," and then pointing to his heart, "This is strong. My faith has not wavered."

"Keep your faith, Patrick. If our faith fails, we will be at an abyss facing the apocalypse."

—•—

Book 4
Chapter 27
Saint-Jean-de-Luz, France
December 17, 1936

It was Christmas Season in Saint-Jean-de-Luz. Strings of lights—some spelling *Joyeux Noel*, others making stars lit in green or red to mark Christ's coming—were hung across the narrow streets of the old port town as the afternoon quickly transitioned to dusk. Xavi stopped at several shops on his way to the address Father Ganbarra had given him. The shopkeepers, some in Basque, and mostly in French, noted the bandage above Xavi's right eye.

"*Monsieur*, are you okay? That bandage needs to be changed."

Xavi neared the apartment. It was neither grand nor totally run down. He knew his mother would hate the plainness of it. He tried to organize his story in his mind, how he got the wound; he was not sure he could play out the lie, and he imagined his mother would wear him down with successively detailed questions.

It's too late anyway, he thought as he knocked. "Mother, it's me."

Opening the door his mother forcefully grabbed and embraced Xavi, "Oh my goodness, Xavi! It is so good to see you. Come in, come in. How did you find us? What are you doing here?"

Pulling back a bit, she gasped. "Your forehead? What happened? That bandage must be changed!"

Xavi set down his packages and followed his mother to the apartment's small bathroom.

"Oh my God, what a mess," she said as peeled off the bandage. She then cleaned and re-bandaged the wound. He could see the questions building up as she finished.

"How did this happen?" she demanded.

"The bishop sent me to France ... on some business ... and I ran into a doorframe—"

"Xavi, that's ridiculous! You are too old to lie to your mother—

270

and you, a priest!"

"Mother, please I can't really say more."

"Can't, won't, or shouldn't?" she snapped back almost immediately.

Xavi paused to parse the alternatives, "Shouldn't."

"I do not like any of this."

"Any of what?"

"The money, this gash on your head—that will leave a scar, by the way—and you, my son, a priest traveling here, there, and everywhere at a time like this."

"There will be a time when I can tell you about it, but not now."

Maria Bidertea stared at him with a combination, of frustration, suspicion, love, and worry. She changed the subject. "How did you find us?"

"Father Ganbarra told me where you had settled."

"I'm sorry about the interrogation, but really, more than anything, I'm just happy you are here."

"I brought you a few things—some treats and a few Christmas presents."

"You need not have done that; and look at our little tree, it's pathetic, but it's the best we could do this year."

Xavi put several items under the small, scraggly tree and handed his mother the other packages. "Please open these, they are for the season."

"What delicacies! Bayonne ham; a nice sheep's cheese; a bottle of Patxaran, your father's favorite liquor; and Basque cake. Oh Xavi, this will brighten our Christmas for sure. Xavi, remember our beautiful Christmases in San Sebastian? Everything was just right there. I am so sorry for you to see us here, here in this shabby little apartment."

"It's not shabby, Mother, and it is best you are here anyway, really it is. Things are still not right in San Sebastian."

"When, when do you think we could return?"

"Honestly, I have no idea. No one really knows where this war is headed."

"Well I guess we should feel lucky to just have any roof at all over our heads. There are thousands and thousands of Basques who fled here when San Sebastian fell."

"Yes, I've heard that."

"It's terrible. There are camps all around this corner of France. The conditions are dreadful, and now, as winter is upon us, it is a crisis. Women, babies, young children, the elderly, all stuck in camps, shivering, trying to avoid death."

"You have firsthand knowledge?"

"Yes. They need doctors, and I help out as I can, but no matter what we do, many will die this winter for certain."

"There is too much of that to go around, but God bless you, Mother, for what you are doing."

"Your father helps too. He teaches the Basque children. No one could have imagined what misery this war would bring. It seems Spain is not big enough to contain all of its suffering. There is too much of it there, and now it has overflowed here to France. They say it is bad in Perpignan as well. But, enough of that. Let me look at you—besides that gash, you look thin and tired. I hate to think of you traveling around with this war on."

"There is no need to worry about me—I am careful."

Xavi's words triggered his mother worry again. "Xavi, I heard you about not asking too much, but please, whatever it is you are mixed up in, please watch yourself."

"I will, Mother, I will, I promise."

"You are my only son. If anything—"

He knew where his mother going and cut her off. "Don't worry, nothing is going to happen to me. Don't worry, Mother."

"Okay, okay. Your father will be home soon, and with what you brought we can make a celebration. It is not as it was in San Sebastian, but for now it is our home—for how long, no one can know."

Book 4
Chapter 28
Salamanca, Nationalist Spain
December 20, 1936

"Come in, come in," Professor Unamuno said welcoming Xavi. Xavi passed the guards and entered the house; Unamuno immediately noticed his head. "What is that bandage on your forehead? What have you been up to?"

Xavi thought for a moment. He felt so alone in his mission. He was a made-up person sent on secret missions interfacing with a man in Perpignan named Jacques Latour—and he doubted that was his real identity either. It was a lonely journey; it was weighing on him. He felt if anyone could understand the shadows in which he moved, it would be Professor Unamuno.

"Can we talk in your office?"

"Of course, of course. Would you like a coffee?"

"No, no thank you."

Unamuno sat behind his desk and Xavi in a red leather chair just in front of it.

"Well, about your head ... tell me?"

"I have been making trips in and out of the Republican Zone."

"Whatever for?"

"To rescue people."

"Are you mad? What people?"

"Priests, nuns ... religious people trapped on the wrong side. There are a lot of them."

"Yes, I can imagine there are."

The basic outline of the secret was out, and Xavi waited as the Professor organized his thoughts to probe in on what it all meant.

"I see you live like some type of spirit moving between two worlds, and you are never really in one or the other, are you?"

"Yes, it has that feeling to it."

"This is an existence I know well. A Basque, teaching at the great Spanish University, revered, yet exiled. Yes, I know some of the life of the spirit world—what it is like."

"I'm sure you do."

"How is it on the other side?"

"Suffering, horror, suspension of reality, erasure of truth."

"As I feared."

"And not just in the Republican Zone. In San Sebastian too. My parents fled to France, a childhood friend, a priest, was murdered by the Nationalists—there is evil everywhere. Where does it come from? Where, Professor, tell me." Xavi asked, pleading to hear some wisdom.

Unamuno rose from his desk and peered out the window to the street below, "It's in our natures, Xavi. Our oldest prayer, the Our Father, asks God to not only lead us from temptation, but to also deliver us from evil."

"Professor, I'm not following you."

"It is acknowledgment of the temptations and evil are all around and that God is the safety net when all else has failed." Unamuno turned back around, standing by the window he looked at Xavi, and he could sense Xavi wanted something more. "Xavi you are from San Sebastian?"

"Yes."

"What is the name of the river that cuts the town in two parts?"

"The Urumea."

"Yes, the Urumea. It's like the Urumea."

"What do you mean?"

"The Urumea is a tidal river."

"That's right. The tides go up and down into the river from the sea."

"Well it's like that. The tide, the sea that is, rises into the river, but it never overcomes the river; and the river flows into the sea, but the river never becomes the sea. Every day, back and forth, the tides and river struggle with one another, neither gaining the upper hand and neither giving up."

Unamuno paused again, "Good and evil, sacred and profane, back, and forth. It's like that. It has always been. It always will be."

"So what is purpose of it all?"

"The struggle. Life is about the struggle. You are Catholic Xavi—you knew both faith and doubt, both river and sea, but in the end, you, and I, we both know, that in the end we win. It is in death we win. That is the ultimate paradox."

Xavi was not fully prepared for what he heard, and he again felt he needed to search for an exit, a place to catch his breath and organize his emotions. "Professor, thank you—I need to get going—there is so much to do before Christmas."

"When is your mass, Father?"

"I am saying the Midnight Mass on Christmas Eve; might I see you there?"

"Yes, I will be there ... out of the shadows, with my guards in tow."

Book 4
Chapter 29
Barcelona, Republican Spain
December 22, 1936

Tomás came to the door; across it loosely hung the greeting of the season: *Bon Nadal.* He rapped the door hard, almost violently, shaking the letters.

"Who is it? Who's there?"

"It's Tomás!"

"I don't want to see you. I told you that! I cannot do another fight about us. There is nothing more to say. We are finished."

"I've moved on, and I've had enough of your condescending lectures, Montse. I'm not here about us."

"What then?"

"It's about the article."

Montse rose from her desk and walked across the room to unlatch the lock. Pausing for a few moments to return to be seated at her desk she replied, "The door is open."

Tomás entered Montse's apartment. He stood while she stayed seated.

"I see you still celebrate Christmas?"

"Of course I do, for lots of reasons."

"We will get to that, too. Enjoy yourself; by next year Christmas will go the way of the churches."

"Tomás, why did you change? How did you go from forward thinking liberal to a Bolshevik totalitarian?"

"I said, enough of that! If you had not been my lover, I would smash your face for what you say."

"How dare you! But after what I saw, the nuns' bones spread on the streets, I would not at all be surprised for you to hit a woman."

"I said that is enough, bitch! I am here for something else."

"What now?"

"The article."

"I'm not sure I want to write it."

"Why not? You have all the pieces."

"You don't want an article. You are looking for a wanted poster."

"In Catalan and in Spanish too. I want a wide net thrown out for that priest, whoever he is."

"Like I said, I don't want to do it."

"You don't have a choice."

"Of course I do! My words are my own."

"Not anymore."

"What are you saying?"

"Our militia has taken over your paper. You work for me now. You will write it or else."

"You fool! You focus on a few people escaping while Franco marches on."

"Montse, be careful. Your tone, your criticism of the Republic is not well received. I can only defend you so far."

"Republic—you have no right to use the word!"

"If not for me, you would already be facing a People's Tribunal. You will write the article about the priest!"

Montse felt kicking from inside her body. She rubbed her stomach, and thought she really was cornered now; she did not have a choice. "Okay, I will start on it today. Is that all? Can you leave now?"

"You will be helping the revolution."

"Enough! Go! Get out!"

Tomás slammed the door behind him and Montse considered the pieces laid out on her desk before her: the statements of the two men who had tracked the so-called priest up the Pyrenees, her interview with the two seminarians who had initiated the hunt, a blurry photo of the back of a man on a steep slope between some pine trees. She also had heard from a friend in Madrid of a rumor that some nuns had made an escape across the line.

It all added up. *It's Xavi. It has to be Xavi. I can't give him up—I can't. How do I write this?* Then she felt the kicking in her stomach again, again stronger.

Book 4
Chapter 30
Salamanca, Nationalist Spain
December 24, 1936

Xavi was in his office preparing his sermon for the midnight mass at the cathedral. Out his window he could see the lights flickering against the thin blanket of snow that covered the city. Winter had come early.

At just before eight p.m., Xavi turned on his radio to hear what General De Llano had to say to Spain on Christmas Eve.

"Merry Christmas, Catholic Spain!

"It has been a difficult year for God's forces, but by our virtue, we are on the march! First, we liberated Seville; then Badajoz; then San Sebastian; and triumphantly, we liberated our brothers and sisters in Toledo. What of the Godless communists whom we fight? What do they prepare to celebrate?"

Llano paused for dramatic effect and then continued, "This communist filth prepares to celebrate nothing! They have no God. They have no Christmas. They have no victories. They are on the run. They will be chased from Spain. We will hunt them down like the filthy stray dogs they are.

"This will end when we reconquest Spain, then we will put them on trial, in exile, or kill them. By God's Grace, we will exterminate this menace from Spain!"

Even by General De Llano's standards, this Christmas Eve rant was shocking. No message of peace, nor love, nor reconciliation, no humility—just hatred. Xavi despised the use of God in this way. *God is not a partisan,* he thought. Disgusted, he turned it off, and went back to put the finishing touches on his sermon.

The cathedral was packed for the midnight mass. The war had brought nearly everyone in Salamanca back to the practice of their faith. It troubled Xavi that people seemed more motivated to faith by fear than by hope; but whatever the reason, the church was full, and the congregants were attentive as he entered the pulpit.

"Merry Christmas, good people of Salamanca!"

"Merry Christmas, Father," the church echoed.

Xavi continued, "We all know, and it must be said, that this has been a very difficult year in Spain."

Most people nodded, and some just bent their heads down.

"Here in a Salamanca, thank God, we have been spared the worst of the war, but even so, nearly everyone here has been touched in one way or another by its miseries and sufferings. Our thoughts and prayers tonight are with our families, loved ones, friends who have been caught up in this nightmare."

There was more head nodding around the cathedral.

"As we contemplate the suffering around us, it is easy, natural perhaps, to doubt, to wonder where God is—has He been lost to us?

"And I too ask this question. I too have been caught in the maelstrom."

The nodding now changed to intent listening.

He continued, "My father was jailed for speaking his language, my language. My parents fled San Sebastian after it fell, and to-night they sit in a tiny apartment in France, dreaming of their old life, and wondering when, or if, they will ever see it once more, and when they will see their only child again."

He paused, and he looked at the crowd. He could see pain on the faces of the mothers, yes it was the mothers who felt the loss of children most deeply. "And I have dear friends who have been killed—murdered—by both sides. There is nothing that one side has done that the other side has not also done."

His tacit acknowledgment of the wrongs by the Nationalists stoked murmurs in the congregation.

"This senseless killing and brutality that is all around us erodes our faith—and yet we still come, and yet we are here."

Taking in the sweep of the crowd he added, "We come in re-cord numbers to find Him, to celebrate the birth of our Lord—and His love is all around."

Heads were nodding again in the cathedral.

"And even I, your priest, the bishop's secretary, confronting these faith-shaking atrocities, seek reassurance. Here tonight we know the message of Christ is love, not hate. That His love triumphs above all."

He paused to pick up some pages from the lectern. "And nothing underscores this message more than this letter which was smuggled out from Republican Spain."

Xavi raised up the letter for all in the church to see. "This letter is from a twenty-one-year-old living in southern Spain. Like most young men in our country before this horrid war broke out, he thought of romantic love, the love he felt for his beautiful young girlfriend. I can see many like him here tonight—and be thankful they sit safely beside you.

The letter is from Bartolomé Blanco Márquez. He was arrested when the war broke out for being active in Catholic youth ministry. He was a threat to no one. He was not a politician, he was not a soldier, he was not even a seminarian, let alone a priest. He was just a young man who loved God, and, who, as you will hear, loved his girlfriend. Bartolome wrote this letter to his beloved girlfriend Maruja from prison in Jaen on October first."

Xavi then paused and raised the letter again, "Allow me to read what we wrote—it is universal:

My dearest Maruja,

Your memory will remain with me to the grave and, as long as the slightest throb stirs my heart, it will beat for the love of you. God has deemed fit to sublimate these worldly affections, ennobling them when we love each other in Him. Though in my final days, God is my light and what I long for. This does not mean that the recollection of the one dearest to me will not accompany me until the hour of my death.

I am assisted by many priests who—what a sweet comfort—pour out the treasures of grace into my soul, strengthening it. I look death in the eye and, believe my words, it does not daunt me or make me afraid.

My sentence before the court of mankind will be my soundest defense before God's court; in their effort to revile me, they have ennobled me; in trying to sentence me, they have absolved me; and by attempting to lose me, they have saved me. Do you see what I mean? Why, of course! Because in killing me, they grant me true life, and in condemning me for always upholding the highest ideals of religion, country, and family, they swing open before me the doors of heaven.

My body will be buried in a grave in this cemetery of Jaen; while I am left with only a few hours before that definitive repose, allow me to ask but one thing of you—that in memory of the love we shared, which at this moment is enhanced, that you would take on as your primary objective the salvation of your soul. In that way, we will procure our reuniting in heaven for all eternity, where nothing will separate us.

Goodbye, until that moment, then, dearest Maruja! Do not forget that I am looking at you from heaven, and try to be a model Christian woman, since, in the end, worldly goods and delights are of no avail if we do not manage to save our souls.

My thoughts of gratitude to all your family and, for you, all my love, sublimated in the hours of death. Do not forget me, my Maruja, and let my memory always remind you there is a better life, and that attaining it should constitute our highest aspiration.

Be strong and make a new life; you are young and kind, and you will have God's help, which I will implore upon you from his kingdom. Goodbye, until eternity, then, when we shall continue to love each other for life everlasting.

Xavi paused after he finished reading the letter. He turned away from the crowd, as even though he had read it several times before, he was again moved to weeping. He brushed aside the soft tears that trickled down his cheeks and turned back around to the crowd. "Bartolome was executed the next morning. This is a story of love and hope, a story that has been played out, over and over again, in one way or another since our Savior was born almost two thousand years ago."

The crowd was silent, except for the sobs which rang out from all corners of the ancient cathedral.

—•—

Book 4
Chapter 31
Salamanca, Nationalist Spain
December 28, 1936

"Xavi, thank you for coming." Professor Unamuno greeted his friend.

"I wish I had more time. I would like to come more often."

"Of course, of course, but you have *two* busy lives. Come sit, sit as we do in my office."

After they had settled in the professor's office, Unamuno continued, "That was quite a sermon you gave on Christmas Eve."

"You were there?"

"Yes, in the back, so as to not make much of a fuss. The letter you read deeply touched me."

"Me as well, Professor, me as well."

"Xavi, I am taking stock these days."

"What do you mean?"

"I never thought I would see days like these. These are the worst days of my life."

"I hope I will never see any worse," Xavi added.

"You know, Xavi, my life seems to be bookended by war and punctuated by exile. Sitting here in the exile of house arrest, nearing the end, I spend a lot of time recalling my life."

"It is an amazing life, Professor."

"I do not know that, but it has been my life."

"It's not over."

"Well I am closer to the ending than the beginning, that I know."

Unamuno's directness, that he always found the way to say the truth simply, often seemed to put Xavi off balance, without a response.

"Do you know my earliest childhood memory?" Unamuno asked.

"No, Professor, I don't."

"My first memory is that of almost being killed by a bomb from the Carlist War that exploded next door to my house in Bilboa. And now my last memories will likely be this horrific war. After that first bomb, as a young man I was intensely religious, and I imagined even becoming a saint."

"I feel you still have a strong desire for faith within you."

"Perhaps … but I have dedicated myself to knowledge. I learned eleven languages, many of which so I could read philosophers in their native tongues. I thought gaining knowledge was the answer, but this was wrong. Do you know that one of my children died?"

"I had heard that one of them died, but that's all."

"Well it is true. My wife and I had eleven children, and one of them died the painful death of meningitis."

"I am so sorry, Professor."

"A pain of this type never completely dissipates, does it?"

"No, I don't imagine it does."

"This loss sank me into a deep depression. I believed God had punished me because I had traded my faith for the pursuit of knowledge. In a dream I saw the Angel of Nothingness dragging me into an endless, spiraling abyss."

"Professor, the Angel of Nothingness …?"

"If not for my wife, I would have been completely lost."

"It speaks to a desire for faith brewing inside you."

"Yes, yes it does. But even after my wife comforted me, and I realized all that God had given, I still could not give myself to the routines and rituals of the church. Even so, I am Catholic. Even so I have faith, … and I also have doubt."

"This is the battle we fight every day, isn't it? This war between faith and doubt challenges us all."

"Like the Urumea. Like the sea and the river."

"Yes, like the Urumea. I will never see it the same way again, Professor."

"So, Xavi, here I sit, I am in exile in my own home. My life started with a war, and now I will die in the midst of a different one."

"Oh, please don't say that."

"It's true. I have seen kings and republics come and go, and ideologues of every stripe shout their shallow ideologies, as if the louder they scream the truer they will sound. Yet, as I near the end of my life in this world, I still struggle. My lifelong battle between faith and doubt is not resolved—it seems it will be not be resolved."

"You are a great man, a giant of learning. You are a pilgrim for truth. This is the most challenging path of all."

"A pilgrim of truth … I like that … in this country of pilgrimage … like Cervantes. Cervantes was another pilgrim of truth, wasn't he?"

"Oh, Professor, you are the expert on Cervantes, not me."

"I believe Cervantes wrote Don Quixote to deal with madness of the two worlds he saw."

"I'm not following exactly."

"You remember the scene when Don Quixote charges at the windmills as if they are giants?"

"Of course."

"And what do you imagine that Sancho thinks?"

"He thinks Quixote is mad."

"Have you ever thought it was really Sancho who was mad? That Quixote, who charged at evils, real, or often imagined, was the sane one? That in Quixote's blind fearlessness lay his sanity?"

Xavi remained quiet.

"In any case, here you are. You are a Basque who works for a Catalan bishop who is in the pocket of Franco, who himself hates the Basques."

"I do not exactly see it that way."

Unamuno, ignoring Xavi's protest, continued, "And what do you do?"

"I am not sure where you are going?"

"You tilt at windmills, too! You become someone else, and you travel to places where you should not travel; you put your life at risk to save people you do not know and who you will likely never see again."

"I do not see myself like Don Quixote, Professor."

"Of course not! You are too humble for that."

Xavi watched as Unamuno got up from his desk and took a book from his bookshelves, and then sitting down again, he wrote some words on the first page of it. "Xavi, this is my copy of the first edition of my book, *The Life of Don Quixote*. Here, take it."

"I couldn't."

"Yes, as a gift. When no one else came to see me in my final exile, you came. You spoke to me in my Basque language. You made me remember the beauty of words and ideas."

"But Professor—"

"Take it. Where I am going, I cannot bring it, and where you are going you will need it."

Xavi took the book and read the inscription Unamuno had written:

To my friend Xavi,

May you always remember that the sanity in the world is in the charging of the windmills, in the facing up to evil

Miguel de Unamuno

Overwhelmed, Xavi tried, but could not fight back his tears. "Oh Professor there is so much evil ..."

Unamuno, leaned forward, peered directly into Xavi's eyes, and put both of this hands on Xavi's shoulders. "Remember this: you may walk away from a fight, but you can never retreat from evil, because if you do, it will hunt you down and consume you."

Once more Xavi sought an escape from the power of the truth Unamuno spoke. "How can I thank you?"

"Keep doing what you are doing."

"I will, Professor, I will. And I want you to remember something also."

"Yes, Xavi, please tell me."

"Remember what Pascal said—"

"'If you are seeking God it means you have already found him,'" Unamuno said, filling in Xavi's words.

"Yes, exactly. Professor, I must go. I need to see about my next journey."

"Be well. Always remember that in the end, in death, we win. It is the ultimate paradox."

"Farewell, Professor."

Book 4
Chapter 32
Salamanca, Nationalist Spain
December 31, 1936

In his office Xavi heard the bells of the cathedral begin to ring; then bells from another church nearby, St. Esteban, perhaps; then bells from another church, and another. Soon the air of Salamanca was drenched in the sound of bells.

The knock on his door was faint and difficult to hear against the chiming that filled the air.

"Come in."

"Oh Your Excellency, I didn't hear your knock with the bells everywhere."

"That's what I came to tell you—"

Excitedly Xavi asked, "The war? It's over?"

"No, it's not the war."

"What then?"

"They are for Unamuno. He's dead."

Xavi made the sign of the cross.

"I knew you would want to know," the bishop said as he left Xavi's office.

Xavi was stunned, sad, and immediately heartbroken. He reached for the book, *The Life of Don Quixote,* as if holding it would keep Unamuno nearby. He reread the inscription and began to wail loudly.

Walking away, back to his office, the bishop heard Xavi but did not return.

Book 4
Chapter 33
Perpignan, France
January 20, 1937

Xavi was defeated by his failure.

After escaping his hunters on the last journey back, the Pyrenees had lost their innocence. He was extra careful on the return back over the mountains to France where he had left his truck. He took unmarked routes; he made his own way, created his own trails. In January, the snow was deep, and the days were cold, colder still in the afternoon when the sun disappeared behind the mountains. Out of caution, and he made no fire. These nights were long and frigid.

"Hello, hello. Jacques, are you here?"

Xavi heard a faint reply from the back of the warehouse. "Yes, I'm back here."

There, Jacques was at his desk, a newspaper, *El Progressiu*, in front of him. "Patrick, you need to see this, you need to read this!"

"Not yet."

Xavi's tone, sharp, almost hostile, caused Jacques to pay more attention to him. "Patrick, you look worn out. Are you okay?"

"No."

"What is it?"

"It's about Jaime Hilario Barbal."

"What happened? Did you find him? Did you bring him back?"

"I found him, but there was nothing to bring back."

"What do you mean—nothing to bring back?"

"Jacques, I went to the address you gave me, but he was not there."

"So you came back?"

"No."

"I decided to stay. I decided to try find him. I heard he might

287

have been taken to Tarragona. I made some inquiries about him, and finally I found my way to his lawyer."

"That wasn't safe, Patrick."

Xavi ignored the comment and continued on, "And the lawyer told me Jaime Hilario's story. He told me much more than you had told me."

"Like what ..."

"I will fill in the details, but the net of it is that Jaime Hilario Barbal was a person of inherent goodness, piety, and decency. I cannot imagine we live in a world where anyone would want to harm a man like him."

"Patrick, when the war started there was a massacre of religious and devout lay people all over Republican Spain. We do not yet know all the cases—well I should say individuals—who were murdered for their faith, but the total is in the thousands, tens of thousands. In addition, thousands more have been imprisoned. Jaime Hilario was just one of them."

"Perhaps, but he was the one I was charged with saving—but I couldn't. I failed, and I want you to hear his story, I want you to feel what I felt at the end."

"Patrick, are you angry with me?"

"I'm not sure with whom I'm angry—but I am angry, and tired, and Jaime Hilario is dead."

Jacques gasped at the word.

"I don't want to carry it all alone, so you need to hear it."

"Patrick, I know it is difficult."

"I'm not sure you do. I am not sure my bishop does either. But you are going to hear it, anyway."

"I'm listening."

"Jaime Hilario was born not far from here in the Catalonian Pyrenees. He came from very modest means and heard God's calling from a young age."

"So many simple men seem to hear God more clearly."

"Perhaps, but Jaime Hilario heard the call even though he was nearly deaf."

"He was deaf?"

"Yes, and his hearing problems were so acute that he could not became a diocesan priest. Instead, he became a teaching brother and devoted himself to teaching underprivileged young people. Do you see the irony Jacques? He was persecuted by people who proclaim their allegiance to the working class because he taught poor children!"

"I had heard he was a teacher or something like that."

"Yes, and after sixteen years of teaching his hearing problems grew worse to the point that he could no longer continue in the classroom."

"What then?"

"He became a gardener for the brothers. "

"A gardener?"

"He served those who are called to serve. What simpler, more humble life could there be than that? At the end he spent his days tending the flowers and the fruits of the trees."

"So how did a gardener get caught up in this mess?"

"I think God wanted him to be a martyr."

"A martyr?"

"When the war broke out, a series of events transpired which can only be seen as God's hand at work."

"What happened to him?"

"He was on the way to see his family, and at a train station he was identified by some Judas—there seem to be so many of them—as a religious brother. In Catalonia that alone was crime enough to be arrested. Why is it now that good and evil both seem to be so accentuated?"

There was no answer to the question, and Jacques, caught up in and stunned by the story, said nothing.

"The prisons are overflowing with prisoners, so he was moved to a ship anchored off Tarragona. Can you imagine a world where the prisons overflow with innocent men?"

"It seems to be the world we have."

"In any case, he was lucky to have a lawyer."

"A lawyer? Really?"

"Yes, it seems that in his case. they wanted to create the veneer of a fair process."

"Hmm, odd ... as mostly these men are just executed."

"In any case, his lawyer told me that he was brought to trial— what a sham of justice? What men could be worthy to sit in judgment of such a gentle person?"

"Trial? What happened at the trial?"

"He was told that if he renounced his vocation and stated he was just a gardener, that he would be set free."

"But he didn't, did he?"

"No. His lawyer told me that he begged him to do it—even if it was false renunciation. He said he wouldn't, but listen Jacques, listen carefully because this touched me, and it is important—he said *he couldn't.*"

"Couldn't?"

"He said his vocation, and his deafness for that matter, they were all gifts from God, and to reject these would be the same as to reject God. So, no he could not reject his gift vocation. He could not reject God."

"I'm listening. What happened? He was killed?"

"Yes—and I was there for it."

Jacques gasped for a second time, and then turned away. "I need a drink. Can I pour you one too?"

"No, not now, maybe later, I need to finish this."

Jacques poured a glass of the *marc* and took a long sip, and then Xavi continued.

"I found out where the executions were *performed.* What a word, *performed.* It was at the cemetery in Tarragona called The Mount of Olives. What irony, The Mount of Olives. In any case, I watched the place for several days. I watched several of these *performances.*"

Jacques face turned pale.

"On the third morning I saw them bring him to the cemetery. I recognized him from a blurry photograph his lawyer had given me. It was just him and his executioners. The sun rose over the hills, and it was cold. The executioners were not more than boys. Their commander was older, maybe in his late twenties He had a rough voice, a mean tone. He ordered the boys to raise their rifles ..."

Xavi paused again, seeming to leave Perpignan, returning to The Mount of Olives. "And then I heard Jaime Hilario call out, *'to die for Christ friends, is to live.'*"

"They killed him?"

"No, no that was not it."

"What then?"

"When the command was given to execute him, the first two volleys failed to hit him. And, as if the boys knew that Jaime Hilario was a saint, they seemed to be overtaken by fear and grief, and they dropped their rifles and ran away."

"So how was he killed then?"

"The Commander, who even from a distance I could sense had an evil aura, came forward, to point blank range, and there he cursed Jamie Hilario, and emptied his pistol into him."

"Oh my God …"

There was a long silence in the room, which Xavi finally broke. "I'll take that drink now."

Jacques filled a glass for Xavi. "Patrick, there is something else you need to know."

"What else could be important after this?"

"It's the paper, *El Progressiu*. There is an article about you."

Xavi had a sip of the drink and took the paper.

Who is the Mystery Man Rescuing Priests? and Religious?
Montserrat Costa

Barcelona

Reports have been surfacing from all over the Republican Zone of a mysterious man who is said to be executing daring rescues of priests, nuns, and other religious. Through interviews with four people who have seen or spoken to the man, it appears he is a priest. He is said to have been heard speaking Catalan and French, so while his nationality is not known, he is thought to be living in either Catalonia or France.

Most recently, he is known to have taken at least four seminarians over the Pyrenees to France. He is also thought to be dangerous, as he attacked two brave comrades who were tracking him. In physical appearance, he is said to tall, dark haired, handsome, with an athletic build.

So it seems that in our time of war, of revolution, we have a real Pimpernel in our midst, and one cannot

help but be reminded of the famous rejoinder from by
Baroness Orczy:
> They seek him here, they seek there
> Those damn Frenchies seek him everywhere
> Is he in heaven or is he in hell?
> That damned elusive Pimpernel

So who this man, this priest, this pimpernel? And
what he is doing rescuing the religious in hiding in
Republican Spain? No doubt, this man, this priest, this
pimpernel, is both a hero to those he rescues, and an
outrageous afront to Republican authorities. He is in
both heaven and in hell.

Finding, arresting, and bringing him to revolutionary
justice is crucial to the authorities, and to hear them tell
it, perhaps it as crucial as the war itself. ...

The article continued on with the standard diatribe against the
church, and how it must be wiped from Spain, and the like.

"Patrick, you have been outed."

"No. I know Montserrat well, and I know what she did here."

"What she did?"

"Yes, I have known Montse for nearly fifteen years. This article is illusory. She left out important things that she would have
known from the interviews. And the Scarlett Pimpernel? Why a
reference to such a highly bourgeois novel? She is mocking the
authorities in Barcelona."

"Whatever, but still they are hunting you."

Somehow, the article, the feeling that Montse knew about his
missions, it lifted Xavi's spirits.

"Well, also now I have a scar." Xavi added with a small smile.

"With all this, Jaime Hilario, the article, I hate to ask you this."

"Jacques, what is it? What do you need?"

"The Nationalists are descending on Malaga. I am afraid that in
the run up to the battle there are people we know there that could
be found out, could be slaughtered."

"With a good night's sleep I will be ready to go."

"Good. In Malaga there is a Monsignor and two priests who
need you. "

"Need you." The words further fortified Xavi. Having purpose kept him going.

"We believe they are in hiding at *Calle la Serna* 10. With everything that has happened, with the article, please be careful. Please, there are so many who need you."

———•———

Book 4
Chapter 34
Perpignan, France
February 14, 1937

Xavi maneuvered the badly damaged truck back to its home base in Perpignan.

"What happened to the truck? Are you all right?" Jacques greeted him.

"Yes, yes, I am fine."

Jacques slowly circled the truck and silently inventoried the damage: blown out windscreen, bullet holes here and there on its body, two wheels circled by spare tires.

"Patrick are you sure you are all right? The truck is a mess—what happened? Did you get the monsignor and the two priests out?" Jacques fired his questions in rapid fire.

"The priests, always the priests!" Xavi barked.

"Why are you taking out whatever happened on me?"

"May we share a *marc*?"

Perpignan was full of Catalans and teeming with spies and snitches. Jacques was simply happy to have Xavi back; he gave no thought of who might be watching, as he brought two glasses with the strong liquor.

"Jacques, I'm so sorry, I have no right to snap at you."

"Don't say another word about it. Have a sip and tell me what happened."

"Getting to Malaga was no problem."

"Good."

"I arrived there on February second and spent the next day getting settled and planning my route of escape. It was that same day that the Nationalist forces launched a massive assault on Ronda fifty miles away."

"Yes, I heard General de Llano on the radio."

"That sadist! He played two roles: he oversaw the assault, and he gave a nightly play by play on the radio. His broadcasts were a disgusting combination of hyperbole, threats, and callous, haughty gloating."

Jacques was shocked at Xavi's choice of words. "Sadist, really?"

"Yes, sadist. It is not only the Republicans who commit atrocities, Jacques—you know that, right?"

"I suppose I have been more focused on one side of the coin than the other."

"As is almost everyone. Everyone has their own side, and then they pick and choose their stories, their own truth—"

"Their own facts?"

"No, not that. It's just that we seem to choose only to focus on one idea of truth ... the truths that appeal to us. Why can't people hold two ideas, totally conflicting, in their mind at the same time? Life is like that; it's complicated."

"Do you know anyone who can?"

"Yes. Professor Unamuno and Montserrat Costa, and they are both gone to me."

"Señora Costa ... the journalist?"

"Yes."

"You know her well, then?"

"Very, but we are not talking about her. I had a job to do in Malaga."

Jacques could see that Xavi wanted to return the story of his mission, so he helped guide him back, "Yes, Malaga—what did you find?"

"The city, for whatever reason, was caught off guard by the sudden beginning of the assault, so much so, that there were still upwards of fifty thousand civilians in the city, mostly women and children."

"Where were the men?"

"Dead for being Nationalist, or with a rifle bent on killing them."

"I see ..."

"On February fourth, the attack was joined from the north, and by the sixth the city was surrounded. The Republican defenses were a shamble. The city rapidly descended into a mix of terror, fear, and hopelessness. Whatever happened in Badajoz, or was made up, it serves the purpose of creating dread in the people."

"What do you mean?"

"Well in Badajoz there was some kind of atrocity. Believe me, I know all about it, like I was there," Xavi said, recalling Jaime's confession.

"I don't understand. You were in Badajoz?"

"Not exactly, but in any case, when the Nationalists march on a city, they warn the people to surrender, or else."

"Or like Badajoz."

"Exactly. I saw it in San Sebastian and now at Malaga. It works too. The fear in front of their advance is palpable. By the February eighth, the Nationalists streamed in from the west and the north, and a mass of civilians, and an army if you will, finally fled to the east. It was a crush of humanity. Thousands headed up the coast on the N340 road towards the next major Republican town, Almeria, about one hundred twenty miles away."

"But what of the monsignor and the priests you set out to rescue?" Jacques asked.

Xavi was irritated by the question. "By now I am quite certain they have been liberated and are fine."

"You saw them?"

"Yes. They were confused about the chaos all around them, but overall, they were fine. I told them to stay put as I expected that they would be liberated by the Nationalists in a matter of a day or two. They were relieved."

"Good, good. But how did the truck get in such a state?"

"Jacques, the exodus towards Almeria was a hell—"

"Oh, Patrick, tell me ..." Jacques said, now voicing true concern.

"First, you must understand that this exodus had no military value. It was civilians—primarily women, children, and elderly—in the thousands. They were mostly on foot. Mothers carrying children, elderly being helped along as they could be. This deluge of the downtrodden walking over one hundred miles would have been heartbreaking enough, but added to the horror were the marauders, like wolves hunting in a pack. There were more Italians than Spanish; they gunned them down from the air, shelled them from their ships off the coast, and eventually troops pursued them from the rear."

"*Quelle horreur!*"

"It was. I did what I could to help. I loaded up the truck, three or four in the cabin, and a dozen or more crammed into the back. I made trip after trip."

"They must have been relived to get to Almeria."

"Not completely. They were homeless, terrorized, and shell-shocked. They were unwelcome refugees drawing the Nationalists on their tails."

Xavi paused for another sip of the *marc*. "Jacques, the real horror was the roadside."

"The roadside?"

"It seemed that for everyone who managed to escape to Almeria, there was a dead body rotting along the road. When I tell you I saw thousands of dead bodies, unattended, creating an unforgettable stench, lying in the sun, uncovered, I am not exaggerating—and yes along the way the truck was battered."

"It can be repaired."

"Yes, it can be repaired. It was mostly from the strafing of the planes. After a while I began to recognize the noise of the oncoming menace, and I learned the terror would pass. Somehow, in all of this, I felt God wanted me to save as many of these helpless as I could. I knew it was not my time."

Xavi paused for a few moments to let Jacques absorb all he had said before he continued. "Jacques this is not the end of this episode."

"What else could have possibly happened?"

"I stayed in Almeria for a few days to help with the survivors, and each day a few more people who had stayed after the city had fallen trickled in. The stories of retribution were gruesome. Men were murdered and women violated in the vilest ways. As bad as was the exodus, those who remained had it worse."

They both stopped for a moment to take a drink of the strong liquor and to digest what had happened along the N340.

After several moments Xavi continued on, "Jacques, they do not teach us about this depravity in university, or in the seminary. There are unimaginably horrible demons on both sides—some of them Republicans killing priests, some Nationalists murdering civilians. This evil should never have been released. It now moves freely all around us."

"Yes, I know, they do not prepare us for this."

Xavi studied Jacques and thought, *who are you Jacques Latour?* He was struggling separating truth from fiction, Xavi from Patrick.

There was nothing to add, nothing to say as they finished their glasses; they stared off in separate directions.

Book 4
Chapter 35
Salamanca, Nationalist Spain
March 31, 1937

It was eight p.m., and as customary, Xavi and the bishop met in the bishop's office and turned on the radio.

"Good evening my fellow *Espagnoles*. Today is another momentous day in the second reconquest of Spain. Our troops fresh from their glorious victory in Malaga, today launched the campaign to free the north of Spain. We will push the treacherous Basques and their communist scum allies into the Cantabrian Sea. Soon all of the north will be rid of this menace. From Pyrenees to the Atlantic, Spain will be cleansed of the twin cancers of separatism and communism."

"Malaga!" Xavi spit out in disgust.

"Excuse me, Father?"

"Your Excellency, I am Basque."

"I know, Father."

Xavi turned his head, and looking directly in the bishop's eyes, "Do you consider me a cancer?"

"Father! Of course not. Remember I am a Catalan!" the bishop snapped. "We need to unify Spain."

"The solution for disunity is not more divisiveness."

"True, but sometimes things must get worse before they get better."

"Break a few eggs to make an omelet?"

"This is all a messy business. The launch of the campaign for the north of Spain is big news. When our troops are successful in this campaign the balance will be tipped. Once we gain the ports, the mines, and the factories of the north the rest of Republican Spain will fall. It will be inevitable."

"Yes, Your Excellency, so it seems—and also the Basques will be

299

crushed," Xavi added sadly.

"Father, who are you?"

"Excuse me, Your Excellency?"

"Father, I have enormous respect for what are you doing, but I also need—demand—your loyalty. So, I ask you again, who are you?"

"You command my loyalty, Your Excellency, if that is what you are asking."

"I am not accustomed to having to ask, but, yes, I am."

"But with all due respect, Your Excellency, I have already seen tremendous heartbreak in my country, the Basque Country. My parents are in exile, and friends, fellow priests, murdered—all part of solving the so called 'Basque Problem.' I can only imagine the additional terror yet to come in the north."

"Father are you having trouble choosing a side?" the bishop asked forcefully.

"No, Your Excellency, no."

"Good. The Nationalists are on the march, and the Republicans are torn asunder by their infighting, by their, let me use this word, 'lust,' for ideological purity. When this war ends, you can do great things in our church."

"Who I am is a priest."

"Of course."

"What I mean is a simple priest. I do not aspire to your station, Your Excellency. I am no politician. I am just a priest."

"Before I reproach you, let me give you an opportunity to explain or apologize," the bishop said sternly.

"I am your secretary, and you are my bishop. I take my loyalty and my duties seriously in both elements of my vocation. I am in your service in this office, and I am in your service on the missions in the Republican Zone as well. I can see the challenge of your responsibility. You must shepherd your church through a holocaust, on the edge of a razor blade. I cannot imagine the compromises and alliances you have had to make to survive this dark time. I would not trade my challenges for yours."

"Thank you for your clarification, Father. It is a complicated world, and sometimes one would prefer to be able to have different friends, but, for now, I do not have this option."

"I am sure this is true. I remain a dedicated priest. I am also a Basque, and my heart weeps for my country."

"I am sure it does, but please remember your loyalties, your duties; the war continues, and there will be casualties. It is the way of this world."

"Can you excuse me, Your Excellency, there is something I must attend to?"

"Of course. I am satisfied that we understand each other."

"Yes, Your Excellency."

Xavi left the Bishop's Palace; he wanted to move on, and to forget the conversation. He walked across the street to the cathedral, and once inside, to the small chapel of St. Martin. Almost all the candles were dripping with warm, melted wax. He was happy to find one that was unlit, and he lit it. As the small flame from the wick began warm the wax, he prayed. He prayed for the Basques; he prayed for all the people of Spain.

Kneeling, he lifted his head to study the fresco. *The Last Judgement* painted six hundred years earlier. The angels were blowing their horns, their music calling souls from their tombs—calling these souls home.

"Oh God, let it be thus—let all of them, all of us, hear the angels' horns blow."

Book 4
Chapter 36
Saint-Jean-de-Luz, France
May 1, 1937

For a few days, the war seemed far away to Xavi. He had rescued four priests from Valencia, shepherding them to the fishing village of Port Sa Platja, and then onto a sailboat to Nationalist-held Ibiza. There were no problems; the rescues went as planned. Xavi knew his routines now.

Once away from the coastline off Valencia, he felt liberated. It was his first sail in the crystal blue waters of the Mediterranean. It was joyful. The smell of the salt air, the fresh winds, the warm sun in the cloudless blue skies, the stunning beauty of Ibiza opened his eyes back up to a world where war did not rampage. This simple pleasure pushed what he had seen in the last nine months to a recess of his mind. For a short time Xavi felt some relief from the war.

After returning through Perpignan, he made his way to see his parents. He rode a train across southwest France; the countryside was exploding in a magnificent springtime bloom. He senses were reawakened, and he realized how numbed the war had made him.

He was joyful when he knocked on his parents' apartment door. His mother, surprised and ecstatic, embraced him. "Oh, Xavi!"

"Where is Father?" Xavi asked.

"He is in the bedroom. He is getting ready to listen to the horrible general on the radio."

"You get General de Llano here?" Xavi asked quizzically.

"Yes, it is a filthy addiction."

As Xavi entered the bedroom the broadcast was just starting, and he was quiet so as to not disturb his father.

"Good evening fellow *Españoles!* By now you may have heard of the atrocity of the bombing at Guernica. The red scum has hit a new low! They themselves have bombed this ancient city but have had the audacity to brazenly lie about it. They blame Nationalists for this attack. This lie to portray our noble crusaders as cold-blooded killers is an attempt to curry favor with foreign devils ..."

Xavi's father furiously shut off the radio. He was so angered by the broadcast that he seemed unaware of how special it was to see his son. "That is a lie," he bellowed out.

"Hello, Father," Xavi said.

"Oh Xavi, I am so sorry, but this is so upsetting. All of it."

"I know."

"That bombing in Guernica happened five days ago, and since then the reports have been trickling into to us here. The main themes are very consistent."

"What do you hear?" Xavi asked.

"Xavi, you know Guernica."

"Yes, well."

"It is a town that holds so much history and tradition for our people. We Basques have gathered there for as long as anyone can remember, around the ancient oak tree there, to hammer out our differences and make our laws. It is a mystical place."

"I don't understand, Father, the town has no value in this war."

"Exactly. Beyond that, they chose Monday, the Market Day, when so many people would be out on the street. One can only conclude that Franco knew bombing this place, on this day, would kill many Basque civilians. First, they killed our priests; then they forbade the speaking of our language, sending us fleeing into exile; and now they attack our ancient places, the roots of our culture."

Xavi's father paused, winding up for a second toss. "They want to exterminate us."

"Or bring us to heel at least," Xavi interjected.

"Then there is the bombing itself. Franco used Hitler's Luftwaffe to do his dirty work. The city was defenseless and wave after wave of German bombers descended on the town, flying so low their Nazi emblems could be seen. Xavi, untold numbers of innocent people were killed and injured. It was a pure act of terror, done to send a message to the people of Bilboa to surrender, or else—die!"

"Like Badajoz ..."

"Yes, like Badajoz. And now this jackal, General de Llano, has the audacity to suggest it was a Republican plot. What swine they are."

He knew all of the basic elements of the story his father told were likely true. It was terrible. It was an act of terror. Xavi was hardened now by what he heard from Jaime about Badajoz; what he had seen on the road from Malaga to Almeria. In fact, he had seen worse, much worse. He could not share these horrors with his father, and he knew there would be more atrocities to come. He detested what he felt, or rather what he was having difficulty feeling—empathy. He felt the war was hardening him and straining his ability to feel compassion; he detested it.

"It is war ..." And after saying it, he hated the words that had come out.

His father studied him, and asked, "How do you do it?"

"Do what, Father?'

"Work for the bishop who is deep inside Franco's pocket."

"This is all not so simple. Someday I will be able to tell you what I have seen. Can't we forget about it for the day while I'm here? Can't we have a meal, like a family, without this damn war all the time?"

His father's eyes grew large in shock to hear his son curse. "I'm sorry, Xavi. You are right. Can you help your mother set the table while I open the open the wine?"

"Like the old days."

"Yes, like the old days."

———

Book 4
Chapter 37
Salamanca, Nationalist Spain
June 20, 1937

T he bishop was anxiously pacing around his large, formal office. "Father, the *Generalissimo* should be here any minute.
Speak only when spoken to, be deferential, and above all, do not
say anything about the Basques!"

"Yes, I understand," Xavi replied.

When General Franco arrived with several of his assistants,
what stood out about him was his absolute ordinariness. He was
small of stature and spoke with a squealing, high-pitched voice.

Xavi knew that Jaime admired Franco, but in the first minutes
of meeting him he couldn't see it, he couldn't see what there was to
admire. He lacked the physical charisma, the presence that great
men possessed. Unamuno had it. He remembered that the professor could capture a room with his grey presence, without even
saying his first word.

What were his compensating attributes which had enabled
Franco to rise to lead the Nationalists? How had he come to the
precipice of ruling all of Spain?

"General this is my private secretary, Father Bidertea. He is the
priest I have been telling you about. He is the one who has been
doing the daring missions to save many religious."

"Yes, Father, I have heard of your exploits. When all of this is
finished, we will make sure your bravery is properly recognized."

"Thank you, sir," Xavi answered respectfully.

"Bidertea … is that Basque?" Franco asked.

"Yes sir, it is. My father is a Basque and my mother, like the
bishop, is a Catalan." Xavi, calculating a way to preempt a fol-
low-up question, added, "I am first and foremost a Catholic."

"You are an unusual cocktail, Father."

The bishop, wanting no further discussions of Father Bidertea's background jumped in. "Please sit down and let's discuss the Bishop's Letter."

"Yes, the letter. Yesterday Bilboa fell, and soon all of the north will be liberated. This will be over soon. The Republicans are staring down the barrel of a gun, and it is just a matter of time before Barcelona and Madrid capitulate," Franco said.

"God help us that be true," the bishop added.

"It will be, and now we must begin to think about rebuilding Spain after the war. Spain must regain its legitimacy so that it can take its rightful place among the great nations."

"The Bishop's Letter—" the bishop tried to interject.

"Yes, the Bishop's Letter. How is it coming? When will it be done?"

"Father Bidertea is just now working to get all the bishops to sign it."

"Good. Our cause has been put in an unfavorable light by the international media. The press and many so-called entertainers, film stars, and writers—like the American Hemingway—they have all enthusiastically endorsed the Republican side."

"And Hemingway passes himself off as an expert in Spain because he has seen a few bullfights." The bishop smirked.

"These foreigners, they know so little of the true situation here, the causes of the war, the atrocities committed against Catholics, and the control the puppet masters in Moscow exert."

"They choose their truth," the bishop said, agreeing with Franco.

As the words came from his bishop's mouth, Xavi chewed on the irony of "choosing a truth." The letter would have no mention of Nationalist atrocities. No apology. No quarter given.

Franco continued on with his diatribe, "They romanticize the Republicans, they see them as democrats, rather than the radicals they truly are. This letter needs to begin to fix this, to frame the war in different terms."

"We agree—" the bishop said, but the General continued on.

"We are fighting a crusade for Christianity here."

"Yes, it's a crusade," the bishop said in full agreement.

"Why can't they see that? Do they want Spain to be Red, like Russia?"

As the bishop and the general went back and forth on the letter that the bishop had helped to pen, Xavi began to see some of Franco's strengths emerge. He was intelligent, calculating, and a good listener. Franco seemed to possess an unusual mixture of caution and boldness.

After the consensus was reached on the next steps, Franco left. There was no small talk, no socializing. The bishop and Xavi were suddenly left alone with the subject of the letter hanging in the air.

"Father, you heard the *Generalissimo*; you are managing the letter; where are we?" The bishop asked with urgency.

Xavi found the letter clumsily written, too long, and overly complex, but as most of it had come from the bishop's hand, Xavi carefully navigated a course for the answer to his bishop's question.

"Your Excellency, as you know so well, the letter covers a complex topic."

"Yes, that's true."

"It makes many well-articulated points, but yet, if I am to be candid in my critique, Your Excellency, I would say it does not fully address several important issues."

"I'm listening, Father, you have my attention," the bishop said, suspiciously, eyebrows raised.

"I see four issues which, I believe, if adequately addressed, would significantly improve the letter."

"What are these issues?"

"First, the importance of the impact of the extreme, grinding poverty which exists in our country, particularly in the south, and the urgent need to address it; the glossing over the issues with the Basque people; a lack of full respect that the elections between 1931 and 1936 were democratic, free, and fair."

"Father that is only three issues. What is the fourth?"

"Your Excellency, I am particularly sensitive to the fourth issue. Namely, I do not believe the letter highlights for criticism the violence and repression on the Nationalist side. I have seen and experienced this violence myself—in the Basque Country and, horrifically, on the road from Malaga to Almeria."

"There is no place in our letter for that!"

Xavi replied with the tone of someone surprised to have been so summarily dismissed. "As churchmen we should not distinguish the horrors wrought against the clergy and religiously minded from the murder of Basque priests tending their flock, or what rained down on the poor souls on the N340."

"Please do not think you need to remind me that I am churchman, Father! Your humility is in danger of becoming a haughty condescension."

"Excuse me, Your Excellency ... it's just ..."

"It's just what?"

"It's just both sides have engaged in forms of terrorism."

Xavi could see the bishop was cornered. He could see his frustration was building with him. "Your Excellency—"

"Stop, Father. Do not patronize me! You may be right, yes you may be right—but these views don't square with those of General Franco."

Xavi thought about continuing on, prosecuting his upper hand, but he could see that the bishop was not Unamuno, and that this was not a real discussion. "I understand, Your Excellency."

Then, returning to a stern tone, the bishop added, "This is not a topic to be brought up with the general or his assistants. It would create problems for you—and also for me."

Xavi left the bishop. He was resigned, not angry. He knew that there were limitations to his relationship with the powerful man for whom he worked. He knew these limitations, due to differences in position, background, and experience, could not be bridged.

Book 4
Chapter 38
Biarritz, France
September 3, 1937

Few people in Spain, Nationalist, or Republican, had holidays during the war. Every day was a struggle. There was not the time, or money, or the freedom of movement to visit the seaside, the mountains, or the countryside of glorious Spain. War had sucked the life out of the country.

Xavi was no different. In addition, he carried the burden of two jobs. So the taking of two or three days with parents on his way back to Spain from Perpignan was a guilty pleasure. These days along the French Basque Coast with his parents were moments to savor. To be near the sea, and more than anything, to just be away.

The last time Xavi had been in a boat with his father they were escaping in the dark of a sad night. This day could not have been more different. Setting out from St. Jean-de-Luz to Biarritz in a small, borrowed sailboat, it was a perfect day. There were a few puffy clouds on the far horizon and the sea was calm with a breeze brisk enough for sailing, but not so strong as to warrant too much work on the boat.

For Xavi, feeling the breeze, taking in the sea-scented air, being with his father—for the moment it felt like a different time, the time long before the war. He was able to forget about Patrick, about sneaking back and forth over the Pyrenees as an impostor, as a ghost. A time before the wanton violence, the air strikes, the burning of the convents, and the arduous missions. A time before hatred and death descended on Spain.

But in these days, the war could never be far away. Once the breeze filled the sails his father could not avoid it.

"Xavi, I read that Santander has fallen."

309

"Yes, and soon the resistance in Asturias will collapse as well. The rout is on."

"How did this all happen? The Republicans started with the better hand."

"They have squandered it with their infighting and petty rivalries. And, Father, the Nationalists are more professional, more focused, more unified, more ruthless than the Republicans."

"And Xavi don't forget the help they are getting from the Germans and the Italians."

"Yes, that too, I'm sure," Xavi said then went quiet. *Germans, yes that too.* "Franco and the German Ambassador were just in Salamanca," Xavi commented.

Xavi saw General Franco more in Salamanca. In fact, the bishop had turned his palace over to the general to use as his headquarters there. Salamanca, other than having a famous university, was at its heart a provincial town. Franco had put Salamanca on the world's map.

"Really, the German Ambassador in Salamanca?"

"The *Plaza Mayor* was packed to welcome them. The crowds were jubilant, it was if they were the conquering heroes of old."

"Disgusting. Fascist birds of a feather."

They changed subjects back to the boat, the breeze, the dinner they would have in Biarritz, but soon, as it always did, the conversation came back to the war.

"How much longer will it go on?" his father asked.

"Maybe a year, maybe a bit more, unless the British, the French, or the Americans jump in to help the Republicans. It's all but over," Xavi responded.

"What will happen when it ends?"

"I am not exactly sure, Father. But from I have seen, I would guess Franco will not easily give up the power he has gained. Perhaps he will crown himself as head of a state. Not quite king, but not far from it."

The boat continued to carve its way toward Biarritz, splashing through the calm blue sea. Xavi's father studied his son. He had left home for Salamanca fifteen years earlier in 1923, and he realized he had lost touch with the arc of his son's life, his points of views, and his compass headings.

He thought long and hard, and then asked, "Xavi, how do you do it?"

"Do what, Father?"

"You know."

"No, I don't know."

"Serve the bishop?" He paused because it hurt him to say it, "Serve Franco?"

"It is the bishop who had you freed—"

"And he also suggested we flee."

Xavi wanted to snap back, but he caught himself. "Really, Father, I serve God. It's complicated. It looks different on the inside."

"Tell me then, from the *inside*?"

"You saw the Bishop's Letter in the paper?"

"Yes, and my first reaction is that your bishop prefers to use three words when one would do just as well."

"I agree, but that is not the point."

"What is the point then? We are two educated men having a discussion, let's end this dance about the letter. I am your father, and I want know what you think."

"Okay then, I will tell you exactly what I think."

"Good, Xavi, I would like that. I want to know."

"First of all, and most importantly, this conflict in Spain is a part of a grand, bigger struggle between irreconcilable ideologies: the Christian world and the godless world."

"We are not at university, Xavi—"

"No. We are not, but we are not two fools at a bar either." After he said those words, he realized that while he loved his father like a son, they were now equals having a serious discussion.

"Spain is a replay of what played out in Russia," Xavi added.

"You believe that?"

"I do. There is not a middle ground. The Bolsheviks, and believe me they are prominent in this, particularly in Catalonia, they want to destroy Christianity; they want to destroy the Catholic Church."

"That seems a severe point of view, like the bishop talking."

"No, Father, you are wrong." He said in a matter-of-fact manner, with no disrespect intended. He paused to see that his father had taken no offense and was indeed listening to his son as an equal.

He continued, "You want facts and figures, here you go: twenty thousand churches and chapels destroyed or plundered; six to eight thousand religious killed—that is forty percent of all our priests, and eighty percent in some dioceses."

Noting his father was taking it all in Xavi added, "You want to know what is worse?"

"What?"

"Thousands of religious went into hiding and now are pursued, hunted, like dogs. And if they are found they are almost always killed on the spot without trial."

Xavi was so close to revealing it, to revealing his double life. He wanted to tell his father, but quickly he could see it would be a self-serving revelation, that it would only bring more worry to his parents.

"Beyond the killings of the religious, we estimate three hundred thousand laymen, twenty thousand or more in Madrid alone, have been killed because they are conservative or religiously oriented."

"That's a sad accounting, Xavi."

"Truly. And what irony it is that while the Bolsheviks scream their love for the poor, it is the clergy who actually are poor and who do the good work for the poor. Did you know that at the start of the war over ninety-five percent of our seminarians were poor, or very nearly so. Yes, I need no more proof of the irreconcilably of these two worldviews."

"No one can justify killing innocent priests and nuns, no one, but what about the attack on the Republic, a democratically elected government?"

"Unfortunately, the Republic has an uncleansable, original sin."

"Original sin?"

"Yes, original sin. From the very beginning the Second Republic was aggressively hostile to the church and the values on which our country rests. It not only set out to do noble things, to lift the poor, but also to destroy the church in Spain, to destroy the values that make Spain, Spain."

"Are you saying you don't support the democracy, Xavi?"

"No, that is not what I am saying. What I am saying is that a mission with noble purposes built on a foundation of hatred cannot survive. What I am saying is the hatred always overwhelms nobility. Remember I was in Madrid in a convent that these fanatics tried to start alight."

"Yes, I remember … but still Xavi, does that justify the coup of a democratically elected government?"

"Father, Even Unamuno supported the coup."

Bringing in Unamuno, a fellow Basque, an intellectual giant, quieted his father.

"Public order had broken down; political violence was rampant. Our society was on the verge of complete collapse," Xavi added.

"But a coup, Xavi?'

"No one can justify a coup, but, Father, I have seen so much up close."

"What do you mean?"

"Working for my bishop I have seen many Nationalist generals. I have met Franco himself several times."

"And what of these men?"

"They are powerful men, practical men. For the most part, they are not ideologues. Here is how I see it—"

"I want to know how you see it."

"It is inevitable that men of power, men who love their country, would not sit by while they witness the country they love fall into complete ruin."

"That's sounds like a rationalization."

Xavi responded without changing tone, man to man, "No, it's just the truth. It's just the way the world is. That is how I see it."

Xavi's father went silent, appearing to be focused on tacking the boat into Biarritz. After a few minutes, he returned to the discussion. "Xavi, I hear all you say, but I am still confused?"

"By what? By what, Father?"

"Please hear me out."

"I'm listening."

"Xavi, who are you?"

"I don't understand…"

"Seeing what has happened in our Basque homeland … seeing what has happened to your own parents … you can still support the Nationalists? You still support that bastard Franco? Xavi, who are you?"

In his silence, as the boat tacked along, Xavi's father had conjured up a mighty, meaty counter punch.

"Father, I am heartbroken by all that has happened to you and to Mother—"

"I know you are Xavi. I know."

"And the war in our Basque homeland is a tragedy. I, myself, visited the angel of death to Inaki's parents, remember?"

"Yes, and I cannot imagine you having to do this. I thought what a horror for my dear son when this happened." his father said as he reached out to touch Xavi's shoulder.

"It was not easy, but back to the discussion; I live in a world where one must choose between the alternatives that exist. I am not like some of the bishops who did not sign the letter, or, God rest his magnificent soul, Unamuno, who imagined some third way. There is no third way."

"Third way?"

"In the here and now there are only two choices: The Nationalists, or a Soviet style revolution which will decimate my church and erase our history. I chose the Nationalists. And regarding Franco, he is a bastard, a cunning, devious bastard, but, unfortunately, he is a necessary one."

Xavi's father's face showed that he was stunned by what his son had said.

"And to your question …"

"Which one?"

"Who am I?

"I am a priest. I am a Catholic. I am a follower of Jesus Christ. That is who I am. I am doing the best I can do in a fallen world, and for better or worse, for now I work for an extremely powerful bishop."

"For now?"

"Yes, for now. When this war ends, I am going to leave the bishop. I want a parish again. Malaga, I think. I think I could do some good there, in Malaga."

"Malaga? Why Malaga?"

"The people there will need help when this is all done."

His father felt both outdueled by Xavi and so proud of his son for doing the outdueling. "Xavi take the boat. You bring it into port. These days on the sea, in the breeze are too precious to be spent talking only about this war. Who knows when we will do this again? Let's get to Biarritz and find some fresh fish to eat and a good bottle of wine to drink."

Xavi took the rudder and directed the boat to the harbor.

Book 4
Chapter 39
Perpignan, France
November 21, 1937

Xavi marched into the warehouse and called out for Jacques. "Patrick, I'm back here."

He went back to Jacques' office where he found him reading *El Progressiu*.

"Anything interesting?"

"Not really, but I'm glad you are here. Sit."

"I was told it was important."

"It is. I need you to go to Barcelona ..." Jacques let the word float in the air.

"Barcelona?"

"Yes, I know, I dread having to send you there, but it's urgent."

"If you say it's important, it must be."

"The request comes directly from the Vatican."

"What? Who can be so important to catch the eye of the Vatican when there are thousands of other worthy men and women still stranded in harm's way elsewhere?"

"A priest. Father José Maria Escriva."

"The founder of *Opus Dei* ..."

"Yes. He and a small group of his followers are on the run and they need to be helped over the Pyrenees. If he is killed this new order will be destroyed."

"I thought he was dead."

"So did I, but he is not. He has powerful friends in Rome."

"He is in Barcelona?"

"Last we heard he was in the Chilean Consulate there, but honestly, I'm not certain."

"I know my way around Barcelona; I can be careful."

316

"It is the most dangerous place in Spain for a priest, and I hate sending you, but I have my orders."

Xavi considered the word "orders," and what it meant, but decided instead to close down the topic.

"Okay, I will start out tomorrow."

"Thank you; be careful."

"Don't worry about me. I am in God's hands."

"Yes, so it seems."

"Jacques, I see you were reading *El Progressiu*."

"Yes, every day."

"Have you noticed anything from *señorita* Costa?"

"Montserrat? Not in months. I think the article about you, the mystery man, was the last article I recall seeing from her. Maybe she left? Maybe she made it here to France?"

"She's not the type."

"Not the type?"

"No, she's not the type to be forced from her home, or to cut and run."

"To leave a civil war is not a form of surrender, Patrick."

"For her, it would be."

"You admire her—"

"Greatly. If she had wanted to escape Barcelona, she would have done so at the beginning of the war."

"It wasn't that easy."

"Her family has the means. She decided to stay."

———

Book 4
Chapter 40
Andorra la Vella, Andorra
December 2, 1937

It was cold and Xavi was exhausted from trudging up the mountain and through the heavy snow. He assumed he had made it over the border to Andorra. He stopped and turned back, and in the far distance he could hear the men who had been following him. He felt safe now. He did not think they would cross over the border.

Ahead he saw the flickering of lights in a small Inn. One last rugged stretch up the Pyrenees to surmount. Whether José Maria Escriva was there or not, he was stopping. He was at his physical limit.

Xavi opened the door to the inn and kicked off the snow from his boots.

"Come in, come in, it's too cold to be out there," the deskclerk called out in Catalan.

"Thank you. Is this Andorra?"

"Yes, you are in Andorra."

"Oh good. Do you a room for the night?"

"Of course. Few people come up here now, with the war, and the snow. Your passport please.

"I see. Patrick Azerbergui. You are from the French *Pays Basque*, but your Catalan is perfect?"

"My mother is Catalan."

"I see. What you are doing out here? We only get smugglers and people escaping the war."

Xavi thought of choices and changed the subject. "Neither," Xavi said as the clerk eyed him carefully. "Is your restaurant open? I haven't eaten but a piece of cheese all day."

"Yes. Give me your pack, I can show the way to the dining room."

"Thank you, but I'd prefer to keep it with me."

"As you wish," the clerk said, noting the scar on Xavi's forehead. "This way."

The restaurant was rustic. The tables and chairs were of unfinished wood, and various implements from the mountains—snowshoes, a rifle, skis, an animal trap—hung from the walls. Two tables were occupied: at a large, long table sat seven men; on the other side of the room was small table where two men sat across from one another.

"Just two groups tonight?" Xavi asked.

"Really one. They all came in together as one group."

"Hmmm."

"Yes, the big group speaks Spanish and the other two Catalan. Here is your key. I will be back shortly to take your order. Something to drink while you wait?'

"A *marc* to warm me up, and then a beer."

Xavi studied the tables. He was trying to work out the combination in his mind. The seven men at the large table were gaunt, almost emaciated, and one of them matched the description he had been given of José Maria Escriva. But the two others did not fit. He could not work it out.

As Xavi ate his dinner, he picked up some the conversation of the two men speaking in Catalan. "... return to Barcelona ..." "... next trip ..." "... how much we get per head?" The other table, with the seven men, was almost silent over their food.

Finally the two Catalan-speaking men left, and he was alone in the restaurant with the seven others. He made his way slowly towards their table and noted that each of the seven watched him intently, suspiciously.

"I have been sent to look out after you." Xavi said in a whisper.

"Who sent you?" the man who looked to be Escriva replied, taking command for the group.

"I can't say."

The men squirmed. "Okay then, for whom have you been sent to look?"

"José Maria Escriva."

"It would be odd to find him here, wouldn't it?"

"Maybe it would, and maybe it wouldn't. These are odd times."

"Meet me in my room in fifteen minutes. Room four. Knock twice."

"Okay," Xavi replied.

Xavi made his way up the stairs of the inn to room four. He knocked once, paused, and then again.

"Come in."

He entered the small room and found himself face to face with the man he thought to be José Maria Escriva, surrounded by the other six men, each holding something from the room poised as a weapon: a glass, a book, a wooden coat hanger, a belt, etc.

"Don't worry I am a friend."

"In these times no stranger can be a friend," Escriva answered. "Who are you?"

"I have been sent to make sure you reach France safely. May I go to my bag to show you my ID? I am a Spanish priest."

"Slowly."

Xavi maneuvered his pack under the watchful eyes of the men. "See, here is my ID. I work for the Bishop of Salamanca."

The men studied the ID; they spoke in hushed tones to one another, and finally their anxiety gave way to relief. Father Escriva took the lead and the others watched with intent interest, in silence. They seemed like his Praetorian Guard.

"Yes, yes I am Father Escriva, and these are six of my fellow members of *Opus Dei*."

"Good, I've been trying to catch up with you for almost two weeks." Xavi replied.

"Really?"

"Since Barcelona. How long have you been on the run?"

"Since Barcelona, or before that?" Escriva asked.

"Since the beginning …"

"I have been in hiding since the day the war broke out in 1936."

"Almost a year and half?" Xavi asked with an air of astonishment.

"Yes, every day for almost a year and half."

"That's a lot of days."

"Indeed it is."

"How did it start?"

"I was in Madrid when the coup happened. It was chaos. The

killing was everywhere. Gangs roamed the streets looking to kill anyone wearing a cross, or watch, or a gold ring. Criminals were released and sought out judges to settle scores, and of course the most hunted of all were the priests and religious."

"Yes, I know."

"How do you know?"

"You are not my first. I was in Madrid in August 1936. I saw it too."

"Hmmm ... you are no ordinary priest."

"I want to know about you. Father, how did you hide?"

"The first thing was to get out of my clothes, my collar. I knew I needed to blend in, so I changed into street clothing. In those first days I felt truly hunted. Every new footstep was a terror. I moved houses every few days."

"And you are well known."

"Yes, a wanted, well known man in Madrid is not a comfortable place to be, Father. They hunted me, and they even hanged another man in front of my mother's house who they falsely thought was me."

"Your poor mother ..."

"I haven't been able to see her—can you imagine?"

"No, well yes ... I have seen things too—but first more about you."

"Moving from house to house became too risky, and it also endangered the friends who sheltered me."

"What then?"

"I have a friend, Dr. Soils, who runs a psychiatric hospital in Madrid. "

"You lived in an insane asylum?"

"Yes, for six months. But that became unsafe as the hunters ramped up their efforts to find priests in even the most out-of-the-way hideouts."

"What then?"

"I, well, me and my brothers here, were able to get to the Honduran Embassy in Madrid, and from there we were able to get some forged documents."

"And then you made it to Barcelona?"

"How did you know?"

"I caught your trail there. I was a couple of days late, and you were already gone when I got there."

"We had some money, so we paid some men to get us here."

"You are lucky."

"We know, but how do you mean?"

"Those men. The two here in the inn, they are likely traitors, men looking to be paid twice."

"Twice?"

"Once from you, and once from the men who were hunting you."

"Were we followed?"

"Yes."

"How do you know?"

"I know how it sounds."

"How what sounds?"

"Hunters. There were other men on the trail. They were hunting you, and, likely me too, or maybe just me."

"What?"

"Yes, they followed me into the mountains, but I have been in these mountains since I was a child, so I was able to send them in a circle."

"Did you lose them?"

"No, but I put them off your trail long enough for you to get here to Andorra. They won't come here. The Andorrans won't put up with the war spilling over into their country. We will be safe here tonight, and in the morning, I will get you to France."

Father Escriva dug his right hand into his pocket. "See this?"

"What is it?"

"It's a sign from the Virgin Mary. It is a fragment, a carved flower, from a desecrated altar piece. We found it on the trail."

"It's beautiful, a flower, a rose."

"They desecrate, but She persists. The rose is the sign of the Virgin. When we came across it, we knew Our Lady was watching us."

"That's a beautiful thought."

"It is more than a thought, Father," Escriva said in a tone that was almost a reproach. "She sent you."

"No, Father, that is too much."

"Do not doubt the power of prayer, the power of intercession."

"My job was to lead you to safety, and I feel blessed to have caught up to you."

"We are too, we are too."

"There are many important people who are concerned about you."

"None more than you, Father."

Xavi was silent, he did not know how to respond, as Escriva continued.

"And I am no more important than the baker, the tailor, or the housekeeper. That is the point *Opus Dei*, to see God in the everyday things we all we do."

"Yes, I suppose that is true. May I ask you a question?" Xavi asked. "How did you do it?"

"Do what?"

"Keep going every day since the war started?"

"*Opus Dei* is my vocation, Father, my destiny. I need to keep going. It is like breathing."

"And Father Bidertea, do you do much of this?"

"If you mean to try to help people like you, well then the answer is yes."

"Then I can say you are doing the *Opus Dei* too."

"I guess that's right."

"And so I have a question for you."

"Yes."

"And why do you do it? Why do you march up and down mountains, evading the hunters, through the snow and cold for people you don't know?"

Xavi thought hard about the Escriva's question. "I have a vocation, too."

"Yes, indeed you do. Bless you, Father. You will be in our prayers."

Xavi left for his room. There he gazed out the window. In the dark of the night the snow continued to fall. For all the fatigue, and sometimes failure, tonight was a good night. All of his traipsing across Catalonia and up into the Pyrenees led to a good thing. He felt a sense of purpose, and he wept tears of humble joy.

—•—

Book 4
Chapter 41
Salamanca, Nationalist Spain
December 28, 1937

Xavi heard an unusually forceful knock on his door. "Come in," he said. "Oh, Your Excellency, I did not know it was you. Please sit down."

The bishop took a seat in a small chair next to Xavi's desk. "I know you have barely returned from your last trip ..."

"Anything, Your Excellency, what is it?"

"As you have heard from General de Llano, Teruel is under attack."

"I heard that. I had to look it up on a map."

"Yes, it is a cold, bleak place."

"Why Teruel, Your Excellency?"

"The Bishop of Teruel himself."

"The bishop is still there, really?"

"Yes, he is still there—the fool!"

"Is he a friend?"

"An acquaintance. We come from different worlds."

"Excuse me?"

"Anselm, Bishop Polanco, is an Augustinian missionary. He has served all over: China, Japan, Peru. He is more comfortable digging ditches than wearing a miter. I have no idea why he is still there. Teruel has been on the border of this war for a year and a half?"

"Maybe he believes it's his vocation—"

"That's not the point! We need to get him out. Do you know how many bishops have been murdered so far?"

"About ten I would guess."

"Twelve. And he cannot be number thirteen. We can't let the Republicans put his head on a stick."

"I can see that."

324

"You need to get him out—just in case the Republican offensive succeeds. There is no need to go through France; all the territory between here and there is in Nationalist control. I need you to leave tomorrow."

"Yes, I will leave in the morning, Your Excellency."

Book 4
Chapter 42
Teruel, Nationalist Spain
December 31, 1937

Xavi rechecked his map. Teruel, in the region of Aragon, two hundred miles east of Madrid, was a provincial capital, surrounded by, well, really nothing. The city was a small peninsula of Nationalist territory surrounded on three sides by a hostile army. In the map of divided Spain it was almost like a Nationalist thumb print jutting into Republican territory.

But now, fate had put this desolate place on the center of the world stage. For the Republicans, this was to be the victory they could feed to a hungry International Press. This was to be the place where the tide of war would turn in their favor … or at least, that would be how the headlines would read.

As the bus bounced along to San Blas, Xavi thought of how odd it was that this small, provincial capital, known for nothing but its rocky surroundings and extremely harsh weather, was now at the center of the world's attention. *Why have I been brought here?* he thought.

There were no longer direct routes, buses, or trains, to Teruel. It took Xavi two days to get from Salamanca to San Blas. From there he still had five miles to make on foot to Teruel.

It was three p.m. on New Year's Eve when Xavi exited the bus. He was alone in the desperate cold, overwhelmed and debilitated. He had never felt cold like this. *It must ten below zero, or colder,* he thought.

With the sun low in the winter sky, and cold piercing him like thousands of needles, he set off on foot for Teruel. There was no one in sight.

The cold was inescapable. It was exhausting. Xavi walked backwards into the wind; he pounded on his arms with his fists, and

326

stomped his feet, but it did no good. He wanted to lie down and go to sleep, but he knew if he did, he would never wake up, he would die a silent, frozen death. He continued on.

Just before reaching Teruel, he stopped to change his identify—to become Patrick Azerbergui, thinking he would be safer as a French aid worker than a Spanish priest.

As he entered the town, Republican soldiers were everywhere. There were thousands of them. They were mostly huddled in small groups around fires. Shivering hands out over the flames, the soldiers paid no attention to Xavi. He moved freely inside the city. The cold had silenced all the guns.

"*Parlez vous Francais? Tu hablas Frances?*"

"No. No. No."

Until he heard a *"oui"* in reply.

"*Bonjour, mon ami,*" Xavi addressed the man.

"*Bonjour,* comrade. What brings you here to this God-forsaken place?"

"I'm an aid worker from France; I'm here to help the Republic."

"Good to have you. Where are your supplies?"

"They are outside the city—I need to assess the situation here."

"We are overwhelming the fascists. They have been pushed back into the center of the town, over there," the soldier said, pointing to a cluster of buildings.

"I see ..."

"Yes, they are now confined to just four buildings: The Governor's building, the Bank of Spain, the Convent of Santa Clara, and the seminary."

"They are surrounded."

"But they won't surrender. We've tried, but they won't give up."

"What happens next?"

"Nothing for the moment. It's just too cold, but when the weather turns a little better, it will be just a day or two before we overrun them. Their situation is hopeless. Almost all of them who are left will be dead in a few days."

"So it would seem."

"I need to get back to my men. Good luck, comrade, get yourself around a fire."

Xavi waived the man goodbye, and after the soldier disappeared in the dark cold, Xavi slinked his way towards the buildings the soldier had pointed out. No one paid attention to him. Amongst the cold, the darkness, and the blowing snow, Xavi moved easily through the city.

Nearing the convent, he suddenly felt the cold steel of a gun barrel against the back of his head. "Stop. Move no farther. Who are you?"

"May I turn around?"

"Slowly."

He turned around, and he could see the man was in Nationalist uniform, and in Spanish he said, "I am here for the bishop."

"Here for the bishop?"

"Yes, I've been sent to rescue the bishop."

"Are you insane?"

"I have a job to do."

"And this job entails sneaking through the Republican line in the coldest weather in twenty years?"

"I told you, I have to get to the bishop."

"Well, no one could make up your story. Inside!"

Even inside the convent, the cold could not be held away. Xavi waited in the vestibule amongst statues of saints, and he wondered if their stone garments might provide them any warmth. Across the room, the soldier and his commander went back and forth for the better part of a half an hour, examining his ID and his pack.

"You say you are Spanish, but your passport is French."

"I can explain that; may I have my pack?"

"Okay, but remember, two guns are pointed at you."

After a few moments he maneuvered into the secret compartment of the pack, "Here, here, look at this. It's my Spanish papers."

"Xavier Bidertea, a priest, and you work for the Bishop of Salamanca?"

"Yes."

"Maybe you are a priest. Okay, come with me."

He followed the man to a small room with a crucifix on a bare wall, a few cots, several desks. Two imposing men occupied the room. One was an officer in an unpressed, unkempt uniform jacket; the other man wore a simple priest's coat and collar and a large wooden cross across his chest.

The officer took command. "Well, what do we have here? Are you Patrick Azerbergui, or Father Xavier Bidertea?"

"Both, really." Xavi replied.

"You saw the situation outside! I am down to just a few handfuls of men. We don't have time to play word games."

"Can I explain?"

"You'd better." The officer demanded.

"I am Xavier Bidertea, a priest, and the Secretary of Bishop Pla y Deniel of Salamanca—"

"Enrique?" the priest said, surprised.

"Yes, His Excellency Pla y Deniel. He sent me here from Salamanca."

"What? Why?" Both men exclaimed in unison.

Xavi looked directly at the priest. "To rescue you. I assume you are Bishop Polanco?"

"I am," said the priest.

"And I am Colonel Rey d'Harcourt. I am in charge here, and I am still trying to work this out."

"What?" Xavi asked.

"Who you are, really? How did you get here? What do you want?"

"I am who I say I am. I am Father Xavier Bidertea. I have been sent for Bishop Polanco."

"Then who is Patrick Azerbergui?"

"He is the identity I use when I move in and out of the Republican Zone."

The men's jaws dropped again in unison. "What?"

"Yes. Since the beginning of the war, I have been doing rescue missions of religious—"

"Do you have some sort of death wish?" the colonel asked, rhetorically.

"Father, how many trips, how many missions?" the bishop asked.

"Maybe six ... no, let me think. This is my eighth trip."

"I'm impressed," the colonel said.

"As am I," Bishop Polanco added.

"No, I am the one who is impressed."

"About what?" asked the colonel.

"This ... Teruel ... What you are doing here?"

"You mean that we are holding out in this God-forsaken cold?" the colonel asked.

"Yes. Why here, why Teruel?"

"The Republicans' only real success in the first year and half of the war has been to keep the Nationalists from taking Madrid. Other than that, month by month, we advance. So now, they are focused here. They need a victory. Really, they need a headline."

"Other than the cold, what's the situation?"

"Two weeks ago the reds launched an attack against us with an army of one hundred thousand men or more. We are just a few thousand here defending Teruel."

"You said a headline?" Xavi asked.

"Yes, a headline, a story. They want to show heads on posts for the whole world to see. Hemingway was already here, writing articles about the resurgence of the Republicans ..."

The colonel paused. "And they want my friend here; they want the bishop," Colonel d'Harcourt said, pointing at Bishop Polanco.

The young officer who had brought Xavi to the room chimed in, "But they will need to continue to wait."

The colonel continued, "Yes, they will have to wait."

"But we have to get the bishop out. That's why I am here. In this weather, it will be easy to slip past them and make it back to San Blas."

"So Enrique sent you, did he?"

"Yes, to get you out."

"I know Enrique well. I have been to beautiful Salamanca, to his palace there. He would not enjoy here, would he?"

"No, I don't think he would."

"Well, Teruel has been on the frontier since the beginning of the war, and if I did not leave in the last year and half, I will not leave now. Tell him, tell Enrique, I prefer the cold sleep on a hard cot amongst my men to the warm sheets of his palace. Tell him!"

"You're not leaving?"

"No. I will not skulk through the streets, disguised, defrocked, defeated, back to Salamanca."

Xavi realized he was in the presence of a great man. "I understand. I will tell him."

"And they will have to get me too." The colonel added.

"But your situation—"

"What situation? We fight to hold on."

"Hold on to what?"

"These four buildings are Nationalist Teruel. We will fight to hold them, and we will fight to protect the bishop—to the last man. "Did you hear me? To the last man."

"Yes, I heard, but for how long?"

"However long it takes. Right now the cold is our ally, and we know Franco is on the way."

"There are other forces at work in this world besides you and your bishop, Father. Franco was about to launch an offensive on Madrid when this all happened. Hearing of our situation, he canceled this mission; now he has columns of men racing here to relieve us."

"Can you hold on?"

"We will fight; we will do our duty. Franco is a man of a few strong absolutes: no communism and give no ground. He told us emphatically—no giving up. We will fight … to the end."

"God bless these men," Bishop Anselm Polanco chimed in.

"Yes, God bless these men is right. Fighting the reds, and worse, the cold. I never imagined so many amputations from the cold," the colonel added.

Xavi's eyes once more returning to the bishop, resumed, "Eventually—"

"Don't start again, Father. I am not going. These are my men. This is my flock. They, and God, will protect me."

"Yes, but—" Xavi started another counterargument before the bishop again cut him off.

"I am an Augustinian. I have been a missionary all over the world: China, the Philippines, Peru, Columbia. Mission is akin to vocation."

"It is." Xavi nodded.

"This is now my mission, my vocation. You wouldn't give up your vocation, your mission to save people, would you?"

"No."

"Not under any circumstances—even in grave danger?"

"I have not."

"Then we understand one another. St. Augustine tells us that when all are in need, it is the greatest among us who must lead the way."

Xavi was outgunned by the ultimate weapon: the moral superiority of two great men.

Xavi looked at the bishop. "Your Excellency, I understand. Can I help in any way?"

"Pray for our strength to hold out. Pray that if we are captured, that our faith may stand the test of captivity. And pray that if we face the firing squad, we will know the Lord is just moments away."

"Grab a cot, Father. You must get some sleep now. Tomorrow you will need to escape back from where you came. It will not be easy," the colonel said, closing down the discussion.

Xavi laid himself down on a cot and pulled a thin wool blanket over himself. Even inside the cold was paralyzing, yet he knew he was in the presence of a hero and a saint.

Book 4
Chapter 43
Salamanca, Nationalist Spain
January 3, 1938

Xavi left at dawn on New Year's Day from Teruel. When he rose from his cot in the convent, he peered across the room to see Bishop Polanco on his knees in silent prayer. He did not disturb him. Leaving the convent, in the dark, he had no problem sneaking back out of town. The Republican soldiers feared the cold more than any surprise attack.

The cold followed Xavi for two days all the way back to Salamanca. He did not begin to feel warmth again until he set foot back into the bishop's residence.

The door to the bishop's office was closed. He knocked.

"Come in."

Xavi entered; a fire was raging in the fireplace. "Come, Father, sit, warm yourself. No one has seen this much cold in years."

"Thank you, Your Excellency. It was a long trip."

"I'm sure it was. Where is Anselm?"

Xavi had been dreading this moment for several days. "He is not here."

"Where is he, then?" the bishop said, beginning to raise his voice.

"In Teruel."

"What! Did you find him?"

"Yes, I made it to Teruel. I found him."

"Where is he then?"

"He would not leave."

"Would not leave?"

"No. He wanted to stay with his men, his flock."

"Teruel will fall any day now, Father!"

"Yes, a day or two after the weather warms enough for men to begin killing each other again. It seems the devil prefers milder weather."

"Don't be smart with me! A day or two?"

"Yes. Their position is dire."

"He will be captured, paraded out of town, put in front of a mock trial, and then probably executed."

"They may capture him, but they won't be able to touch him."

"I have no idea of what you mean, Father."

"Your Excellency, I was in the presence of a saint."

"A saint? Father, I think that judgement is well above your station."

"You know when you know. If not a saint, then a genuinely great man at least."

The bishop was now visibly agitated. "More likely he will be a symbol of your failure, and not one Franco will appreciate, great man or not."

The frequency of his disagreements was growing, but until now Xavi had never felt anger. The bishop's words and tone touched a nerve. He was enraged, insulted, and on the verge of saying something from which there would be no path back. "You'll excuse me, Your Excellency, I have something else to which I need to attend."

"As you wish." The bishop said with his tone expressing his desire for Xavi to leave as well.

Xavi marched from the office, out of the residence, through the cold air to the cathedral, and down to the Chapel of St. Martin. The old stone church was frigid too. He lit a candle and prayed for Bishop Polanco and Colonel D'Harcourt. And he prayed he would be able to hold his temper with his bishop until the war ended.

Book 4
Chapter 44
Salamanca, Nationalist Spain
February 21, 1938

Xavi glanced up from his work at the firm knock on his door. "Come in."

Xavi rose. "Your Excellency, please sit down."

"No, no thank you."

"How can I help you, Your Excellency?"

"I just came back from my palace."

"You saw *Generalissimo* Franco?"

"I did. We had a number of items to discuss, and he provided me the update on Teruel."

"Teruel, he must be pleased—it was liberated."

"Not completely. He described the battle in great detail. He spoke of the cold and deep snow. He told me of retaking the town—that there are many thousands of dead soldiers frozen, entombed in the ice until springtime."

"Yes, it was a terrible place—"

"He detailed the massive cavalry assault through the Republican defenses, and the key moment when our cavaliers slashed through the line."

"In the snow?"

"Yes, in the snow, and he spoke with great satisfaction of retaking the Republicans' prize. He hates the Americans. Hemingway and the singer Paul Robeson were there to celebrate when the town fell. He loathes the international press, and he loved wiping their smug smiles off their faces when the Nationalist flag was replanted over the town."

"But what of the bishop and the colonel?"

"I am coming to that. They are gone."

"Gone?"

"The *Generalissimo*'s mood changed, almost to anger, when he recounted what happened to them."

"What, where are they?"

"It seems that that the colonel and his men fought hand to hand, floor to floor until the end."

"They surrendered?

"No, they were overcome. Your friends, *your heroes*, they were taken. They were frog marched out of town. They were jeered at and spat upon as they left."

The bishop, face to face with Xavi, moved slightly closer. "I thought you should know." The bishop then turned and left the room.

Xavi gave no thought to his bishop leaving without saying goodbye. He thought only of Bishop Polanco and Colonel D'Harcourt being marched to their Calvary. As with Jesus, no amount of jeering or being spit upon could diminish their dignity.

Book 4
Chapter 45
Salamanca, Nationalist Spain
April 15, 1938

Nearing eleven a.m., the sun was not quite yet fully overhead in the eastern sky of a warm spring day on the Mediterranean Coast.

Jaime and his men raced through the little fishing village of Vinaros. Few people were about when the Mediterranean Sea came into sight. The sea was crystal blue, and the sun shimmered brightly on it.

"Captain, we are at the sea. We've come a long way from the snow and ice of Teruel, haven't we?" one of Jaime's men exclaimed as he ran along beside Jaime towards the water.

"A very long way." Jaime replied with a smile.

"The Republicans are cut in two. Barcelona and Madrid are separate islands. It won't be long."

"No, it shouldn't be now," Jaime added.

Jaime stopped near the water's edge, dropped his gun belt, and made his way for the blue water. He dove into the clear sea. The cool water washed over him. He wanted the sea to cleanse him of the war, of all that he had seen, first at Badajoz, and then at Teruel—cleanse him, like a baptism.

Book 4
Chapter 46
Salamanca, Nationalist Spain
October 2, 1938

As Xavi and the bishop reentered the Bishop's Palace, Xavi wondered what mixed emotions ran through the bishop's soul? How did he feel about returning to his residence? What deal had he made with Franco in return for giving up his palace? Did he feel any disgust seeing Hitler's photo in his old personal office? And, above everything, were all the compromises worth it?

"Father, as I told you, there will be many important people here. Remember that."

"Yes, Your Excellency," Xavi said as they entered the grand hall of the palace.

Xavi counted fifty-sixty chairs, and in the front of the room were easels with various maps of Spain. The bishop mingled in the room with the country's future leaders: generals, members of the provisional government, other bishops, important industrialists.

The group took their seats, and the air was filled with the low din of conversation. They waited for General Franco to arrive. Xavi thought it had the feeling of a crowded gate of thorough-breds, anxiously jockeying for position.

Franco entered from the back of the room, and all stood as he marched toward the podium. They turned towards him and raised their arms out in the Fascist salute. Xavi kept his arm at his side.

Franco raised his hands to capture the group's attention. "Welcome, my friends. Welcome to this conference to discuss the future of Spain. Today we will look forward to what happens next after this war is finished."

Rapturous, adoring applause broke out. Among so many accomplished people, Franco's small stature, and high-pitched voice seemed even more out of place to Xavi.

Franco put his hands out again, this time to quiet the crowd, "Thank you, thank you, and before we get started, I have some important news."

The crowd went quiet in anticipation.

"I have news from Munich. The Allies have signed the Reds' death warrant. They have made an agreement to not intervene in Czechoslovakia. The French and English have no appetite for war."

The crowd created a loud murmur. "They will not come to the aid of the Reds. This rabble is done. Even now, the International Brigades are withdrawing from our country."

More thunderous applause rang out through the room, the applause being so loud that perhaps the saints in the paintings and statues watching over them might be awakened from their long sleeps.

Franco let the applause roll over him, enjoying the adulation. Finally he quieted the crowd.

"Thank you, thank you. Now, I want to turn the floor over to our Minister of the Interior, Ramón Serrano Suñer, to review the situation in the Ebro."

As Serrano Suñer took the podium, he cut a dashing, commanding figure. He had had his own perilous escape from the Republicans before making his way to Salamanca. He had been imprisoned at the beginning of the war, escaping, and then fleeing to France dressed as a woman.

Serrano Suñer began. "Teruel was a disaster for the Reds. As at Toledo, they spent too dearly for a gemstone that they could not hold. After Teruel, we raced to the Mediterranean, and we cut their territory in two. We are readying for an assault on Catalonia. To be fair, they are finally fighting, but it's too late for that. We are slowly grinding them down. In another few weeks, a month at the most, they will be finished, exhausted, and Catalonia, Barcelona will await us, virtually unguarded."

More loud applause rang out.

And so the afternoon went: self-congratulations, optimism for the future, and hubris. As the session wound down and moved its way to a cocktail reception, Franco retook the podium, congratulated the speakers, and asked for questions.

"Can it end quickly? Can we make a peace?" one of the bishops asked.

"There will be no peace agreement," General Franco barked in his high-pitched voice. "Only a total surrender. An unconditional surrender—and it will come slowly. We need to squeeze the red blood out of our country. The more Reds who are killed in battle, the fewer to deal with after the war is done."

"*Generalissimo*, what about the Germans? What if war comes to Europe, will we be drawn in?"

"No, no. We and the Nazis are only aligned around our hatred of communism, but from there our world views diverge. Their religion is this perverse sense of Fatherland. We are Catholics. They cannot seem to understand how deep this runs in us, and that we are not interested in replacing a true religion with this new mythology they have created. We have no interest in that. We have been useful to each other, but once the war is finally won, we will need to look out for Spain first. We will have a country to rebuild and we will need good relations with the British, the French, and even the Americans."

With that, the meeting ended, and the group began to make its way to the reception.

"Your Excellency, I am sorry I cannot stay for the reception, but there is so much work waiting for me."

"Don't let us keep you, Father."

In truth, Xavi needed relief from the crowd; he needed air. Xavi was troubled as he made his way to *Plaza Mayor*. Franco lacked any sense of reconciliation or real vision. He was all cunning and pragmatism.

Xavi loved the medallions in the square. He took note of the greats of Spanish history: El Cid; Isabella and Ferdinand; Saint Teresa; Cervantes; so many giants for one square. Soon he imagined the little man with a high-pitched voice would hoist himself up onto a medallion, that Franco would make himself their equal.

Book 4
Chapter 47
Le Petrus, France
October 14, 1938

Bonjour, Madame Chenot."
"*Bonjour,* Patrick," *Madame* Chenot cheerfully called back as Xavi entered her *Auberge.*

Xavi had grown to adore her. She was a warm, simple, wise countrywoman.

"More supplies for the Spaniards Patrick?"

"Yes."

"*Bien sur,* but I think soon I will no longer see you as this war will be coming to end soon—*n'est-ce pas?*"

"Perhaps, but there will still be many people in need, even after the war ends."

"*C'est vrai. C'est vrai.* The usual, Patrick?"

"Yes, yes please."

As Patrick waited for his onion soup and charcuterie, he could not help but notice the auberge was full of lean, hard-looking men—most of them clearly having weapons in their packs. There were about twenty of these men around four of *Madame* Chenot's tables. Some were speaking French, others German, some English, and others still were speaking languages he could not make out—eastern European languages, perhaps, he thought.

"Who are the men?"

"They are withdrawing from Spain, from the war."

"International Brigades?"

"Yes, that's it. Every day for the last several weeks, I have had groups of them coming here on their way back home from Spain. They say the war is over. They say Franco has won."

"Your little *auberge* sounds like the Tower of Babel."

"It's true. They come from all over—and a lot of Jews, too. Once

341

they cross over the mountains they stop here for a good meal."

"No problems?" Xavi said pointing toward their tables.

"They can be a little noisy, but they pay their bills, so they are okay with me."

On his way back from the washroom he bumped into one of the men.

"Désolé, Monsieur," Xavi apologized to the man.

"Pas de problème. You speak French?"

"Qui, I'm a French aid worker. I have been delivering supplies to the Republic."

"Good to meet someone on the same side. I am Philippe Fignon," the man said as he stuck out his hand to Xavi.

"And I'm Patrick, Patrick Azerbergui."

"Unfortunately, I think your job will be done soon."

"What do you mean?"

"It's over. It's done. Franco has won. Any day now it will be over."

"You fought with the Republicans, Philippe?"

"Yes, we are all members of the International Brigade. Don't eat alone. Come sit with us."

Xavi signaled *Madame* Chenot to bring his meal to the men's table, and Philippe introduced his friends. "This is Lars from Norway, Nikola from Czechoslovakia, and Gunter from Germany."

Xavi said *"Bonjour,"* and the replies came back in English, French, German, and Spanish.

"How do you all communicate?"

"Pointing a gun at a fascist doesn't take much communication." Philippe laughed.

"No, I guess it wouldn't."

"Madam, another bottle! Patrick, where is your glass? No true Frenchman eats without a glass of wine," Philippe barked out with a smile.

"Well I guess I wasn't being much of a Frenchman, then was I?" Xavi replied, thinking how easy Philippe was to be with.

Philippe called out to *Madame* Chenot again with a laugh, "And another glass too. We need to spend this Republican money before it turns like bad milk."

Xavi liked Philippe and the others. They were hearty, good

spirited, straightforward men.

"When did you get to Spain?" Xavi asked.

"July 1936—right after it started. The four of us met on the train to Madrid. There were two others, but they are in ground now."

"Madrid?"

"Yes, we held Franco off for two and half years, but what's left of the Republic is crumbing around us. Any day now."

"*Madam*, bring some bottles, *marc*, vodka, whatever local liquor you serve here!" Philippe shouted out.

Madame Chenot brought five shot glasses to the old wooden table and filled them with the clear liquors. Shortly thereafter the emptied glasses pounded the wood, followed by, "Ahhh," as the men finished their shots of the rough liquors.

After the warm liquid passed through his mouth, Patrick asked Philippe a question, "How did you find the Spanish?"

"Crazy. Disorganized. But more than anything—immensely likeable."

"Crazy?"

"Yeah, anarchists versus communists, Catalans against Castilians, and the Basques—who can figure them out? And talk about disorganized. But mostly, I will remember them as sympathetic, likeable people."

"Oh Philippe, I think you like everyone."

"Not the fucking Fascists! They are serious, bad-ass men. In all, I would guess about fifty thousand of us came to Spain, and we leave about twenty thousand of our brothers in the Spanish dirt because of those assholes."

Philippe then opened his shirt and said, "See this? I took one in the shoulder, and it hurt like hell, but I got it patched up and got back out to the line."

"Ouch."

"Another round for the men we left in Spain. *Madam*, more drinks!"

"Where is home, Philippe?"

"For me, the north of France, near Lille."

"Judging from the *auberge*, the men came from all over?"

"Yes, all over really, Europe and the United States, too. When the war broke out, we came."

"Why Spain?"

"It was the fault line with Fascism. I thought if we don't stop this virus there, who knows to where all it will spread, and I guess now it will be all over Europe. I imagine I will be fighting Germans soon."

"I see, you hate Fascism, but Philippe you are not a man of hate?"

"Hmmm, an aid worker, huh? Most of us dream of building a new world, a real worker's state: Communists, Trotskyites, trade unionists, anarchists ..."

"Quite a group." Xavi added.

"Intellectuals and workers, dreamers, and men who experienced the exploitation of capitalism with their own two hands."

"What camp are you?"

Philippe grabbed Xavi's hands. "Feel these hands? These hands were made on the docks in Lille."

Xavi felt Philippe's hands; they were strong and rough.

"Patrick, your hands are soft ..."

Madame Chenot arrived with more drinks and hovered above the men, watchfully.

"Yes, soft, almost like a priest." Philippe paused, and then roared in laughter.

"Patrick, may I speak with you?" *Madame* Chenot said as she looked directly at Xavi.

"You know the *madam*?" Philippe asked.

"I come here often—with my truck. Excuse me a moment."

Xavi went off to a quiet corner with the woman.

"Patrick, I speak Catalan. In this part of France most of us speak it."

"Excuse me?"

"I read *El Progressiu* ..."

"Uh huh ..."

"I read about the priest helping people escape."

"Yes."

"Your trips, and the scar over your right eye ... You should be more careful; rumors are beginning to swirl about this mysterious priest. These men are all atheists. These men hate the real you. You need to leave before all that drink kicks in, before something goes wrong, something slips out. Tell them you need to make a delivery for me in Perpignan. Leave now."

Xavi, well on the way to becoming drunk, had just enough sense left to hear her plea.

"You are right. I should go."

Xavi returned to table.

"What did the *madam* want?" Philippe asked.

"I do some errands for her, you know, to make a little money on the side, and she needs me to get to Perpignan to make a delivery."

"But not before one more with us. *Madam!*"

"Just this last one, Philippe."

After the glasses hit the table Xavi got up and circled the table, shaking each man's hands until he reached Philippe. He and Philippe grabbed each other on the shoulders, looked each other in the eye, and then they bear hugged.

"*Bon voyage, mon ami,*" Philippe said loudly.

"You as well; you as well."

Xavi left the table, made for the door, and there, *Madame* Chenot intercepted him.

"Be careful, Father."

Xavi leaned over and whispered into her ear, "God Bless you, you are like a guardian angel."

—•—

Book 4
Chapter 48
Near Tarragona, Nationalist Spain
December 24, 1938

C aptain de la Calzada, we need you now."
  "One minute," Jaime shouted back at the colonel.
Just enough time to write Xavi a few words for Christmas, he thought.

> *Dearest Xavi,*
>
> *What a year it has been...*
>
> *Here I sit in Catalonia, not far from Tarragona, after fighting through the freezing snow and ice of Teruel, making the easy march to the warm, blue Mediterranean, and surviving the horrific Battle of the Ebro. Like St. Paul, I am trying to run the good race.*
>
> *Xavi, the final battle is beginning. We are making our way to Barcelona. Soon this will all be over. I pray I survive so I can see my father and the vineyard again, see Montse again, and see you again—and return to Badajoz.*
>
> *Merry Christmas,*
>
> *Jaime*

———

Book 4
Chapter 49
Salamanca, Nationalist Spain
January 22, 1939

The letter from Paris caught the bishop's eye. The envelope was bulky; he opened it, and inside was a letter and the envelope of another letter, that one addressed to Xavi. He took out the sheets of fine stationery and began to read.

Paris

January 13, 1939

Dearest Enrique,

Oh what sad and terrible times these are.

Elena, Joan, and I left Barcelona for our home in Paris in the first days of the war, and we have not been back to Spain since. Montse has remained in Barcelona during the war for reasons she should best explain. Even though we have been out of harm's way, we have suffered greatly. Jordi has been in prison, and our home has been ransacked, with every treasure accumulated over many generations gone or destroyed.

But I do not write you to bemoan our travails when millions of others of our countrymen have been killed, maimed, or even more harshly displaced. Enrique, I am writing you to engage you to be a courier; I need you to get the enclosed letter to Xavier Bidertea with all haste.

Fondly,

Luisa

P.S. I look forward to when these horrible days are behind us and when we can all gather together for a meal and recall the serene days of our childhood.

It was difficult to get mail from one zone to another, and Montse had made significant effort to get a letter from Barcelona to Salamanca … *It must be something important,* the bishop thought. He rose from his desk, left his office to immediately to seek Xavi out. He found his assistant in his office.

"Your Excellency, how can I help you?"

"Father, I have an important letter for you. It is, by the way of her mother, from Montserrat Costa."

"I see …"

The bishop handed Xavi the letter and left his office.

"I will be available if you need me, Father."

"Thank you, Your Excellency."

Xavi opened the letter. Montse no longer wrote on fine linen paper, but on simple sheets from a notepad. Nonetheless, he handled the pages like a delicate treasure.

> *Barcelona*
>
> *December 31, 1938*
>
> *Dearest Xavi,*
>
> *How terribly sad this time has been.*
>
> *So much has happened since I saw you last, but it is about one enduring thing I write you. Xavi, I have a daughter. She is so beautiful and precious to me! My daughter, Maria, named after your mother and the Virgin Mary, is about a year and a half old.*
>
> *Over the last two and a half years I have seen so many things I never thought I would see, things I couldn't even imagine. Xavi, I have to come to believe in terrible times like these, as in a civil war, that one must pick a side about God … for or against … and I have chosen faith. I want to give this treasure to my daughter.*
>
> *The situation here is perilous. Barcelona is exhausted from war, and it is about to fall. There is a dark, foreboding mood in the air, and I fear chaos will soon again descend upon the city. I have seen successive waves of terror over the last two and half years, and it feels that the settling of scores and the lawlessness will return any day. Xavi, you cannot imagine the horrors I've seen.*

Xavi paused a moment to imagine what Montse must have seen. He had seen much of it in Catalonia too: churches destroyed, tombs opened, gangs roving the streets, and now the war on her doorstep. He read on.

> *With little Maria it is impossible now to leave the city and get*

over the Pyrenees. I have also made many enemies with my articles, I am afraid. I do not know if I will survive this chaos ... in truth, I do not think I will live to see what comes next after all of this is over.

Xavi paused again. *I need to go. I need to get her out.*

I have nowhere else to turn, and I only want one thing: for Maria to be baptized. Xavi, there are no priests to be found anywhere in Catalonia (even the beautiful abbey we visited at Montserrat was desecrated, and its monks killed!). And so, I ask you to come here to baptize Maria.

Xavi, I know you can come ... I know, and I have known for some time, that you are the mystery person who has been slipping into Republican territory to save priests and other religious.

Each time I heard a rumor of a priest or nun being saved, I cheered you. I knew from the beginning that only you would have the courage and ingenuity to do what you have done. God bless you, noble, selfless, Xavi.

I know what I am asking you to do. I know how difficult and risky it is for to come here, but I can't see another way; and beyond that, Maria's father hates God ... if I die, the door to her faith will be closed.

Xavi placed the letter down for a moment to consider all that she has said ... *It must be Tomás,* he thought.

Motherhood changes everything, and I no longer care about what will happen to me, but only for Maria. Even though I have not been devout, I want to give her the gift that I treated so cavalierly.

Should you receive this letter, and should you make it back to Barcelona, you can find Maria and me at Carrer de la Victoria 10, Apartment 4a.

With Deepest Affection,
Montse

Xavi, letter in hand, got up from his desk went to the bishop's office. The door was open, the bishop was waiting.

"Xavi, please come in."

"Xavi." he heard the word, his name, and at this moment, the bishop was different. He was waiting for him like a friend, like an ordinary priest—not as a prince of the church, not as a clever politician—his face seemed less stern, his tone was empathetic.

"It's Montse."

"I know."

"She's in trouble. She's still in Barcelona."

"She's my goddaughter, too."

"What do you mean?"

"She's not only special to you, Xavi."

"She touches everyone."

"Yes, she always has."

"I need to go."

"I know you do. Go in the morning. I will make sure you have what you need in Perpignan."

Book 4
Chapter 50
Perpignan, France
January 25, 1939

Perpignan was overrun by Catalans.
First, in the summer of 1936, came the exodus of conservative Catalans; now Republicans and other leftists fleeing the impending retribution of the onrushing Nationalist troops had descended on the city.

The stories were all the same: Barcelona and Catalonia were about to fall, and chaos reigned. The large cities were lawless; the routes out were treacherous, and the passes over the Pyrenees were nearly unpassable as the winter snow accumulated. The recently arrived, the nearly dead souls that had trudged over the mountains as their country was collapsing in mid-winter, came to find only a new life of poverty and uncertainty. It was a better choice than waiting for the wave of terror the Nationalists would bring.

This flood of people was unwelcome, but there was nowhere else to go. Perpignan, overwhelmed with refugees, was now a microcosm of the Spanish Civil War itself; arguments between Spaniards on opposite sides of the politics frequently escalated to fist fights. The local authorities did their best to keep the warring sides in opposite corners.

Xavi imagined how much gruesome fear there must be to propel these people to run: first, the fear of the roving gangs feasting on the carcass of a wounded city, then, inevitably, next the Nationalists would arrive. Would it be like Badajoz or Malaga?

With each day the reports circulated of the Nationalist advance. Any day now they would be in Barcelona. Xavi knew one thing: the border was about to close, and he needed to get across it before it did. He needed to get to Montse and Maria.

Entering the garage, Xavi noted the relief truck. "Jacques are you here?"

"Patrick is that you?"

"Yes, it's me. I need the truck."

Jacques wasted no time. "Don't go! It's too dangerous!"

"The keys, Jacques. I need the keys to the truck."

"You don't have to go!"

"I do, actually, I do."

"The bishop called—"

"So then you know all about it?"

"I know some of it. I cannot know everything. There is too much to know about señorita Costa."

"I have to go, Jacques."

"I know. I knew I would not be able to talk you out of it, so I loaded the truck."

"Thank you for that."

"Patrick, the border is going to close any moment now. You could be killed—killed by either side."

"It's my last crossing."

"Patrick, there is no talking you out of this?"

"No."

"Okay, okay, then please remember this address: *Carrer de l'Argenter* 25, number 2c. It is an apartment we have in Barcelona. You should be safe there."

"Thank you, Jacques. I need a pen and piece of paper."

"Of course, here you are."

"Thank you for everything my friend, but if I do not make it back—"

"Patrick don't say that."

"This is the address of my parents in Saint-Jean-de-Luz. If I am not back in four or five days, please go see them. Go to them and explain where I went, what I have been doing. They deserve to know."

Jacques looked away from Xavi; he did not want him to see his eyes welling up.

"Promise me, Jacques."

Jacques, glassy eyed, turned back towards Xavi. "Yes, I promise, but ..."

"But what?"

"I don't really have the words, Patrick."

"The words for what?"

"To say goodbye."

"Enough of that."

"Do what you are called to do, but at least let me shake your hand, Patrick."

The men shook hands. Jacques eyes were roiled by water.

"Jacques, I must go. I have one more stop before I cross the border."

"Here are the keys. Be safe, Father, be safe."

Xavi left the garage and Jacques receded from view. As he drove up the mountains there were many women and children on the road heading the other way, towards Perpignan. They had crossed the Pyrenees in midwinter, mostly on foot—it was over one hundred miles from Barcelona—as there were few cars or trucks left and even less gas available to fill them. They stared at him from the road in his truck. Shivering, barely moving, their faces were sunken, gaunt, with lifeless eyes, nearly dead. He drove on until he reached *Madame* Chenot's *auberge*.

"Patrick!"

"*Bonjour, bonjour Madame* Chenot."

"What are you doing here?"

"Going to Barcelona."

"No! No one is crossing over to Spain now."

"I need to go before the border closes."

"It is full winter, and with the state of the war it is too dangerous! Stay here, let me make you a plate?"

"No, I'm not here for that. I can't stay."

"Then why did you come here, if not for a plate?"

"I wanted to see you, to give you a small token for all the kindness you have shown me."

"That wasn't necessary, Patrick."

Xavi handed the woman a small box. She opened it.

"A Saint Teresa medal … what a treasure … can you help me with the hook in back?"

Xavi attached the hook that secured the chain.

"There, it goes with my St. Bernadette of Lourdes. Two great saints together with me all the time."

"Yes, all of the time."

"But, Patrick, somehow, all of the sudden I feel such a great sadness, like this is a final goodbye."

"For a Christian there is no such thing as goodbye—only *à bientôt.*"

"Oh, Patrick, you pass over these mountains and back like a ghost in the night. I will never forget you. Hug me, Father, hug me."

They embraced, and *Madame* Chenot felt a cool breeze come upon her, as if it were the Holy Spirit.

"I must go now."

Xavi jumped up into the truck and backed away. Through the windshield he could see she was weeping.

In the late afternoon Barcelona was like a ghost town. There was rubble everywhere, and the streets were deserted except for a few armed, menacing young men here and there.

As Xavi drove nearer into the center of the city, the combination of debris and barricades was too much to continue on in the truck. He abandoned it and made his way to apartment 4A at *Carrer de la Victoria* 10   on foot. He was determined.

Approaching the door, he felt excitement, and a little trepidation, to see Montse again. The door to her building was open; the concierge had long since abandoned his post. He rang the bell to her apartment and waited.

"Who is it?"

"Montse, it's me. It's Xavi."

"I knew you'd come! The elevator is broken; you will need to take the stairs."

On his way up he wondered how he would find her. How would she be? And even, he wondered, about how she would look? Would she be as he remembered her? So beautiful, so vital? Or had the war wounded her too?

He knocked. He heard footsteps, her footsteps. The door opened, and there she was with Maria in her arms, held close to her.

His first impression was shock. Her beautiful, long dark hair was gone, now being cropped short, unwashed, uncombed, and unstylish. Her beautiful figure was lost to the war. She was thin as a rail.

"Oh, Xavi ..."

He felt ashamed that his immediate judgments were so shallow, but he could not help the feeling that part of the woman he had known and loved had been lost.

"I'm so happy. I knew you would make it here, somehow."

"This must be Maria. She is adorable. May I hold her?"

Montse gave the baby to Xavi. Maria settled with ease into his arms as he held her close. "She likes you! Oh of course she does."

"Come sit down. There is no coffee to be had, but I have a bottle of cheap wine and two clean glasses."

"That would be nice, Montse."

"Let me put Maria down for a nap, and then we can talk."

Several minutes later Montse came back with wine and the glasses.

"Xavi let me look at you. ... You look mostly the same, thinner ..."

"Going up and down the Pyrenees will do that."

"And that scar above your right eye—how did that happen?"

"For now, let's just say I ran into your godfather's sternness."

She laughed. "Yes, he is a serious one. Oh, Xavi, it's good to laugh again ... with you. And how do I look to you?"

"Well ..."

"I know my hair is awful."

"You look both happier and sadder at the same time."

"The happy part is easy—it's Maria. She saved my life in so many ways. And yes, I suppose sad, too. I don't see surviving this, the chaos that is coming when the Nationalists arrive in a few days."

"Montse don't ... I can get you ... you and Maria ... out of this, away from here. It is what I do."

"No sadness, not right now. You look wonderful to me, a grown version of the handsome man I met in Salamanca. I can still recall that first meeting in the square—do you remember?"

"Like it was yesterday."

"It was fifteen years ago; can you believe it?"

"I had caught a glimpse of you just before we met; you were on the street, and then there in the *Plaza Mayor* with my mother and Jaime—"

"Under the Cervantes medallion."

"Yes, under the Cervantes medallion."

"How is Jaime? Do you hear from him?"

"He is near here somewhere."

"In Barcelona?"

"He wrote me at Christmas, and he was near Tarragona then, so I suppose he too could be close to Barcelona now."

"How strange … maybe we are all to meet again … and your mother, tell me about Maria?"

"Sadly, she is in the *Pays Basque* in France, in Saint-Jean-de-Luz."

"But why?"

"My father—his teaching of the Basque language—they had to flee San Sebastian."

"I'm so sorry. I loved their home, your home there."

"It sits empty now."

"It's hard to know which of these dueling fanatics I despise more, the communists and anarchists here or Franco's men."

"I shouldn't comment on that—your godfather might be listening somehow."

They both laughed loudly.

"And what of your parents' beautiful estate?"

"They left for Paris in the first days after it all began, and their home, it was soon vandalized, ransacked, and overrun. I went once, and it broke my heart. The furniture was gone, the walls bare, even the curtains were torn asunder. I couldn't go back, but it did make me realize something."

"What was that?"

"You know I grew up privileged?"

"It was obvious, Montse."

"Well, it wasn't the money, or the material possessions that was the privilege."

"What then?"

"It was the beauty of the life before all of this that is gone now. They have destroyed the beauty. That is what I miss, the beauty."

"After it all started, what did you do?"

"It's a long story."

"For true friends time does not exist."

"Oh, Xavi, I've missed you so …"

"Yes, Montse, I know, I have had some very dark days too …

but tell me."

"When it started, in July 1936, I was pregnant with Maria, but I didn't know it."

"Is Tomás the father?"

"Yes, yes he is."

"Where is he now?"

"Gone. I kicked him out when the war started. Oh, the horrors of those first days ..."

"I did see some of it too, Montse; I wasn't just in your godfather's palace."

"I know that, Xavi. In any case—"

"But why did you stay?"

"At first, out of my hubris."

"Hubris?"

"Yes, that I believed I was part of the story."

"Part of the story?"

"Yes, I felt I had helped to create the story, and I needed to stay to shape the events that were unfolding.... But after the first several days it became clear that the story was quite different from the one I had envisioned."

"How so?"

"It was not a fight to save the Republic, but rather, just underneath, extremism was boiling, and it overheated into a revolution. The wanton terror, the destruction of the churches, the skeletons on the street, ..." She paused, looked away for a few moments. "It sickened me, and that is why I kicked Tomás out."

"How so?"

"He rationalized it; he justified it; and worst of all, he reveled in it. I saw that in reality he was a sadist, not an idealist."

"But still you stayed in Barcelona."

"Yes, I continued to write, and then I realized I was pregnant. I had purpose."

"I was in Perpignan often and saw *El Progressiu* there, but at some point, maybe in the middle of 1937, your articles seemed to disappear."

"They did. I started to question what was going on—how our march towards a liberal democracy had morphed into a revolution. I was shunned for saying that which had to be said."

"Like what?"

"Well, first, the false trials and executions of the rebel generals who had started the coup, and then the lunacy of their obsession with Toledo—there is nothing at Toledo. These people, these fanatics, value theatre, propaganda more than anything. They produce nothing real—nothing except hatred, that is. And then Maria saved me for the first time."

"Saved you?"

"Yes. They came to arrest me, but by that time Tomás knew he was the baby's father, and he intervened for me—well, for Maria, really. He hates me and is obsessed by me. You must be careful coming and going here. He has me watched."

"Don't worry, I've learned to see into the shadows."

"Yes, I'm sure you have. In any case after that, Maria was born just before the second revolution."

"Second revolution?"

"May 1937. For a week or so another terror descended here. The communists, if we are being honest, Soviets really, grew tired of the power of the anarchists."

"I didn't follow all the nuances of the politics."

"The anarchists are loony utopians, and this became a threat to the communists who believe in command, control, and strict discipline. A short, fierce little war broke out between them, and now the communists are in control. If I had to choose between left wing fanatics, I would choose anarchists like Tomás—at least they like a good *fiesta*." And then she laughed.

"That was May of 1937…?"

"Yes, after that Maria was my focus. It was fine here, gloomy, but fine, until March of the next year."

"What happened then?"

"The Italians came from the sky."

"Italians? Sky?"

"Yes, for three days straight the sky was filled with their planes, marked as Nationalist, dropping bombs specially designed to kill civilians."

"I think I heard Franco say something about this once."

"Probably, it was a horror from Mussolini. He is even more evil than Franco. Since then, we wait."

"Wait for what?"

"Wait for it to end. Wait for the Nationalists to come. Wait for the retributions. Wait to die. I'm exhausted, I'm waiting for my time."

"No! Montse, I can you get you and Maria out!"

"Oh it's so good to see you, Xavi. Who could have imagined all that has happened to us? So much we have seen in our sad country."

"I am trying to remember when I actually last saw you … It was at my ordination in 1931, wasn't it?" Xavi asked.

"Yes, that was an emotional day for both of us. But no, I came to see you in Salamanca after the massacre at Casas Viejas."

"Now I remember … you were worn out by it all, even back then."

"Oh Xavi, so much has happened. I have lived three lifetimes since then. I was so hopeful, so idealistic before the war. I believed I was in the midst of something big, and perhaps in a small way, through my articles, helping to build a new and better country. We had such wonderful ideals back then. Justice, equality, a future of boundless opportunity for everyone. And Tomás and I were happy, or as happy as we could be given that there was only so much of me that I could give him…" Her voice trailed off.

"We lived in a different world then."

"I had no idea that there was such hatred. What enormous well-spring of evil is needed to compel people to kill, to rape, and even to desecrate tombs? This hatred shocked and frightened me. The joy people took from it smelled wicked to me. I had not thought of these words: 'evil,' 'the devil,' since I was a small child. I thought these ideas were medieval and had no place in a progressive, modern country. I was wrong. They exist."

They both went silent, taking a pause to shift the gears of the conversation.

"And you, Xavi, tell me about you?"

"There's not much to say, really. Just after the war started the bishop tapped me to rescue priests, nuns, and other religious people who were trapped by the chaos. It has been a blessing. Other than the two seminarians in Girona that you know about, I have met so many people of faith who have humbled and inspired me. I thank God for giving me this blessing."

"My God, Xavi, you have always been too modest. What you have been doing—and I am sure I don't know the half of it—is noble, heroic, inspired. It is saintly. I knew as soon as I spoke to those seminarians it was you. The way they described the man's physical appearance, his self-assuredness, his grasp of French and Catalan. I said to myself, 'It is Xavi! It has to be him!' You must believe me that I did not want to write that story. They made me."

"I never thought otherwise, Montse."

"I tried to kill the story, but it was the one thing about which both the communists and anarchists agreed: they wanted the story out; they wanted you exposed; they wanted you captured, paraded around, tortured, and then executed. So in any case I did my best to put them off the trail by leaving out important details."

"I know, I know …"

"How many times have you crossed over to Republican territory?"

"Let me count … I think this is my twelfth trip."

"Oh goodness, it seems so dangerous, Xavi. Priests are still hunted here like animals."

"Montse, I don't understand something?"

"What?"

"After it all crashed down, why didn't you leave, go to Paris to be with your parents?"

"I tried once, but Maria got sick, and I had to turn back. Since then, Tomás keeps close tabs on me and Maria. And now, anyways, it is too difficult to get out."

"Do you want to get out?"

"Yes, anywhere but here, but I doubt I will. I didn't ask you here for that."

"Where to, Montse? To Paris with your parents?"

"No, not Paris. I cannot face another war. I have thought about going back to Salamanca."

"Salamanca?"

"I was happy there. There was beauty there. … Has it changed?"

"No, Montse, it's as it was."

"Even now I can close my eyes and see the way the sun shines off the soft stone of the buildings. I can imagine the array of domes, cupolas, beautiful cloisters, and arches all around. There I would have my godfather, the bishop, and of course you would be there too," peering directly into Xavi's eyes.

"We can talk about that tomorrow, Montse, after the baptism, but you know, no matter what, I will not abandon my vows."

"Yes, yes, I know, Xavi, and I do not wish to be a temptation. It's, it's just you are the only person who gives me any comfort, any peace. I have thought that this presence, even if it just in the common air we would breathe, would make me a calmer, better mother."

"Montse, I am sure after the baptism we can plot a way out and back to Salamanca, if that is what you want."

"Yes, I want to go back to Salamanca ... with you."

The conversation paused, not out of boredom, but out of satisfaction. They covered so much ground so quickly, the way only true friends can.

"Montse, I need to get going before it gets too late."

"The later it gets the more foreboding the city becomes. The night is ruled by ghoulish goons."

"I saw a little church near here; though it looked badly damaged, it seemed like we could use it for the baptism. I think it is named *Sant Pere de les Puelles.*"

"Yes, I know it. It was almost completely destroyed, but we can get in."

"Okay, Montse, let's say we meet there with Maria at eleven a.m.?"

"Perfect. One other request, Xavi."

"Or course, anything."

"I need you to hear my confession before you baptize Maria, just in case—"

Xavi quickly interrupted her. "No, Montse, don't say that, but yes, I will hear it."

They embraced, said goodbye, and he left the apartment. In the early evening Xavi headed toward the address on the *Carrer de l'Argenter* that Jacques had given him. Hiding nearby, in the shadows, behind a pile of rubble, a man, smoking a cigarette, intently watched him leave Montse's building.

Book 4
Chapter 51
Barcelona, Catalonia,
Republican Spain
January 26, 1939

The winter sun cut its way through the mist. In the cool morning air Jaime read from a small, leather-bound Bible:

It happened that I was on that journey and nearly at Damascus when in the middle of the day a bright light from heaven suddenly shone round me.

I fell to the ground and heard a voice saying, "Saul, Saul, why are you persecuting me?"

I answered, "Who are you, Lord?" and He said to me, "I am Jesus the Nazarene, whom you are persecuting."

The people with me saw the light but did not hear the voice which spoke to me.

I said, "What am I to do, Lord?" The Lord answered, "Get up and go into Damascus, and there you will be told what you have been appointed to do."

"Captain de la Calzada, we need to get going."

"How far are we from the city center, from the *Plaça Catalunya*?"

"About ten miles," the soldier answered.

"Okay, give me a minute."

Jaime read this passage often, and he particularly contemplated the words, "'What am I to do, Lord?' The Lord answered, 'Get up and go into Damascus, and there you will be told what you have been appointed to do.'"

Quo vadis? What I am to do today, Jaime thought?

Jaime closed the Bible, kissed it, and marched towards the men, the jeeps, and their truck.

"The city is exhausted, and today it will fall; but be careful; be on guard for snipers and the last few hangers-on. It is still dangerous here. *Vamos!*"

In her apartment, Montse prepared Maria for the day. Yet again, she made little Maria a bowl of rice, which now, in the waning days of the war, was the staple of her diet. She also laid out a simple white, cotton dress for her to wear to her baptism.

Montse gazed at little Maria, so playful and happy. "Oh darling, you will be so beautiful in your little white dress."

As Maria cooed back, Montse remembered pictures of her own baptism, the ornate baptismal dress, the ceremony at the cathedral. Maria's little white dress was so plain in comparison to the gown she had worn for her own baptism.

Oh how far the family had fallen during this war!

A few blocks away was the simple apartment on the *Carrer de l'Argenter* with just a bed, a bathroom, and a small kitchen. Xavi sat on the bed and he pulled his small pocket Breviary from his backpack. He began his readings of the day:

I have fought the good fight, I have finished the race, I have kept the faith. Now there is in store for me the crown of righteousness, which the Lord, the righteous Judge, will award to me on that day …

He said specific prayers, by name, for a long list of people he cared for: his mother, his father, Jaime, Montse, and now little Maria. He prayed for the bishop, though, being so different, it was sometimes difficult to find the right prayer for him. He prayed for the people he had helped to save, that they might find rebirth in their salvation. He prayed for those who were gone from this world, that they know peace: Professor Unamuno and Inaki. He also knew he needed to pray for those who hated him, "Forgive us our trespasses as we forgive those who trespass against us." There had only ever had one person on this list: Tomás.

He finished his morning ritual with one "Hail Mary" and one "Our Father." He made the sign of the cross and then checked the items he had packed for the baptism: a small container full of Holy Water, a scallop shell he gathered on his first journey on the Camino Santiago to hold the Holy Water he would pour over Maria's head, some Holy Oil, a candle, and a narrow scarlet stole. He also packed a baptismal gift for Maria, a small medal of the Virgin of Pilar, the Patron Saint of Spain.

At just before eleven o'clock Xavi came to the church. The portal had two doors separated by a marble column. Above the portal, the sculpted figures had been hacked furiously, severely damaged, but he could make out a spear pointing groundward at the tail of a dragon. It was St. Michael slaying the Satan dragon. He recalled the verse from the Book of Revelation:

> *...Then war broke out in heaven. Michael and his angels fought against the dragon, and the dragon and his angels fought back. But he was not strong enough, and they lost their place in heaven. The great dragon was hurled down—that ancient serpent called the devil, or Satan, who leads the whole world astray. He was hurled to the earth, and his angels with him...*

The desecration and destruction of such ancient, beautiful figures in a few minutes of fury: Who? ... Why? But still, St. Michael was there; still Satan was defeated. It comforted him to think one simple truth about his faith: *In the end, we win.*

He pushed one of the doors open, and inside he waited for Montse and Maria. Amongst the rubble he found the confessional and the baptismal. Little of the stained glass remained in the church's windows, and through the gaping openings the light of the late morning sun streamed in.

Moments later Montse entered the church with Maria. They were radiant.

"Little Maria is so beautiful in her white dress."

"Oh, Xavi, you are so sweet to say it. It is not what I would have imagined, but it is perfect for the day."

"Montse, you, too, look so happy."

"I have not been this happy in two and half years—truly, I haven't."

"Good, good, are you ready?"

"Yes."

Montse knelt in the confessional, holding Maria in her arms. Xavi was seated on the other side of the confessional screen that separated them.

"Bless me, Father, I have sinned. It has been many years since my last confession. ... Where should I start?"

"Please start with the really significant events of the last few years."

Montse paused in thought for a few moments. "My articles were hurtful."

"Oh dear, Montse, that is not a sin. You sincerely reported what you saw and wrote what you believed to be true."

"Yes, but I hurt people, like my aunt, with the article I wrote about Casas Viejas."

"There is no sin in what you wrote. I was there too, you remember?"

"I remember."

"I saw what you saw—that your aunt and uncle were, however inadvertently, a part of the system that held these poor people down is not disputable. When this war ends, our faith calls us to bring greater justice and equality to our country."

"Okay, okay I understand," and she paused again.

It was uncomfortable for her to speak to Xavi about Tomás, but she knew to make a true confession that she must. "For years I ignored my faith and the practice of it," she said, working her way to the core of what was troubling her heart. "And then there is my relationship with Tomás."

Montse paused and Xavi asked, "What about the relationship?"

Montse knew it had to come out, so she pushed herself on. "I stayed in a relationship, an intense sexual relationship, being unmarried, with a man I did not fully love."

She paused again. "Father, must I be behind this screen? Must we be *separated?*"

"No, Montse. We can sit beside one another in a pew."

"Thank you, Xavi, I would like that."

They moved to one of the few undamaged wooden benches in the church and sat next to one another, as a few feet away, Maria toddled back and forth in the church.

Montse continued on. "I did not, could not, give him what he so willingly gave me. Up until the end of our relationship, I could neither leave him nor give myself fully to him."

She paused again, took a breadth, and finished. "In a way, the whole time I was with him I was unfaithful to him."

Xavi averted his eyes and asked, "Why did you stay?"

"I was afraid."

"Afraid of what?"

"Afraid of being alone … I never got over you …"

Xavi needed a bit of space to think. "It's a joy to watch little Maria run about, isn't it?"

"Maria, Maria darling come back this way." Montse called out.

Xavi drew a very deep breath. "Montse, I will always be there for you, always, and many times I have wished to be there with you as you want—but I can't be. I took a vow. I made a promise."

"I know, Xavi, I know …"

"To love is not sinful, but your deceit is."

The word "deceit" stung Montse.

"You misled and hurt Tomás very much, and that was sinful."

"A sin," a second blow in succession. She was stunned by the word "sin," but she knew he had chosen the right, the appropriate word, to describe what she had done. She had sinned.

"Is that all, Montse?"

"It is the major things. It's a start; it's a step back."

"Yes, it a step back, an important step. And I would like you to consider a few things."

"What things?"

"The Urumea."

"The river in San Sebastian?"

"Yes. I pass this idea to you from Professor Unamuno."

"Oh, the great professor …"

"Yes, the great professor."

"What about the river?'

"How the tides and sea and go back forth, neither overcoming the other."

"I can see it …"

"Or said another way, like in Ecclesiastes:

What profit has a man from all his labor in which he toils under the sun?

One generation passes away, and another generation comes;
But the earth abides forever.
The sun also rises, and the sun goes down,
And hastens to the place where it arose.
The wind goes toward the south,
And turns around to the north;
The wind whirls about continually,
And comes again on its circuit.
All the rivers run into the sea,
Yet the sea is not full.

"Help me understand what you are saying?"

"Vanity is vanity, all is vanity."

"I'm still not following."

"Going forward, slow down. Take note of the harmony in the world, use silence more often, listen for the tranquility in the world. Avoid the vanity of things."

"Yes …"

"And most importantly, your family. Now you have Maria, and your parents, and Elena and Jordi. Focus on them above all else. This war, these politics, they are vanities which consume us."

"I see it, Father, I do."

"I can feel your yearning, Montse. I felt it in your letter. Each day, like a pilgrim, take a step. For your penance I ask you to say one deeply felt 'Hail Mary' and one deeply felt 'Our Father.'"

"I will do that."

"And two other things: raise Maria in the faith."

"I will, and what is the other thing?"

"Seek Tomás out. Make amends to him. Promise me."

Xavi could see the distress this request caused Montse.

"He is a monster."

"But it was your sin."

She turned away for a few moments. "You are right." *His will be done on our earth as it is in heaven.* "Yes, I will find Tomás."

Xavi conferred his absolution. Montse beamed and they left the pew for the broken baptismal font. Montse picked up her daughter and held her in her arms.

"Is Maria ready?" Xavi asked with a smile.

The beautiful little girl signaled her readiness as she squirmed in Montse's arms and called out, "Mama ..."

Next to the battered stone basin, Xavi took out the water, the shell, the oil, and the candle from his pack. He put on his scarlet-colored stole and gave Maria the little gold medal he had brought for her.

Montse, who had seen so many elegant and expensive things in her life, was deeply moved by the simple medal. "Oh, it is such a treasure!"

"May we start?"

"Yes, we're ready."

"Baptism is our first sacrament. It is a building block of our faith, and it frees us from the stain of original sin. It is a gift to us. We recall John the Baptist, and in fact Jesus himself who said, 'Go therefore and make disciples of all nations by baptizing them in the name of the Father, the Son, and the Holy Spirit.' This baptism will make an indelible imprint on little Maria's soul, and Montse, with this baptism do you commit to pass on our faith to Maria?"

"I do," she replied solemnly.

"Who will be Maria's godparents?"

"My sister Elena and my brother Jordi will be her godparents. They will be part of the community of support for Maria."

Xavi then proceeded with the baptism. "With this oil I make the sign of the cross to signify the gift of the Holy Spirit. I now light this candle, and I give it to Maria so through Christ she may illuminate the world for her."

Finally, he took the small container of water out of his bag, being careful not to spill it. He blessed the water and three times he filled the scallop shell and poured the water over little Maria's head. "I baptize you in the name of the Father, the Son, and the Holy Spirit. Amen."

Maria began to giggle, and she smiled and glowed in her mother's arms. Montse, Maria, and Xavi embraced.

"At this moment there seems to be no war, no hatred, no hunger—only happiness. There isn't another thing I could want. Thank you, Xavi. I will never forget this. I will never forget that you came."

"Oh, Montse ..."

"Can you come back to my apartment? I have prepared a few things, as one can in this time, for a little celebration. We can talk about how to get Maria and me to Salamanca."

"I would love to celebrate and talk of your new life in Salamanca. Let me pack up, and then we can go. Montse, you should have the shell and candle."

"What treasures you've brought us."

Xavi packed his things. In the rush out he neglected to remove his scarlet stole, and, also, perhaps because Montse made him feel so comfortable, on this day that he had forgotten to take off his Saint Sebastian medal which lay beneath the stole and his shirt.

When Xavi, Montse, and Maria stepped out of the church, they heard a loud voice. "Well, well, who do we have here? My daughter, her mother, and her boyfriend the priest."

"Tomás, what are you doing here?" Montse confronted him.

"Xavi, it was you all along, wasn't it?" Tomás raised his hand, bringing the half dozen rough men behind him to halt.

"Tomás, what are you talking about?" Montse's voice raised to a shout.

"The war is almost over, but hunting season is not yet closed. Xavi, you have roamed our country with impunity for too long. Your adventures here are over. Grab him!"

At that, four of Tomás' companions descended on Xavi. Xavi dropped his pack and began the fight. He knocked two of the men to the ground, but in the end, they were too many for him. He was subdued.

"Tie him to that column."

"Tomás, what are you doing?" Montse struggled to get to Xavi, but one of the men pulled her back.

"Father, you are from San Sebastian, aren't you? Let's see you do your best impression of your city's patron saint."

Xavi was tied to the marble column. He struggled underneath the desecrated stone carvings of St. Michael spearing the dragon, his scarlet stole in vivid contrast to the grey marble and piles of rubble.

"Tomás are you crazy?" Montse shouted out, as several of the other men held her and Maria.

"I am going to do to what is done when the hunt is successful, and the animal is cornered. Strip him down but leave his stole…

it will go well with his blood." The medal on Xavi's now bare chest caught the light and glinted in the late morning sun. "Now you look like your city's Saint. Let's finish your martyrdom. Aim the guns."

"Tomás—no, no don't!" Montse screamed.

Xavi remained calm. "Tomás, I pray for you now, as I have prayed for you before. Killing me will not ease your pain; it will not ease the hatred you feel. Only Christ's love can free your pain, let me help you."

"Enough of your nonsense. Kill him!"

Simultaneously, Montse shrieked, Maria wailed, and Xavi, in his mind's eye, clutched the medal from Inaki's father, and said, "Tomás, may God be with you—*long live Christ the King!*"

At that moment, Jaime and his men were but a few blocks away from the small church. "Captain, those were shots!"

"Yes, from three or four rifles," Jaime replied.

Then he heard another set of volleys … and then, finally, after a few silent moments … a single shot.

"To the sound of that gunfire," Jaime gave the order, and the convoy raced off. In a less than a couple of minutes they came to the church.

On arriving at the scene Jaime yelled out, "Oh my God!"

There he saw his friend tied to the column—dead—his body crumpled down and riddled with bullets. Next to him, attending him as best she could, was Montse, with a small child sitting on the ground nearby, crying hysterically.

One of his men shot down one of Tomás' gang. Jaime cried out, "No! That is not the way! Capture them and take them into custody. They need to stand trial for what they did."

Tomás and his men were cornered. As Jaime moved towards him, Tomás edged his way next to the portico.

"Tomás, you can't escape."

"I will not give you the pleasure. Long live the Revolution!" Quickly, he put his pistol to his temple and blew his brains out.

His brain splatter horribly soiled Montse and Maria—both on their clothes and across their faces. It was chaos. Xavi slumped down on the column, Tomás dead in a pool of blood spilling from his head, and Montse and Maria covered in blood and brain matter.

Jaime rushed to Xavi. He freed him from the column. Montse clutched Xavi to her, holding him as if in a Pieta.

"Lieutenant bring some clothes or blankets, or whatever we have to clean the blood off," Jaime barked out.

The soldier brought a blanket and cleaned up Montse and the child as best as he could.

"Montse, what are you doing here? Why was Xavi here?" Jaime asked.

Sobbing, she said, "I brought him ... I brought him here."

"But why was he here?"

"He came to baptize Maria. How will I ever be able to forgive myself?"

With the war in its final convulsion in Barcelona, Jaime knew two things: Xavi's body must be attended to properly, and Montse and Maria needed to be taken out of the city.

"Montse, Montse. We need to get you out of here, out of Barcelona. Do you have somewhere to go?"

"Not exactly. I was thinking of going to Salamanca, but now I'm not sure," Montse said as she still sobbed heavily.

Montse's body convulsed so intensely from the sobbing that Jaime was not sure she could hear him. "Montse, can you hear me?"

"Yes."

"We need to get Xavi's body in the truck. We need to take him back to Salamanca. Can you accompany him? Can you take him back to the bishop?"

After a few moments she responded, "Yes ... yes, I can do that." She looked up at him. "What about you?"

"I will find you. I promise I will find you." Jaime turned to one of the men. "Lieutenant, load the father in the truck."

"Sir, sir, we need that truck."

"It's an order! And you are to go with it. Also, you are to take the woman and her daughter, too. Deliver all three of them—safely—to the Bishop of Salamanca! Do you understand?"

"Yes, Captain."

Several minutes later Jaime watched the truck leave. As it sped away, he could still hear Montse's sobbing and Maria's wailing in the distance.

Book Five

Redemption and Healing

Book 5
Chapter 1
Salamanca, Nationalist Spain
January 30, 1939

Responding to the knock on his office door the bishop called, "Come in."

Sister Monica, one of the sisters who tended his residence, entered. "Your Excellency, there is a woman here asking for you. She says she is your goddaughter."

The Bishop looked surprised. "My goddaughter?"

"Yes, Your Excellency, and she has a small child … and, Your Excellency, she is in a terrible way."

"Send her in." The bishop's mind raced as he heard her footsteps approach, but he was not prepared for how badly Montse appeared. At the first moment she stepped into office, his heart sank; all of her beauty and vitality had been drained away. But beyond that, he was disturbed, almost repulsed, that her and her daughter's dresses were stained with dried blood. She wore the remnants of death. He knew she was here to deliver terrible news.

Upon entering the bishop's office Montse, holding a sleeping child in her arms, sank into a chair, and even before she spoke her face began to tremble. "He's dead. His body is in the back of the truck. He was murdered."

Then Montse collapsed to the ground. Maria fell with her with mother and began to cry loudly.

"Sister Monica, Sister Monica, come, come quickly!"

Book 5
Chapter 2
Salamanca, Nationalist Spain
January 31, 1939

It was about two p.m. when Sister Monica informed the bishop that Montse was finally waking up.

"Thank you, Sister, and how is the little girl?"

"Oh, she is so beautiful, and she has become an immediate favorite of the sisters."

The bishop knocked on the door of the guest room where Montse had been sleeping, "Montserrat, it's me, may I come in?"

"Yes, come in."

When the bishop entered her room, she was still in bed. "Montserrat you have been sleeping for almost a whole day. Are you feeling a bit better now?" he asked with true concern.

"Yes, yes, oh I was so exhausted. Where is Maria?"

Relief came over Montse's face when she heard the bishop say, "She is fine. She is entertaining the sisters."

"I want to see her. I would like to get up now, but I have nothing to wear."

"I had Sister Monica go out and buy you and your daughter— she is named Maria, I hear—some things. I would not expect them to be too stylish, but they should do for now. Please come to my office when you are dressed."

Forty-five minutes passed and Montse appeared in the bishop's office in a simple, shapeless grey dress. "Can you have the sisters bring Maria now?" Montse asked.

"Yes of course," the bishop replied, and in several minutes Sister Monica came in with Maria beaming in her arms.

"Oh Montserrat, she is such a beautiful little girl. May I meet her?"

Montse then held Maria in her arms and moved her close to the bishop. "Maria, this is my godfather ..." Somehow the word, "godfather" sent Montse back to the baptism and her face sank with sadness.

"What's wrong, my dear?"

"Oh, I have so much to tell you. Can we walk, perhaps around the *Plaza Mayor*?"

"Yes, but it's chilly outside. You can borrow a coat from one of the sisters, but I'm not sure what we have for little Maria."

"It seems she will be fine with Sister Monica."

They made the short walk to the *Plaza Mayor* in silence, and once there they ambled around its perimeter.

"I brought him, Xavi, to Barcelona," Montse started out.

"I know. I delivered your letter to him."

"I had him come to Barcelona to baptize Maria because I thought I would be killed."

"He, more than anyone, knew the risks."

"I knew he would come. I knew what he had been up to during the war."

"You did? How?"

"Yes, early on in the war the rumors began to swirl about a mystery man moving in and out of Republican territory performing daring rescues of religious."

"That was Xavi."

"I know. With each rescue his notoriety grew; the way he moved in and out with such stealth, he was like a ghost. I caught onto his trail. I knew from the descriptions that it had to be Xavi. I even wrote an article about him."

"You wrote an article?"

"They made me. I did my best to mix up some of the details. I hated to write it. I tried to protect him."

"I can't imagine the turmoil you must have felt."

"I loved him."

"I know you did. ... I know you did."

"But in the end ..."

"No, Montse, everything happens for a reason."

"I can't see any reason in this," she said as her eyes welled up.

376

"Sometimes it takes a lifetime to know the reason for things."

"Oh God, to carry this pain, this guilt for a lifetime …"

"There is healing, there is redemption, my child."

"How?"

"Slowly, step by step, through faith."

"I can't see it. I can't see the purpose of any of it."

They walked several dozen paces in silence and then the bishop picked up the conversation again. "Can we talk of Barcelona?"

"Give me a moment …" she replied, turning away.

She dabbed her eyes with the back of her right hand and then turned back around. "Okay."

"Tell me, as you can, what happened there."

"I'll try, but I'm not sure how far I can go."

"Take your time, dear, take your time."

"It was two days ago. He came to baptize Maria, and I told him I wanted him to hear my confession."

"A confession?"

"Yes, I thought I would not survive … but now it is he who is dead. I'm sorry, I need a moment," Montse said walking away from the bishop.

When she rejoined the bishop, they walked along a bit more and she added, "Xavi was a priest to the end."

"I believe it."

"You would have been proud of him."

"You have no idea how proud of him I am."

Montse stopped to look into the bishop's eyes. At this moment she saw him as her godfather, and not as the most powerful bishop in Spain. She could see that his eyes had welled up too.

"Well afterwards, after he baptized Maria, as we were leaving the church, Tomás and a gang of his men jumped him … I'm sorry, give me another moment," as she turned away again.

He gently stroked her shoulder to comfort her.

"He tried to fight them off, but … but they were too many."

They took several more steps under the medallions in the direction of the *Café Novelty* before she continued. "After that, it all happened so quickly. They tied him to the portal of the church and stripped his shirt off—"

"Oh…"

"Finally Tomás gave the command to shoot. Tomás' men shot their rifles twice, then … I'm sorry, I need to rest."

"Sit Montse, sit down. Sit at the table here. I will go inside and have a waiter bring us two coffees."

Everyone inside the *Café Novelty*, the waiters, the patrons, were all shocked when the bishop walked into the *café*. "Your Excellency, Your Excellency, what can we get you?"

"Two coffees, for just outside, please."

"Of course, of course, anything, Your Excellency."

A waiter brought the two coffees and, after taking a sip, Montse continued. "Xavi lay crumpled after the first two volleys from the rifles, but … but that was not enough for Tomás."

"I don't understand, not enough?"

"He hovered over his crumpled body. He taunted him, kicked him, spat upon him, and then took his pistol out and shot him point blank in the forehead."

"Oh my God …" the bishop knocked over his coffee, and then he crossed himself. A waiter approached to clean the table, but the bishop waived him away.

Montse began sobbing again, and the bishop did his best to console her. For those in the *Café* and around the plaza, it was odd to see this important man, this man that they had seen as impervious to suffering, show such compassion. He looked completely human.

"I'm sorry. I'm sorry to behave like this … in public."

"Montse, Xavi, well, he was special." The bishop said in a consoling tone.

"And I'm the one responsible for all of this."

"No, Montse, you need to stop thinking that. There are much bigger forces at work here."

"Could I get some water?"

"Of course, waiter, a glass of water please."

After Montse took some water, the bishop asked, "And so how did you get here, here to Salamanca?"

"Just after it happened, a group of Nationalist soldiers arrived. By chance—"

"Nothing happens by chance, Montse."

"No I don't think it was chance, either. The soldiers were led by

Jaime de la Calzada."

"Your old friend, Jaime?"

"Yes."

"And Tomás, what happened to him?"

"He died the loud coward that he was. He killed himself. There they lay next to one another, dead, the saint and the coward. And, so in the end, it was Jaime who saved me again."

"Again?"

"Never mind that. He saved me and Maria and he had one of his men bring us here. Could we walk around the plaza? It has been so long since I have …"

"Of course."

"Yes, it was Jaime. He saved us. He saved Xavi's body." Montse paused in front of the Cervantes Medallion, "you know we met right here …"

"I don't follow you?"

"It's a story for another day. In any case the journey here was a horror. First, passing through places like Teruel which have been completely destroyed, then long stretches of the deadness of winter, all the while holding Maria in her blood-stained dress," Montse said, sobbing openly again.

"I can't imagine …"

In fact, he could not imagine. Xavi never shared his work with the bishop, and having spent the war in tranquil Salamanca, it all had been largely an abstract concept—like pieces moving on a giant chess board. He spent his days on the politics of the church; he met with men like General Franco, conferred with other bishops, and increasingly, he planned for what would come after the war.

"Have Xavi's parents been told?" Montse asked.

"No, I don't believe so."

They walked a bit more, enough so that Montse regained her composure. "What comes next? What about his body?"

The bishop changed his tone, become more formal, more stilted. "I have spoken to the Bishop of San Sebastian and to General Franco's office already this morning."

The words "General Franco" immediately transformed Montse. Her body language and tone veered to being defensive, almost hostile.

"Why General Franco's office?" Montse said with repulsion.

"His funeral will be in San Sebastian, and because it is coinciding with the ending of the war, it will be a particularly important event for the Nationalists. Father Bidertea is a hero and a symbol of the new Spain."

Montse emotions were raw, and she flew from deep sadness towards hot anger. "Xavi served no one except God. You should know that better than anyone, Your Excellency."

"Excuse me, Montserrat," the bishop responded incredulously.

Montse stopped and glared at the bishop. "What is at your core, Enrique, the compassion you showed at the café, or the politician planning to parade Xavi's body like a *Semana Santa* float?"

"Montserrat, you have no right!"

"I have every right! I think it is best that Maria and I go. I will go to France to tell his parents. Maria and I will leave in the morning."

The bishop could see that he had missed his goddaughter's turn of emotion, and he changed tone again, but it was too late; the skirmish was over. Montse was gone. "Perhaps, it is best. I will have my driver take you."

Book 5
Chapter 3
Haro, Nationalist Spain
February 1, 1939

Montse and Maria got in the back seat of the bishop's car. The leather seat of the spacious black sedan was comfortable, a far cry from the truck which had carried them from Barcelona.

"*Buenos días, señora.* I am *señor* Martinez. I am the bishop's driver."

"*Buenos dias, señor.* What is your first name?"

"José."

"Okay, José, we are going to be together for quite a while, let's be less formal please. I am Montse, and this is my daughter Maria."

"She's lovely ... I am told we are driving to Saint-Jean-de-Luz, France."

"That's right, but we must make a stop in Haro in La Rioja first."

"Yes, *señora.*"

And so they were off. The bishop's sedan was nearly alone on the road. It roared past the ancient cities of Castile: Valladolid, Palencia, Burgos. The fields to either side of the road were brown, dormant, and there were long barren stretches between the towns and villages along the way. After about four hours they arrived at Logrono, and the landscape began to change. They were now in La Rioja, and everywhere there were vineyards; they too were dormant and appeared sad. Like Spain, they were awaiting the moment to reemerge, to regain their vitality, after a long, cold winter.

As they neared the de la Calzada house, it all came back to her in her mind: the wine harvest, when the sun was warm, and the fruit was red and ripe, heavy on the wines. She recalled the joy of picking the grapes, stomping them, the singing and the dancing with Xavi, Jaime, and Don Pedro de la Calzada. It seemed so far away, a different time and place, and she hoped the vines were just dormant, and not dead. Everything was filtered by her deep sadness.

Coming to the old house sitting above the vineyard, a thought came to her: *This is Jaime's house. Jaime.* He had saved her twice. The prickly young Spaniard she had first met in Salamanca was the one who had been there to rescue her at the two worst moments of her life. *How strange and unknowable life is,* she thought.

Montse and Maria exited the car, and she instructed *señor* Martinez to turn it off as she did not know how long she would be.

"Yes, *señora*, but we will still have about three hours to go before we get to Saint-Jean-de-Luz."

"We will get there when we get there. I have something important to do here," she replied curtly.

Montse, with Maria in her arms, knocked on the front door; they were greeted by the housekeeper, "Oh *señora* Costa, is that you? It's so good to see you."

"*Señora* Gomez, it's good to be back."

"What a beautiful little girl! Come in, come in. Let me get *señor* de la Calzada. In the meantime, please sit down."

While she waited, she was reminded what a handsome house it was. Several minutes later Don Pedro came to the front room of the house. He was grey and significantly aged since the last she had seen him.

Before even saying hello he blurted out, "Is it about Jaime? Is he dead?"

"No, he's not dead. I saw him four or five days ago."

"You saw him?"

"Yes."

"Montse, I'm so sorry. It seems people only visit anymore to deliver terrible news."

"But I do have news about Jaime." Montse could see the relief of hearing that his son was alive lighten Don Pedro's face.

"Oh dear God, please forgive me. Is this your daughter, Montse? She's beautiful."

"She's my little Maria."

"She's adorable. I have been in such pain that I have lost even my most basic manners. Would you like a coffee?"

"Don Pedro, I have much more to tell you, but yes a coffee. We hardly saw it in Barcelona."

"Montse, please come sit down. Where are you coming from?"

"Salamanca."

"Salamanca? You must be exhausted."

"Yes …"

The housekeeper brought coffees to a table in the living room near where they were sitting. Maria immediately took to the old man, teasing him and crawling on him in his chair. Little Maria seemed to lift the sadness that was all about the room.

"Montse, can you tell me more about Jaime?"

"He saved me and Maria."

"Oh my God—what, how?"

"Don Pedro, please, I do not want to recount all of those details just now, but I want you know it was Jaime who saved us. He saved me."

"Where was this? Is he all right?"

"Yes, he is fine. It was in Barcelona. There is too much to tell just right now, but Xavi, well, Father Bidertea, had sneaked into Barcelona to baptize Maria—"

"Xavi, was in Barcelona? It's too dangerous there for a priest!"

Montse broke down, weeping into her hands.

"Oh dear girl, what is it?" Don Pedro said, taking Montse in his arms like a father.

She sobbed. "Yes, and now he's dead."

He whispered faintly, "Oh, my God," as he cradled her.

Through her sobs she finished the story. "If Jaime had not come at just the moment he came, I too would be dead now, and Maria would be lost. He is a hero."

Don Pedro did not know what to say. There were too many conflicting emotions swirling about.

"Don Pedro, can you watch Maria for a bit."

"Of course, of course."

Montse went to bathroom and splashed water on her face. She looked in the mirror; she had the awful recognition of her haggard appearance. What had become of her face? *Where has the life gone?* she thought. But at that moment she thought something else too: she had been saved; she had a role; her part had not yet been played out.

When she returned from the bathroom Maria and Don Pedro were playing peek-a-boo. It was a simple and beautiful game to watch from across the room.

"Montse, I see a fancy car and driver out front. Where does it come from? Where are you going?"

"The car and driver belong to the Bishop of Salamanca"

"Xavi's bishop?"

"Yes, his bishop. I need to get to France to tell his parents what happened."

"Oh no, really? They are in France?"

"More wreckage from the storm. They fled San Sebastian when it fell."

"My dear girl. What a journey you still have in front of you. It is mid-winter. It's too late now to continue on. You and Maria must stay here tonight."

"Yes, but we must also make a bed for *señor* Martinez."

"*Señor* Martinez?"

"José … the driver."

"Of course. I will call Mercedes to make up a bed for him."

"I am exhausted. I will try to remember the last time I slept here. I will try to sleep with those happy memories."

Book 5
Chapter 4
Saint-Jean-de-Luz, France
February 2, 1939

It was late morning when the car arrived at the address Montse had been given for Xavi's parents in Saint-Jean-de-Luz.

"Should I stay and wait for you, *señora?*" the driver asked.

"No, my daughter and I are finished with the bishop's car. *Señor* Martinez, José, please drive safely back to Salamanca and thank the bishop for his generosity."

With that, she and Maria got out of the car and took the small bag that had all of their belongings, including the baptismal candle and the shell which Xavi used to pour the water on Maria.

Montse found the apartment and knocked.

Maria Bidertea answered the door; she looked grey and drawn. "You are here about Xavi, aren't you? Where is he? He is dead, isn't he?"

Montse felt assaulted and she buckled. In a moment all the things she had planned on saying evaporated. Her mind was a muddle. "Oh, Maria ..."

Just then, as Xavi's father entered the room, Maria Bidertea stormed out of the small apartment. "Montse, dear, it's not you. It's not about you ... is that your daughter?"

"Yes."

"Come in, come in, sit down. Can I get you or your daughter something?"

"No, we're fine, thank you, but I'm sorry I upset Maria so much."

"It's not you. Yesterday, a Swiss man came here."

"A Swiss man?"

"Yes, from some charity in Perpignan,

"Charity, in Perpignan ...?"

"Yes, and he told us the story of what Xavi had been doing—

doing during the war ..."

"You didn't know?"

"No. He never said a word."

"He was a hero ... maybe even more than a hero ... right until the end."

Montse's words floated past Xavi's father. "We had no idea what he was doing—or that he had left for Barcelona a few days ago and had not returned. Neither of us slept last night."

"I saw him there—"

"You did? The Swiss man did not mention it. He just said he had gone to Barcelona and had not returned."

"Yes, it's why I am here." She said sadly.

"And why are you here, exactly?"

"To fill in the details."

"Oh no." Xavi's father's face went blank.

"I'm so terribly sorry to bear this news."

Xavi's father got up and went to another room. Several minutes later he returned. "Before we go on, please, I want to meet this beautiful little girl."

So it was his father; he was the seed of Xavi's humanity, Montse thought. "She is Maria, too."

"How dear! May I hold her?"

"Oh, of course. She connects us all to Xavi."

"How so?" he said as he took the little girl in his arms.

Montse took a deep breath, "Xavi baptized her. That is why he was in Barcelona."

"Oh my God."

Just then Maria Bidertea returned. "Oh my God, what?" Maria exclaimed.

Maria Bidertea overwhelmed Montse again. To her right, Xavi's father, to her left, his mother, each of them waiting for the horror to be told; and she, both the narrator of and a main character in this fierce, too-true tragedy, wounded, forced herself to go on. "Yes, Xavi was in Barcelona a few days ago. He baptized Maria."

"It's your daughter? She's Maria too?" Maria Bidertea asked.

"Yes ... That's why Xavi came."

"Is she *his* daughter?" Maria asked pointedly

"No! He came as a priest."

"I want to hear the story. I want to hear it all, but I do not want it to enter here, to enter our house."

"I understand, I do." Montse said respectfully.

"It isn't much, but it's where we live. Let's go down by the shore to talk."

The winter sun was bright, but it did not provide much warmth as the four of them walked along. Montse started the retelling from the day the war began: her kicking out Tomás, her pregnancy, how terrible life had become in Barcelona, how she had learned of Xavi's double life, convincing him to come to Barcelona. She sought no refuge from her part in his demise.

Finally, as the sun fell lower in the sky, she talked about the confession she had made and little Maria's baptism. Recalling these sacred rituals, the beauty among the rubble, comforted her and provided her the fortitude to continue on—to recount what happened next.

Maria Bidertea pushed her for details, and Montse responded, omitting nothing.

After hearing the words, "Then the rifles fired," Maria stopped it. "I'm sorry—I can't take anymore right now. Let's go home."

When they returned home, Maria Bidertea went directly to her room. "It's not much, but you and Maria can sleep on the small bed in the second bedroom. Stay for as long as you need." Xavi's father said with a comforting touch to her arm.

His touch brought relief to her pain. How odd it was how each person reacts to tragedy so differently. It seemed the war had pushed the whole country to its limits, and some responded in anger, others with self-righteous arrogance, and here, in a simple flat in Saint-Jean-de-Luz, she experienced regenerating compassion.

"Montse, it's not your fault. Xavi was called. You just happened to be there."

—-·—

Book 5
Chapter 5
San Sebastian, Nationalist Spain
February 9, 1939

At noon, the cortege departed from just in front of the Cathe-dral of the *Buen Pastor*. Xavi's body lay in a coffin on the open, horse-drawn carriage. The carriage was bestrewn with flowers, and the coffin was draped with the blue and white flag of the city.

Which flag that would cover the coffin was just one of the many conflicts that emerged in the planning of Xavi's funeral. The Bid-erteas were caught in an intense political crossfire among warring factions that wanted to use Xavi's death as symbol of the new Fas-cist Spain, or of Basque identify, or of an extraordinary Catholi-cism. At the end of the day it was deemed that the flag of the city would be the symbol least likely to offend any of the sides whose emotions were so pitched.

The procession moved slowly down the axis that connected the Cathedral of the *Buen Pastor* and the Basilica of *Santa Maria*. The basilica was Xavi's church, and it was here, and not in the cathe-dral, that Maria Bidertea insisted her son's funeral mass should take place.

The sad silence was only broken by the clopping of the hoofs of the horses that drew the carriage. Two bishops accompanied him: The Bishop of San Sebastian and the Bishop of Salamanca. Fol-lowing them were a number of priests, including Father Extebarri.

Father Extebarri was back from France for the ceremony. His inclusion in the funeral had been another point of tense conten-tion. Maria Bidertea insisted on his participation in their son's funeral, but government officials initially said no, as they had branded him a Basque terrorist. After much back and forth, it was agreed that he would be able to come for the service but would have to leave Spain to go back into exile in France the next day.

It was but one example of the government agreeing to look the other way for one day at the symbols of what had become known as "Basqueness."

Following the carriage were the Biderteas, along with Montse and her daughter, Maria. They were all dressed in black, and the women covered their faces with black veils. They were harbingers of grief.

Hand in hand they walked, like a black chain. Xavi's father, then Maria Bidertea, then Montse, then Maria. Over the week since she had recieved the horrific news, Maria Bidertea had come to see Montse as not the cause of her son's death, but as another victim of the war, another tragic soul who had been caught up in an un-controllable conflagration. She had come to realize that Montse too had been in grave danger, and she had just barely escaped with her life. As Maria Bidertea's hostility waned, the affection she had always felt for Montse reemerged. She had reconnected with her as a daughter. Maria Bidertea had once shared the same dream for Xavi that Montse also held in her heart. They were united in a common grief.

It was about two miles from the cathedral to Xavi's home church. The processional street was packed. Both sides of it were crowded with mourners, sometimes as many as ten-deep. No one remembered so many people coming out for anything or anyone in San Sebastian.

They came to say goodbye to Xavi. For the last two and half years the city had had so little to celebrate; it had felt like a grey cloud had permanently descended over it, like an occupied land. Today, with the winter sun shining brightly, they came out in the thousands. They came out to celebrate a local hero, and to signal to the Nationalists that their "Basqueness" was submerged, but not exterminated.

The conflicting sentiments underpinning the funeral were evident along the processional route. Many called out goodbye in Basque, *"Agur,* Xavi." Others crossed themselves as the coffin passed them by, and a few raised their arms in the fascist salute.

Finally, the procession arrived at the basilica. As she reached the steps, Montse looked up at the statue of Saint Sebastian high above the church entrance. The Saint was carved remembering the moment of his martyrdom. He was tied to a post and pierced with arrows. Seeing the statue, for a moment she lost her breath, painfully recalling the moment of Xavi's death. It was too early in the day to break down, so she steadied herself and moved up the steps to the church, little Maria in hand.

Inside the church was packed, overflowing, waiting for the procession to arrive. The first row on the left was reserved for the Biderteas, Montse, and Maria—and for Jaime, who had not yet arrived, though he promised he would be there.

To the right were rows of Nationalist officers and other officials. In the front row, opposite the Biderteas, was Ramón Serrano Suñer. Serrano Suñer, General Franco's brother-in-law, and the Minister of Interior of the Fascist regime.

Oh what an outrage! Maria Bidertea fumed: one of the men responsible for hounding her and her husband out of Spain was now here to celebrate her son.

"Where's Jaime?" Maria Bidertea whispered to Montse.

"He'll be there; I know he will. He promised," Montse whispered back. And just then he appeared, taking his seat with the family. He was in complete contrast to the Nationalist officers in their best dress uniforms, cleaned and pressed. Jaime was muddied and had the look of a soldier just off the battlefield.

"Where have you been?" Montse asked.

"Not now—later," Jaime responded softly.

Deep into the mass, before the Eucharist was consecrated, from above in the choir loft, the choir began the Procession of Saints:
Kyrie, eleison
Christe, eleison
Sancta Maria, ora pro nobis
Sancti Michael, Grabriel, et Rafael, orate pro nobis

Oh, God, I remember those chants, as Montse thought of Xavi's ordination in Salamanca.
Sancte Augustine, ora pro nobis
Sancte Benedictine, ora pro nobis
Sancta Teresa, ora pro nobis
Sancte Xavier, ora pro nobis...

By the time the choir chanted out *Sancte Xavier, ora pro nobis,*

...Saint Xavier, pray for us..., there was not a dry eye in the crowded church, and there were whispers throughout, "Maybe our Xavi is a saint." Montse, tears streaming down her cheeks, thought not of the saint, but of the man she loved. Twice she had heard this chant, and twice she had lost him.

When it came time for taking communion, Montse, and nearly everyone else, come forward to take the Eucharist. At that moment, it was as if the idea of communion, of being in communion, now seemed to hold more meaning than ever in the backdrop of the war, and with Xavi's coffin stationed before the altar.

After the mass ended came three eulogies. Bishop Pla y Deniel took to the platform first.

"Xavi was a hero of the new Spain," he started, making eye contact with the Nationalist luminaries in the front row. The powerful, smug men nodded, and at that moment Montse again felt contempt for her godfather and his bowing before the Fascists.

This is how you remember the man who served you? The man who went where no one else would go? Yes, Enrique, that really is your core. You may know many languages, and have grand erudition, but you lack the character that made the man you eulogize, she thought.

After the bishop came Father Extebarri. Father Extebarri was in perfect contrast to the bishop. He was warm and engaging, and he addressed the congregation with a few words in his native Basque. Hearing their language spoken out loud, after two and half years of its silence, aroused them to full attention, like sunflowers hit by the sun.

Father Extebarri switched to Spanish and took the assembled crowd back to Xavi's boyhood. In rich, colorful detail he highlighted how even at a young age Xavi showed skill, courage, and leadership; and that other boys, even though they were nearly peers, deeply revered him. Finally, he recounted how he owed his own life to Xavi. How on two occasions Xavi had saved him, the second time fleeing from death, escaping the Nationalists, taking to the sea in a small, open boat in the middle of the night.

The crowd nodded. They all knew about these escapes ... and the ones that had failed.. Montse leaned over and whispered to Jaime, "The generals went from triumphant to surrounded in just a few instants, didn't they?"

Father Extebarri finished, "God bless you, Xavi. I will miss you." He climbed down from the pulpit clearly shaken by the words he had delivered.

Father Extebarri was followed to the pulpit by another priest, a man no one seemed to know. "Who is he?" the crowd murmured.

"*Kaixo*, hello, my friends. I am here to give a eulogy to a man I never knew."

The audience became unsettled in their seats. The man then continued in Spanish heavily accented in French, "My name is Monsignor Jacques Latour. I did not know Xavier Bidertea, but I have the great honor and blessing of knowing a man none of you knew, Patrick Azerbergui. Who is Patrick Azerbergui you ask? Let me draw him for you by telling the stories of some of the people he saved. People who likely would be dead now, but for Patrick."

He looked to the crowd and called out, "Sister Clara, where are you? Please stand up with your other sisters."

There, a few rows back, Sister Clara and four of her sisters stood up. All of the eyes in the church were drawn on them.

"Thank you, Sister Clara. Sister Clara and her sisters were trapped in Madrid in the early days of the war, and it was Patrick who made his way from Salamanca through France, back into Spain, and into Madrid, to save them. He went during the time when the hunt for religious people was most intense. When good people thought only of how to flee the inferno, he rushed into it. And caught in this raging fire were Sister Clara and her sisters.

"Let me paint for you the picture of their escape. After night fell, during a firefight, he shepherded the sisters across to Nationalist territory. Then he crawled back across the no man's land to the Republican line."

The crowd listened with amazement. "Xavi did that?" people whispered.

"When I saw him next, I asked him what he recalled, and do you know what he said?"

People were shrugging and shaking heads, "no" in the crowd.

"He told me, 'their singing.'"

"'Their singing,' I asked?

"'Yes, in the night as the gunfight stopped, they sang like angels,' he said."

"Singing in the night like angels—that was Patrick." Jacques had skill, he was a natural orator, and so he paused to enable the crowd to build the picture of it in their minds, to imagine the singing.

He continued on, and many of those he had saved were there: The seminarians from Girona, the *Opus Dei* priests. He pointed each of them out and then recounted how Xavi had saved them.

"And it was not just religious, or Nationalists he saved." Then Monsignor Latour had a group of people who looked quite common, poor really, to stand.

"By chance, having heard of Patrick's death, these people rode a bus for two days from Almeria to get to the service. They are not priests, or nuns, and some of them have no faith at all. So why are they here you ask? Because Patrick saved them too.

"Desperate, given up for, on the road out of Malaga, hunted from three sides, it was Patrick who saved them. It was Patrick who shielded them from death, who got them to Almeria."

Everyone knew what Malaga meant, what it was code for. The crowd was buzzing, and the generals were perplexed and uncomfortable as Latour continued.

"As you can hear, I am not Spanish, and I am not here to pick a fight, or take a side, but I tell you these people that you see among you were caught in the unimaginable horror of the forced evacuation of Malaga. There, facing severe deprivation, and under attack, it was Patrick who made trip after trip in the truck he used to deliver relief supplies—the cover he used to slip into Republican Spain—to save dozens of people at their most vulnerable moment. Patrick did not ask which side they were on. He did not ask them what their level of faith was. They were in need; he could help. It was simple to him."

Latour, even in his halting Spanish, was connecting with a powerful story. He paused again and then continued, "And then, as the war was winding down, Patrick made one last trip. For a friend, and for his friend's daughter, into the most dangerous place in Spain—Barcelona in the final days of the war. Here, after giving a little girl her Catholic Baptism, fate caught up with Patrick, and, well, you know the rest. That is why we are all here on this sad day.

"So before I end, let me fill in some of the puzzle pieces for you. I am Swiss priest, a monsignor, who was in the Vatican in 1936 and who was asked by the Pope himself to organize a rescue mission to save as many of the Spanish religious in danger, caught on the wrong side of the war, as possible. I set this mission up. I created a network of people who helped and a charity which served as our cover. All of it was organized around one person's faith and courage. That person, I knew only by his false identify of Patrick Azerbergui, is who you know to be Father Xavier Bidertea. Xavi to most of you."

He paused again. "And one last thing."

The crowd was in rapt attention.

"It is something which connects Xavi to this city and to the events that have torn this country apart for the last few years. High above the entrance of this church is the statue of Saint Sebastian, the patron of this city. He is bound, tied to a post, pierced with arrows. He was martyred for all time, and after his martyrdom, Saint Sebastian became the saint called for intercession against plagues.

"Xavi was also martyred. He was bound and tied to a church pillar, pierced not with arrows, but with bullets. Join with me to call on Xavi's memory for intercession against the plague that has descended on this country. There would be no better way to remember Xavi.

"May God rest his soul." Monsignor Latour stepped down from the pulpit and the funeral ended. The choir sang the last verses from Psalm 23:

The Lord is my shepherd; I shall not want.

He maketh me to lie down in green pastures; he leadeth me beside the still waters.

He restoreth my soul; he leadeth me in the paths of righteousness for his name's sake.

Yea, though I walk through the valley of the shadow of death, I will fear no evil: for thou art with me; thy rod and thy staff they comfort me.

The crowd left the church; all were subdued and moved, and most of them openly weeping.

After the ceremony hundreds of people crowded into the public rooms of the Hotel Maria Cristina, whose exterior walls were pockmarked with civil war battle bullets. They came to pay last respects, to say a few words to Mr. and Mrs. Bidertea, to tell stories of Xavi, and to take a small step towards healing.

The first person to seek out the Biderteas to express his sympathy at the reception was Ramón Serrano Suñer. Handsome, elegant looking in his dress uniform, perfectly groomed, and graciously polite he approached the Biderteas. "I am so sorry for your loss. Your son is a great hero to Spain. We are rebuilding our country around men like him."

Maria Bidertea was silent, and Xavi's father jumped in graciously "Thank you sir. Thank you for coming."

Serrano Suñer added, "I am aware that you have left Spain, but I also want you to know that you are welcome back whenever you wish and as you wish. No questions asked."

Maria Bidertea jumped into the conversation and asserted her willfulness. "Under cover of night we fled our grand apartment, just three blocks from here, in this beautiful city to live in a tiny flat in a foreign country. Thank you for your offer, but we are happy where we are. We are building our life there."

"I understand, *señora*, as you wish," Serrano Suñer replied, and then left the reception with the other Nationalist officers in tow.

After that, many of the people who owed their lives to Xavi sought his parents out. They retold their stories; they hugged; they cried; and many made promises of dedicating their lives to Xavi.

During a lull, the Biderteas, Montse, Maria—behaving like a trooper—and Jaime were huddled together off to the side. Xavi's old friend Martin stopped by; for once his sadness overwhelmed his natural smile and effervescence.

"Martin, how we can thank you—" Xavi's father started.

"There is no thanking today. Today is for Xavi. He was one of the great ones. He really was. I wanted you to know," he said as the Bishop Pla y Daniel arrived. "I see I'm now out of my league—I should go. Goodbye, if you ever need anything, you know where you can find me." He bowed formally to the bishop and hurried away.

The bishop nodded to Martin and greeted the Biderteas, Montse and Maria. He focused in on Jaime. "Jaime, you look like you are just off the battlefield?"

"Yes, Your Excellency, I am. I had one last thing to do in Catalonia before I raced here. I was on a mission you should know about."

"What? Please tell me."

Jaime then recounted his last few days. "We were tipped off that the Commander of the Nationalist forces in Teruel, and the Bishop of Teruel were being held in a prison north of Barcelona. My unit was given the mission to free them."

"Did you find him? Did you find Anselm? How is he?" the bishop waited anxiously for more of the story.

"Yes—too late."

"What do you mean, too late?" the bishop said in a demanding voice.

"When we arrived, they had just been murdered. Their freshly-dead bodies were in the prison yard, lying face-down in the mud, riddled with bullets."

"Oh my God, may they rest in peace." He paused and added, "Did you know that Xavi also tried to save the bishop?"

"No …"

"He went to Teruel in dead of the winter, during the battle, before the city fell, but the bishop sent him away?"

"I never knew. He never told me; we may have crossed paths coming and going from that sad place."

Montse chimed in, "I wonder how many of these stories only Xavi knew. I wonder how many people are living today because of him that none of us know about, that none of us will ever know about."

Just then Monsignor Latour interrupted in French. "Please may I introduce someone who also knew your son? She served Xavi many times at her auberge."

Madame Chenot immediately connected with Maria Bidertea, woman to woman, mother to mother, "*Madame* Bidertea, I knew your son more as a man than as a priest. He was so kind; he was so gracious."

She paused and put her hands to her chest, touching one of the medals she wore; she then took it off her neck. "Before he left for Barcelona, he gave me this medal—you should be so proud of him. I miss your son deeply, but you should have this medal." She gave the Saint Teresa medal to Xavi's mother, then they shared a moment, hugging and weeping.

As the crowd began to thin out Maria Bidertea found Montse.

"Where will you go now? Even though our apartment is small, you and Maria may stay with us as long as you wish."

"I can never repay you for how you and your husband took us in. I am so grateful for the love you have given Maria and me."

"No, Montse, it is you and Maria that have started to bring life back to our home."

"Dearest Maria," Montse said, "Thank you so much. I feel the very early signs that I am healing. But I want to be in Spain; I need to be in Spain. Spain is my country."

"Yes, Spain—but where will you go?"

"I think I would like to spend some time with Jaime's father in his vineyard. I am hoping that watching the vines come back to life will allow me to find some peace. I need to focus on my daughter now. Maria, wherever I am, I will be with you. We will be forever connected by our love for Xavi. No one loved him as we did."

"No, no one could."

"Montse…"

"Jaime, where have you been?"

"Circulating, giving you some space."

"You seem sad."

"I am. I need to go. I need to get back to the war."

"The war …"

"Catalonia will fall in a few days, and then Madrid will follow. It's all but over now."

"You really have to return?"

"Yes."

"When will I see you again?"

"Walking towards the vines."

"You promise?"

"I do."

"Goodbye Montse…"

After Jaime left, Maria and Montse embraced and wept one more time, Don Pedro found them.

"Are you ready, Montse? Are you ready to go to the vineyard now?"

"May I have a few minutes to myself? Can you watch Maria?"

"Of course, anything, Montse."

Montse left the ballroom of the grand hotel. She passed through its lobby and out the entrance, then she crossed the street. She walked the few steps to the *Puente de La Zurriola*—the last bridge across the Urumea River before it meets the Cantabrian Sea.

She made her way to the middle of the bridge. There, just fifteen feet or so above the rushing water, she leaned over the railing. She watched the battle below, as back and forth the river and the sea pushed against one another, neither overwhelming the other.

Epilogue

On April 1, 1939, in a simple communique, General Francisco Franco declared the war over. As Franco said it would be, the Nationalists won an unconditional surrender over the Republicans.

This emotionless notice followed nearly three years of intense war, that came after five years of increasing chaos subsequent to the abdication of King Alfonso XIII and the establishment of the Second Republic in 1931. Spain descended into chaos and wanton violence. Forces on the left and the right first threw punches, then counterpunches at one another, until the punches escalated to gunfire, and gunfire escalated to unspeakable atrocity.

By July 1936, a number of right-wing generals had had enough. They launched a coup on July 18, 1936. The coup against a democratically elected government in Europe was seen as an outrage and a dangerous expansion of fascism by the international community.

The coup failed. A stalemate ensued. The stalemate devolved into a civil war. Slowly, then more rapidly, the Nationalist forces led by General Franco, and aided by the Germans and Italians, routed the Republican forces. In truth, the Nationalists were more organized, more professional, more unified, and more ruthless.

In the war's aftermath, Franco ruled as an authoritarian dictator for almost forty years until his death in 1975. Franco had deep hatred for, and suspicion of, left-wing politics and separatism. As the war ended, at least five hundred thousand Republicans fled Spain for France. After it ended, many tens of thousands of Republicans were imprisoned or put into forced labor. At least thirty thousand were executed.

Spain avoided WW2, but it remained shunned, outside the international community, until the 1950's. Once Spain emerged from the shadows, aided significantly by the United States, economic growth exploded. Only Japan grew more rapidly that Spain from 1959 to 1974.

Franco believed in a unified Spain, and he outlawed the speaking of the Catalan and Basque languages. But the Basques would not be subdued.

For almost sixty years, ending in 2018, a Basque terrorist group, ETA, and the Spanish Military waged a dirty war. Thousands were killed, or assassinated, including in 1973 the Spanish Prime Minister Luis Carrero Blanco. An ETA cell exploded a bomb that sent Carrero Blanco's car one hundred feet into the air as he left morning mass in Madrid's chicest district.

After Franco died, Spain made a peaceful transition to democracy. Its democracy has flourished for over forty years.

As I finish this book, a far-left wing government, democratically elected, is in power. In Catalonia, the fires of separatism rage again, while the Basques watch the Catalans sympathetically. On the right, a new party, Vox, has emerged echoing Franco's themes.

In the *Plaza Mayor* of Salamanca, General Franco's medallion has been taken down—he is erased from the Pantheon of Spanish heroes.

Outside of Madrid lies the *Valle de Los Caidos*, the Valley of the Fallen. There, Franco built an enormous basilica, burrowed deep inside a mountain, marked with a five-hundred-foot cross that can be seen for miles. In the basilica, forty thousand Spanish victims of the civil war are buried. Only two Spaniards had marked tombs: José Antonio Primo de Rivera, and Francisco Franco.

On October 24, 2019, following years of wrangling between the left and the right, Franco's body was disentombed from the basilica. Ingloriously, his body was flown by helicopter to a small family plot.

Back and forth it goes—like the Urumea, the river and sea push against each other, as they always have—as they always will.

Appendices

Appendix 1: Map of the Camino Frances

El Camino Santiago, Source: Caspin.com

El Camino Santiago

The ancient pilgrimage to venerate the remains of the Apostle Saint James in Santiago de Compostela is called the Camino Santiago. The main route of the Camino Santiago through Spain is called the Camino Frances. The 'French Way' starts just over the Pyrenees in Saint Jean Pied de Port, travels across northern Spain, to Santiago de Compostela, and then ends at Finisterre on the Atlantic Coast.

Appendix 2: Geographical Maps

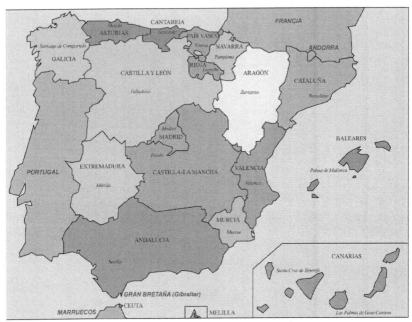

Spain and its Regions, Source: www.WorldHistory.biz

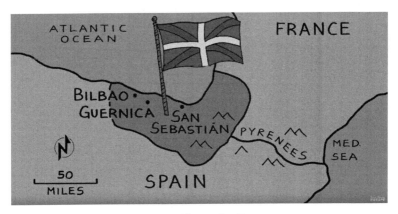

French Pays Basque, Source: About the Basques

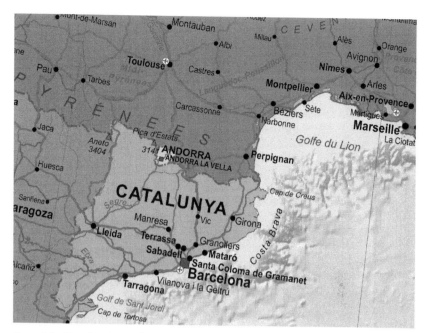

Spanish Catalonia and Neighboring France/Perpignan,
Source: Wikipedia Commons

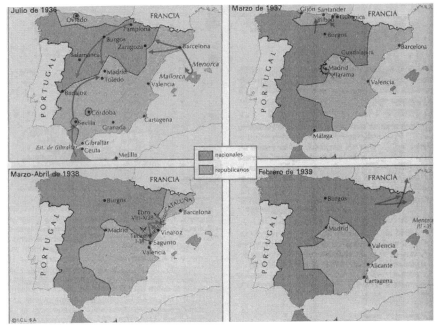

Appendix 3: Civil War Maps

End of July 1936

The Nationalists had immediate success after General Franco's invasion from Spanish Morocco, which was coordinated with a military uprising in the North.

October 1936

After their initial success, the Nationalists gains were slowed in the Fall of 1936.

October 1937

Eighteen months into the Civil War the Nationalists controlled all of the north of Spain but had failed to regain control of its two largest cities: Barcelona and Madrid.

May 1938

By May 1938, after the Battle of Teruel, the Nationalists drove to the Mediterranean, splitting Republican Spain.

February 1939

Following the fall of Barcelona and Catalonia, the Republicans territory continued to be squeezed down, holding only two large cities: Valencia and Madrid. Madrid finally fell to the Nationalists on March 28, 1939; Valencia fell on April 1, 1939, ending the war.

Acknowledgments

I owe many thanks to a number of people who generously read and commented on the early drafts of the book: Chris Mortensen; John Ackerman; Ella Leary; Thayer Baine; Christine Tomas. Also, to my friends in Spain whose grandparents lived through these horrors: Enrique; Papa; and JM. And finally, my editor, Judy Geary, who pushed me over the finish line.

Thank you all.

Historical Images
Relevant to the Story of Holy Ghost

These images were harvested from Wikimedia Commons. Unless otherwise labeled, these files are licensed under the Creative Commons Attribution-Share Alike 3.0 Spain license or the Creative Commons Attribution-Share Alike 4.0 International license.

San Sebastian
Promenade of La Concha Beach
Source: Arquivo de Villa Maria,
Angra do Heroísmo, Açores

Salamanca Cathedral
Author: Briana Laugher

Walls of Avila
Author Choniron

Roncesvalles
Author: Cherubino

Monastery of Montserrat
Author: Orlith1

Portrait of Miguel de Unamuno
by Maurice Fromkes
Source: Museo del Prado

Holy Week in Seville
Painting by Alfred Dehodencq
Source: Carmen Thyssen Museum

La Sagrada Familia/Gaudi Cathedral
Author: C Messier

Plaza Mayor Salamanca, Spain
Author: Zarateman

Mural of Guernica

Guernica is infamous for the first use of the Luftwaffe's bombing force against a town and Picasso's famous painting. After such a long time there is little evidence of the bombing but there is this large tiled version of the painting by Tony Hisgett from Birmingham, UK

Manuel Azaña, Republican Leader
Narodowe Archiwum Cyfrowe, 1-E-6356,
originally published in Ilustrowany Kurier Codzienny.
Author: unknown

Jose Antonio Primo de Rivera
Author: unknown

Francisco Franco in 1930
Source: Biblioteca Virtual de Defensa RETRATO FO-
TOGRÁFICO DEL GENERALÍSIMO D. FRANCISCO
FRANCO BAHAMONDE (MUE-120279)
Author: unknown
Public domain dedication

Lincoln Brigade:
Americans Supporting the Republican Cause
Author: unknown

Hemingway at Pamplona,
Spain in 1925
Source: John F. Kennedy Library,
Ernest Hemingway Collection,
Author unspecified

Running of the Bulls,
Pamplona, Spain
Author: Inaki Larrea

Urumea River, San Sebastian...
where the river and sea meet
Author: Xabier Cañas

Basilica of Santa Maria San Sebastian, Spain
Author: Roberto Chamoso G
This is a photo of a monument indexed in the Spanish heritage
register of Bienes de Interés Cultural

Meet the Author

Kelly **Conway** holds degrees in Economics and Finance from UCLA and USC. He has built numerous technology companies, and he holds twenty patents on using software and big data analytics to analyze linguistics to understand human behavior.

Mr. Conway has been travelling to Spain since 1979, and has visited there more than fifty times since. He has travelled to every region and corner of Spain, and he has been a pilgrim on the Camino Santiago seven times.

Holy Ghost is Mr. Conway's first novel and is the result of his experiences in Spain, and extensive research conducted about the events that occurred there between 1923-1939.

When not in Spain, Mr. Conway resides in Vero Beach, Florida.

Made in the USA
Middletown, DE
17 September 2021